AIR AWAKENS

BOOK ONE OF THE AIR AWAKENS SERIES

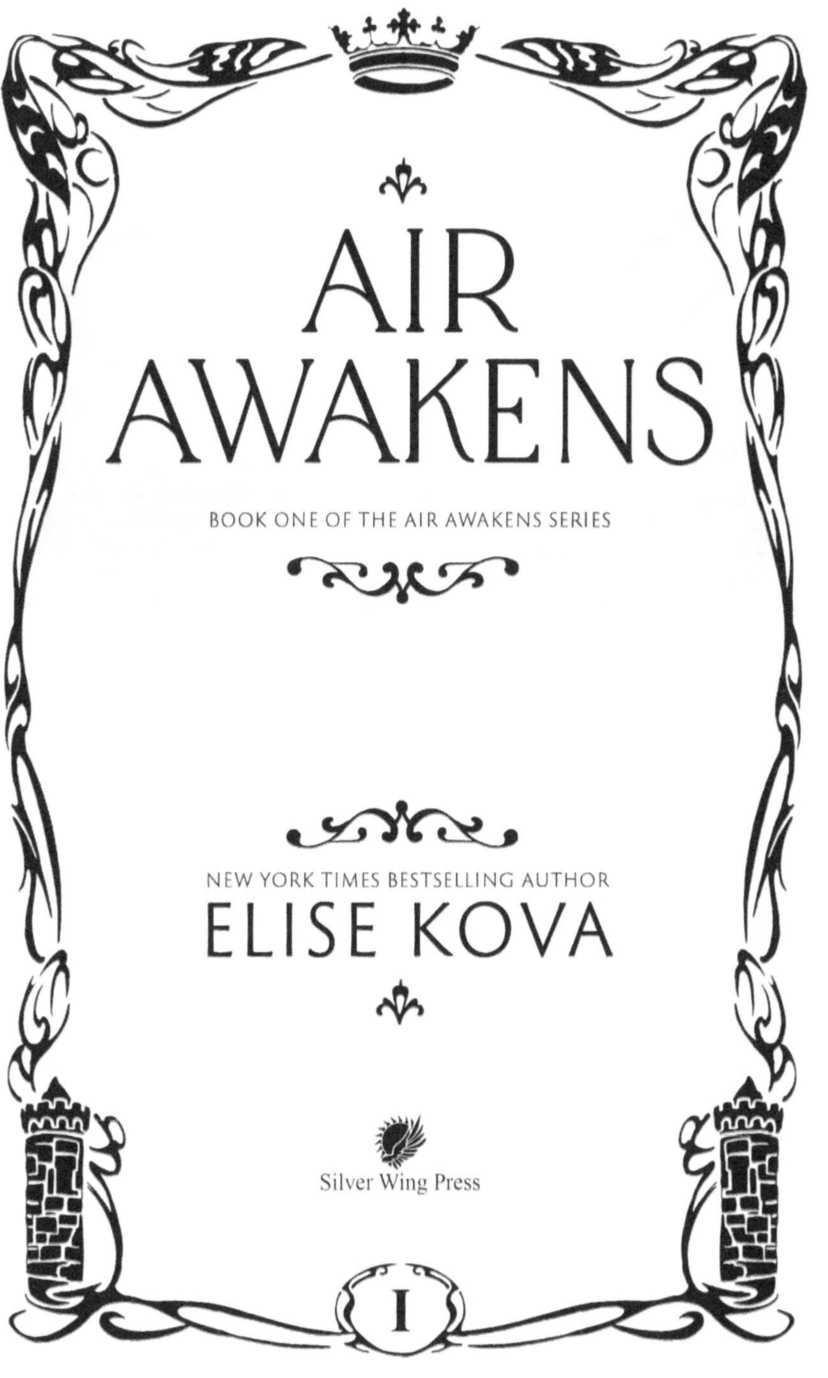

AIR AWAKENS
BOOK ONE OF THE AIR AWAKENS SERIES
NEW YORK TIMES BESTSELLING AUTHOR
ELISE KOVA
Silver Wing Press
I

Published by Silver Wing Press

2025 Cover Artwork by Niall Grant
Original Cover Artwork by Merilliza Chan
Scene Artwork by Polar Engine Studio
Additional Character Artwork by Alice Duke
Edge Design by Painted Wings Publishing

Editing by Monica Wanat
Proofreading by Kate Anderson

ISBN (paperback): 978-1-949694-68-0
ISBN (hardcover): 978-1-949694-67-3
eISBN: 978-1932549942

2025 Ten Year Anniversary Edition

CONTENTS

ALSO BY ELISE KOVA

~

See the most up to date list of all of Elise's books and find where to get them on her website at:
https://elisekova.com/books/

~

ARCANA ACADEMY

Arcana Academy

DRAGON CURSED

Dragon Cursed

AIR AWAKENS UNIVERSE

Air Awakens Series

Air Awakens
Fire Falling
Earth's End
Water's Wrath
Crystal Crowned

Vortex Chronicles

Vortex Visions
Chosen Champion
Failed Future
Sovereign Sacrifice
Crystal Caged

Golden Guard Trilogy

The Crown's Dog
The Prince's Rogue
The Farmer's War

A Trial of Sorcerers

A Trial of Sorcerers
A Hunt of Shadows
A Tournament of Crowns
An Heir of Frost
A Queen of Ice

MARRIED TO MAGIC

A Deal with the Elf King
A Dance with the Fae Prince
A Duel with the Vampire Lord
A Duet with the Siren Duke
A Dawn with the Wolf Knight

LOOM SAGA

The Alchemists of Loom
The Dragons of Nova
The Rebels of Gold

∼

NEVER MISS A RELEASE

**Get exclusive giveaways, review copies, and a <u>free gift</u> on
sign up by subscribing to Elise Kova's newsletter:**
https://elisekova.com/subscribe/

This book is for ...

*Alicia Davis, Kiri, Kay, IridescentSoul, Elanor Crumwell,
RomanceObsessed, DarlingFaye, PowerMadGirl, yesiamhuman,
queencarrot, Prodigee123, doc2or, Seriah Black Sheep, Your Loyal
Bookworm, shinju asuka, puffgirl1952, musicboxmetaphor, shari,
bfl2ma, Valerie, XtremeAngell, Mirirowan, Rebecca, prathyu, Alyss20,
TwiinzRJ, Vyra Finn, Ozymandeos, Lady Altrariel, Ulsindhe,
gizem524, musicalfishieXD, devonamorgan, blueeyesbrightsmile,
Estheranian, Michelle Fang, Rizzy, Tessa, Sekhra, JustAnotherGal,
Ashley, Izzy, Blanket Baby, hopewriteinspire, rosewood,
appleeater1313, Wonderlander, A fan, Mizz Dustkeeper,
lalalaughter101, LazyFakeName, carmensimagination, avery, avid
reader, Mousey, Emmie, FreakinMarisa, Death's Sweet Kiss, Kaf,
Sephirium*

... and everyone else who was with and supported me from the
start. Without you, there would be no story.

THE
MAIN CONTINENT
VANGAR
THE CRYSTAL CAVERNS
SOLARIN "THE CAPITAL"
RIVEND
THE GREAT IMPERIAL W
MO
OPARIUM
LYNDUM
PACA
SHAN
LEOU
THE FINSHAR DELTA
HAS

THE CRESCENT CONTINENT
THE BARRIER ISLANDS
THE WEST
MHASHAN
QUI
NORIN
XIA
LAU
SILME
YON
THE CROSSROADS
ORE
ANTO
POHEAT
THE PASS
DAMACIUM
SORICIUM
LAKE IO
ALDA
THE NORTH
SHALDAN

CHAPTER I

Summer storms were common in the capital and Vhalla Yarl had endured their visits in the seven years since she had moved from the East, but lightning and thunder were never welcome guests.

The burst of light through the shutter slats hadn't set her heart to racing tonight; it was the solemn, low cry of a horn resonating off every post in the city that slowed her world with each reverberation. The noise faded before resounding once more.

Vhalla jumped to her feet, rushing to the small archer's slit that served as her window. Unlatching the shutter proved to be a poor idea as the wind grabbed it, slamming it against the palace stone so hard that she thought it would rip from its hinges. The shutter was quickly forgotten as horns echoed their call on the palace wall below, and Vhalla blinked into the howling wind.

Horns could only mean one thing.

Her dark brown eyes—flecked with gold—fixed on the Imperial Gate far below as it opened to allow a military party to race inside. Leaning out as far as she could, Vhalla ignored the rain splattering her cheeks, straining to make out the shifting shadows of soldiers home from the front.

Had they won? Was the war against Shaldan over?

Vhalla's heart beat harder. Through the intermittent flashes of lightning, she only made out twenty horsemen.

Victory rode through the city in full force with sunlit pennons fluttering in the wind. Victory waited until better weather for their parades. Something was wrong. This was a messenger party, a delivery, an escort, a—

Vhalla's mind went blank.

Palace servants rushed to meet the party and, by the flickering light of their torches, Vhalla was able to make out people. An Imperial White cape draped the haunch of a horse.

A prince had returned.

The servants helped the slumped royal from his saddle, pulling off the limp and sluggish body. She couldn't hear the words shouted over the storm, but they seemed frantic and angry. Vhalla stood on her tiptoes, doubled at the waist and drenched halfway down her back, craning out the window until the injured man was carried away. Pulling herself from the rain, she closed her shutter and ignored the small puddle around her feet. One of the princes was injured, but which one?

Endless cerulean eyes filled her mind. Prince Baldair, the second son, had stopped into the library right before returning to war. Vhalla had never met a member of the Imperial family before, but all the tales told about the Heartbreaker Prince had been true.

She gripped the front of her sleeping shift and forced herself to breathe deeply. The prince didn't even know who she was, Vhalla reminded herself. He had certainly forgotten the library apprentice whom he had caught mid-air as she had clumsily slipped from one of the bookcases' towering rolling ladders.

Now palace clerics were called, servants were woken to fetch blankets and stoke fires, apprentices of the healing arts would work all night, and all she could do was stand in silence.

Vhalla pushed away slick strands of hair sticking to her face. Roan was right; she was foolish for ever thinking of the Heartbreaker Prince. Vhalla was not the type of girl Prince Baldair would be interested in, she was far too plain.

The door slammed open. A petite blonde with ringlet curls stood breathless in the doorframe. Vhalla blinked at the woman, a woman Vhalla seemed to have summoned with her passing thought.

"Vhalla... library. Now," Roan panted. It was like she spoke another language, and Vhalla's body failed to oblige the command. "Vhalla, *now!*" Grabbing her wrist, Roan pulled her down the dimly lit halls, giving Vhalla no time to even dress properly.

"Roan. Roan! What's going on?" Vhalla demanded as they rounded a tight corner.

"I don't know much. Master Mohned will explain," Roan replied.

"Is it the prince?" Vhalla blurted.

Her friend paused, turning. "You *still* have the Heartbreaker Prince on your mind? It's been—what, two months?" Blue eyes, slightly darker than the prince's, rolled at Vhalla.

"It's not that. I—" she struggled, a hot flush rushing to her head.

"And why are you all wet?" Roan blinked, assessing her friend for the first time. Before Vhalla could answer, they were winding through the narrow servants' passages again. "It doesn't matter; just don't get water on the books."

The Imperial Library was housed within the palace, a part of the mountainside capital city of the Solaris Empire. Gilded, cherry wood bookcases, which stood taller than four men perched upon each other's shoulders, housed the vast knowledge of the Empire. Stained glass ran along the vaulted ceiling and, during normal sunny days, cast a kaleidoscope of color upon the floor.

Now, however, the library was swathed in darkness. Each apprentice stood by a candle at the central circulation desk in various stages of dress.

Her eyes passed over the motherly Lidia and briefly landed on the girl Cadance before falling on Sareem. Vhalla stared at his olive skin, a richer hue than hers, on display without a shirt. He was surprisingly toned, and Vhalla struggled to remember when her childhood friend had become a man. Sareem's eyes caught hers, and he seemed almost startled. Vhalla quickly looked away.

"We need every book on the magic and poisons of the Northern Sky Citadels of Shaldan. Bring them here. We shall read through them and take notes on what may be useful before forwarding them to the clerics." Master Mohned spoke as guards began to light more candles throughout the library. He looked every year of his ancient age, his long white beard unruly like the spindly roots of a tiny plant. Noticing the library apprentices all stood, mouths catching flies with shock, he snapped, "This is an Imperial Order! Go!"

Vhalla took a running start at a rolling ladder, using momentum to glide the length of a bookshelf. Her eyes scanned the titles, and her hungry hands plucked books. With three manuscripts cradled in her arms, she sprinted back to the central desk, depositing them on the floor before repeating the process.

The piles grew and sweat dotted Vhalla's brow. The master often scolded her for reading during work, but seven years of disobedience had burned a large list of titles into her mind. Book titles appeared before her eyes faster than her feet could carry her to them.

When the third stack of bound parchment stood taller than she, Vhalla noticed the other apprentices had stopped searching and claimed places on the floor to begin confirming the contents of each manuscript. She placed a palm over the stitch in her side. Their piles were so small. She could think of five tomes in potions alone that Sareem had missed.

The prince occupied her mind as she retrieved more books, his face in the forefront of her thoughts. His injuries must be serious if the clerics needed research beyond their common knowledge. Vhalla bit her lip, staring at her towers of books before the desk. What was wrong with him?

"Vhalla."

She missed the master's weathered voice while running through more titles in her head. There was one missing, *there had to be*. Was it in mysteries?

"Vhalla."

The prince's life could slip between their fingers due to missing only one line of text. Vhalla ran the back of her hand over her forehead. Sweat or water rolled down her neck.

"Vhalla!"

"What?" she replied sharply, staring at Mohned. Vhalla instantly realized her disrespectful tone.

The master let it slide. "That's enough; we have enough. Help us research. Write down anything you find of use."

Master Mohned motioned to the floor, and Vhalla took her place between Roan and Sareem. The library staff ignored all rules and decorum as they grabbed from a communal pile of quills, ink pots, and parchment in the middle of their circle.

Vhalla pulled the first book into her lap. "Master." She raised her head, turning away from the pages sandwiched between her trembling fingers. The sage looked at her through his spectacles. "Who's sick?"

"The prince."

Those two words were all the master needed to speak for

Vhalla's throat to feel drier than the Western Waste. She wished she had been wrong.

He was in the palace, somewhere beyond her reach. He needed help, and she was no one. Vhalla was barely above the servants who swept the halls and mucked the toilets as punishment for petty crimes. But maybe her years of reading could pay off and she could actually do something.

Vhalla grabbed another piece of parchment. Her quill roughly marred its blank surface with streaks of ink. This was all she could do. It was all she was ever good at. She could read and perhaps pass on some knowledge to a cleric who would save a man she hardly even knew.

Snapping a quill, Vhalla cursed and threw the broken tool aside before reaching for another. Sareem shot a curious look toward her, but the girl was a world away. The more Vhalla wrote, the calmer she felt. The quill was like an extension of her being and she forged the ink to her will as if she were under the spell of the words.

Slowly, the books began to grow in a new stack. Each had a note behind the cover, listing information she had found that she thought may be helpful. Vhalla hardly noticed her vertical workload diminishing as soldiers began to carry books out, armfuls at a time. She also did not turn to say goodbye as her friends wearily departed throughout the night.

Though her energy was fading, the more books that left the room, the more she was compelled to read. Gradually, warmth budded within her. Slowly at first, then growing with each passing hour until it flourished into a blazing heat.

The sound of the last book closing woke her from her trance. Vhalla blinked at her empty ink-stained hands. In the sunlight, she turned her eyes toward the heavens, and she stared tiredly at the magnificent rainbow of colored glass that ran the length of the ceiling. Dawn had arrived, and she could not even remember the night. Two hands clasped themselves tightly around her swaying shoulders.

Blinking the haze from her eyes, Vhalla looked at the man who appeared suddenly before her. An unfamiliar face stared back. He was a Southern man with icy blue eyes, a goatee, and short blond hair. While he wasn't menacing, she was certain that he was no one she had ever seen.

"This is the one?" He spoke to someone else, though his eyes were fixed on her.

"It is, minister," another unfamiliar voice replied.

"Thank you. You are dismissed," the Southern man ordered. Footsteps faded away with the sound of clinking armor.

"Who are you?" Vhalla's tongue found life again, the daze of feverish heat fading. She tried to make sense of who this man was and why he was touching her. Her eyes settled upon a crisp black jacket. It contrasted starkly to the morning light. No one in the palace wore black.

She felt dizzy. *Almost* no one wore black. "Wait, you're a—"

"No questions here." A large hand, clammy and cold, clasped over her mouth. "Don't be afraid; I'm here to help you. But you need to come with me."

Vhalla looked up at the man with wide eyes. She breathed sharply through her nose and shook her head in protest against the silencing palm.

"I must speak with you privately, but the Master of Tome will return soon. So, come with me." He slowly peeled his hand from her face.

"No." She almost fell backward. "I won't go with you! You shouldn't be here, I won't go there." Her mind was jumbled from panic, heightened by the night's exertion.

The man grabbed her once more with an annoyed look and a glance over his shoulder.

Vhalla opened her mouth to call out for help, but all she

inhaled was a strong herbal scent from the cloth that was suddenly pressed against her face. Right before she lost her struggle with her remaining consciousness, Vhalla saw the symbol embroidered on the man's jacket as he leaned forward to pick her up. Stitched over his left breast was a silver moon with a dragon curling around its center; split in two, each half was off set from the other. She had never seen it with her own eyes, but she knew what that ominous image meant: a sorcerer.

CHAPTER 2

It felt as though someone had taken an axe to the back of her head, split it open, and allowed her brain to leak out upon the unfamiliar pillow. Vhalla groaned and cracked open her eyes. Her face felt hot, and not from the sunlight that streamed through—in Vhalla's opinion—an enormous window.

The previous day came back to her in a rush. She sat and grabbed her temples as a chill raced through her. The prince's return, finding every book she could think of, practically passing out while reading, and the man and his strange black jacket—it all came back with sickening speed.

Vhalla looked around the room cautiously, as though a specter may lurk in any shadow. The walls were the palace's stonework, fitted and mortared. A decorative edge ran around the top of the room, unlike her own unadorned chambers. Sculpted dragons danced around moons.

Her eyes finally settled upon a small glass jar hanging from an iron hook bolted into the wall. Flickering within was a tongue of fire. There was no oil or wax to fuel it, no source for the flame. It simply hovered within its container.

She scrambled to her feet, bolting for the door. Her hands closed around the metal handle, and she tugged vigorously. The sound of iron on iron filled the room as the lock engaged and the door refused to budge. It was louder than the panicked scream stuck in her throat. The memory of the black-coated man flashed before her eyes; Vhalla blinked it away.

Taking a step back from the locked door, she frantically looked around the room. There was a bed, a small table, and a chamber pot. She ran to the window, throwing open the glass and looking downward. It was a dizzyingly straight drop to the ground far below.

The sound of the door latch disengaging brought her attention back within the room, and Vhalla plastered herself against the far wall. A sorcerer had taken her, and she did not want to believe where. The door swung open and a vaguely familiar pair of icy eyes met hers.

"Good to see you're awake." The man smiled cordially. "How do you feel?"

"Who are you?" Vhalla was so close to the wall that it would be impossible to fit even a piece of parchment between her back and the stone. She eyed the man warily. He wore different clothes today; long robes atop a tunic and trousers. Over his left breast was a patch that reaffirmed her panic: a black swatch with a broken moon.

"Do not be afraid." The man raised his hands unthreateningly. "No one will hurt you."

"Who are you?" Vhalla repeated. She knew by his floor-length robes and belled sleeves that the man was of higher rank than she, as almost everyone in the palace was. Vhalla struggled to keep her voice as calm and respectful as possible. She failed.

"Wouldn't you like to sit down?" He continued to ignore her question.

"I'd like to know who you are," Vhalla repeated slowly, her

eyes glued to his left breast. A nail chipped as she dug her fingers into the stone. "Why did you take me?"

"My name is Victor Anzbel," the man finally revealed with a small sigh. "I am the Minister of Sorcery, and you are in the Tower of Sorcerers. I took you because I need to speak with you, and doing so upon the library floor was not an option. Forgive me, but it was already dawn, and we didn't have time for relaxed introductions there."

"Wh-what could you possibly need to speak with me about?" Vhalla stuttered, leaning against the wall for a wholly different reason. She was in the Tower of Sorcerers speaking to the Minister of Sorcery. She must be dreaming.

"Please, come." He motioned to the door. "I do not wish to discuss this across a room."

Without waiting for her response, the man walked away, leaving the door open behind him. Vhalla heard his boots upon the stone floor in the unknown beyond. She didn't want to leave her wall. Her wall was safe and stable.

Sorcerers were odd and dangerous; they kept to themselves and left normal people alone. That was why they had their own Tower, so they kept out of sight and mind. Everyone in the South had always told her so. It was the last place *she* belonged.

"Would you like black or herbal tea?" the minister called nonchalantly from the other room.

Vhalla swallowed. Perhaps if she stayed still long enough she could become part of the wall and vanish from the world.

"I have cream and sugar also."

Vhalla weighed her options. There were two ways out: the window or the door. The former involved a long fall to certain death. The latter involved facing the sorcerer who had kidnapped her. She didn't like either of her options.

Vhalla inched forward toward the open door, wringing her hands into the sleeping gown she still wore. She didn't care if it was against Southern fashions, *she'd give anything for a pair of trousers.*

The minister was busy at a far counter in the connected room. A kettle sat over another unnatural flame as the man fumbled with jars of dried herbs and mugs. It was a workroom of sorts with a table, more beds, and bandages. Vhalla recognized some clerical salves and her eyes fell on a row of knives. Was she to be part of some living experiment?

"Ah, there you are. Please, take a seat." The man half turned, motioning to the table. His eyes held a youthful spark to which Vhalla was unaccustomed. She had always thought palace officials were ancient, like Master Mohned, but this man couldn't be more than ten years her senior.

Vhalla slunk along the far wall, careful not to bump into anything. She almost jumped out of her skin when her feet fell on something soft. Nothing more than a rug accounted for the plushness beneath her. Vhalla blinked at it. It was far nicer than what decorated the library. She curled her toes into the soft fibers.

"So then, black or herbal tea?" the man persisted, as though nothing about their situation was strange in the slightest. His hand hovered over the kettle, one mug already steaming.

"Neither." Vhalla had not forgotten the cloth he used to make her unconscious.

"Are you hungry, perhaps some food?" He accepted her refusal with grace, but left an empty mug on the countertop where he worked.

"No." Vhalla studied him carefully as he sat in the chair opposite her. The minister curled his fingers around his mug with an annoyingly relaxed little smile.

"If you change your mind you only have to say the word," he offered.

Vhalla's throat felt too gummy to do little more than nod. Tea would be nice, but the Mother Goddess in all her shining glory would cease to rise for dawn before she accepted anything from this man.

"What's your name?"

Vhalla bit her lower lip, torn between respecting the official sitting before her and the fear that threatened to set her balled hands to shaking. He could easily find out her name, she reasoned. Though forcing it between her lips was harder than confessing her darkest secret. "Vhalla," she answered. Perhaps if she obliged him he would let her go. "Vhalla Yarl."

"Vhalla, it is a pleasure to meet you." He smiled over his tea.

She tried to keep her face blank, something she was never really good at.

"I know you have many questions, so I will try to explain things as simply as possible. First, allow me to commend you on your efforts on our prince's behalf."

Vhalla nodded mutely. The library seemed like a different world. The only reminder that it was real was her clothing, the ink stains on her hands, and the fever heat still radiating throughout her body.

"Last night, I was summoned by the clerics to inspect the prince's magical Channels," he continued. "As a Waterrunner, they needed my knowledge."

"Prince Baldair doesn't have magic," Vhalla interrupted. She didn't understand the strange squint to his eyes.

The minister stroked his goatee, sitting back in his chair. "Prince Baldair is still at the front," he said finally.

Vhalla could not stop her mouth from falling open. If Prince Baldair wasn't in the palace, then that meant the prince she saved was...

"It's Prince Aldrik?" Every servant's whisper and mean spirited-word about the snobbish heir to the throne echoed in her ears. *That was the man she had struggled all night for?*

"It is." The minister chuckled, amused by her confusion and shock. Vhalla shut her mouth quickly. "While I was examining him, there was something peculiar about a certain set of notes tucked under some of the books' covers. Once the prince was stable, I had time to properly inspect them. They were crafted by a magical hand," Minister Victor explained, leaning forward. "Imagine my surprise when they were not from any of the Tower apprentices conducting similar research on our prince's behalf, but from the library."

"That's impossible."

"When a sorcerer makes something, trace amounts of magic might be left behind," the minister elaborated. "Especially when that sorcerer is not yet properly Awoken and their power Manifests itself in unexpected ways."

"I don't understand." Vhalla wanted to go home. She needed this man to say whatever it was he wanted to and then let her go back to her library. Work had already begun for the day, and she was late.

"Vhalla, you are a sorcerer," the minister finally said outright.

"What?" The world ground to a halt, and the silence weighed upon her shoulders.

A memory flashed before her eyes, a young girl standing before a farmhouse, begging for her father to stay. But he had to go; the Empire had called for soldiers to fight the magic taint that was seeping into the world from the Crystal Caverns. Vhalla remembered her father's leaving.

"What?" her voice was sharper, stronger. She was on her feet. "No, you have the wrong person, the wrong books. My notes must have gotten mixed up with someone else's. I'm not a sorcerer. My father was a farmer, my mother's parents worked in the post office of Hastan. None of us are—"

"Magic is not in the blood," the minister interrupted her hasty words. "Two sorcerers can give birth to a Commons," he explained, discussing those with and without magic. "Two Commons can give birth to a sorcerer. Magic chooses us."

"I'm sorry." Vhalla was laughing as though the world was one giant joke and she was the punchline. "I am not a sorcerer." She started for the door despite not knowing where it led. Her logical facilities weren't quite functioning. She just wanted out.

"You cannot run from this." The minister stood as well. "Vhalla, your powers have begun to Manifest. You are older than the normal age of such Manifestations, but it is happening." He blinked a few times. "Even now, I can see traces of magic woven around you."

She stopped, halfway between the minister and the door, and wrung her hands. Just because he claimed to see it did not mean it was there. *He might be lying*, Vhalla insisted to herself. Could she trust the word of a man who abducted her?

"Your magic will continue to grow. Nothing will stop it, and eventually you will be Awoken to your powers in full. It will be either at the hands of another sorcerer guiding you, or your powers will simply unleash themselves." The minister's tone held no levity. But the lack of jest made it no easier to believe.

"What could happen?" The nervous energy within her sought an outlet. Her whole body trembled as she waited for the answer.

"I don't know." Minister Victor reached for his mug of caramel-colored liquid, taking a long and thoughtful sip. "If you are a Firebearer, perhaps you light a candle with a glance. Or you could set the entire Imperial Library ablaze."

Vhalla nearly lost her balance and collapsed, the words knocking the wind from her. She shook her head, as if she could cast reality away.

"I want to go home," she finally breathed.

"I am sorry, Vhalla, but you should stay—"

"I want to go home!" Vhalla's cry interrupted him. Through

burning eyes she glared at a man to whom she should show respect and subservience.

He let her catch her breath before he spoke. "Very well," Minister Victor said with a soft and thoughtful voice.

"Really?" Vhalla's fingers relaxed, her fingernails leaving crescent moons in her palms.

"I can see this is a decision that will not benefit from force." He held up both hands in a sign of surrender. "Usually when I bring a budding sorcerer into the Tower, they come around. I had hopes that I would be able to show—"

"I don't want to see it!" Vhalla nearly shouted. Her hand went to her mouth, as if to take back the rough and rude words.

"Perhaps, some other time." The minister smiled.

As he led her out the door, Vhalla's eyes remained on her feet. The hall was a sloping downward spiral with doors at random intervals on either side. There were no windows, and she presumed the light to be from more of the unnatural flames that she had seen in the previous rooms.

Vhalla did not want to look at any of it. She didn't want to take anything away from this place, not even a memory. She didn't want to have anything in common with the strange Tower people who currently gave her and the minister a wide berth. Biting her lip, Vhalla choked back a sob. She was tired, and she did not have the energy for this sorcerer's lies. He was mistaken, and when she returned to the real world she would never have to think of this place again. Bringing her hands together she fidgeted with her fingers.

Yet, despite her mental and emotional withdrawal, Vhalla did see. She saw the endless rugs of dazzling patterns that lined this hall. Where one rug ended, the next began; her feet never even touched stone. She saw the start of ornamentation upon the walls, sculptures embellished with iron and silver, forming shapes she stubbornly would not permit herself to look upon.

Vhalla saw the feet of those who passed, boots and polished shoes. Why did sorcerers have such nice things when the slippers she owned were almost worn to holes? When her windows were archer's slits and her halls were barren, cracked, and roughhewn?

The minister wordlessly led her down a side hall. The stones began to shift into shapes and colors she was more familiar with, the lighting dimmer. Vhalla looked up, finally, as they stopped. Before them was a narrow, pointed dead end.

"Minister?" Panic blossomed in her anew.

"The Tower lives and dies by the moon, by the Father who keeps the realms of chaos at bay and guards the celestial gateway in the heavens above," he informed her cryptically. "When you have calmed down, I know you will come find us again. Most Manifesting sorcerers do, when they think logically."

"Will you take me by force again if I don't?" Vhalla took a half step back, strongly doubting she would ever seek out this man and his Tower by choice.

"My apologies for that." The minister had a glint in his eyes of what she almost believed to be sincerity. "I didn't see any other way to speak privately with you. I thought if you were in the Tower you would be willing to see what it held for you."

"I would have listened..." Vhalla looked away in annoyance. She wasn't sure which frustrated her more: his actions or the fact that he was right about her not being willing to mingle with sorcerers.

"Very well, I will see you soon I'm certain," he said lightly; little seemed to bother Victor Anzbel. Vhalla wondered how many times he had performed this same dance with another.

The minister held out a hand, motioning toward the dead end. Vhalla blinked at him, but he said nothing else. She stepped forward hesitantly. Reaching out a palm, she expected to push some form of hidden door. Her fingers vanished right into the stone.

Vhalla gasped and she looked back to the minister for explanation, but he was gone. She barely suppressed a shiver before plunging herself into the magic wall.

Emerging on the other side, Vhalla instantly recognized her location. The stone behind her looked the same as it had every day as she'd passed it growing up. Squinting, Vhalla noticed something she never had before—a circle, cut in two, its halves offset from the other—the broken moon of the Tower. How had she missed it all these years?

Timidly, she reached a hand forward, and it vanished back into the false wall. A spark of curiosity blossomed within her. What magic could do this?

Vhalla quickly put the thought from her mind. Too curious for her own good, the master had always scolded. Magic was dangerous. She reiterated the hushed words she had always heard on Southerner's tongues: *magic was risky and strange.*

She headed for the library as fast as her feet would carry her.

CHAPTER 3

It was far easier to feign normalcy when she was in her drab apprentice robes being scolded by the master for arriving almost four hours late for her duties. His words were restrained and her punishment was nothing more than being reprimanded in front of Roan, who sat at the desk transcribing. The other girl looked at Vhalla with curiosity; a glint in Roan's eye revealing she didn't buy Vhalla's excuse of oversleeping. The master did give it heed, however, after the prior night's excitement.

The master assigned Vhalla the most boring task there was in the library: alphabetization. Most of the staff resented the chore, but Vhalla found the dance of her fingers along the spines therapeutic. This was her world of safety and consistency.

"Vhalla," a voice whispered from the end of the aisle. Sareem glanced up and down the intersection where the shelves met. He motioned for her to follow, and she was down the ladder without a second thought, winding through bookshelves behind him toward the outer wall.

"What is it, Sareem?" Vhalla asked softly as they reached her window seat.

"Are you feeling well?" he asked, motioning for her to sit at his side.

"I'm fine." She could not meet his eyes as she sat. How could she sum up the unorthodox events of her day?

"You're lying," Sareem scolded. "You're a bad liar, Vhalla."

"It was a long night. I'm tired," she mumbled. That much was true.

"It's not like you to be late. I was worried." He frowned.

"Sorry to worry you," Vhalla apologized.

She had known Sareem for almost five years. He had started his apprenticeship only two years after her and they have been fast friends. Certainly she could trust him.

"Sareem, do you know any sorcerers?"

"What?" He leaned away, as though she had made some kind of threat. "Why would I associate with sorcerers?"

"I know your father is from Norin. I hear magic is more accepted in the West. I thought that maybe..." What began as a rushed excuse quickly lost its momentum.

"No." Sareem shook his head. "I don't know any sorcerers, and I don't plan to."

"Right," Vhalla agreed half-heartedly. She felt cold.

"What book is your head in now?" Sareem tapped her chin with his knuckles, bringing her eyes back to his. Vhalla attempted to make up some explanation but he wasn't about to allow it. "I know you, Miss Yarl." Sareem wore a satisfied smirk. "Read all you want, fine. I can't judge you for it, not after it likely saved the prince. But don't go seeking out sorcerers, all right?"

Vhalla couldn't stand his caring gaze.

"They're dangerous, Vhalla. Look at our crown prince. His mood is tainted by his flames, or so they say." Sareem rested a palm on her head, holding it there for a long moment. "Vhalla, you're warm."

"What?" She blinked, fretting that somehow he felt the magic within her.

"You're fevered." Sareem's hand had shifted to her forehead. "You shouldn't be here. We should go tell the master."

"I feel fine."

"No, if you strain yourself it will only get worse. Autumn Fever will be upon us before we know it, and you should keep up your strength." He was helping her up when she caught movement on the edge of her vision.

Vhalla's eyes shifted. At the far end of the shelves stood a figure shadowed between the beams of light cutting through the dust from windows. Her heart began to race. A black jacket covered the person's shoulders, the hem ending at the waist, and the sleeves stopping just below the elbow. She couldn't suppress a fearful chirp.

"Vhalla, what is it?" Sareem regained her attention, and by the time he turned to follow her wide-eyed stare, the person was gone.

"N-nothing." Vhalla struggled to keep her voice stable.

Sareem helped her back to the main desk, where he was, in turn, scolded for not working. Her friend disappeared back into the stacks with a small grin in Vhalla's direction. The master affirmed Sareem's claims by placing a wrinkled palm on her forehead. With father-like worry he sent her back to her chambers early to rest.

Alone outside the library, Vhalla quickly found the statue that was spaced far enough from the wall to allow someone to side-step behind—and disappeared. Vhalla knew every crack in the walls, every uneven stone beneath her feet, and every servant passageway. She had been walking this route for almost seven years since her father traded an opportunity to advance from foot soldier in the militia to palace guard after the War of the Crystal Caverns; a trade he had made to see that his daughter had a better future than a farm in Cyven, the East.

Her hand paused upon her door handle; footsteps at the far end of the hall called her attention. A group of servants and apprentices passed along one of the passageways' crossroads. She squinted past them, farther down still. A pair of eyes stared back at her. Vhalla disappeared quickly into her room, throwing herself upon her bed. Sleep would not have come so quickly were it not for the exhaustion that seeped from her very bones.

Her sleep was restless and filled with a vivid dream.

She dreamt she felt the night air upon her skin as she stood before the palace-side library doors. Torches flanked them, their carved surfaces set shadows dancing in unnatural ways. Through the crack between the doors she felt the cool, musty air of the library beyond, like the breath of a sleeping beast.

The doors did not obstruct her; like the fake wall in the Tower, they allowed her to pass through with ease. Vhalla soon found herself in the moonlit library. She turned, starting for her window seat. Her heartbeat fluttered faster than a hummingbird's wings. There, she had to go there.

The world began to blur, the bookcases fading into a haze. Everything slipped around her as she raced toward her destination. Upon her favorite perch sat the hunched figure of a man. Hazy and shadowed, she could not make out his features and, when he finally turned, the movement was pained. Surprise tensed his shoulders, and Vhalla could only make out a pair of dark eyes set upon a blurry face, struggling to focus on her much as she was struggling to focus on him.

"Who are you?" The man's words were as deep and dark as midnight. They resonated directly into Vhalla's core, and it fractured the faded world around her.

Wait, Vhalla cried. Wait! Only air passed through her lips.

Everything surrounding her lost its sharpness and began to crumble beneath her feet. She fell into darkness.

Vhalla awoke with a start, her covers upon the floor from thrashing about in her sleep. She pressed a palm to her forehead. Her skin wasn't fevered, but it was clammy from night-sweats.

It was a dream, she insisted while readying herself for the day. But nothing seemed to be able to calm the nerves upsetting her stomach, not even the familiar scratch of her rough spun woolen clothing. She had worn the same clothes for years, though Vhalla was suddenly tugging at her robe's sleeves uncomfortably.

She had a similar dream the next night, and the night after that, each time more vivid than the last. She ignored the shakes the dreams left in their wake. Vhalla blamed it on the black-clad figures who seemed to stalk her every movement—just beyond the edge of her vision. She did not go a day without seeing a sorcerer swathed in black, but only out of the corners of her eyes.

They stood at the edge of a bookshelf, the junction of a hall; sometimes they passed through doors that would be locked when she tried the knob. No one else ever saw them. Not Roan, who sorted books with her. Not Sareem when he walked her back to her room after dinner, meals that sat too heavy in her stomach.

The feel of eyes upon her became as common as breathing. What they wanted from her—they did not say. What they were waiting for—they did not reveal.

Vhalla ignored her suspicion that she already knew what they sought.

One day, she was working alone in the library when the hairs at the nape of her neck rose on end.

At the end of the row stood a woman. She wore a variation of the Tower's apprentice robes that Vhalla had only seen once or twice before. The black jacket still ended at her waist, but the sleeves were capped over the shoulders. Vhalla could not guess the significance of having different styled robes; library apprentices all wore the same.

The woman did not move, she did not even seem to breathe. Dark brown eyes, almost black, were set upon deep tan Western skin. Black hair fell straight around her face with a horizontal fringe cut right below the woman's brow. Her hair was longer in the front and shorter in the back, exposing her neck.

It was the first time Vhalla had seen one of her watchers long enough to examine their appearance. She didn't know what she had been expecting, but the woman looked like any other Westerner. Wasn't she always told that sorcerers were different from normal people?

"What do you want?" Vhalla whispered. Her eyes watered, she did not even allow herself to blink for fear the woman would vanish.

"Have you ever read any of these?" The woman had a thick accent, holding her *a*'s and *y*'s like those of the West. Vhalla had heard traces of it in Sareem, even though he had been born and raised in the South.

"These?" Vhalla repeated carefully.

"These books," the woman clarified. "Have you ever read any of them?"

"Of course I have," Vhalla retorted defensively. People did not often question her knowledge of the library, especially when it came to her reading.

"And you still fear us?" The woman squinted slightly, tilting her head.

Vhalla subconsciously took a step away. "I-I don't fear—" The woman's approach stilled her words. What would this person do to her? Vhalla looked over her shoulder to make sure Sareem or Roan weren't nearby. She jumped when she looked back—the sorcerer stood right before her.

"This one." Pulling a manuscript from the shelf, the woman passed it to her. "Read this."

"Why?" Vhalla accepted the manuscript from the woman with hesitant fingers. She read the title quickly: *An Introduction to Sorcery*.

"Because you are too smart to be so afraid of what you are," the dark-haired woman replied simply, turning to walk away.

Vhalla blinked, reeling from the strange interaction. "Wait," she called a little too loudly. "What's your name?"

The woman stopped. Vhalla clutched the book with white knuckles, holding her breath. Dark eyes assessed her, silently thoughtful.

"Larel." With that, she vanished down the rows. Vhalla did not even try to pursue.

By the time the closing bells rang out across the library, Vhalla's neck ached from being hunched over reading for so long. She had acquired additional manuscripts on magic to aide her on the more complex points. One was on magical Affinities, the other on sorcerers' history.

Retrieving her worn bookmark from the powder blue sash holding her robes closed, Vhalla put it delicately between the pages. She returned the manuscript to its place on the shelf, stacking her references on either side, out of order. No one else would be reading in the section of mysteries.

The next morning she trailed behind Roan as they walked through the palace. War was still being fought in Shaldan, and they had received a shipment of books to process from a conquered city. The guards had refused to carry the heavy crates up to the Imperial Library. Why two of the smallest girls in the palace were sent instead was a mystery to Vhalla.

As they descended through the outer wall, she began to wipe sweat from her brow. The library opened into the town at one of the palace's highest access points and was always cooler, even in summer. The stables were farther down along the capital's main road.

"Did you know that when we first began to worship the Mother, all the Crones were Firebearers?" Vhalla blurted out suddenly, recalling the prior day's reading.

"What?" Roan blinked, turning. "What's a Firebearer?"

"I..." Vhalla opened and closed her mouth like a fish, formulating words. The last thing she wanted to do was admit to reading books on magic by explaining Firebearers. Ignoring Roan's question she continued on. "Well, I didn't know this, since the Empire invaded Cyven to spread the word of the Mother."

"I know the history of the Empire's expansion." Roan laughed lightly. "It's not that long."

"Right, well, I always thought that worshiping the Mother Sun came from the South, since the Emperor says his wars are to rid the world of heathens. But it's actually Western. King Solaris names himself Emperor, invades Mhashan, takes their religion, and uses it to claim Cyven and now Shaldan," Vhalla mused aloud. "But, he's doing it to spread a faith—or at least he claims —that isn't originally his."

"All right, what are you reading?" Roan hummed in amusement.

"Don't you think that's interesting?" Vhalla asked, dropping all mention of sorcery.

"I do." Her friend smiled. The expression quickly turned into a teasing grin. "I also think someone's been reading strange things when they should be working."

Vhalla looked away, guilty as charged. Her friend only laughed, nudging her side. Roan was less than a year older than Vhalla, and they had always looked out for each other. When they met seven years ago, only Lidia and another man, who was now long gone, worked as library apprentices. Two eleven-year-old girls hardly had any interest in twenty-somethings; Vhalla and Roan had taken to each other out of necessity and kinship in the written word.

Rounding a corner, they came to a small landing that overlooked the ground below. Vhalla ignored a shadowed figure on the edge of her vision. The stables were two large buildings built into the walls of the castle, each on either side of the main road leading up to the palace. They stretched on for an impossibly long time, and she always felt a little awe at all the horses, carts, and carriages they could contain. Presently, most of the stalls stood empty due to the strain the war was putting on the Empire's resources.

After their brief escape into the sunlight, the women returned inside and descended a short, spiral staircase and exited out a small door onto the rocky, dusty ground. By the smaller portal were two, massive, opulent doors that Vhalla knew were for decoration over function. Behind them was a viewing room where the Emperor would—from time to time— allow common folk to speak of their troubles, on those rare times when he wasn't off at war. She had only stood in that throne room once before when her father had first brought her to the capital to ask the Emperor to exchange his promotion into the palace guard for an opportunity to find an apprenticeship for his daughter.

The first six stalls belonged to the Imperial family. All but two were empty. The Empress's mount, a beautiful white mare, stood stoically in place. In the adjacent stall resided a Warstrider that snorted as she passed. Vhalla stopped, captured by the beast's eyes.

"I hear the soldiers call it the *nightmare stallion*." Roan was suddenly next to her, also studying the oversized creature as she spoke. "I think it comes—in part—from the prince's reputation, but I hear the beast is pretty foul toward most."

"His reputation?" Vhalla looked quickly at a plaque on the stall door. *Prince Aldrik Solaris.*

"He's a sorcerer. It makes people uncomfortable. Magic is something that should stay within the Tower." Roan tucked a piece of lemon-colored hair behind her ear.

Vhalla had always been jealous of Roan's hair and generally everything else about her. Vhalla's hair was a boring brown mess of frizz and untamable waves; Roan's fell in beautiful curls. Southerners were lucky with their light skin and features. Even the Gods were shown that way. Vhalla felt perpetually inadequate compared to Southerners and Westerners. Those in the East usually had straw-colored skin with dark brown eyes and wavy hair. Nothing was fantastic about her.

"They say the prince's eyes glow red with rage," Roan murmured.

"What do you think?" Vhalla whispered, looking up at her friend.

"I don't know. I've never seen a battlefield, and when I have seen the prince, his eyes have never been red." Roan put her hands on her hips, squinting at the horse as if it would give her some secrets about its owner. "But I think that in every rumor there is a small piece of truth."

They started walking again, closing the distance to the cart section of the stables.

"Then, do you think it's true he's a bastard?" Vhalla asked quietly, not wanting to be overheard by any others walking about, particularly those in black robes she suspected to be lingering in the shaded stalls.

"I don't know if it matters. The Emperor married our late Empress before she showed. Who is to say whether or not she was with child before their wedding bed? But the Emperor claims the prince is his legitimate heir and, since our first Lady

Solaris walks the lands of the Father now, no one can say differently." Roan shrugged.

Vhalla nodded, recalling a book she read on the Imperial family when she was fresh to the capital. After conquering the West twenty-five years ago, the Emperor quickly took a Western bride to his bed, tying loyalties with blood. But there were always whispers surrounding the wedding to the youngest daughter of the late Western king when she had two older, eligible sisters. Her death, while giving birth to the Empire's crown prince within one year of the wedding, had only made it worse.

Upon reaching the cart section, the young women met the Master of Horse. After navigating through greetings and polite chatter they retrieved the books they had come for. The crates that held the manuscripts were too heavy to carry, and the contents had to be split into smaller boxes, the rest to be retrieved at a later date.

It took almost triple the time to cover the same distance back up the palace. At first, both girls seemed to be playing a game of denial and determination, but once Vhalla suggested they take a breather, those breaks became something that occurred liberally throughout the rest of their ascent.

After parting ways with Roan at the desk, Vhalla disappeared into the books to pretend to work. She retrieved her manuscripts from mysteries without thought, carrying them over to her window seat. It wasn't until everything was set out that Vhalla noticed the piece of paper folded around her bookmark. She looked around quickly, there were no black-clad observers.

A tingle shot through her fingers as she touched the paper, prompting a sharp intake of breath. The book fell open-faced to the floor, forgotten. Vhalla stared at the foreign, slanted, tight script.

To Vhalla Yarl...

CHAPTER 4

Deep lines appeared between Vhalla's brows as she studied the note. The writing was unfamiliar. Lidia's slanted the other direction. The master's was far spikier. Sareem's wasn't half as lovely. Cadance was a child, and her writing showed it. Roan's was the closest, but Vhalla knew how Roan formed every capital letter from years of penmanship classes together.

No, this wasn't anyone from the library.

To Vhalla Yarl,

To the one who denies her heritage and seeks out danger by dismissing the tutelage and open arms of the Tower of Sorcerers. To the foolish girl who risks her life and the lives of those around her by walking about, Manifesting freely. To she who is so selfish that she would inconvenience her peers by making them babysit her every movement.

It is time to stop pretending. It is time to become serious about who you are and your future as a sorcerer. Enough time has been wasted already.

She stared numbly at the antagonistic note. With a cry she crumpled and threw it across the window seat, watching it bounce off the opposite wall. Had it been the woman, Larel? The note seemed nothing like her, but what did Vhalla know? What did she know about any of them?

Vhalla ignored the crumpled parchment for the rest of the day before reluctantly picking it up, folding it, and placing it beneath her sash as the closing bells rang. Sareem linked arms with her, walking toward the mess hall, but Vhalla quickly excused herself, encouraging Roan and the young man to go ahead. She wasn't hungry and meals were the first thing she sacrificed when her mind was full.

Alone in her room sitting in dim candlelight, Vhalla inspected the note over again. Every word sent red heat to her cheeks. Before she could stop herself, Vhalla was reaching for a quill and ink.

Of the phantoms stalking my waking hours, I don't know which one you are, but you know nothing. I am no sorcerer. If this is Larel, you may speak with me in person as you did last time. I am not about to indulge someone so cowardly that they will not even sign their name. I am reading books on magic purely for—

FOR WHAT? Vhalla's quill paused. Why was she reading the book the sorcerer had handed her? There wasn't any point to it. It wasn't as if Vhalla would—or could—ever use the knowledge it contained.

—personal intellectual improvement and learning. Go bother someone else.

SHE DROPPED her face into her palms. This wasn't who she was. Vhalla muttered a curse under her breath. She did not speak harshly to strangers—or even those she knew. This was the Tower's fault. Were it not for their persistence with wearing her down with every waking hour, Vhalla would not be so exhausted. She crumpled the note once more and threw it into her closet, trying to ignore it.

Her exhaustion was not helped by that same recurring dream. Every night she chased shadows and asked hazy figures for names, only to have her words vanish into wind.

The next morning she shrugged on her apprentice robes, not even trying to run a brush through her hair.

Grabbing her reply off the closet floor, she resolved to give this sorcerer a piece of her mind. She hardly cared if she offended some random apprentice in the Tower of Sorcerers. The note went in *An Introduction to Sorcery,* and Vhalla expected that to be the end.

She was wrong.

The person exceeded her expectation in their stubbornness.

Yarl,

I am not stalking the halls. I do not slink or dodge. I am waiting to see if you are even worthy of my time. I am not a phantom with little better to do than keep an eye on your wellbeing. I am <u>the</u> phantom in the darkness.

However, if your last note and desperate attempts at research really are any indication, you are not worth an iota of the ink on this

*page. Perhaps you should do the sorcerer community a favor and
Eradicate yourself before you embarrass us all?*

THAT SHOULD HAVE BEEN the moment when she stopped writing. That should have been the moment when Vhalla threw her hands in the air, marched to the Tower, and demanded to be Eradicated. At least, after looking up that Eradication meant the removal of a sorcerer's powers and not some horrible death sentence.

But Vhalla had little that she called her own. She did not have clothes, gems, or precious metals. She had never even eaten fresh fruit other than what her mother had grown around their farmhouse when she was a girl. Vhalla did have one precious thing though: her knowledge. And she would be cursed before she would let an apprentice of the Tower show her up intellectually.

To the one who declares themselves "the phantom,"

Perhaps I should demand to be Eradicated! I read about the War of the Crystal Caverns; the magic unleashed there was not only capable of warping men's minds and bodies into abominations but it is also written that the magic was set free by sorcerers' meddling. It was a two-year war against monsters that kept my father from my mother and I as she lay sick and dying. War and horror spawned and fueled by magic.

Perhaps the world should be Eradicated!

Vʜᴀʟʟᴀ ʜᴀᴅ ɴᴇᴠᴇʀ ʙᴇᴇɴ ᴍᴏʀᴇ certain that she should rid herself of whatever magic she may possess. Everything she had always been told was right, and it only took half a book on the history of the Empire's most mysterious war to understand this. Magic changes things; magic made more men die at war; magic could turn a human into an abomination.

Vhalla shoved the books back on the shelf in self-righteous anger.

Anger fought a battle with amazement when this person was stubborn enough to pen out another reply.

Yarl,

You were reading about the War of the Crystal Caverns? Was your interest in history sparked by your introduction to magic or your misplaced vendetta against it? In either case, allow me to elaborate on your reading. Perhaps, in this, you may be right. There are good men among the wicked in this world, donning the fleece of the innocent. He who set free the power that warps the hearts, minds, and bodies of mortals was certainly wicked. The actions of this man should condemn only him, not all who wield magic. It was also because of sorcery that the war could be ended and the power resealed in the Crystal Caverns. Soldiers – your father – came home because of the magical warriors of the Black Legion.

Consider that, when you wish to be Eradicated. Are you going to be the sorcerer who could have saved lives but chose instead to be no one? When a sword is thrust into someone's gut, do you blame the sword or the knight who wields it?

When will you stop being afraid, read, and learn more about who you are?

VHALLA STARED AT THE NOTE. She did not know what was more agitating; this person's tone or the fact that they were right. Vhalla confirmed their claims by actually finishing the book she started the day prior. The Black Legion, the war sorcerers of the Empire, had been integral to sealing the Caverns and their dangerous magic once more.

Were those sorcerers any different from any other soldiers? No, her quill paused for a moment, hovering over her blank page. Were sorcerers very different from the people she called *normal*?

Phantom,

I've moved away from the introduction; I want to learn more about what sorcerers do, what magic is. I found a book on magical Affinities. As I understand it, the early sorcerers in the West believed that magic came from the Mother Sun in the form of her elements, so they harnessed and trained those elements. This is why Crones were the only ones with fire Affinities, called Firebearers.

Then I began to research Groundbreakers next. It seems with their abilities to mend wounds, charge magical salves, and create potions would be most useful.

Vhalla Yarl

As MUCH AS Vhalla did not want to, she found the words of her challenger's notes embedding themselves into her head. At every opportunity over the next weeks, Vhalla withdrew to sneak down the long rows of books into the aisle of mysteries. As the pile of notes in her closet grew, so did her awe and appreciation for her phantom's seemingly endless knowledge.

Yarl,

What is magic? I am afraid you will not find that answer in these books. It is a question more suited for theologians and philosophers.

Am I to commend you for pointing out the obvious? Tell me why Groundbreakers can do these things and maybe I shall grace you with further correspondence.

The phantom

VHALLA VIGOROUSLY RESEARCHED an answer the rest of that afternoon and the day after. How dare this person push her so far, further than even the master had ever pushed her, to pursue new knowledge? Something about their words seeped deep into her. Pride swelled in her chest when she found something that may be considered acceptable by her phantom. It was undeniable: she wanted to impress her phantom.

Phantom,

While not exclusive to their Affinity or proximity to Shaldan, Groundbreakers will often times possess magical sight. This gives them the ability to locate afflictions in the body and to diagnose illness. But, as the writing illustrates, this is not exclusive to Groundbreakers. I could not find anything beyond that.

Vhalla Yarl

WITHOUT REALIZING IT, Vhalla's days began to fall into a repetitive cycle of work, a note from the Phantom, and sleep. She found a rhythm in managing her work to maximize the amount of time in her window seat. The more she read, the more she realized that she had never contemplated the ways of the magical world. She was disappointed in herself as a scholar, and that only served to fuel her continued research. Vhalla had always considered herself intelligent, at least above average. But could she even make that claim if she ignored a whole field of study with a closed mind?

Yarl,

I see your tone has changed. Very well, now that you are showing some appropriate humility, I shall indulge you. A Groundbreaker possesses an Affinity for the earth, but if they are lucky they also possess an Affinity of the self that gives them the ability to inspect a person better than any cleric. Affinities of the self are lesser known, and the literature is sparser as a result. However, what we do know is that every natural Affinity bears a unique Affinity of the self, even if not all sorcerers of an elemental Affinity possess the skills.

The phantom

DESPITE HERSELF, Vhalla began to contemplate Affinities. If she was indeed a sorcerer, what Affinity would she have? At night, when writing by candlelight, Vhalla stared into the flame, wondering if she could make it move and dance as the Firebearers in her books could.

Phantom,

I wonder, do all people have an Affinity? Is every man and woman an untapped magical being? Is everyone simply waiting to Manifest?

I have been reading about the history of magic and it seems sorcery is connected with some of our oldest traditions. I never realized that the mirror that passes from one Head Crone to another was intended to be a vessel for keeping the Mother's own magic within.

The writing on the Crone's mirror led me to find a work by a man named Karmingham. He discussed magical transference via conductors and storage via vessels. Is anything a sorcerer touches a magical vessel?

Sincerely,

Vhalla Yarl

SOME DAYS she would reread the notes. She'd stare at that slanted, tight script and wonder whose hand wrote it. No one ever came forward, from Tower or library staff. The longer the game went on, the more she began to think he really was a phantom haunting the library. She would joke with herself that he was the same man who had been lurking in her dreams for weeks.

Vhalla Yarl,

Your tone has changed. Are you beginning to consider sorcery with something more than your prior ill-conceived, ignorant notions?

I regret to inform you that not all people have a magical Affinity. Most are simply close-minded Commons who fear something only because they do not know and cannot understand it. You are special. Magic has chosen you, and it is time you accept that.

I am impressed that you picked a work like Karmingham and deciphered it. Perhaps something has sunk in these past few weeks.

You are correct; a magical vessel can either conduct or store magic. It is impossible to have an item that does both. But vessels are difficult to create, even for experienced Waterrunners. While unintentional vessels are possible, they are highly uncommon because a sorcerer's will must be very strong to form one. More often, a vessel is created when a sorcerer leaves a magical trace in something he or she makes. Not true power, but like an inky fingerprint upon a blank page.

The phantom

HER DREAMS BECAME A GROWING problem that Vhalla ignored by daylight. Every night, she dreamed of trying to reach a figure in the darkness. The only explanation was that those dreams were a result of the mysterious notes.

Dear phantom,

Your praise warms me in an odd way, despite your bleak outlook on the world. I think it should be a sorcerer's obligation to share magic with Commons, as you seem to call non-magical people, in a way that is easy to understand—like you have done with me.

I am not special. I have never been someone who is special. But perhaps you are right that my tone has changed these past weeks under your tutelage.

Here is my question for you today: Why is it that Affinities seem to prefer geographical regions?

Sincerely,

Vhalla

WHILE THEY CONTINUED to exchange notes through the introduction book, Vhalla's reading now extended far beyond that primer. There were times that she wanted to share her notes with Roan or anyone. But then Vhalla remembered what the writing signified. No one other than her phantom would share her enthusiasm for magic. Well, no one other than her phantom —and other sorcerers in the Tower.

As a result, in an odd way, her phantom was becoming easier to confide in and speak openly to than her closest friends. The anonymity fit Vhalla's inquisitive mind and she found it easy to reveal things about herself.

> *Vhalla,*
>
> *Call me bleak; I call you naïve and optimistic. Shall we deem it even?*
>
> *I do not praise you to warm you; I praise you so that you may continue to learn. But you may take what you will from it.*
>
> *No sorcerer seems to know why Affinities favor geographical regions. It is known that the majority of Firebearers are from the West, Waterrunners from the South, and Groundbreakers from the North.*
>
> *You think you are under my tutelage. Do you consider me your teacher?*
>
> *Sincerely,*
> *The phantom*

Vhalla wasn't sure how to respond, so she spent that night tossing and turning. If she confessed she had begun to see the phantom as a teacher, did that make her a sorcerer? The girl within her ran in terror at the thought. But after their correspondence began, there was also a budding woman inside her who faced the idea of being a sorcerer with a level head.

. . .

Dear phantom,

Perhaps I do consider you my teacher. The last sorcerer I spoke to drugged me and spirited me to the Tower. At least your worst offense is your sharp tongue and that you have not told me your name. Who exactly are you?

You covered South, North, and West. But, what of the East?

Sincerely,

Vhalla Yarl

"Vhalla!" Roan gave her a shove as they wandered toward the library from breakfast.

"Roan, sorry, what?" Vhalla mumbled, rubbing her shoulder.

"What is it with you lately?" Roan studied her up and down.

"I'm tired." The truth of her words seeped into them.

"Yes, you are, but I have seen you tired before. This is different. You keep weird hours, and only pick at your food during meals, if you take them at all," Roan argued.

Vhalla shrugged.

"Even Sareem has noticed something is wrong. He asked about you; he's noticed your habits," her friend muttered, her voice flat.

Vhalla continued to stare forward. Roan's words were distant, like she was speaking under water. Who cared about Sareem? There were more important things on her mind. One such thing was the fact that sorcerers no longer seemed to be stalking her waking hours.

"Don't tell me," Roan whispered. "You and Sareem—are you an item?"

"What?" Vhalla blinked, summoned back to life. "Sareem and I? No."

"Really?" Roan hummed. "He clearly cares about you, and he comes from a good family. You know his father was Norin's ship builder."

Vhalla nodded.

"And he's handsome in that Western way. I always thought Southern blue eyes were striking on Western skin..."

"Excellent," Vhalla murmured, half-heartedly.

"Really, not Sareem then?" Roan asked again.

Why did she care so much? "No, not Sareem," Vhalla confirmed.

"But it is a boy?" her friend teased, laughing at the idea of Vhalla romantically involved with someone.

Vhalla almost tripped over her own feet, earning a slow, penetrating stare.

"Is it? By the Sun, is it a boy?"

"I don't know what you're talking about." Vhalla looked away.

The blonde's hands clasped on Vhalla's shoulders, and soon Vhalla stood in a small side hall.

"Roan, we're going to be late."

"Then tell me faster, so we're not." Roan grinned.

Vhalla focused on the freckles dotting Roan's nose rather than the uncomfortably eager look her friend was giving her.

"I thought you weren't interested in boys after..."

"Narcio?" Vhalla sighed. He had owned her heart for a few months, and Vhalla had been young enough to think it was love. She didn't regret her time with him, but things just hadn't worked out. Vhalla wasn't exactly good at relationships as she preferred to spend more time with books than people. Still, Vhalla wished she knew what became of the man whom she had lain with for the first time as a woman. "I'm not a Crone. Of course I'm still interested."

"So who, what, where, when, how?" Roan persisted.

"There isn't much to tell," Vhalla sighed, finally relenting. "I don't know his name, I don't even know if he is a he..." she revealed softly, looking into the neighboring hallway to see if anyone walked too close.

"You're making no sense." Roan loosened her grip.

"It's complicated, but it's special. I've learned a lot; he's *really* smart, and witty, too... in a mean sort of way, sometimes. But he is someone who seems to understand just how to push me, and yet I can't seem to figure out anything about him." She stopped herself before rambling on and giving away too much.

"But, how do you not know?" Roan scrunched her eyebrows.

"I've never actually met him." Before her friend could ask, Vhalla continued, "We communicate through notes in books. That's all." She turned and quickly continued down the hallway to the welcomed escape of work.

"Wait, so that's why you're always running off lately? And carrying your satchel?" Roan pointed to the leather bag on Vhalla's shoulder that she subconsciously gripped tighter. "To write notes to your secret lover?"

"Not my lover," she remarked sharply.

"Fine. But, Vhalla, this is weird," Roan whispered. Before Vhalla could offer up some kind of retort, her friend continued, "But it is kind of exciting."

They parted ways upon arriving at the library. Vhalla quickly learned her task for the day, completed it, and headed toward her window seat. Her hands were eager to find a book with a note tucked within.

Dear Vhalla,

The East's Affinity was air. They were called Windwalkers, but there has not been one for one hundred and forty-three years.

I have already told you who I am. I am the phantom in the darkness.

Sincerely,

The phantom

LATER THAT NIGHT, Vhalla fought sleep. In one hand she clutched the cryptic note, the other ran through her long hair, snagging on tangles.

She was tired of these games. Despite the trenchant and dry nature of her phantom, she did not want their correspondence to end. Her eyes drifted closed, and she was no closer to a resolution of the battle raging inside her.

SHE STOOD in the empty hallway before the torchlit library doors. Normally she entered at a run, but this time she walked. There was no need to run; it would all be the same anyway. She passed through histories, down the hall of mysteries, and a little farther still to her window seat.

There she saw him, a black shadow illuminated only by the light of a single flame hovering magically at his side. He didn't move and, for the first time, she didn't try to speak.

In the silence Vhalla studied him. This night her dream became sharper, clearer. By not trying to speak, the dream remained stable long enough to make out features that normally were shadowed and fogged. The man was older than she by about six to eight years. His shoulder-length black hair was slicked back, away from his face and set with something that gave off a dull shine in the light.

"You are early tonight." A deep voice hovered in the silence.

Vhalla was confused. I'm early? *she wanted to ask, but only air escaped from her mouth.*

"You have to try harder," he sighed, pretending to inspect the book he had propped against his black-clad knees.

Try harder? *Still only air passed through her moving lips.*

"Tell me your name," he commanded.

What?

"Tell me your name," he demanded again, agitation clipping his words.

Vhalla.

"Tell me your name!" He snapped his book shut and turned to her. She could almost see the fire behind his coal-colored eyes.

Don't slam books closed! *She found her voice, and it echoed through the dream from her to his ears.*

VHALLA FELT his laughter resonating through her as she woke with a start.

Sitting, she tried to control her ragged breathing. It was hopeless and something wild took her.

She was up, on her feet, and down the hall in a flurry of motion. Vhalla didn't even think twice as she put her shoulder to the solid library door to push it open. A faint flicker of light glittered off the lacquered shelves.

Her sudden stop almost caused her to tumble forward into the man on the window seat—*her* window seat. Her chest rose and fell with each gasping breath, and her side hurt slightly from the sprint, but her eyes locked onto him. She stood there in silence for a long moment, the stunning clarity of the world around her reminding her that this wasn't a dream.

Slowly, he put his hand on the seat and turned, piercing her with his eyes. A knowing smirk spread across his face as he commanded her with only his stare. Minutes or hours could have passed before he spoke.

"I knew you would come."

CHAPTER 5

Reality hit Vhalla like a slap across the face. Pinned to the man's breast was a symbol she knew well. She would know that symbol—a symbol that hovered over her every waking hour—better than any in the world. Crafted in gold gleamed the blazing sun of the Empire.

She stood barefooted and in her nightgown before the crown prince, the second most powerful man in the world. He shifted his feet to the floor, nonchalantly placing his book on the bench. Moving his elbows to his thighs, he rested his head in his palm with one dark eyebrow arched, as though he had already become bored.

His eyes held her to the spot with an unbroken gaze. They simply stared at each other and, while Vhalla felt her anger slowly rising to a boil inside, his demeanor was perfectly calm. As time dragged on, it gave birth to her nerves. Whatever had possessed her vanished, and she realized this was a dangerous course of action. She was playing with fire.

"Y-you, you knew I would come?" Vhalla finally stammered

out, wishing her tongue would obey her more eloquently before a prince.

"Oh, without doubt." The prince's voice was soft but she could feel it reverberating through her bones.

"How?" She blinked.

"Oh, Vhalla." He chuckled and it made her tense. "Since when have I simply told you things?" He stood and she looked up at him, realizing he was head and shoulders taller than she, even taller than his brother. "I have never fed you information; you are far too *smart* for that. Where is the sport?" He rounded her, peering down the bridge of his nose. Vhalla felt like wounded prey snared in the trap of far bigger game. "Think, Vhalla. How did I know you would come running to me?"

"I don't know," she whispered.

He paused behind her, leaning close to her ear. Vhalla could feel the small hairs on the back of her neck move as he spoke.

"Vhalla." She barely suppressed a shiver at his voice on her skin. "Show me that big intellect for which the world seems to praise you."

"The dreams," she breathed deeply and closed her eyes. He leaned away from her, and she let out a small sigh of relief.

"Very good." It was a compliment, but it didn't feel sincere.

"What about the dreams?" She turned to face him. A flame hovered magically over his shoulder. Her fascination with the tiny fire was only halted by her inability to catch her breath when she looked at *him*.

From this angle, the light was at her back and she could study his face properly. He had high cheekbones and a pronounced nose, his face was narrower and more angular than his brother's. All of his facial structures were distinctly Western, save for Southern pale skin that seemed paper-white even in the orange glow. Nothing about him was traditionally handsome yet, for it all, he was astonishingly striking.

"Not thinking again," the prince drawled, leaning against a bookshelf and looking bored anew.

"I don't know," Vhalla said weakly.

"Of course you do." He yawned.

"No, I don't," she insisted, putting her hands on her hips defiantly.

"Then I thought wrong about you. You are boring, like everyone else." He shrugged and turned, starting down the row of books.

Frustration and helplessness twisted her insides as she watched him go. She had no business speaking to the crown prince.

"Wait!" Her curious mind objected to that obedient, rule-abiding voice within her. "Wait, my prince!" She scampered after him, blocking his way.

A small smirk played at the corner of his mouth. The arrogant royal had known she was going to chase after him.

"They weren't just dreams," she forced herself to continue. He crossed his arms over his chest, cocking his head to the side. "I don't know what they were, but they weren't *just* dreams."

"Well, that is something; twenty percent I would say. Not yet passing marks." One corner of Prince Aldrik's mouth curled upward.

Vhalla stood dazed; she really didn't know anything more than that. *But*, she thought, *there had to be more*. How had he known?

"You knew, the dreams. When I was dreaming, you knew that I was here," she realized.

"Very good. Now we are getting somewhere, my budding Windwalker." His eyebrows rose and his grin turned into a smile that Vhalla assured herself wasn't a sneer.

"Windwalker?" she repeated dumbly.

"You have heard this word before," he reminded her.

"Sorcerers, from the East," Vhalla breathed. "But you said there aren't any more; there haven't been for over a century."

"There were not," the prince corrected.

Vhalla frowned. "You said—"

He cut her off. "I am still your *prince*. You would do well not to forget that, *apprentice*. Do not question me so," Prince Aldrik spoke low and slow.

The expression fell from her cheeks. For the first time Vhalla felt terrified of the man. His proximity gave off a fearsome heat that sent a chill through her. He straightened. She grabbed her hands and wrung them together.

"Forgive me, my prince." Vhalla lowered her eyes, unable to handle the intensity of his gaze any longer. He turned, walking deeper into the library. "Where are you going now?"

"Stop asking questions and follow," he ordered with a sigh.

She quickly crossed the distance between them. Vhalla looked down at her feet as she followed behind the mysterious being that was the crown prince.

In that moment of silence, she could appreciate exactly how odd it all was. It was some ungodly hour of the night and a library apprentice was being led by the crown prince to some mystery location. Fear and curiosity compelled her, making her all the more entranced with the man before her. Vhalla had every right to fear the prince and yet, after weeks of exchanging notes, she found him less frightening than she had the Minister of Sorcery.

She was certainly going mad.

"I would have expected you to have put it together. I had you reading books on Affinities to push you toward a realization." He sighed again, letting out his disappointment. "You seemed so close, too; some of your questions made me think you were wondering about your own potential Affinity. Surely one of your Manifestations has given you a hint."

"I still don't believe I am really a sorcerer. I haven't had any—Manifestations. Nothing about me is magical," Vhalla whispered, thinking back to the Minister of Sorcery. "Reading the books, I've always loved reading. It was easier than talking—like a child playing games."

"You are a child." He looked her up and down with apparent disapproval. "But we are *not* playing games." She put her hands together and began to fidget. "And stop that!"

He slapped at her fingers then grabbed her chin, forcing her face up to look at his. The jerking motion was painful, and she barely managed to suppress a whimper. Vhalla was fairly certain he would've liked that even less.

"You are a sorcerer—albeit a small, untrained, helpless little slip of a sorcerer—but still a sorcerer! Stop shrinking or you will be an embarrassment to the rest of us," he scolded at her shocked and helpless expression. His grasp slowly loosened, then relaxed until he was holding her chin with only his knuckles and thumb.

"Your Affinity is air," Prince Aldrik revealed softly, dropping his hand and turning away from her dumb stare. There was a sudden and surprising gentleness about him, but the moment was fleeting.

"Air?" she repeated, her face hot from his fingers. His touch had felt different than his brother's contact. Even months after Prince Baldair had caught her in the library, she still remembered the feeling of his calloused fingers on the backs of her knees. Then again, everything about the princes was night and day.

"It is like walking around with a parrot. No, I take that back, the parrot would be better conversation." He sighed and pinched the bridge of his nose.

"How do you know?" Vhalla was forced to ask.

"Affinities of the self," he answered cryptically.

Vhalla did not have time to ask anything further, a gasp stopping the words in her throat.

They had reached a wall bearing a tapestry. The prince pulled apart the molten metal of the tapestry's frame, heated by only his fingertips, revealing a secret passage behind. He smirked at her expression.

"You did not think servants were the only ones with hidden ways of getting around, did you?" He chuckled darkly and entered the narrow passageway.

Vhalla glanced over her shoulder, *she could still disappear into the library*. She could go home. The light of the prince's flame began to fade as he continued on without looking back. She never knew exactly what beckoned her to step into the passage after him, just before the secret door closed with a heavy clang.

"Where are we going?" Vhalla asked again.

"We are going to show you what you stubbornly refuse to believe, little parrot," Prince Aldrik answered, his hands folded behind his back.

"I'm not a parrot." She frowned. "And I'm not a sorcerer."

"Your problem—" the prince began as he started climbing up the pitch-black passage. Vhalla was left no other option than to follow closely behind the magic flame that hovered over his shoulder as the only source of light. "—is that you rely entirely on books."

"What's wrong with books?" she was forced to ask.

He stopped, turning on his heel to stare down at her. "What is wrong is that you *cannot* learn how to *really* do things from books." He ignored her open mouth, continuing, "They are starting points for principle, theory, and concept. Your mind understands, but your body does not know until you perform the act yourself. Without action and practice, your hands will not oblige. Experience is a far greater teacher."

"Tell me, Vhalla, have you ever made love to a man?" He closed the distance between them as he spoke. With a single step, the crown prince was painfully close after asking such a personal question. "Tell me, have you ever pleasured yourself?"

Vhalla swallowed hard. Her brain betrayed her and she thought of clumsy experimentations on lonely nights. The guard, Narcio, flashed upon her mind without her command. Fleeting pain and the memories of brief satisfactions brought a hot flush of embarrassment to her cheeks, *as though she would tell anyone any of that.*

"Whatever it was, I doubt it was very good," he sneered down at her. She wanted to hit him. "I will tell you why it was not. Because, Vhalla, you think and you watch, but you never do. You can read all the books in this library, be wiser than the master himself someday, and then you will die having never really done anything. You will have only ever lived through everyone else's experiences."

Vhalla stared up at him, at those cold judgmental eyes that threatened to pick her apart and lick her bones clean. Looking away only provided minimal relief. He was still there assaulting her senses. Resisting the urge to fidget, she brought her hands together, squeezing them tightly.

"So then, how do I *do*?" she asked, still avoiding his eyes. It was a potentially dangerous question, given their recent conversation.

"You follow me, and you stop ignoring what is right before your eyes." They continued walking up a swirling staircase into the heart of the palace. Sometimes they would curve off as the path split before heading up again. There were no windows, no lights, no ornamentation, no signs. She was well and truly lost.

By the time they stopped, Vhalla felt dizzy from going up all the stairs. Above them stood a wooden door impeding their progress. The prince unbolted it and pushed open the hatch. Like ice water running through her hair and down her shoulders, cold wind poured down into the stairway. It forced her to blink tears from her eyes and shield her face.

"Come," he ordered, and she obliged.

They emerged into the night air in an impossible place. The wind took the breath right out of her lungs. They stood on a small landing, barely large enough for the two of them.

It felt like the top of the world.

They had climbed straight up through the servants' halls, the public areas, past the Imperial Housing, to the top of one of the golden spires that she had only ever looked upon from far below.

Vhalla could see the castle stretching outward beneath her, its many tiers cascading down the mountainside and into the capital. The distant, flickering lights of the city mirrored the stars in the sky. Vhalla could see the dual peaks of the mountain, and if she stretched her vision toward the horizon, she could see the Great Southern Forest, which hid a road that could take her home.

"What do you think?" He had moved behind her. Even at such close proximity she could barely decipher his words through the howling wind.

"It's amazing," she breathed.

"I have heard it was said that the Windwalkers were the children of the sky."

His words barely registered as she looked upwards at the heavens. It was an engrossing scene, as though she was at the very place where the earth and sky met. Vhalla took a tiny step forward, sweeping her gaze back to the glittering city below.

Perhaps it was her enchantment with the wonder surrounding her. Or, perhaps, it had been the wind filling her ears. Whichever, it masked his last footsteps. The prince placed his hands lightly upon her shoulders.

"Trust me," he demanded, his lips barely brushed over her ear.

Vhalla did not even have a moment to turn her head before he pushed her effortlessly into the empty air beyond.

CHAPTER 6

She plummeted through the air in a surreal trance. Her shoulder hitting the golden rooftop jarred her back to life with a sickening crunch. Vhalla half tumbled, half bounced small distances down the slope of the roof, desperately trying to grab a handhold. But the pitch was too steep, and each desperate grab resulted only in a fingernail being pulled back or ripped off. Soon there were no more golden shingles and there was nothing left to reach.

Vhalla had heard stories of one's life flashing before one's eyes in the moments before death, but all she saw was the round moon overhead, staring down at her. As the wind whipped around her body, she began to twist in the empty space. The celestial body departed her field of vision as she spun head over heels. It was replaced by the ground rushing to meet her.

She was going to die.

She opened her mouth to scream but the force of the wind pulled her voice from her, flooding her lungs.

She tried to turn herself to fall toward a nearby balcony, a landing, or even a decorative moulding. Her body slammed against the castle wall, succeeding only in knocking all the air from her lungs with a cry of agony. Then she was falling again. Her small frame smashed against an arch before tumbling back into the night sky. She searched for a stone that would catch her, but every attempt tossed her back to her death.

Her vision blurred and blood smeared her hands. She held out her arms; the ground was close now. She could only see the sky above but she knew it had to be over soon. Vhalla groped at the empty air, clinging to nothing but the wind slipping through her fingers.

An explosion rang out through her—and she sat upright, jolted awake.

Vhalla instantly regretted opening her eyes. The world looked hazy, both too bright and too dark; the colors twisted, and her eyes had trouble focusing. She turned quickly, retching over the side of the bed. Hot bile splattered on the vaguely familiar floor. The process of vomiting caused her abdomen to object to the tightening spasms, and she let out an agonizing cry as she fell back onto the bed in a heap.

Her entire body felt wrong. It felt as though someone stole her soul from her old body and placed it in a different one. Nothing matched up, nothing obliged in the way it should, and everything worked in ways it shouldn't. Her brain felt scrambled, and under the fingers clutching her abdomen she felt the sickening angles of broken ribs. She likely shouldn't be lying on her side but it hurt if she moved, and it hurt if she didn't. So she only endured her current position over risking any change.

Through the sliver of light between her eyelids, Vhalla tried to orient herself. The first indication she should panic was the window; it was three times larger than anything she had ever seen before in the apprentices' and servants' halls. When her eyes found the dragon moulding around the top of the room,

Vhalla tried to scramble out of bed, making unreasonable demands of a broken body.

Muffled voices and quick steps approached on the other side of the door before it burst open for two figures frantically approaching her. The older man she recognized instantly—the Minister of Sorcery. But the woman was a surprise. Vhalla blinked at the fuzzy shapes of the people.

"Larel?" Even her own voice sounded strange to Vhalla's ears, and she struggled not to retch again. The dark-haired woman departed quickly from the room. Vhalla grimaced. The woman should be ashamed of her role in Vhalla's current state. If it wasn't for Larel thrusting that book in her hands, she would have never met the prince.

"Don't talk," the minister demanded sternly. Vhalla cracked her eyes open against her better judgment. His hand ran between her forehead and her shoulder. Vhalla did not have the strength or will to fight against his touch as she would have wanted.

The minister rolled her onto her back, and Vhalla's body objected painfully. With a scream, she tried to push him away. This man, his world of magic, and all the sorcerers within, were nothing but pain.

"Vhalla." She stilled at the sound of her name in his mouth. "You need to believe me now. I am here to help you." The minister's voice was gentle, more than it had any right to be.

"You have to get down—and keep down—some bone regrowth this time."

This time? Vhalla was so confused and so tired, she closed her eyes. Sleep was much easier she realized. All this could go away if she closed her eyes and pretended to no longer exist.

"No, Vhalla stay here."

"How?" She could barely manage one syllable words, but he seemed to understand.

"I said don't talk." He shot her a cold glare. "Prince Aldrik brought you here after you Awakened."

Awakened?

Vhalla heard a commotion behind him and struggled to open her eyes again. Larel had returned, apparently not ashamed in the slightest, with a bucket and mop. It was actually Vhalla who felt ashamed when the woman began to clean up her spew that puddled on the floor.

"Larel, the blue vial," Minister Victor demanded. She nodded obediently and scampered from the room. Vhalla permitted herself darkness again. "No, Vhalla, you have to stay awake now." The man shook her shoulders slightly, where only a small touch sent waves of pain down to her toes. She whimpered in protest. "*Vhalla.*" His voice was sharp—demanding, and the stern tone reminded her just enough of another man's voice that she wanted to throw up all over again.

But it did the trick, and Vhalla obliged him, opening her eyes slightly. She had tunnel vision and didn't even see the female sorcerer passing the vial to the man silently. He turned and slipped his arm under Vhalla's shoulders, propping her up. Vhalla shook her head violently, remembering the last time she sat. Her brain only rattled around in her skull, threatening to make the blackness at the edge of her eyes all-consuming.

"Stop, stop, *stop*," the minister ordered, holding her close to him with one arm and pressing the vial to her mouth with the other. She didn't want to drink; she wanted to sleep. However, his insistence yielded her eventual surrender, and Vhalla gulped down the syrupy liquid with a small cough. It flowed through her like fire and she heard someone screaming as the minister threw the vial to the floor with a shattering noise and took her in his full embrace. It wasn't until she was cognizant of thrashing against the firm arms holding her that she realized the screaming was coming from her own mouth.

The agonizing cries gave way to eventual sobs as the burning slowly passed and she went limp, relying entirely on the support of the man whom she wanted to hate. Vhalla cast aside all decency and she simply wept against his chest. Somewhere he was talking; she could hear and feel it.

"—too susceptible to magic now. We tried—help you be more comfortable. But your—magical passages are too—and broken to—handle any more being—on you." She hated magic, her original opinion was reaffirmed anew as her mind began to level from the potion. "Vhalla —ten, you had two broken ribs — — left side and the right side of your —cage was shattered. Your hands are a wreck. Your left shoulder was shattered, and your right was dislocated. Your spine was all out of alignment, and your hips were fractured along with one of your legs." Vhalla laughed into his chest with an insane rasp.

"You will be fine," he assured her gently. Now he was the insane one. "But since we are healing almost exclusively with non-magical clerical potions and salves, it'll take some time." The Western woman had shifted Vhalla's pillows so she could sit in a more upright position and the man gently returned her to them, taking a green bottle. "This one is next; it shouldn't hurt."

True to his word the chalky liquid went through her cracked lips and caused no immediate discernible change in her overall state.

"Water," she rasped softly and he nodded. He poured a small cup from a clay pitcher on the bedside table. The minister brought this to her lips also and held it there so she could take a few long gulps.

"This is not how I wanted to meet you next. Believe me, Vhalla," he started, placing the cup back and taking a third strangely shaped vial from the silent woman. "I wanted to give you time to come to terms with what is happening. I have seen people run if forced, and I thought you would benefit from distance. When I found out the prince had taken an interest in you, I felt I had little to worry about."

Vhalla rasped in bitter laughter. She had begun to think that perhaps magic would not be so frightening after all his notes. It was ironic that the man holding her shattered form was the man she should have trusted all along.

"Prince Aldrik didn't know how to tend to your current... *condition*," Minister Victor bit out the last word before pausing. "So he brought you to me three days ago."

Vhalla coughed on the last sip of liquid in the vial that was pressed to her mouth. "Three days?" she managed, rather proud that two words could pass her lips.

Victor nodded. "I wasn't sure if you were going to make it. The second morning we forced you to sleep as you were thrashing and screaming too much to keep you awake," Victor recounted dutifully. Vhalla's mind was overloaded and the horrors hardly registered anymore. "But putting you to sleep disrupted the healing of your magical Channels when you kept reliving your Awakening."

"Awakening?" she asked.

"Awakening is when a sorcerer's powers first Manifest in full." He studied Vhalla for a moment before adding somewhat apologetically, "It's normally a bit gentler."

Larel came in with yet a fourth vial, and Vhalla shook her head. She didn't think her shrunken stomach and battered body could handle any more. After delivering the potion, the woman retrieved the bucket and mop, vanishing into the outer rooms.

"This is the last one for now," the minister promised, so Vhalla relented. The world seemed to slowly stabilize, though Vhalla still felt like she would rather be asleep than awake. "Good," he encouraged as she finished the last drop. "Now please, try to keep those down; no sudden movements."

Vhalla gave a small nod. "May I sleep now?" she asked weakly.

"No," he said, which earned him a whimper. "Almost," Victor assured her. "I have one more thing to try. I hope that it will make you feel better."

She was helpless to object with anything more than a shake of her head so she relented without fuss. If these people had planned on killing her, they wouldn't be exhausting themselves to keep her alive.

Victor left the room for a moment. He returned with a wooden case that he held with great care. Sitting, he placed it in his lap and popped open the latch. Within it were many stones of different shapes and colors. Vhalla wondered if it was simply the strangeness to her vision or if the stones actually shined and glittered unnaturally, as though a cosmos of stars swirled within. After a moment's consideration, he pulled out one of the shining rocks and placed it on her forehead. She was too tired to feel silly and, out of necessity, already trusted him completely. He took a similar stone and placed it on her stomach.

Vhalla's eyes snapped open. The world was suddenly clear again. Her vision shifted back into focus, her ears heard a beautiful stillness.

"Don't talk," he reminded her, "but I take it that helped a bit." She hoped the flick of her eyes was enough of an acknowledgement. "I am going to leave those there for a little, so try not to move much. Not that you should be moving anyway." As if she could. "And yes, you may now sleep."

Vhalla closed her eyes with a small sigh and felt her body relax a fraction before slipping back into the welcoming darkness.

It was night the next time Vhalla woke. Her room was empty save for a small bowl of fruit, a loaf of bread, and a series of vials on the table next to her. She slowly eased herself into a seated position. The stones had been removed, but her vision seemed to be holding steady. The world shifted a little, but her stomach remained settled—she considered it a small victory. Vhalla assessed the food cautiously. Bread and fruit would hurt more than bile coming up.

Her hand paused mid-air so she could assess the bruises and scratches that marred her skin. Even the moonlight made her feel uneasy as she involuntarily recalled the last time she had seen the celestial body. Vhalla retrieved one of the small red fruits and brought it back into her lap, a strawberry. She smiled faintly.

Long ago, her mother had planted some strawberry shrubs near their home. Every year they had eaten the few sweet berries the plants yielded. Despite their love of the fruit, neither Vhalla nor her father seemed to have the energy to maintain the plants after her mother died from Autumn Fever. She hadn't eaten a strawberry since then. Even if they had been available to apprentices, Vhalla didn't know if she would have been emotionally willing.

A few stray tears dripped into her palms as she looked down at the tiny fruit. She was so far from home—felt so small and broken. Her body was foreign to her, to the point that her mind didn't even recognize it. She had something in her, magic that she had never known and didn't think she wanted.

She wasn't supposed to have to deal with this. She was a library apprentice, no one—less than. Exhaustion consumed all of her emotions, and she couldn't even summon anger. She simply wanted to feel normal again, whatever that meant now.

Choking down a sob, Vhalla took a bite of the fruit, chewing thoughtfully. That was when she heard the muffled discussion through the door to the room beyond. Invisible beetles crawled beneath her skin. The resonance of one voice was unmistakable, causing Vhalla to nearly gag on the fruit.

Staring down the door, she debated if she had the strength, mentally or physically, to know what was being said. On legs that could barely support her, Vhalla stumbled over to the door to lean against it. Ear pressed to the wood, she could make out the two male voices.

"Really, Aldrik, what were you thinking?" the minister asked.

"I do not have to explain myself to you, *minister,*" the prince sneered.

"You could have killed her." Minister Victor voiced Vhalla's fears.

"I could not have killed her," the prince retorted, utterly confident.

Vhalla knew that the prince was rumored to have a silver tongue. But there was a peculiar sort of agitation to his voice, as though he were truly offended the minister would even suggest it.

"How did you know?" the minister demanded. "She had hardly Manifested more than trace magic on those notes. There was no way you could have known her Affinity."

"Then you underestimate my prowess." Vhalla could hear the click of boots across the floor as the prince paced the room.

"Certainly," the minister remarked with bold sarcasm. "I only ask because I have this wild idea that you may have some insights into her that you are neglecting to share, *my prince.*"

"Victor," Prince Aldrik sighed dramatically. "You think I would lower myself to trouble with a plain commoner like her?"

"You troubled yourself enough to write her notes," the minister pointed out.

Vhalla hadn't thought about it, but it was strange that the crown prince had sent notes to an apprentice.

"She is the first Windwalker in almost one hundred and fifty years. Of course I would trouble myself." His tone had turned cold and calculating.

"Well, the next time we have a new Manifesting sorcerer, I will be sure to ask you to assist, what with your mysterious powers of deduction on Affinities," the minister commented dryly. There was a long silence, indicating the prince was finished indulging the minster on this matter. "However you knew, the fact remains she is a Windwalker. I confirmed it."

"You felt the need to confirm it when she survived a fall from the palace spires?"

Vhalla could almost see Prince Aldrik rolling his eyes with his tone alone.

"I used crystals upon her," the minister continued, ignoring the prince's sarcasm.

"You *what*?"

Was that worry that Vhalla heard in Prince Aldrik's voice? She thought back to the shimmering stones that Minister Victor placed upon her forehead and stomach. Those were crystals? They couldn't possibly be the same as the taint-causing stones from the War of the Crystal Caverns. They had helped her, not hurt her.

"We should tell the Emperor." Minister Victor seemed to be well versed at overlooking choice comments from the prince. "He will want to know. He could use her in the war."

Vhalla's heart began to race. The idea of her at war was ludicrous. She had never even hit a person in play or sport.

"No." As if the prince picked up on her panic, he squelched the idea sharply. "I will deal with my father, Victor. I do not want to catch wind of you breathing a single word to the Emperor about her."

"Very well," the minister sighed. "Aldrik, I can only theorize on what your grand plan is for the girl, given our histories. I know what we read, what we studied—"

"Victor," the prince growled dangerously.

"I remember wishing we had someone like her," the minister

continued, ignoring the warning tone. *What did these people want with her?* "I would be false if I claim to have not had similar ideas cross my mind already. But she will need to be trained first. We will need—"

"She is not your concern," Prince Aldrik snapped. "I will oversee her training."

Vhalla rested her forehead against the door, reminding herself to breathe. It did not seem like she would escape the prince anytime soon.

"Larel will be her mentor, and she will report to me. I thank you, minister, for keeping your distance."

Her heart was racing, and the adrenaline replaced the pain. How had he known her Affinity? Why had the prince decided out of all the sorcerers that he had control over, she would be the one he would make his pet? Vhalla's face twisted in agony. She should be Eradicated, certainly that was still an option.

"Now, if you will excuse me, I would like to check on her." The prince's footsteps neared the door.

"My prince, please let her rest." Vhalla's opinion of the Minister of Sorcery was steadily improving.

But nothing stopped the prince if he wanted something, and Vhalla took a step away from the door, glancing around frantically. Once more she was reminded how trapped this room made her feel. She had yet to stumble back to the bed when the door opened.

Dark eyes met hers, and Vhalla looked up uncertainly, caught in a whirlwind of apprehension and fear. Would he know that she had been eavesdropping? She couldn't imagine the prince would take kindly to it.

"You're awake." He breathed the words and his eyes softened with what looked like relief. Though Vhalla was certain she was mistaken.

"I am." She nodded, her voice no longer sounded wrong.

"I'm glad," he said softly.

Vhalla squinted up at him, not caring about how bold it was. "*You*, you're glad?" Anger stammered her words as she glared at the tall man dressed all in black.

"I am, Vhalla—"

The prince took a step toward her, and Vhalla took a step back.

"No." She shook her head. "No, don't come near me. Never come near me again." Vhalla's voice was rougher than she had ever heard it before. She didn't care that he was the prince, and she didn't care that the minister stood as an observer.

"Vhalla." The prince had the audacity to have the start of a smile on his face. Who did he think she was—some ignorant child? "This is not a time for anger; we should celebrate."

"You—pushed—me—off—a—roof." Vhalla wished she had a more dramatic word for *roof* because it didn't seem to quite cut to the truth of the matter.

He laughed.

Vhalla had never struck someone before, but he was making an appealing case.

"You are fine. See how quickly you are healing now? You will be better than fine soon. I will even teach you myself." He outright smiled, as though he was bestowing some great honor upon her.

But Vhalla did not smile. She took another step away and swayed as the world was suddenly unstable. She had been on her feet for too long.

Prince Aldrik was there in a moment, his hands on her upper arms for support. "Stop this foolishness," he said, his deep voice gentle. "You know you should not be standing. Let me help you back to bed." His sudden kindness made her want to scream.

"Don't touch me," she whispered.

"Vhalla—" The lightness was beginning to slip from his face.

"Do. Not. Touch. Me!" she cried, pushing his hands off and taking a step back. Vhalla stumbled, her world tilted, but her feet held onto the floor with all the force of her rage. "You threw me off a roof!" Her voice had risen to a near shrill. "You didn't tell me! You didn't warn me!"

"If I warned you, it would not have worked. If I had warned you, then you would not have done it." He crossed his arms over his chest.

"Of course I wouldn't have!" She threw her arms out and swayed dangerously again, but regained her balance. "I trusted you to be my teacher! I did not trust anyone else, but I trusted you as my prince! I trusted you because you asked!" The confession caught in her throat as she choked it out. Vhalla wasn't sure if she only imagined his eyes widening by a fraction before darkening.

"And you were right to; I Awoke you to something great." His voice grew colder.

"I didn't want this." She looked down at her bruised and broken form.

"You asked for this!" he snapped.

"My prince, please, this isn't..." The minister saw the conversation deteriorating before his eyes, and he took a step in from the doorframe.

"I didn't ask for this! I don't know what I wanted but it wasn't this!" Her rage kept in the tears, and in that moment she swore he would not see her cry. "I am confused. I am broken—"

"You will heal, better than you were before," Prince Aldrik assured her.

"I was fine before," Vhalla protested.

"You were boring. You were worse than boring. You were normal and content. I gave you a chance for greatness." He looked at her harshly.

"What would've happened if I hadn't been a Windwalker?" Her words quieted the air.

"I will not indulge such nonsense." He brushed off the question.

"Do not toy with me anymore," she spoke slowly. "What would have happened?"

He stared at her a long moment. "If things were not as they are and you were not a Windwalker, then you would have fallen to your death." Prince Aldrik shrugged as though the thought had crossed his mind, and he couldn't have been troubled to care.

"You bastard." The words were out before she even had time to consider them, but after spoken she hardly regretted them.

"What did you say?" Prince Aldrik snarled.

"You, *my prince*," she sneered in kind. "You are a self-centered, egotistical, self-absorbed, narrow-sighted, vain, self-important—" she felt her anger finally reach its boiling point "—conceited *bastard*!"

The window next to them shattered, flooding the room with a gale peppered with shards of glass. She hardly seemed to notice as the minister braced himself against the wind. The prince stood motionless, staring at her darkly from behind a thin screen of flame that broke the wind and protected him from the shattered glass.

"Calm down," he growled.

"You can't tell me what to do anymore!" she screamed.

"I can tell you whatever I want. I am your prince!" he shouted and the thin fire that protected him lashed outward.

Vhalla raised her hands to shield herself from the flame. The fire passed over her palms and face as little more than heat—but it broke her concentration. The wind died down and, with it, Vhalla collapsed to the floor, her energy spent.

The prince looked down at her, a stone mask across his

features, judgment burning in his eyes. "Stay there," he spoke slowly. "Stay on the floor where you belong. You are like a pathetic little worm who only wants to sit in the dirt when I was prepared to give you a chance to grow wings and fly."

"My prince," the minister said firmly, but was easily ignored.

"I chose you, and you threw it away," Prince Aldrik snarled.

Vhalla stared up at him. This was the prince she had expected. Not the mysterious intellectual phantom, and certainly not the awkwardly kind man who had first entered her room.

"So stay there, with the filth you so happily chose."

He stormed out of the room. Vhalla's face stung, and she swallowed hard. The minister hovered uncomfortably.

"Leave, please," she whispered. Ignoring her wishes, the minister knelt by her side. "Don't," she said, staring at the shattered glass from the window. "Just... leave." She had no right to command him, but there was nothing left in her to care about that fact.

"Vhalla," he said softly.

It was too kind for what she felt. She wanted nothing more than for him to scream at her and leave, too. Or throw her out the window and finish what the prince had started.

"Go," she demanded. He stayed. "I said leave!"

Finally, with an audible sigh, the minister stood and left.

Vhalla never heard his footsteps walking away from her door. She knew that he stood right outside as she collapsed among the broken glass and cried out, sobbing, until she had nothing left to feel and the darkness took her again.

CHAPTER 7

Vhalla twitched her fingers. There was a bug on her that was intent on disturbing her sleep. When it refused to go away, she twisted in the opposite direction; it frustratingly followed her hand. Almost fully awake, she tried to withdraw and heard a low *shhh-ing* noise come from the bedside.

Cracking her eyes open, she realized that she was back in the bed. It irked her that they had lifted her off the floor and placed her back among the soft pillows and blankets. She would've rather spent the night on the ground. Thinking of what she said to the prince's face, she groaned.

"Does it hurt?" a faint voice whispered next to her.

Vhalla turned back. It was the Western woman, Larel. She was changing the bandages on Vhalla's arm.

"What do you care?" Vhalla remembered what the prince had said. Larel was to spy on her and report to him. The Westerner before her fraternized with the enemy.

"I care very much," Larel replied easily. "Does it hurt?"

"Why?" Vhalla continued to ignore her question. Everything

hurt. But she wasn't certain what was physical and what was emotional.

"Because you are to be my protégé." The sorceress had a flat way of talking, thick with a Western accent.

"I don't want to be your protégé." Vhalla looked away in childish protest.

"Very well," the woman said lightly. "We can change that after you're healed."

"What?" She turned her head back slowly to the dark-haired woman. The movement was accompanied by a deep ache in her shoulders.

"After you've healed, you'll meet others in the Tower," Larel explained. "If you do not wish for me to mentor you, then you can have your pick of a new mentor, someone you are more comfortable with."

Vhalla stared at the bruises and scratches on her flesh. It was true, she was a mess. Underneath the bandages, her skin was a grotesque rainbow of red, yellow, purple, and blue. Wounds were so prevalent she could not even catch sight of the natural tint of her skin.

"Have you done this every night?" Vhalla finally asked. The woman had a gentle hand.

"Almost," she said as though it were nothing.

Despite herself, Vhalla cringed. She didn't care about this sorceress, she told herself. But the idea that someone had been changing her soiled clothes and tending to her needs, naturally put guilt in her mind.

"I'm sorry to be a burden," Vhalla whispered. Magic had only made her a more pathetic being thus far. A soft breeze brought her eyes to the window; the glass had not been replaced and the crisp smell of winter was beginning to change the night air. Summer was gone, and fall was already upon them.

"Prince Aldrik told us not to fix it." Larel missed little. Vhalla winced at his name. "Are you cold? I could bring you another blanket."

"It's fine." Vhalla *was* cold, she was always cold. But her lingering pride would not allow her to be more of a burden. "I guess he's going to make my life as uncomfortable as he can."

"If the prince wanted to make you uncomfortable, he could, and would, do far more than not replace a window," Larel pointed out.

It was a truth Vhalla did not want to believe. To believe it meant the woman was right. The fact that Vhalla was still in bed receiving treatment meant the prince did not want her to be uncomfortable, even after what she said.

"What relationship do you and the prince have?" Vhalla asked boldly. The prince had appointed this woman as her mentor. Larel was the one who gave Vhalla the book that the prince left his notes in.

Her gold-ringed hazel eyes met Larel's dark ones. Vhalla may be a bad liar but that wouldn't stop her from looking for a lie in others.

When Larel spoke, there was no sign of hesitation or fear. "We were apprentices in the Tower together," Larel said simply, returning to rubbing salve on Vhalla's skin.

"The prince was an apprentice?" Vhalla blinked. She expected apprenticeship to be something that was below royalty.

"How else would he have learned?" Larel had a small grin. "I know how he seems. But he's not truly malicious—not normally —and almost never to people like us."

"People like us?" Vhalla repeated doubtfully.

"Sorcerers." Sweeping dark bangs across her forehead, the woman glanced up.

Of course, Vhalla thought. She was one of them now, and there really was no more denying it. The fall should've killed her, and if the prince hadn't intervened, something did.

"Magical people are often feared by Commons. Even you feared us," Larel said thoughtfully.

Vhalla could only nod. She was conflicted over the woman's use of past tense with regards to her fear. Though, at this exact moment, Vhalla did not feel afraid. She felt sad. Something in her was different. Roan, Sareem, Master Mohned; they wouldn't understand, even if she tried explaining.

"The prince knows this," Larel continued. "He knows how hard it is, better than most. He's had more than his fair share."

"So now I'm supposed to feel sorry for him?" Vhalla spat, becoming far more venomous than she would've wanted.

Larel stopped and looked up at Vhalla strangely for a long while. "Yes." She returned to her work, and Vhalla felt her jaw go slack. "And he should feel sorry for what he put you through," Larel added faintly. "Awakenings can be scary, but they shouldn't hurt, at least never this bad. I think, I think he was caught up in the promise of what you are."

"What I am?" Vhalla mused, remembering the unexpected conversation she had overheard. "You mean a Windwalker?"

Larel nodded. "I don't think you understand, Vhalla. You are the first Windwalker in generations. Many theorists have gone so far as to postulate that the East is magically dry. That the source of magic for the Windwalkers had been destroyed when no one connected to the Channel for so long." Larel picked up a bottle of the salve and worked it across Vhalla's open wounds. "You fly—no pun intended—in the face of everything people have been saying for well over a century."

Vhalla wanted to feel special. She wanted to feel important. She wanted to feel she was special and important to the crown prince, of all people. But she only felt like an object. She was jarred out of her destructive cycle of thought when Larel placed salve into a particularly angry gash.

"Sorry, I should've warned you." The woman continued on with her work.

"I'm sorry you have to do this," Vhalla replied. On the scale of sorcerers, Larel had wronged Vhalla the least, and she seemed to be cleaning up everyone else's mess.

"I don't mind." She began padding a few wounds with cloth scraps before starting on the clean dressings. "Yes, you have been more work than most of my peers' Awoken apprentices. But I think your story is already far more profound than most of us can ever hope for."

She paused to smile, and Vhalla was taken aback by the woman's features. She was stunning when she smiled. The straight black hair framed the warm visage perfectly as it curved around her face. She had dark brown eyes, almost black, and Vhalla had to look away before she was reminded of another set of slightly darker Western eyes.

"So what happens next?" It seemed a natural question. Vhalla needed to start approaching things logically. Her emotions had been running wild for far too long, and it had gotten her nowhere.

"Once you are Awoken, there are only two options. Your powers will continue to Manifest. You've already seen how they can be tied to your emotions when it's this fresh." Vhalla looked back to the window, realizing for the first time what had really transpired. "So you must learn to control your powers or Eradicate them. I likely shouldn't say, but the minister is planning to offer you a black robe."

"But I am a library apprentice," Vhalla said weakly, feeling homesick.

"Things change." The woman shrugged. "But it will be your choice. The minister will not force it on you."

"I doubt that," Vhalla mumbled. She wasn't sure if the

sorcerers of the Tower knew how to do anything without force. "What if I choose to be Eradicated?"

She had read about the process of exhausting a sorcerer's magic to block their Channels to power. While she didn't understand it fully, it didn't sound painful as described in the library book. It couldn't be any more painful than the agony she was already in.

"I would urge you to reconsider." When Vhalla glared at the woman, Larel added, "But I think it should be your choice." Larel sat back, reorganizing her supplies.

Vhalla stared blankly out the window, wishing the stars could tell her what needed to be done.

"Prince Aldrik," Larel started gently, seeing Vhalla visibly flinch at the mention of his name. "He told me that you were very bright. That you were surprisingly smart for an apprentice."

"He would phrase it like that, a compliment in an insult," Vhalla remarked dryly.

"He meant it," Larel assured her. "I believe it to be true as well." Vhalla looked uncertainly at the woman as she stood. "Don't make this choice without putting that intellect to use. If you have questions, you can ask me or any other sorcerer."

There was a seed of guilt in her stomach as Vhalla looked up at the woman. She had been kind to her. Vhalla picked at the seams on her blanket. "Thank you," Vhalla mumbled. "I don't think I would be as well as I am now without your help," she added earnestly.

"You are welcome," Larel accepted the gratitude. "Now rest. When you feel well enough, there is a library here in the Tower that you can use."

The woman smiled at Vhalla's expression when she mentioned the library. But the sorcerer said nothing more and departed. With a soft sigh, Vhalla shifted the pillows and laid back.

As much as Vhalla wanted to, she couldn't muster any anger toward Larel. The woman had been too kind to her for that. Plus, it was nice to have someone speak openly and honestly to her about these matters. Vhalla's best guess was that the Westerner didn't seem to be mindlessly following Victor's or the prince's orders.

As much as Vhalla wanted to ignore them, Larel's words had struck something within her. Apply her intellect to the world before her. Vhalla worried about what would happen if she did. Sighing again, Vhalla allowed her wounded body to relax and her eyes to droop closed. There was always the morning to make life-changing decisions.

But the morning came and went, and Vhalla was no closer to deciding how she felt about anything. The pain had mostly subsided and, with it, her rage at the situation. She was still sore at a certain prince, but she no longer felt the need to hit things. Around lunch, Vhalla decided it was time to get out of the room she had occupied for days on end.

When she stood, the world stayed exactly where it should be. Other than a general dull ache, there was no pain. She tried a circle around the small space; when she didn't retch, she considered it a success. Taking a deep breath, she opened the door that led out into the other room.

Vhalla was surprised to see that it was vacant. Larel, the minister, and—most thankfully—the prince were nowhere to be found. Remembering what Larel had told her about a library, Vhalla crept through the space toward the second door.

Vhalla observed the hall. To the left, it sloped up; to the right, down. At frequent intervals hung the glass bulbs with flames inside, casting the path in a warm glow. She stared at the sculptures that lined the walls at random intervals.

It was artwork.

She closely inspected the carved stone. Apprentices and

servants didn't display artwork in their halls. Were there other noble members of the Court beyond the minister?

The reliefs told stories Vhalla had known since she was a child. Most of them were religious in reference, surrounding the Father. Vhalla saw a man grasping a dragon's head, forcing it to eat its own tail; the creation of the moon. The Father protected his lover's world from the chaos of the realms beyond.

Vhalla instinctively started upward, but when she remembered her last interaction with heights, she turned on point to head down instead. It was the same path she had walked with the minister weeks ago, but now she took the time to see this world. The doors were arched at the top with iron handles and upon each hung a silver plate. Some had names; others simply had symbols Vhalla did not recognize.

On occasion, the hallway branched off into common areas, practice grounds, and so on. Some stood empty; some were occupied. The few times she passed someone, they greeted her kindly and kept on their way. No one thought the girl in the white gown with bandages was strange.

A certain smell lingered on the air. It tickled her nose and beckoned her onward. She couldn't place it at first, but as her step quickened and the scent became stronger, she realized what it was with a smile. It was the smell of dusty leather and parchment. She turned to see the central circular room that housed the Tower's library.

The Tower was large and round, and by most standards this would be considered a sizeable library. But it was only the size of about two and a half wings of the Imperial Library. Nevertheless, it comforted her more than anything else had to date. A blond-haired boy, who looked no older than Vhalla, worked, placing some books back on the shelves; he glanced at her as she entered.

"Ah! Welcome!" he said with a grin, almost dropping the books in his hands to rush to meet her.

Vhalla didn't know how social she felt, but she smiled politely and took his hand. His robe was collarless, and his sleeves were longer than Larel's, almost down to his elbows. He had wavy hair, silly in the way it was messily cut. That, and his goofy grin, seemed to ease the tension in her shoulders.

"Hello," she replied.

"You must be the recent Awoken."

Vhalla nodded. If everyone had heard of her, no wonder the others she passed in the halls weren't surprised by her condition.

"I'm sure you have lots of questions. If I can help you find anything, just let me know. Fritznangle is the name, but that's a mouthful so most people call me Fritz. Don't be shy, okay?" He grinned again. Realizing he was still shaking her hand, he stopped with a laugh.

"It's nice to meet you, Fritz. I'm Vhalla." She smiled. He was more energetic than the normal librarians she'd met before. "Are you the master of this library?"

"Master of the library? Oh, no. We don't really have one. I guess the minister officiates over the library as the formal curator. Do we say curator for libraries? Anyway, I do look after it if that's what you're asking. No one else will, I don't think."

Vhalla couldn't suppress a small giggle, it was the first time she laughed in a week, and it made her whole body feel lighter.

"I never knew there was a library in the Tower." She assessed all the books.

"I guess you wouldn't really. I mean, it's private you see. Got some great stuff—originals. I've heard it would rival the Imperial Archives." He said it like it was nothing. Vhalla was practically salivating.

"Hey, do you want to see? You'll be a black robe soon, right?" He took her hand and led her farther into the books. "You don't have one on yet, but when you're all healed up I'm sure they'll initiate you and then this will be your home also."

Vhalla stopped, and he turned as her arm refused to budge.

"I'm not a black robe." She looked at her feet. "I should go."

"Wait." He stopped her. "That's, well—I mean. You're here. And, well, do you want to see anyway?"

"If it's all right?" she asked, turning back to face him. Even if it was a library for sorcerers, Vhalla would never refuse books.

"Yeah, come on." He smiled again.

Once more taking her by the hand, he led her to a table that stood against a tall window in the back. Vhalla put her hands against the glass and looked outside, trying to figure out the library's location in the palace. She knew the Tower of Sorcerers had its own entrance on the ground somewhere, but it merged with the palace as it ascended, making it difficult to discern its exact location as other housing and structures grew around it.

"So what are you?" he asked, picking some books off shelves. "A Firebearer? A Waterrunner? A Groundbreaker?"

"A Windwalker," she said without turning. It was getting easier to say, and Vhalla didn't think she was happy about that fact. But it also didn't upset her as much as she expected.

"A—what?" He walked over to her. "Sorry, I didn't hear you right. One more time please?"

"A Windwalker," she repeated, glancing at him.

He put his hand against the window frame and took a long breath. "Are you sure? I know the Awakening can scramble the brain a tad and, well, we don't hear things right. You know how it is." Fritz continued to stare at her in disbelief.

She looked at him, slightly annoyed that he was ruining her moment of reuniting with books by being so daft. "My Affinity is air. I don't know much, but everyone has told me that makes me a Windwalker." She spoke very slowly and tried to accentuate each word.

"You're serious," he choked out. She nodded in frustration. "Oh by the Sun, you're serious." He snatched her hand again and shook it vigorously. "This is an honor. An honor! To meet you. I wondered why the minister was so tight-lipped about the newly Awoken. A Windwalker. A Windwalker here, in the capital, safe, in one piece. Not burnt up to little bits."

"You're hurting me." Vhalla smiled through a grimace, rubbing her throbbing shoulder as he relinquished her hand apologetically. "What do you mean, not burnt up?"

"Well, given the history of Windwalkers..." Fritz trailed off, as if she understood what he was talking about. She didn't, and he finally realized that fact. "Wait, you don't know the history?"

"I've read some on the history of sorcerers," Vhalla answered vaguely. He was giving her that same feeling that the prince had, guilt at ignoring a whole area of knowledge for years.

"Tell me what you know." Fritz smiled and the resemblance to the prince was gone. "I'll help fill in the rest."

Vhalla took a deep breath. "Well, I know that Windwalkers are—were—from the East. I am Eastern. I know there hasn't been one in a hundred-something years and that some people thought there wouldn't be any more."

"That's the basics." Fritz smiled. "But only just."

He led her along with gentle hand tugs and slow steps through the books. His palm was cool, but not uncomfortable. Vhalla allowed herself a small smile. It was about time she met a sorcerer with a gentle and happy manner.

"Over here—this section is our histories."

There were no rolling ladders, and Fritz was left scurrying for a nearby foot stool. At least the bookshelves were only half as high as the ones in the Imperial Library; it took a ladder with twenty rungs for Vhalla to reach the tops of those. "Windwalkers... There hasn't been much new material since— well, there haven't been any Windwalkers in some time. Books are rare too; Mhashan didn't want any left."

"Mhashan? The old West?" Vhalla blinked, wondering what the Kingdom of Mhashan had to do with Windwalkers.

"I won't explain it well." Fritz shook his head doubtfully. "Here, read this."

Vhalla looked at the title of the manuscript the messy-haired librarian placed reverently into her hands: *The Windwalkers of the East*. It was an old manuscript, and the library apprentice in her noted immediately that the book would need to be rebound soon. A quick flip and the inspection of a few middle pages proved that at least the ink was still legible.

"Thank you." It was like a breath of fresh air. Something about holding a book again made her feel better.

"Don't worry about it!" Fritz smiled a wide and toothy grin.

"Can I read here?" Vhalla had no interest in returning to the room where she had been recovering.

"This *is* a library." He chuckled.

Fritz led her over to a window with a wide bench placed before it. It wasn't quite a window seat, but it was close enough that Vhalla instantly relaxed into her new surroundings.

Flipping open the book, she diligently started reading at the first page. Vhalla did not count a book as read unless one's eyes fell on the very first word of the first page and the very last word of the last.

Her brow furrowed, and her fingers trailed over the script. She tucked some flyaway hair behind her ear only to have it fall in her face again.

Something was amiss.

The writing was familiar. It was slightly less jagged, less spiky than what she knew. This was written by a steadier hand, likely a younger hand. But it was impossible. Vhalla blinked at the title page.

The Windwalkers of the East

A collection of accounts from The Burning Times
Composed by Mohned Topperen.

CHAPTER 8

Mohned Topperen. The name had to be a mistake. Perhaps, it was a very common name, and Vhalla did not know it. Why else would the Master of Tome's name be in a book on magical history? Then again, the master could boast authorship of more than a hundred manuscripts. Why should he have a problem writing on magic?

Vhalla paused, suddenly feeling very small. This whole time she was fearful of sorcerers when the man who was her mentor, who had been like her father in the palace, had written about them long before she was even born. She leaned against the wall, her head swimming. What was wrong with her?

Mohned had raised her better. Her father had raised her better. Vhalla had lived in the South for so long that the Southern fear of magic had seeped into her. Yes, sorcerers were different. But the South had been different, and she hadn't feared moving into the palace. She had been excited at the prospect of expanding her knowledge. Her world had grown and, as a child, she had accepted that better than as a young woman.

Why did growing up shrink her mind?

"Vhalla?" the library boy whispered softly, sitting next to her.

"Yes?" She blinked at him, worried that her magic was acting up again; he was inexplicably blurry.

"Hey, you okay?" He placed a hand on her knee, and Vhalla stared at the foreign contact. It was strangely welcomed. "You're crying."

"Sorry." She shook her head, looking away, rubbing her eyes in frustration.

"Don't apologize. It must be a lot." Vhalla nodded mutely as he spoke. "Were you in the palace before this?"

"I was," Vhalla answered, finding talking helped work out the lump in her throat. "I was a library apprentice. I've lived here since I was eleven. Almost seven years now..."

"That's good." He smiled. Vhalla stared at him, puzzled. Before she could ask what was good about her situation, he elaborated. "Some of the new apprentices are dropped off by their families. They've never lived in the palace before—or even out of their homes. The worst is when their family disowns them, as well."

"Disown? Their own family?" Vhalla blinked. She didn't know what her father really thought of magic, but Vhalla wanted to believe that nothing would make him abandon her on a doorstep. He had been teary-eyed leaving her in the South.

"They're afraid." Fritz shrugged. "They don't think it's natural, even though people can't choose magic."

"Is that what happened to you?" Vhalla asked.

"No." Fritz chuckled. "No one in my family is a sorcerer, but they hardly minded. My sisters thought it was hilarious when I couldn't stop randomly freezing things."

"Freezing things?" Vhalla mused aloud. "That would make you a-a—" She couldn't remember the proper name. "You have a water Affinity."

"A Waterrunner," Fritz filled in the blank helpfully. "Okay, right, well, I'll let you read. I just wanted to make sure you weren't in pain."

"Don't." Vhalla grabbed the hand resting on her knee as he went to stand. "Don't leave." She looked away, a flush rising to her cheeks. Vhalla didn't want Fritz to go. He was the first stable person in the whole Tower, and she needed someone warm and genuine right now. Something about his Southern hair and eyes reminded her of Roan.

"All right," Fritz agreed with earnestness, settling next to her. "I'll read with you; it can't hurt to brush up on my history."

They began reading together and Vhalla appreciated that he read almost as fast as she did.

The story of the Windwalkers started centuries before the last Windwalker died, during the great genocide that was known as The Burning Times. It was a rich history of Cyven, the old East, that Vhalla had never been taught, despite being born there. The story was incomplete in some areas, being taken from oral histories, but it wasn't until Vhalla reached the middle section on The Burning Times that she began to have questions.

"I don't understand. The King of Mhashan was invading Cyven?"

"Mhashan could have been greater than the Solaris Empire if they had kept Cyven, some say," Fritz confirmed.

"Why didn't they?" The book took a distinctly Eastern viewpoint, and the explanations for the West's actions were lacking.

"King Jadar claimed the invasion was to spread the word of the Mother Sun." History was clearly a favorite area for Fritz, by the way he spoke, and through the animation in his hands. Vhalla wondered how many nations would use the Mother as an excuse for conquest. "But really, what he wanted was the Windwalkers' power."

"Why?" Vhalla tried not to sound too eager. The prince's and minister's conversation was still fresh in her mind.

"I don't really know," Fritz replied apologetically.

Vhalla felt her chest deflate. Whatever the reason, the king had enslaved every Windwalker found by his armies and a specially trained secret order of knights. In the process, most of the East was put to the flame. There came a point when the Windwalkers admitted defeat, hoping to spare the rest of their people. Compared to the West's military, they were disorganized and weak. After the king accepted their surrender; after the last of the sorcerers were in irons, he burned every remaining resistance, or love for those, with the air Affinity. It was as though he wanted to erase them from the earth.

Vhalla stared at the words, realizing she was nearing the end of the tale. The last quarter of the book focused on what the West did with their captives. Live experiments and forced labor that churned the contents of her stomach sour.

"Why would they do this?" she whispered.

"I don't know." The Southern man patted her knee. "But it was a long time ago. Things are different now."

"How have I not known this happened?" Vhalla tried to wrap her head around what she had just read.

"In my history lessons, they always told us that the East made all magic taboo following The Burning Times. Cyven was afraid of drawing the wrath of the West anew so they banned magic, discussions on magic, or books on it," Fritz explained. "Eventually, magic was forgotten by the average person, and the laws became social norms."

Vhalla stared forward, the book gripped loosely in her palms. The chatty Fritz stayed silent, letting her process everything that she had just learned. If she had been born more than a century and a half ago, the West would have killed her for her magic. She had something that kings killed for. But Vhalla still didn't understand what made her magic more significant than any of the other Affinities. It frightened her. But she also recognized that it was something she must uncover before the prince, the minister, or even the Emperor could uncover—if they hadn't already.

However, the energy flowing through her veins was not all fear.

Excitement, Vhalla realized. The girl in her who had never amounted to anything other than an avid reader, now had something that kings killed for. She had power, and her curiosity surrounding it finally surpassed exhaustion and fear.

"Fritz," Vhalla said suddenly. She stood, swayed a minute on weak knees, but planted her feet firmly on the ground. "How do I use magic?"

"What?" The blond-haired man was startled by the sudden flurry of movement.

"I am a sorcerer, right? I can use magic then. How do I do it?" Vhalla feared she would lose whatever possessed her before she even saw the truth.

"I'm not a teacher," Fritz cautioned.

"Do your best." Vhalla gave him a weak smile. She remembered the last man she had considered her teacher. Fritz couldn't do worse.

"Are you sure you're feeling up to it? You're still kind of messed up. No offense, but I don't want to tax your body." Fritz swayed from one foot to the other.

"Please," Vhalla pleaded, her resolve about to vanish. "I need to know."

"Fine, fine." Fritz placed his palms on her shoulders and turned her around gently to face one of the glass bulbs that was positioned on either side of the window. He leaned forward, pointing at the flame. "Look there, look close. I'm no magical teacher, please realize. So I'm sorry for any bad advice I'll give

you. Now that I've warned you, you can't blame me. I was told half of magic is visualizing what you want, and the other half is allowing it to come to pass. Does that help?"

"Maybe?" Vhalla said honestly.

"I don't know how it works for Windwalkers. I'm a Waterrunner, so I feel the water in me to help open my Channel. So, feel the wind in you, I guess?"

"This isn't going to work," she muttered doubtfully. Her conviction quickly vanishing.

"Yes, it is. You haven't even tried yet." He gave her shoulders an encouraging squeeze.

Vhalla stared at the glass. The fire kept burning within, and she shrugged.

"You call that trying?" He gave her a gentle nudge. "If looks alone could stop fire, then that would've done the trick."

Vhalla scowled, and she closed her eyes, taking a breath. She had no idea how to go about this and felt rather silly for even trying. She took another slow breath. Vhalla heard the air passing through her, felt it enter her body, felt it give her life.

Hesitantly, doubtfully, she tried to imagine the position of the bulb in front of her, the fire inside. The picture formed before her almost as clearly as if her eyes had been open.

Magic, she had magic within her.

She would accept that. Hadn't she been kidnapped and pushed off a roof to force her to accept it?

Vhalla thought of the prince, her mood instantly souring. She had summoned magic then. That pig-headed infuriating man had made her summon magic. If he could bring it out of her, then she would be damned if she could not bring it out through her own will. Inhaling sharply, she snapped open her eyes just in time to watch the fire blow out, and the bulb shatter.

"You did it!" Fritz's hands were off her shoulders, and he was clapping them together like a madman.

"I broke the bulb." She stared at the shattered glass on the floor. Thinking of the prince led her to breaking things. It wasn't really impressive—or healthy.

"Who cares? We have a lot more." Fritz laughed; something about his laugh was infectious, and she smiled despite herself. "You *are* a Windwalker!" He took both her hands in his and spun her around a few times until she felt dizzy, but slightly giddy. "Next, do that one."

Vhalla turned to the opposite bulb and repeated the process, this time trying to think of the wind staying only within the glass, but never actually touching it. She tried to quell her emotions some, but still reach from the same font she felt when her mind turned to angry thoughts of the crown prince. The bulb shuddered before cracking and breaking. This time, there were significantly fewer pieces.

"You're amazing, Vhalla!" Fritz cheered.

His words and the world around her were lost as Vhalla stared, mesmerized by the shattered glass. She had done it, more or less. Magic had been scary, mysterious, painful, or intellectual. But this was the first time she could've described any moment as fun or rewarding. For once, it felt good.

And, for the first time in her life, Vhalla felt strong.

"Vhalla," a familiar voice broke her trance. "I'm sorry, I stepped out for some lessons and training and you were gone."

She turned to look at the Western woman approaching quickly. Vhalla saw genuine concern in Larel's eyes. It was tempered with a look at Fritz, noting that Vhalla had not been alone.

"How do you feel?" Larel asked, inspecting her bandages.

"I'm fine." Vhalla braved a smile and was surprised to find her face still moved as she expected it to.

"She's better than fine!" Fritz clasped a hand over her

shoulder, and Vhalla grimaced as it shot sharp pain down her arm. "Look, Larel, the Tower's first Windwalker broke a bulb!"

"Really?" Larel half stepped around Fritz to inspect Vhalla's accomplishment, if it could be called that. "Do you feel fine?"

"I do." Vhalla nodded, rubbing her shoulder where Fritz had given her his painful version of encouragement. "Well, other than the obvious."

"You need more potion." Larel nodded in agreement. "I'll tell the minister about your success and then we'll get you food and medicine."

"Come visit me again, okay?" Fritz asked hopefully.

Vhalla fidgeted with the bandages on her hands and fingers. She did not want to go back to that lonely room just yet. Things had been feeling normal; a strange and different normal, but normal nonetheless.

"Can I eat with both of you?" Vhalla asked timidly.

"Of course you can!" Fritz bounced. Larel had a small and knowing smile, but spared any comment and simply nodded.

VHALLA SAT NEXT to Fritz in the Tower's dining hall. She was surprised to find that they had their own kitchens, and the apprentices took turns cooking. Fritz explained that, as a result, they got to try all kinds of food from the different regions of the continent.

The strawberries hadn't been a fluke. Not only was the variety apparently better, but the quality of the food was as well. The meat was fresh, and it was actual cuts. Not the reject pieces, riddled with chewy fat and tendons, that she would get in the normal servants' and apprentices' dining hall. The vegetables were so fresh they still had a crunch. Vhalla felt cheated.

Larel noticed her disapproving stare within moments, and

Vhalla wondered if the power to read minds was part of a Firebearer's Affinity, as Larel found herself quickly explaining the cause of the differing food system.

There was a saying that Vhalla had heard before: The Tower takes care of its own.

Sorcerers knew how hard life could be, and they stuck together as a result. The Tower had a large number of sponsors who, after training, had gone out into the world and earned their fortunes. But they never forgot the start the Tower gave them and regularly sent coin and gifts to take care of the current apprentices. The cycle repeated itself generation after generation.

She sat between Larel and Fritz, and they did a good job of steering the conversation around her so that she only participated as much as she felt like. Larel spoke with other Firebearers, who wore capped sleeves and collared jackets. Fritz seemed engrossed in his own world talking to the man, Grahm, at his side. From the corners of her eyes Vhalla saw the mens' thighs touch briefly as Fritz leaned in. Was she simply imagining the warm glow radiating between them?

After the meal was over, Larel escorted her up to her temporary room, and Vhalla appreciated the artwork in the halls all over again. She tried snuffing a bulb, but only succeeded in shattering it.

"Really, Vhalla," Larel sighed, though she didn't sound genuinely upset. The other woman held out a hand, and the glass shards briefly burnt white-hot and disappeared.

They entered the workroom, and soon Vhalla was settling beneath the covers. Larel had five more potions for her patient to take and three bandages to replace.

"You'll speak with the minister tomorrow." The Western woman looked at Vhalla's bruising. Even Vhalla was surprised at how fast her skin was healing now.

"What will happen then?" she braved to ask.

"I don't know." Larel shook her head. "But I'll be here to help with whatever it is, as long as you don't mind me as your mentor."

Vhalla stared at the dark-haired woman for a long moment. She remembered her harsh words nights ago. Perhaps they had been deserved, perhaps not. Things had changed, and as much as Vhalla had been trying for years to grow into a woman, right now she needed her inner child who embraced the world shifting around her.

"I don't mind," Vhalla whispered. "If you still don't mind being my mentor."

Larel only smiled.

CHAPTER 9

Vhalla met the dawn the next morning. It hadn't been pain or discomfort that woke her early but apprehension for what the day would hold. Vhalla had spent almost a week in the Tower. Granted, half of it she had been unconscious. The minister had stopped to see her twice more when she was awake, overseeing her healing personally.

Her opinion of the Minister of Sorcery had improved with his efforts to heal her, but Vhalla still remembered his conversation with the prince. The minister kept assuring her that she could trust him, that he meant her no harm. Vhalla hoped that he was sincere.

She met the minister in the room adjacent to her temporary chambers. Vhalla sat in the same chair she had occupied weeks ago. This time a mug of steaming tea was placed before her, which Vhalla timidly—bravely—sipped. Unsurprisingly, it was high-quality. *Superior food is something I could grow accustomed to,* Vhalla mused, as she absorbed the tea's aromatics.

"I am glad you are feeling better," the minister started after acquiring his own tea. "Better enough that I've already heard rumors of my apprentices and mentors taking dinner with the first Windwalker." Vhalla avoided his stare, guilty as charged. "Which means, we need to speak on your future."

She wasn't sure what to say.

"I am sure Larel has already explained most of it to you. But, you are a sorcerer now, your place is here in the Tower. We have worked hard to create a place that is a haven for sorcerers of all ranks and skills. You will be allowed to practice freely and will be taught how to control and apply your new skills." He folded his hands, placing them on the table.

"Now, to accept the black robes, you will have to resign your current position in the library. That is not to say you could not patronize the library in your spare time. But you would move here, into the Tower, to live and work among your new peers." He produced a piece of paper from within his robes that was a formal decree of change in apprenticeship. It had four blank spaces for signatures.

There it was, laid out so neatly.

"And if I refuse?" Vhalla found herself asking. The minister paused, and Vhalla tried to decipher what flashed across his eyes. "Can I be Eradicated?"

"Vhalla," Minister Victor began slowly. "You are the first Windwalker in nearly one-hundred and fifty years." Her heart began to race. "I would think that—"

"Is it not my choice?" she asked quickly.

"It is." The minister knew already he would get nowhere by forcing her.

Vhalla settled into her chair with a soft sigh. "Minister," Vhalla began, "the Festival of the Sun is coming." If the changing colors of the trees below her window were any indication, the Empire's largest celebration would start within the month. "I realize I am in a place to ask little but... may I have until the end of the festival to make my decision?"

"Vhalla." The minister pressed his fingertips together. "I am sure you can now appreciate the dangers of having an Awoken and untrained sorcerer around the palace."

"But wasn't the majority of the danger from not knowing how I would wake to my magic?" Vhalla asked timidly. "Now that I have Awoken, there's less of a risk."

"No, you have seen how your emotions can influence your magic without training to suppress that natural response," the minister said, and her heart sank. "I will need you to make your decision today."

Vhalla frowned. She stared at the icy blue eyes of the minister, remembering his conversation with the prince. Whatever they wanted from her, she was not about to give it easily.

"Then I choose to be Eradicated," Vhalla announced boldly.

"Vhalla—" Victor began slowly.

"Was it not my choice?" she cut him off. "If I am forced to choose now, then I will make the safest decision and choose to be Eradicated."

"You are the first Windwalker," the minister repeated in dumb shock.

"It's a shame, isn't it?" Vhalla swallowed her fear to maintain her bold front.

He stared at her for a long moment. Vhalla gripped the hem of the cotton slip they had put her in. She had to stand her ground. If they truly needed her, the minister would not allow her to be Eradicated. Pushing him was dangerous, but Vhalla needed to know the truth.

"Very well," the minister gave in with a sigh. Her heart thumped in her chest. "You may have until the end of the Festival of the Sun to make your decision."

She was right. Whatever they wanted, it involved her magic.

Vhalla had one month to find out why, and then decide if she would keep her magic.

"Thank you, minister," Vhalla said politely.

Within the hour Larel returned her clothes. Placing the clothes upon the bed, Vhalla looked at them in surprise. Her robes looked the cleanest they had ever been; the drab cotton was almost white. She picked up her maroon tunic to find that her finger no longer fit through any holes in the seam.

"We mended them also," Larel noted.

"Thank you." Vhalla had not seen any servants in the Tower, which meant that the apprentices were sharing the work in all areas, just like they were the cooking. She wondered if whenever Larel said *we* what she really meant was *I*.

Larel excused herself, and Vhalla changed slowly. Lifting her arms caused sharp pains to her ribs, making her wince. Despite her battered, purpled, and scratched body her clothes still fit. She was still the same person, or close enough.

She walked at Larel's side in silence, unable to find words. The other woman had a comfortable way about her, and Vhalla did not feel pressured to speak. Her head was full, weighing her choices, and it hurt to think she only had one month to arrive at a decision.

It should be easy, Vhalla scolded herself. She should be Eradicated and put it all behind her. But, as Vhalla slipped through a foreign door behind Larel, she stole one last glance down the Tower. There was something about this place that Vhalla could no longer deny.

"So you know, the minister informed the library that you fell ill with Autumn Fever," Larel explained dutifully.

"I see." Vhalla nodded, wondering how deep the Tower's influence actually ran in the palace. "Larel, thank you," Vhalla said suddenly. After all the woman's care, Vhalla was leaving without giving the Tower anything in return.

"Take care of yourself," Larel demanded gently.

Vhalla vanished through the fogged wall and stood at a crossroad.

She willed her feet to move, but they wouldn't budge.

Something in her screamed to run back down that dim walkway into the arms of the people who had pulled her from death; the people who knew about the change she was enduring and could help her face it. It would be easier if she never went back to the library. If she never looked upon the faces of those who had been her family since she came to the South.

Mohned's face appeared in her mind's eye. Eyes, milky with age, that still held an intensity as they looked at the world from behind circular spectacles. Guilt registered as a stomach spasm. She couldn't leave like that. So she moved one step at a time back to her old home.

Most of the bandages on her hands were gone but the purple of the bruising was still severe in a few places. Vhalla was glad for her long sleeves, as they hid most of the remaining wounds.

She didn't have much strength to push open the ornate doors of the library, so Vhalla was grateful when the guards took hold from within and pulled them open the rest of the way.

During her absence, the Ministry of Culture had begun their preparations for the Festival of the Sun. Large cornucopia hung from the ceiling. Boughs of wheat accented the titles of each library stack. Even the circulation desk had been decorated in sweet-smelling garlands made of autumn leaves and flowers.

Sareem was the first to notice her as he stood behind the desk, looking over Mohned's shoulders at something. "Vhalla!" he shouted.

The master scolded him lightly, but Sareem was already running toward her. Two arms scooped her up into a big hug, and Vhalla didn't even mind the pain in her ribs and shoulders. Echoing his cry was Roan. She dashed from the rows and hugged her next, then Cadance, followed by a much more mild but smiling Lidia. Even the master walked half the length of the library to greet her.

"How do you feel, Vhalla?" Master Mohned's voice was heard through the din of chatter.

"Much better." She blinked back tears. She knew he asked because of the lie about Autumn Fever, but Vhalla could answer honestly.

"We were all really worried for you," Sareem interjected. Vhalla rubbed her eyes.

"What's wrong?" Cadance's voice was small.

"I just missed everyone a lot, that's all," Vhalla sniffed, frustrated with herself.

"It was only a week and some, Vhalla," Roan said with a smile, patting her back. "Actually, not bad for Autumn Fever."

"It felt like a lifetime to me." She gave them a tired smile, knowing that they couldn't understand.

The master adjusted his spectacles. "Well, I think it should be obvious that we are all pleased to have Vhalla with us again," Mohned began. "Though let's give her some air and get back to work."

With another round of warm words and small hugs, everyone parted ways, save for her, the master, and Sareem. She followed the men to the desk. "I'll give you a very simple task today, Vhalla. Please sort through the section of potions to make sure it's all in place."

Pleased with this task, walking through the library was like reuniting with an old friend. Each shelf was a familiar face. Many books held memories for her as much as holding information. Vhalla spared a glance toward the mysteries section as she plunged herself into the rows about potions and put her situation out of sight, but frustratingly not out of mind. She could go on, she realized, just like this again. Like nothing had ever happened. She could be Eradicated and put magic in the past, like a bad dream.

Her face was wet with tears again, and Vhalla mentally cursed herself for crying so much. A shelf became her support. Sliding down against it, she tilted her head back and looked up at the tall bookcases that held the books she was supposed to be sorting.

As she sat there in the silence, breathing deeply and attempting to regain control of herself, Vhalla became aware of something she had yet to consider. This was the first time she had to make a choice about her future.

Her birthday was in a few days, she realized. She would be eighteen and had never made a decision for herself that mattered. Something about it terrified her; something about it shamed her; something about it pushed her forward.

Picking herself up off the floor, she began to sort books. Her mind was too occupied to read any of them. The work was solace enough this day.

The menial task kept her hands busy while Vhalla's mind did its own sorting in the silence. By the time the closing bells rang, she had vowed that no matter what the future held, she was going to make her own decision. Despite what everyone said about sorcerers, Vhalla's short time in the Tower had shown her differently. She wasn't about to let the whispers of common folk, or of Lords heard through a door, decide her future for her. Vhalla was stronger than that. At least, that was what she wanted to believe.

As the library staff were leaving, a small team from the Ministry of Culture carried in items to finish decorating. Vhalla wondered how soon the festival would start. It was one of the best times of the year, as most of the staff were only forced to work one day, so they could enjoy the festivities.

"Vhalla, come eat with us." Sareem touched her shoulder lightly.

She didn't feel hungry—the weight of the world filled her stomach—but Vhalla found herself agreeing, nonetheless.

The dining hall was a raucous place, full of people from all levels of the palace. It was a cavernous space with long rows of wooden tables. Clanking metal plates and glasses, conversations in a multitude of dialects, and fights and laughter rang in her ears. This reminded her why she normally didn't eat here, but, at the same time, she felt nostalgic for her girlhood years when she had been more social and often ate with her peers.

Vhalla sat with Sareem at her left. Roan sat opposite Sareem. Lidia and Cadance stayed with them too, and the library staff ate and enjoyed each other's company, until Vhalla could no longer contain her yawning.

"Someone is sleepy." Sareem rested a palm on her forehead.

"A little." Vhalla nodded.

"You're likely still recovering from the fever," Lidia pointed out, her motherly instincts showing.

"Right," she agreed softly, looking down at her fidgeting fingers. She was still recovering, which wasn't that much of a lie. When Vhalla's eyes raised again she caught Sareem's. He was squinting oddly and, before Vhalla could ask, he was on his feet.

"Well, I think I should see Vhalla to her room; make sure she's all right," Sareem announced. She looked up at the man's form. When had Sareem grown so tall?

"It's fine, stay." Vhalla stood, ignoring a sideways stare from Roan.

"No, no, I want to see you back," Sareem insisted. He offered her his arm, and Vhalla took it timidly. It wasn't the first time she had walked arm-in-arm with Sareem, but it was the first time when they weren't kids running off to some mischief. She felt a little odd, and it wasn't only because of the fact that Roan's stare followed them all the way out.

They walked down the mostly-empty halls in silence. Vhalla adjusted her hand in his elbow, but he made no indication he wanted it removed. She almost jumped when his tenor voice finally broke the silence.

"Vhalla, you didn't have Autumn Fever, did you?" Sareem asked outright.

Vhalla gaped up at him in shock. "What are you talking about? Of course I did! Where else was I?" she replied with panic.

"I don't know." There was the telltale severity of concern in his ocean blue eyes as he looked at her. "But, I know you already had Autumn Fever when you were a girl, and it shouldn't put you out for a week. Plus, I can see a bandage on your forearm."

She snatched her hand back from his elbow quickly, pushing her sleeve down. Vhalla bit her lip. What could she say?

"If anyone asks about your fever, send them to me," he instructed.

"Why?" Vhalla asked softly, the food in her stomach churning.

"Haven't I told you before? You're a bad liar. It'll be more convincing if you send them to me."

"Why would you do that?" They stopped walking before her door, and Vhalla stared up at her friend.

"Because, it might help you," he answered, glancing away. Something suddenly felt awkward. "I don't know why you're lying, Vhalla. But I trust that you wouldn't be trying to if it weren't important. If you ever need someone to talk to, I will be there."

"Thank you, Sareem." Vhalla shifted her feet.

To her surprise he raised her hand to his lips and kissed her knuckles lightly. "Rest well, Vhalla," Sareem whispered, before releasing her fingers and starting back toward the dining hall.

Vhalla was helpless to do little more than watch him go in a dumbfounded silence.

CHAPTER 10

Two days came and went with such a normalcy that it seemed slightly surreal. Vhalla returned to almost all of her usual duties. The master gave her extra leeway in the mornings to help with her recovery. While Vhalla habitually woke with the dawn, she enjoyed the extra time to relax in bed and dress at her leisure. It caused some guilt, but there was a good deal of that feeling lately, as she felt no closer to her decision regarding the Tower.

Things with Sareem had not changed, after her first night back. At times, she could feel a strange stare coming from his direction. Sometimes, he would sit closer than normal, as they hid from work on her window seat. But neither were prepared to cross the line between them.

She began to look at him differently, forcing Vhalla to think back on Roan's words. Vhalla had so readily dismissed her friend's inquiry about a relationship, but now she thought of it during each of Sareem's glances. Why was he paying so much attention to her? It piled on her list of everything she would eventually sort through.

So, on her birthday, she slept past dawn, curled in bed with covers pulled up over her head. As custom, Mohned had given her the day off, and she took the opportunity to sleep in. She was almost completely healed, but her body still demanded additional rest.

Or rather, it would have demanded additional rest were it not for a knock on her door. Vhalla squinted open her eyes, hoping the person would go away. But after a few moments, the second knock pulled Vhalla to her feet.

She struggled to think of whom it could be. The library staff were at work by now, and Vhalla didn't have a large number of friends. Therefore, it shouldn't have been any surprise who greeted her.

"Larel?" she exclaimed, looking at the other woman in the black coat.

"Hello, Vhalla." Larel flashed one of her dazzling smiles. "May I come in? I wouldn't want anyone to notice me when I've avoided being observed until now."

Vhalla nodded and moved to the side to allow her friend to pass.

Larel walked into the small space and looked around. Vhalla's room was little more than a bed, desk, chair, closet, and mirror, but Larel's eyes went over each. She paused a moment, staring at the closet. Right as Vhalla was about to inquire what the other woman thought she saw, Larel turned with a clap of her hands.

"So! How are you feeling?" Larel led Vhalla back to the bed, and she played the patient obediently.

"Very well," Vhalla responded.

"Good." Larel pulled up the chair to sit across from her and started inspecting the last of Vhalla's bruising. "You really have healed amazingly."

This conversation felt very odd after returning to what Vhalla considered to be the real world. Intentionally or subconsciously, she had hardly given more than a passing thought to magic for almost three full days.

"Have you been experimenting?" Larel looked up from her medical diligence. Vhalla shook her head. "Any reason?"

"I don't know what I'm doing." Vhalla held up her leg for Larel to check the bandage on her calf.

"Hardly," Larel remarked dryly.

"Hardly?" Vhalla tilted her head to the side, her hands stretched behind her on the small bed.

"You broke flame bulbs in the Tower," the Western woman pointed out.

"Fritz was helping me," Vhalla retorted. She instantly felt a pang of longing at the idea of seeing Fritz again.

"Oh, yes, Fritz is such an astounding teacher," Larel mentioned sarcastically and laughed.

Vhalla smiled, despite herself, remembering the Southern man's clumsy nature and efforts to help her understand magic. Larel may not understand, but after the minister and the prince, Vhalla thought Fritz was quite a good teacher.

"Maybe for the best though," Larel continued at Vhalla's silence. "Without a teacher overseeing your efforts, it could be dangerous now that you're Awoken. Has anything strange happened?"

"Strange?" Vhalla repeated.

"Yes, strange. Since you're not actively using magic, then I need to know if your powers are seeking any outlets, such as through your emotions." Larel's dark eyes held a severe note.

"Oh! No, nothing strange." Vhalla paused and Larel did the same. Her eyes fell on her window. "Actually, the wind feels different now. I've kept my windows open a lot since coming back. Well, it's hard to explain; it's like there's *something* in the air. Of course you can feel the wind but..."

"I understand; fire feels different to Firebearers." Larel combed her fingers through her bangs. "I enjoy having fire around me. In the flames I don't feel heat, but I do feel something there, like the essence of the flame."

"You don't feel heat?" Vhalla blinked.

"No. Fire can't burn me unless it's made by a much more powerful sorcerer."

"I see," Vhalla mused softly, watching Larel tuck the last of her bandages back into place.

"Good. Well, nothing seems out of order. I only wanted to check up on you." The sorcerer sat back with a smile.

"You wanted to—or you were sent to?" Vhalla inquired.

"Do they have to be mutually exclusive?" The woman stood. "Oh, and by the way, happy birthday."

"How did you know it was my birthday?" she asked, dumbfounded.

"When you were in our care, the minister sent for all your papers and records. I noticed your birthdate." Larel fussed in a small bag for a moment. "Here." She held out two small parcels.

"What's this?" Vhalla accepted the treasures with both hands.

"Birthday presents, silly."

Larel said it like it was nothing, but Vhalla placed them reverently in her lap. She barely expected her friends to remember her birthday, more or less get her anything. To have someone she barely knew give her not one, but two gifts was amazing.

"Oh," Larel added, "one is from Fritz. I made the mistake of telling him where I was headed this morning, and he was insistent."

"May I open them now?" Vhalla asked.

"Go ahead." Larel nodded, giving a small smile at Vhalla's girlish enthusiasm.

Vhalla placed one to the side, as she had a feeling she already knew what it was. Taking the smaller of the two gifts, she unwrapped the simple brown paper and twine to reveal a beautiful metal cuff. It was thin and turned up slightly on the sides with a small gap in the back to slide her wrist through. She studied it in the light. Embossed upon its surface were foreign runes that Vhalla didn't recognize.

"It's beautiful," she whispered, turning it. Vhalla sincerely hoped her new friend had not spent too much.

"I'm glad you like it." Larel beamed.

"I love it, Larel. Wherever did you get it?" She brought it closer to her face and inspected the writing carefully.

"I made it." Seeing Vhalla's startled expression, Larel added, "Firebearers are often jewelers or smiths. We can temper metal, make flame, keep heat. Not being able to be burned helps."

"These markings?" Vhalla asked.

"They're Western," Larel answered.

Vhalla nodded, feeling overwhelmed. Turning to the other gift with the unassuming wrapping, she discovered an old and ragged book. The title had nearly faded, but the writing within was still completely legible: *The Art of Air*.

"Fritz felt bad because it wasn't a real present you could keep forever," Larel explained.

Vhalla shook her head. "This is amazing," she whispered.

"I thought you'd like it." The sorcerer grinned.

"Please, tell Fritz thank you for me," Vhalla said, still turning the book over in her hands.

"Want to come and tell him yourself?" Larel inquired. "You have the day off for your birthday, right? I'm sure the minister wouldn't object to allowing you back into the Tower, since you've yet to make an official decision."

Vhalla considered it for a moment. She had enjoyed her time with Fritz, and reading with him again would be nice. Perhaps she could even eat more of the Tower's food as a birthday present.

Her eyes turned to the window. The slit in the wall offered little light, but she could see the clouds drifting through the sky upon a fall breeze. Vhalla was overcome with the insatiable urge to be outdoors.

"Thank you for the offer. But I think I would like to be outside today," Vhalla said thoughtfully.

"I understand," Larel nodded and said with a tone that made Vhalla believe her. The dark-haired woman began to move to the door but paused, glancing at Vhalla's closet once more. She opened her mouth briefly as if to say something but when she turned back, her expression changed. "Take care, Vhalla. We're only a call away should you need us."

"Thank you, Larel, for everything." Vhalla smiled.

Larel poked her head out of the room and then crept away.

Wearing one of her gifts, she placed the other in her bag. The days were almost exclusively cool now, and her winter robes had finally arrived. They were spun from thicker wool and heavier materials than her summer and fall robes. Vhalla was perpetually cold, and she welcomed the cloth in all its itchy glory. Just like her summer robes, an open book was stitched on the back of her winter robes, marking her as one of the library apprentices. Vhalla stared at the blue thread. How much longer would she be wearing them?

Vhalla decided that she would actually give some care for her appearance today. It was her birthday, another year older, another chance at maturing and developing womanly habits she had yet to find a taste for. Through her tarnished looking glass, Vhalla moved her head to fit in the palm sized reflection. Her hair seemed marginally better.

Vhalla had one special stop planned before she set out on her day. She headed upward into the sweaty din of the kitchens. It was a bustling place of noise and stomach-growling scents. Vhalla did not often have reason to frequent them, but on her birthday she hoped for one exception.

Lemons only grew in the far West and on the outer islands, so they were a delicacy in the other regions of the main continent. The kitchens served a small cake with tea or lunches for nobles and royals. White sugar glaze on top, Vhalla coveted the spongy yellow sweet throughout the year.

With just the right amount of begging—and luck—she had one palm-sized dessert wrapped in cloth and stashed in her bag for her birthday.

As far as Vhalla was concerned, the palace had three worlds wrapped within it. The innermost world was the lowest in society; it was tucked away in closet-like spaces with servant dormitories, apprentice rooms, and hallways that ran through walls. It was the rough-hewn stone, chipping mortar, and stairs that were not quite evenly spaced. Candlewax dripping down the walls was their artwork and all the pleasurable scents of the plumbing—the palace's and Empire's sophisticated aqueduct system—was their perfume.

Above that world was the public world. This had the showy rooms common folk were permitted to see and the halls nobles and ministers walked through. It was polished and swept with fresco artwork and stone sculptures.

This was where Vhalla walked today. Not completely unorthodox for an apprentice, she enjoyed the beauty of the palace at her leisure. Most of the halls stood empty as Court was in session and the ministers were at work.

Vhalla had never stepped foot in the last world of the palace. Not unless she counted passing through in secret stairwells behind a prince. The quarters for royalty and their high-ranking noble guests were closed off with a gilded gate. The most dangerous guards were posted day and night, keeping out all who would presume to force entry. Vhalla had only set eyes upon the gate once, as a curious girl, before she had been shooed away.

Vhalla did not know what she was looking for. She simply walked. Spiraling upward and downward, she drifted from one thing to the next. She passed one or two other servants, but they asked her nothing and she offered nothing.

Vhalla might not have had a goal when she started this meander, but she knew she had found it when she saw it.

Through an upper window, Vhalla gazed upon a garden she had never seen before, hidden within a palace courtyard. Gravel pathways wandered through the dense hedges, plants, and trees. Many of them were beginning to lose their green foliage, changing into the fall orange and reds. The trees looked aflame as they swayed in the bright sunlight.

She spotted a gate through the windows as Vhalla spiraled around the garden. However, none of the stairwells up or down led her to a passage that connected to it. Frustrated but determined, she found the lowest window she could. It was almost impossible to see over the hedge positioned right before it.

Opening the window, Vhalla stepped over the stone and landed lightly in the garden below. She could barely close the portal behind her and would need to find something to stand on to return later. The wind ruffling her hair, Vhalla plunged through the bushes and into another world.

A breeze swept down the mountainside, stopping Vhalla in her tracks. It was unlike anything she had ever felt before. The world was alive around her, and each gust of air was like the whisper of a lover upon silk.

In awe, she held out a hand, inspecting it as though she could see the air visibly slipping between her fingers. This was more than the soft huffs that managed to breeze through her window. She could not see it, but she could *feel* it. Not in the way that one normally feels a breeze. No, recalling Larel's words, Vhalla could feel the essence of the wind. It was as though she could grab it and close her fingers around something finer than any silk or chiffon.

An upward gust drew her gaze skyward, and Vhalla's breath hitched in her throat. Towering high above her was Imperial Housing. Her whole body tingled at the sight. It was the first time she laid eyes on the golden spires since her fall.

She had no reason to be alive. The spires were astonishingly high with a straight drop down. Vhalla tried to imagine what she might have hit, but nothing seemed to make sense. All the ledges and decorations were to the sides of the tower; it was a far descent before there was anything that could've broken her fall. From her current vantage, she could discern that she would've had to have moved a good six or seven body lengths in the air to have hit anything. It all seemed vastly impossible.

Shaking the painful memories from her mind, Vhalla gripped her bag and began walking through the garden. She had seen an unorthodox structure from the windows and attempting to find it was a much better use of her time, than musing over princes and near-death experiences.

Fortunately, all paths seemed to wind toward her goal and Vhalla's heart beat in a weird rhythm at its beauty.

The building looked almost like a birdcage. Silverwork arched together, holding large panes of swirled glass upright like walls. At its apex stood a silver sun. Vhalla fidgeted with her fingers, thinking. She had only ever seen the blazing sun of the Empire crafted in gold.

The glass had a touch of fog to it. While she could make out hazy shapes and green blurs, it was impossible to discern what was inside. Three silver steps led up to an arched door.

Her hand paused on the silver handle. Her heart was racing but she couldn't place why.

Roses assaulted her senses upon entering. They grew along the outer walls and up a large central post. The temperature within the greenhouse-like structure was warm, perfectly kept for ensuring the Western crimson flowers stayed in bloom.

Her slippers did not make a sound as she walked lightly over to the pillar, inspecting one of the buds. Movement drew her attention past the stunning foliage to a silver bench in the back, opposite the door.

She was not alone.

A man sat hunched over an open ledger and seemed to be deeply engrossed in the notes he was taking. Vhalla's blood ran cold, and she took a step back. This was not supposed to happen. Out of all the people in the world she was not meant to meet this man clad in black, with his slicked back hair and dark eyes.

Vhalla was debating how best to make her escape when his pen stopped and his chin slowly rose. His eyes widened, and his brow furrowed as his lips parted slightly in shock. The deep, rich voice that broke the silence made her teeth grind.

"Are you real?" Prince Aldrik whispered in obvious surprise.

CHAPTER II

With annoyance, Vhalla wiped the confusion off her face.

"Of course I'm real, and I was just leaving." She turned, starting for the door.

"Wait!" He was on his feet, papers scattering across the floor. She looked back at his clumsy and haphazard movement. "Wait."

"Is that an order, my prince?" Vhalla focused her gaze on the door handle. A quiet anger rose in her.

"Yes. No. *No*, it is not. If you want to go, then go; but please, just—wait." He sighed and ran a hand over his hair, and adjusted his long double-breasted coat with the other.

"Why?" she demanded. Vhalla half-turned toward him, her hand still on the door handle.

"Because—" he cleared his throat, attempting to continue with more conviction "—I want to talk to you."

"And if I don't want to talk to you?" she sighed.

"Then go." When she made no motion in his direction, his posture went slack. He knelt and began to pick up his papers.

Vhalla stood in limbo, watching this strange, frustrating, and infuriating man on the floor, collecting his scattered parchment. With another soft sigh, the apprentice within got the better of her, and Vhalla walked over to kneel across from her prince, collecting a few papers within reach and holding them out expectantly.

He looked up at her and took the papers from her hands, his jaw slightly slack and lips parted.

She waited for a moment. Receiving nothing, she stood and turned for the door, frustrated. What had she expected? He was a prince, and—if the palace gossip was to be believed—he never thought of anyone beyond himself.

"I am sorry." It was so soft she barely heard it over the rustling of the trees. Vhalla held the halfway open door. *Surely she'd only imagined it.* She took another step. "Vhalla, *I am sorry.*"

She turned slowly, looking back at him, one foot outside, one foot in. The words sunk into her, and she waited to see if they could be enough to soothe the anger she felt toward the black-clad man.

"I should not have lashed out at you, magically or verbally, as I did," he continued. There was a spark in his eyes that was pleading with her for something she didn't know if she could give. "I was eager—and foolish. I did not think of how it would affect you."

Vhalla took a step back in, closing the door behind her and leaning against it for much needed support.

"I am certain you have heard all of the stories about me." Prince Aldrik rested his folio on the bench behind him. Vhalla wondered why he seemed unable to meet her eyes. "I assure you, they are all true. I am not exactly versed in, in..." He paused, looking for words.

"In creating real relationships with people?" Vhalla finished spitefully. If he wanted to cast her from the palace for her lack of proper decorum, he would have already. She had no idea why he didn't. But Vhalla was ready to find out and wash her hands of royalty.

"I have hurt you with my words—and actions. I know that. And, it likely means nothing to you to say that I did not intend to." He sighed, looking away.

"They say you are the silver-tongued prince." Her voice was fainter than she would've liked. "You already spoke me onto a ledge. How can I believe you now?"

"Because there are things you do not know about us," Prince Aldrik responded cryptically.

Vhalla shook her head—there was no "us" between them. "You could've thrown me to my death and—what's worse—you didn't even care." Her voice broke, and she took a deep breath. Vhalla clenched her jaw; she had been the one who suffered. He had no right to look so pained.

"You are wrong. I did care. I knew you were a Windwalker, so I never realized the possibility of you dying." The prince took a small step toward her. Vhalla glared at the toes of his boots as though they had offended her.

"Fine," she started, trying to turn his logic back on him. "Even if you knew my Affinity—which not even the minister himself seemed to know—how did you know the fall wouldn't kill me; that'd I'd be strong enough?"

"Because air cannot hurt Windwalkers, like fire cannot hurt Firebearers," he pointed out.

"It seems we know almost nothing about Windwalkers. You didn't know that fall wouldn't kill me." She crossed her arms over her chest.

"I knew you would not die, because you saved my life." The prince's voice was slow and deliberate, as if he struggled to speak. Her arms dropped to her side. "When I first arrived home, I was going to die. The... *weapon* that pierced my flesh was laced with a strong poison. Were it not for an immunity I have built up over many years, it would have killed me halfway home. The clerics did not know what to do, so they called on the library and the Tower for any clues as to an antidote or course of treatment.

"I knew it was the end. The clerics could not make sense of the poison and how it had been altered magically to affect me." Aldrik clenched a fist and Vhalla listened to his tale intently. "Yet I began to stabilize as they pulled certain notes from the books. Some were comprehensive, others devolved into gibberish, but somehow they all made sense to me, and I was able to guide my treatment. They were all yours."

"That's impossible," Vhalla protested. "How did you know they were mine?"

"I had the minister ask the guards who wrote them. A guard led Victor to you," the prince explained. "I knew you were exerting a fair deal of magical energy to keep me alive, and I wanted to make sure you were safe."

"What?" she said weakly. The minister had kidnapped her because the prince had been worried for her wellbeing? It was backward and hardly made sense. But if it was true, Vhalla began to paint a different image of that night and the events that followed.

"I was not completely enthused about Victor's methods," Aldrik mumbled. "But he found you, and I knew who to look for."

Vhalla was finally stunned into silence.

"For lack of a better explanation, you wrote magic. I do not know why you did it—or how. But you cared so much about saving me that it forced your powers to Manifest. You made vessels and sent them to me. As utterly impossible as that should be for someone who was not even Awoken, you did it. And if it had not been for that, I would not be standing now." The prince's voice had found strength.

"How do you know?" She found her words once more, still trying to find a flaw in his story. It all seemed so impossible.

"Because when a sorcerer saves another person, a part of them—of their magic—takes root. It is called a Bond. You are likely too recently Awoken to understand it or feel it, but I could." He folded his hands behind his back.

"A Bond?" Vhalla repeated the word in its foreign context.

"Yes, my parrot." The corner of his mouth curled faintly at her scowl. "Part of a Bond is that you cannot bring mortal harm to the person to whom you are Bonded. It is because I carry a piece of you with me. The body refuses to harm itself. If pushing you from the roof would have taken your life, I physically could not have done it."

Vhalla frowned, her still-healing joints aching at the memory of that night.

"But," Prince Aldrik continued, as if reading her mind, "I did not realize the Bond would let me harm you so. I truly believed you would land safely, that we could even speak of it after you did. That was my mistake."

"Aren't you lucky to be a prince and not have your mistakes have consequences?" Vhalla remarked sharply.

"They do," he responded quickly and firmly. "The consequence was the loss of your trust."

Her eyes met his with trepidation. She couldn't help but wonder if his words were carefully crafted to what she would want to hear. As though he could sense her scepticism, Prince Aldrik's gaze rested on her almost sadly.

"How many other people do you puppet?" Vhalla sighed.

"Please explain your question," he requested.

"Larel. The introduction book. Those weren't chance, were they?" She watched his lips purse together. "She told me you knew each other."

"Larel is a friend."

With four words from the prince, Vhalla's jaw dropped. "You have friends?" she couldn't stop herself from blurting out, and her hands went to her mouth as if to hide her outburst. Anyone else she would have expected to laugh.

The prince only shrugged and looked away, painfully awkward. Vhalla reminded herself that she shouldn't feel guilty. But she remembered Larel's words. He had faced the brunt of the stigma against sorcery, despite being a prince. His own subjects seemed to favor *Fire Lord* over his natural titles.

"What about me?" Vhalla dared to ask.

"I already explained what you are to me," the prince responded.

It was just enough to push her back toward the edge of anger. "I don't think you have. Am I another one of your playthings to command? To serve you? To let you train me until you can deliver me to your father?"

The conversation she had overheard came back to Vhalla, the prince and the minister deciding her fate without even asking her. Judging by the furrow to his brow, the prince remembered also.

"You heard?" he asked darkly.

Vhalla swallowed and nodded, suddenly wondering if confessing to such was really a good idea. Prince Aldrik clenched his fist, and Vhalla saw the tiniest sparks of flame flash around his knuckles. He released his fingers with a heavy sigh, and she felt the temperature of the room lower.

"I cannot explain everything now. But I do not plan on telling my father about you. The last place I would want to see you taken to is that sweltering warfront of the North. If I may use your words, Victor was the puppet. Not you."

"Why are you protecting me?" Vhalla asked before she could even think. It did not coincide with his previous actions, if he could be believed at all.

"Because you are the sorcerer to whom I am Bonded. A Bond can never be broken, and it can never be replaced." The prince looked back at her. Vhalla's heart seemed to beat so hard it hurt against her still bruised ribs. "For someone who is so important, I did not treat you as I should have; for that, Vhalla, I am sorry. But whatever you feel toward me, and however justified it is, does not change anything for me. I will still use all the powers I possess to see you safe."

For all his orders and sneers, his commanding presence, and his intimidating always all-black ensemble, Vhalla saw something different. She simply saw someone who was lonely, someone who could likely count their friends on one hand, and perhaps wanted to one day use two hands. He was nothing like the man she first met; the man who wore a mask to meet palace expectations.

She hadn't forgiven him, not quite yet. But perhaps Larel was right, and Vhalla felt a little sorry for him too.

The prince looked away from her, distracting himself with the flowers. But now he held her gaze. The silence fell between them. He stared at her, and she at him.

In time she realized he was waiting for her to pass judgment. He stood, uncomfortably folding and unfolding his hands, waiting.

Vhalla took a deep breath, trying to find the courage to speak. It was easy to be angry, resentful, and argumentative. It was harder to take one step toward him, and then another. She clutched her bag and crossed the space between them, standing before him, and trying with all her might not to fidget.

"I came here to read. If that's all right?" she asked quietly.

"It is." His voice was soft and low, no longer making her grit her teeth at the sound.

She moved around him and sat on one side of the bench. He looked at her like a lost child.

"You were here first. You're welcome to stay," she offered, pulling out her book from her satchel.

He sat down next to her, situating his ledger back on his lap. Vhalla had forgotten the warmth the prince exuded, and she shrugged off her robes, letting them fall over the bench. He glanced at the leggings and tunic that she wore beneath, but spared her any Southern mention of it being inappropriate dress for a woman. Leaning against the wall behind them, she settled with the book in her lap, thumbing to the first page.

"My prince," she murmured. He looked at her. "I'm sorry, also, for the nasty things I said to you." She looked up from the book.

He smiled, and for the first time she felt like it was sincere; that there was no motive, no pretense, and no other hidden emotions behind it. It was little more than the corners of his mouth curling up, but it lit his eyes in a way that Vhalla had yet to see. It made her wonder if she had ever really seen him before. It made her wonder if anyone had ever really seen him before. It quieted the voice in her mind; whispering that all of this was the start of some elaborate grander scheme.

"Call me Aldrik," he said, very matter-of-factly, before turning back to his ledgers. "At least in private." Vhalla felt her jaw drop as his pen began to scratch against the page once more; a familiar slanted script left in its wake. "And you are not a little worm, Vhalla."

CHAPTER 12

Vhalla continued to struggle with her situation. She sat, pretending to read, mulling over the confounding and infuriating man next to her. A thousand questions ran through her head, but she found none worth breaking the silence.

She attempted to read between his words, to find any hidden meanings or motives. But the more she thought of the Bond, the less convinced she felt that he was toying with her. Why else would he have kept her in the palace? If he did not share a connection with her that he deemed important, wouldn't she be gone? Especially after her outburst?

Vhalla glanced at him from the corners of her eyes. She noticed a small bump on the bridge of his nose, as though it had been broken and reset poorly. His pronounced cheekbones shaded the sides of his face in the sunlight.

He lifted his eyes from his work to catch hers. Vhalla looked away quickly, not wanting to be caught staring. *Just act normal,* she scolded herself. But what was normal for an apprentice and a prince?

Shifting slightly, she began to read with intent, pushing the oddity of their situation from her mind. There was something relaxing about this place, the smell and the muffled sounds of the outside world. Her reading was not very dense, and it was actually interesting to learn more about what her magic could do. Vhalla took her time with the pages, committing the points that interested her to memory.

The book was about the applications of air-based magic in a practical setting. Flipping the page, she wondered if she would be able to actually perform any of the seemingly impossible feats contained within. Perhaps, with the right teacher, she may be able to...

Vhalla flipped the page, putting the difficult decisions in the back of her mind.

They continued on like this for a while. She wasn't sure how much time had passed, but eventually she became aware of the weight of his stare on her.

"What?" She peered at the prince's strange expression.

The prince—Aldrik, she mentally corrected herself—opened his mouth to speak, and closed it again, thinking over his words another moment. "What are you reading?" He put his quill down in the open ledger, leaning slightly toward her to inspect the book.

"It's something Fritz gave me, or rather, lent me. It's called the *Art of Air*." She turned back to the first page, showing him the written title.

"Fritz?" His eyes met hers briefly.

"Yes, from the Tower. The Southern boy in the library." Vhalla wondered how much he knew of the Tower.

"Ah." The prince leaned back. "That incompetent nitwit." Now he was back to sounding more like himself.

"Be nice," she chided gently, and he glanced over at her through the corners of his eyes.

"If he was going to break the rules and let a book outside the Tower, there are better ones." Aldrik punctuated his self-serving comment with a scratch of his quill.

She rolled her eyes. "I don't know much, so anything is welcome," Vhalla pointed out.

"Very true. You do not know much," he agreed casually.

Vhalla laughed aloud. "You are a royal pain, you know that?" She shook her head, but she wasn't even angry. Some part of her much preferred this cocky and arrogant side to him over the quieter more insecure glimpses she'd seen earlier. They didn't seem to fit, what little she knew of him. It was safer for the prince to remain a stuck-up royal than someone with a heart and soul.

"You are not the first to think such. You will not be the last." He shrugged, relaxing back into his own work. She looked back down at her book and flipped the page again. He was back to staring at her.

"What?" Mild annoyance was apparent in her voice.

"Do it again," he demanded.

"Do what again?" Vhalla sighed.

"What you just did." Aldrik pointed to the book.

"I know I am a farmer's daughter, but I *can* read." Vhalla glared at him.

"Not read, turn the page." He kept staring at the book.

She looked at him and flipped a page with emphasis. "*Ta-da.*" Sarcasm dripped from the noise.

He raised his chin and stared at her with those endlessly black eyes. "You do not even realize it." He spoke softly at first, their faces close. Sitting back with a laugh, he repeated himself, "You do not even realize it!"

Vhalla was outwardly annoyed with him now. "Thank you, Aldrik the parrot," she muttered.

He stopped laughing and stared at her. She paused, it was the first time she used his name without a title. After a moment he grinned and stood.

"Put it down, I want to see something." He held out his hand to her.

"You're not going to push me off a roof again, are you?" Vhalla instantly wished her tone had been more jovial and less flat.

An unusual mix of emotions crossed his face, and his hand relaxed a little before falling to his side. "You said that you would accept me as your teacher," he spoke softly. She inwardly cursed breaking the lighter moment. "I want that honor again."

He extended his hand back to her and waited. Vhalla swallowed hard. Prince or not, he was asking too much of her in one day. She avoided his intense stare.

"You have to earn it." Vhalla didn't know what else to say. She had trusted him, to lead her, to teach her, and he broke that trust. It wasn't as though it was something she could simply start again on command.

"That is acceptable," was his surprising remark. She looked back to him; he still stood there hopefully expectant.

Vhalla took his hand. His skin was soft and his palm warm; it almost tingled beneath the pads of her fingers. But she had little more than a moment to reflect on that as he pulled her to her feet and out of the gazebo, back into the autumn day.

"How do you feel?" he asked, leading her into the garden.

"Well enough. Larel stopped in this morning and checked up on me. She said I'm healing well," she reported.

Aldrik glanced at her. "If something goes wrong, tell me. I could control your healing when you were in the Tower, but now that you are back in the castle proper it is harder for me to oversee directly." He kept his long strides in pace with her.

"Control over… my healing?" Vhalla considered the implications of this.

He nodded, stopping. They arrived at a small pond.

"After what happened," he paused, "I wanted to make sure you had the best care possible. It was the least I could do."

She stared at him and part of her wanted to yell. Didn't he claim he was not a puppeteer in her life? But she remembered the words of the minister; the prince had been the one who had taken her to the Tower in the first place, and she likely would've died without that.

He cleared his throat. "In any case, back there, you were flipping the pages without touching them," Aldrik announced.

"Huh?" Vhalla said dumbly.

He nodded. "You kept flipping the pages only by moving your hand over the book, but you never actually touched them. You did not even notice." His tone was a mix of excitement and severity. "Your powers are showing, Vhalla."

"That's impossible." She shook her head.

"For other sorcerers, but not for you, clearly." He crossed his arms on his chest.

"I'm sure you could do something even better without thinking about it," she protested and grasped for the idea that what she was doing was not special.

"Yes, I very likely could." He closed the gap between them, looking down at her. She looked up defiantly. "I am the most powerful sorcerer in this Empire. Therefore, I am not a good benchmark of what is *possible* or *easy* to do." He gave a confident grin before strolling around and behind her.

Vhalla kept her gaze forward.

"Tell me, have you ever skipped stones?" He knelt, picking up one of the flatter, circular rocks.

"When I was a child." *Who hadn't?* "Though I can't remember the last time."

He tossed the stone from hand to hand a few times before sending it flying over the still water of the pond. It skipped across the surface three times before sinking. Vhalla intentionally did not look impressed.

"Your turn." He bent down and picked up another stone, placing it in her palm.

The prince walked over to a decorative pile of mountain rocks around one side of the pond, perching himself on the largest. Resting his elbow on a bent knee, he placed his chin in his hand and stared at her expectantly. Vhalla regarded him curiously before she brought her arm back for the throw.

"No, not like that." He stopped her. "Without throwing it."

"How do I..." she started.

"Move it, like you did the pages," he instructed.

"I didn't even know I was doing that," Vhalla said, already annoyed.

"Somewhere in you, you did. I know this is going to be hard for you, but think less." His words did not have a bite to them. "The execution of magic is not something that can be neatly summed up with words. I know you think, and wish, the whole world could be placed down on parchment in-between a strip of leather. But I regret it has fallen to me to inform you that such is simply not true."

He gave her another one of his small smiles. It sparked warmth in her to see him being open toward her and not snarky. That spark quickly vanished when Vhalla looked doubtfully at the stone in her palm.

She held her hand out flat, the small stone in its center. Taking a breath, Vhalla tried to calm her mind and focus only on the afternoon air around her. Closing her eyes, the world materialized around her in the darkness. He was the first thing she saw with her magical sight.

Around the prince there was fire. It burned bright yellow—

almost white—illuminating his features. In stark contrast, was a dark spot in his abdomen; a black scar against the light. Vhalla opened her eyes and slowly turned to him.

"You're not all right, are you?" she breathed. He frowned and she could almost feel him withdraw. "That magic, poison, whatever it is, it's still in you." She pointed at his side where she'd seen the spot. He considered her a long moment, unmoving.

"The stone, Vhalla," Aldrik spoke softly and slowly.

He was shutting her out. Sighing, she closed her eyes. Some things wouldn't change. It'd be foolish to expect them to. He was a prince, and she was an apprentice; some distances could never be crossed.

Her mind focused on the rock this time. *Just like the bulb*, she reminded herself.

The stone shuddered in her palm. *Forward*, Vhalla urged. Her brow furrowed, and she felt a drop of sweat roll down her neck, even though the temperature was nowhere near warm. Frustrated, Vhalla opened her eyes to glare at the insubordinate pebble.

"That way!" she half-pleaded, half-snipped in annoyance.

The moment her opposite finger cut through the air in the desired direction, the stone shuddered to life. Vhalla jumped as it flew out of her palm, soared over the pond, through the shrubs on the other side, and buried itself into the stone wall behind.

Aldrik roared with laughter. She clenched her fists and scowled at him.

"That was amazing." He slowly regained control of himself. "A little too much force, though."

Frustrated, Vhalla picked up a second pebble and held it in her hand again. She connected with it faster this time, but it still refused to move, despite her best mental commands. Lifting up her other hand, she flicked her wrist and it was sent soaring across the pond, though not as far.

Aldrik leaned forward, both elbows on his knees and his hands folded between. His raven eyes followed her every movement as Vhalla picked up the third stone. This time she did not even close her eyes to understand where the pebble was magically. Her fingers twitched, and it fell just to the other side of the water.

The fourth landed in the center of the pond with a dull plop and cry of victory from Vhalla.

Then there were the fifth, the sixth, and the seventh, each of which had a bad angle, moved too slowly, or landed wide again. Vhalla wiped her brow with the back of her hand, noticing her breathing had become labored.

The prince stood. "That is enough for today," Aldrik said thoughtfully.

"But I've almost got it," she protested.

"And are fully prepared to exhaust yourself in your attempt to get it." He offered her his elbow. "Come."

She clutched the eighth stone another second before giving in and replacing it with his arm. Vhalla took a deep breath, relaxing herself.

"We will need to work on your technique," Aldrik explained as they walked. "You do not need to attach magical feats to physical movements."

"It didn't work the other way."

"It will in time," he encouraged her. "Do not become too reliant upon your magic requiring a physical motion."

"Show me?" she asked timidly as they re-entered the greenhouse.

"What am I to show?" Aldrik asked, starting for the bench.

"Your magic, without motion," Vhalla clarified.

"Very well." The prince patted the bench next to him, and she

assumed her prior position. Vhalla did not even realize that she had just made a demand of the prince.

Suddenly his outstretched palm was set ablaze. Tendrils of flame licked up from around his wrist. They circled his fingers and relished the air with their bright dance before fading. Vhalla stared, mesmerized. Aldrik did much the same.

With a timid hand she reached up. The moment her fingers crossed the point of heat, the flame extinguished. His hand caught hers.

"Careful," the prince said thoughtfully. "I would not want you to get burned."

They hovered, the heat of his hand enveloping hers. Her throat felt gummy. Neither of them seemed to be able to fathom words over the ringing silence.

"Right," Vhalla said, breaking the trance first, pulling her hand away and fussing with her cuticles as though they had become the most fascinating things in the world. It was hot enough in the greenhouse that her cheeks were flushed, and Vhalla quickly reached down to her bag underneath the bench, hiding her face.

Placing the leather satchel in her lap, Vhalla unwrapped the lemon cake after only a moment's debate. She wasn't even certain the prince liked sweets, but she still felt compelled to share her spoils with him. Ripping the hand-sized cake in two, Vhalla offered half—the smaller one—to him. Aldrik arched an eyebrow.

"It's a lemon cake," she explained.

"I know what it is." He took it from her hand, sniffing it.

"It's good, I promise." She grinned. He took a bite. "They're actually my favorite."

"Not a bad batch," he affirmed.

Vhalla's chewing slowed. Of course the prince would have eaten the lemon cakes before.

"So, you simply carry a lemon cake with you each day?" he asked.

"No. I'm not supposed to have it, as I'm an apprentice. It could get the kitchen staff in trouble if someone important knew they gave me one." Aldrik smirked. Vhalla continued, hoping that did not come to pass, "But if I beg on my birthday to the right person, I normally get lucky."

"Your birthday?" he asked. Vhalla nodded in affirmation. "Is today?" Vhalla nodded again.

"It's why Fritz gave me the book." Vhalla nudged her bag with her toe. "Larel gave me this cuff." Vhalla held out her wrist for him to see.

He inspected it thoughtfully a moment and Vhalla finished off the last of her lemon cake, using the opportunity to study his features again from the corners of her eyes. Vhalla was actually happy she could share something with the prince. But she wished that thing wasn't a favorite food that she could only eat once every year.

Vhalla was halfway through her book when she noticed her pages had changed from a pale cream color to an orange glow. Sunset blazed above them and threatened to take her reading light away. Closing the book, she bent over and put it back in her bag.

"Finished?" he inquired. He'd been making notes in that black ledger all day.

"Not yet, about half," she responded, standing.

"I was under the impression that you read faster than that," he mumbled over a few quick notes of his own.

"Sorry to disappoint you," Vhalla teased. Smiling around the man who had previously been a source of fear and anger was surprisingly easy.

He looked up at her and closed his ledger, taking a long strip

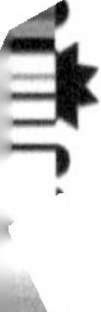

of leather and wrapping it around the outside to hold the papers within.

"Are you leaving also?" she asked.

"I may as well." He tucked the folio beneath his arm.

They started for the door. She did not feel like she was leaving with the same person she had met upon her arrival. Then again, with how her emotions had shifted, Aldrik may be able to say the same.

"How did you get in here?" Vhalla asked, once outside the gazebo.

He looked at her quizzically. "I am the crown prince; I am actually allowed to be here. The better question is how did *you* get in here?" Aldrik wore a small smirk.

"Well, I-I found a way." Vhalla gripped the strap of her bag. He let out a laugh. "I couldn't find the proper entrance!"

"That much is obvious; you are not supposed to know how to get into an Imperial Garden." Vhalla shifted her feet. "But do not let that stop you. It has not until now, clearly." He turned with a laugh and started walking to the gate. Stopping in the middle of the path, Aldrik turned back to her. "Do you need me to let you out?"

The wind picked up at her back, as if encouraging her forward. Vhalla stared down at the black-clad prince. How much did she trust this man? Her thumb ran over the pads of her fingers where he had held her hand in his.

"If it's not any trouble?" Vhalla asked, mustering her courage. She did not understand what the Bond was, not really. He had been right about that. But there was something about the way his eyes fell on her that was different than any other person's gaze.

Walking slowly down the steps of the gazebo, she met those eyes again as he offered her his elbow. Vhalla could not ignore the sparks that shot through her like lightning when they touched.

Aldrik led her through the iron gate and down a passageway, which had her gasping within steps. The floor was not carpet, nor stone; it was white marble set in a diamond pattern with smaller golden diamonds meeting at corners. The arched ceiling was painted in brilliant frescos and the candles flickered magically to life as they walked by.

The prince remained silent as his guest absorbed the wonder in awe. Alabaster statues looked down from high ceilings. Windows made of colored glass and black lead cast bright pictures on the canvas of the floors and walls. It was a world she had only heard of, like a fairy tale that was passed from the lips of one servant to the next.

"This place, is..." Her mind was slowly churning back to being capable of words. "It's..."

"My home," he finished for her.

"I'm not supposed to be here." Vhalla shook her head as they stopped before a small side hall.

"You may be wherever I permit," Aldrik reminded her. Despite his princely tone the words were thoughtful, and he looked at her as though she were the only one he wanted to permit entry. "I would like to teach you more."

"I may enjoy that." Vhalla wasn't sure why she was whispering.

"Come back tomorrow?"

"I can't." Vhalla bit her lip. "I had today off for my birthday, but tomorrow I will be working."

"If you could, would you come?" Vhalla had a hard time deciphering his look. Uncertainty was clear enough, but was there also want?

"If I could," Vhalla replied with a nod.

"Very well." The corners of his lips twitched. "This hall will take you back to the servants' passages. Just head down."

Vhalla took a step backward, her hand falling from his elbow. She turned before his stare made her head feel any lighter and started down the dim hallways away from the world of wonder and magic. The castle morphed around her, and she was lost in her thoughts all the way back to her room. If she could, she would rather learn magic than be in the library. That was what she said, wasn't it? Was it true?

Vhalla rubbed her eyes and pushed open the door to her room. She knew she hadn't eaten much, but she didn't feel that hungry and her hunger wasn't enough to deal with the dining hall.

On her table were three small presents. There was a blank journal from the master and a new quill and inkpot from Roan; Vhalla had a suspicion they had coordinated their gifts. Lastly, a thin rectangular box that had a small note attached:

Vhalla ~

A very happy birthday. While I am glad you got the day off, your presence in the library was missed.

Sincerely yours,

~ Sareem

She gave the note a tired smile. Placing it to the side on her desk, she picked up the box. Unwrapping the used parchment, she found a ruby box within. Vhalla vaguely recognized it. It was from *Chater's*, a clothing shop in the nice area of town not far from the library's public entrance. She had only seen noble ladies walking out of the store, carrying the red boxes with pride.

Vhalla felt strange just holding it.

Slowly, she pulled off the top. Vhalla gasped. Within, were two lovely sapphire gloves. They were fingerless, which suited her writing habit, and extended almost to her elbow. She remembered all the times last winter she complained about her hands being too cold to write. Her other gloves were old cotton things and worn thin with holes from over-use. Her gift was dyed leather and had a beautiful golden thread that embellished the base and sides with an intricate leaf and vine design.

Vhalla couldn't imagine how much they had cost Sareem. She was fairly sure they were close to the same amount of savings she had scraped together. As though she would ruin them with her touch, Vhalla returned the gloves to the box. With a sigh she buried her face into her pillow. What was Sareem thinking?

CHAPTER 13

The next day Vhalla awoke groggy and tired. Dawn came so early. All of the excitement had exhausted her. *My body is still getting used to magic*, she reminded herself. If she was using it at times without even consciously knowing it, then she was potentially wearing herself out more than she realized.

She let out a groan for two reasons. The first was because she realized she had forgotten her winter robes in the garden. She would have to get them back somehow; for now her summer ones would have to do. The second reason was because she saw Sareem's gift once more. Vhalla tugged them on with little thought, ignoring how soft the leather actually was.

"Are those new?" Roan asked as they waited for the master.

"They are." Vhalla nodded weakly in response.

"May I see?"

Vhalla obliged her friend, stretching out an arm over the circulation desk where they both stood. Roan inspected the stitching carefully.

"Vhalla, these are quite nice."

"I think they're from Chater's," Vhalla mumbled.

"Chater's? Were they a gift?" Roan released Vhalla's hand slowly. An expression that was difficult to read crept up Roan's face.

"They were from Sareem." Vhalla looked back toward the palace side doors as though he would appear on command. The two girls were early, and he wasn't.

"He likes you, Vhalla," Roan said thoughtfully.

"I don't think—" Something in the look on her friend's face gave Vhalla pause. Roan was very certain of what she was saying. "Sareem? Really?"

"I think so." Roan nodded.

The doors at one end of the library opened for the master and Sareem, and neither girl had an opportunity to speak after that. Roan was behind the desk with the master and Vhalla was sent among the books, as normal. She told herself that she really was going to seek out Sareem to thank him for his gift; that she wasn't nervous, when he appeared at the end of her row.

"Sareem," Vhalla said, pausing, placing a book on a shelf just beyond her short reach.

"Missed you yesterday." He smiled, crossing the distance between them.

"It was nice to have a day off." Vhalla scolded herself for beating around the bush. "Thank you for the gloves. They're perfect."

"You like them?" His whole face lit up in a way that elicited a twinge of pain within her. "I never had sisters growing up, and well, I was hopeless picking them out."

"You did well," Vhalla reassured.

"Say, Vhalla." Sareem leaned against the bookcase. He picked off his imaginary lint from his robes. "During the festival soon, we'll have some time off. We only have to work one day and well, I was thinking that maybe... you and I could, well..."

Vhalla's heart slowed. This couldn't be happening. Roan couldn't be right. She looked at her childhood friend nervously. Certainly he was attractive. He had filled out and lost some of his boyishness, and his darker skin tone really complemented his lighter eyes and hair. *He comes from a good family*, she reminded herself.

"Vhalla!" The master called from the central desk suddenly. She glanced behind her and back at Sareem. "Vhalla, come here."

"Go ahead." Her friend looked utterly deflated. "I'll catch up with you later. Happy belated birthday, Vhalla."

She hovered awkwardly, waiting for one long moment before the master's call had her running back to the desk. *What had Sareem wanted to ask?* She didn't dwell on it for long as she was quickly distracted by a waiting guard.

"Your presence has been requested by a member of the Court to assess some books," the guard announced, almost mechanically.

"Me? You don't mean the master?" Vhalla looked at the old man who was barely taller than the central desk; one of the few people in the world who was shorter than she.

"They asked for you by name," the guard replied.

"You dare not refuse." The master sent her off easily enough, but Vhalla heard the signs of curiosity in his wavering voice.

The guard had not lied. Vhalla followed him up through the palace and into a stately study. Bookshelves dominated two walls and she was left alone to pick through their contents without clear instruction. One wall possessed four large windows, and soon the scenery competed for her attention.

A side door opened. When a lean figure clad entirely in black crossed the threshold of the room, all else was forgotten.

"Prince Aldrik?" Vhalla blinked.

"I do believe I told you Aldrik was fine in private," he reminded her.

"What are you doing here?" She shifted her weight from one foot to the other as he approached.

"Well, it seems you had forgotten something." Pulling a hand from behind his back, he held out her winter robes. Vhalla felt a foreign bubbling in her stomach and, as if on cue, he continued, "Plus, you told me that if you could, you would come and let me teach you today."

She laughed. She teased him for pulling her from her work, and she scolded him for his use of authority to get what he wanted. But his abduction of her was far gentler than the minister's, and Vhalla found she did not mind being surrounded by opulence. In good spirits, the prince was enjoyable company, and he had her moving a quill from one side of a desk to the other without touching it by the end of the day.

Her phantom was haunting her anew, but no longer with notes. The prince spirited her away the next day, and two days after that. Each time there was some clever excuse, and when those ran out he simply materialized between the shelves in the library and they would slink off together like children.

With his dutiful tutelage, Vhalla began to master basic magic. His palm would rest on the back of her hand, lacing his fingers firmly between hers to keep her hand in place as she tried to attempt magic without physical movement. Vhalla met with little success at this tactic—and a great deal of distraction. He promised her that she would learn something called "Channeling" soon that would make magic easier. But, whatever the technique was, he was holding it over her head until she made a decision over joining the Tower.

In time, Vhalla peeled back the layers to Prince Aldrik, even though he still avoided anything remotely personal. In fact, she knew more about him from what she read in books than what he told her. But what she did learn in person was not written anywhere. Vhalla learned he favored a strong Western-style tea that was almost as dark as ink. She learned that when his lips parted it meant he was surprised, and when his eyebrows rose it meant he was impressed. She gathered very quickly that he did not like speaking of his family under any circumstances.

It took Vhalla a week to realize that, for the first time, she did not actually want to be in the library.

As the master led her back through the shelves toward the heavily fortified door of the archives, Vhalla caught herself staring longingly at a tapestry upon the same wall—a tapestry she now knew led toward a world of wonder and magic that was hers alone.

The hinges complained loudly as they granted access to the master and her. Vhalla followed Mohned into the dim world that was the Imperial Archives. She barely suppressed a cough induced by dust.

The Imperial Archives almost created a library unto themselves. When a book was an old original, rare, or the last copy of its kind, it was moved into the archives for safekeeping. There were five levels to the archives, filled with books and an iron spiral staircase through the middle. Some of the oldest manuscripts and the earliest records for humanity were kept there. Vhalla felt a sense of awe whenever she entered.

Heavy curtains covered every window when no one was present, preventing the light from fading or damaging the manuscripts. Mohned pulled a few of the curtains back, quickly expelling the darkness. Dust caught the beams of light, dancing through the air like tiny fairies.

"There are some Eastern works that are close to falling apart." He led her around the staircase to the second floor down, opening a few more of the curtains as he went.

"Eastern?" she asked.

"Yes, we don't have many older works from the East actually..." the master started.

"Because of The Burning Times?" Vhalla asked offhandedly.

Mohned stopped and stared at her, adjusting his spectacles. "That is quite right, Vhalla," he replied softly. "Haven't I told you to stop reading books when you should be working? You should be careful where you put your nose, Vhalla," he added cryptically.

"Master?" Vhalla asked, confused.

"Ah, here it is." Mohned carefully pulled a large tome off the shelf with two hands.

Vhalla instantly saw where the leather binding was flaking off and helped him gently ease it down onto the table.

"If you finish this one, the other three in this series will also need attention." He motioned to the shelf. "Is there anything else you need?"

"No, I remember how to change bindings," Vhalla said with a shake of her head.

Mohned nodded, and she gave him a small bow as he shuffled back without further word.

Vhalla settled in one of the chairs, carefully starting her work. She wasn't sure how much time had passed before she heard a set of footsteps lightly treading down the iron stairs. They were too heavy for the ancient master, and it was well before closing.

She ignored the heated flush brought on by the frantic beat of her heart. The prince had said he was likely to be busy today. Vhalla knew he couldn't steal her away every day, but she was shamefully hopeful.

Vhalla glanced up and saw a man's boots appear. They were brown, worn, and nothing of quality. Her shoulders slumped.

"Hello!" Sareem whispered.

"Sareem," she replied, hoping she disguised the disappointment in her voice. "What are you doing here?"

"I finished a little early and thought I'd come check in on you." He smiled.

"The master won't be pleased if he finds you slacking off," Vhalla argued.

"The master is behind the desk with Roan, transcribing as always." Sareem shrugged.

Vhalla looked down at her book, tying off one of her stitches. "You should be working," she muttered softly.

"Come now, Vhalla," he pulled up a chair and rested his chin in his palms. "It's not like you've never skipped work." She felt her cheeks flush lightly. "I won't tell if you don't." He winked.

Vhalla rolled her eyes and busied her hands with her work. The apprentice part of her brain reminded her that she had more reason to be with Sareem than Aldrik. She studied him from the corners of her eyes as he settled in a chair across from her. Roan had mentioned his being handsome due to his Western skin, combined with Southern hair and eyes. Vhalla actually thought the reverse to be more attractive.

"So," he began. "I feel like I haven't had a chance to speak to you all week. You've been busy. When I've tried to find you, it's like you disappear."

Her shoulders made a fractional shrug. There was nothing she could say since Sareem already knew she was a bad liar.

"Anyway, I tried to ask before, but we got interrupted. I suppose I've been trying to get up the nerve again." He laughed stiffly, running a hand through his hair. Vhalla felt her breathing shallow. "We'll have time during the festival, time off. Well, I was hoping that—well, we could do something then—just the two of us?"

Roan had been right. Vhalla cursed the girl, her mother, and the Mother in the heavens above. She opened her mouth, about to outright refuse his advances.

Then again, what prospects did she have? She was eighteen

now and had hardly ever been courted. Roan was right again. Sareem came from a good family. Hadn't everyone always told her that marriage came first and love after? Vhalla shifted in her seat, torn over appropriate and desired responses.

His cerulean eyes looked at her hopefully, and Vhalla reassured herself over again. This was Sareem; she had always enjoyed his company. Nothing would change. Vhalla was about to accept his offer when she hesitated.

"I want to show you something," she blurted out. His eyebrows raised in surprise as she stood. Vhalla knew she was dodging the question, but she remembered sitting with him on her window seat a lifetime ago asking about sorcerers... She had to know.

Looking for something, anything, Vhalla finally settled on a small thimble of thread she had been using.

"I need you to promise you won't tell anyone," she breathed.

"Vhalla, I—"

"No one, Sareem. Not the master, none of the other apprentices, not Roan—*no one.*" Vhalla held her breath.

"Fine, Vhalla. I promise." He smiled lightly, and she felt a twinge of frustration at how relaxed he was.

"I didn't have Autumn Fever," she started.

"I know that," he pointed out.

"I know you know," Vhalla sighed, already questioning herself. But she was in too deep. "I was in the Tower."

"The Tower?" He eased both palms onto the table. Her resolve wavered. "As in, *the* Tower? The Tower of Sorcerers?" She dared a nod. Confusion swept across his features. "Why? Did they take you? Did they do something to you?" He was on his feet. "I swear if they touched you—"

"Sit down," she ordered, and he obeyed. "No, they didn't hurt me, they were... helping me." Vhalla made it a point to leave out the minister's abduction, the prince, and the fall. That would hardly help her case, and she wasn't about to explain what she had barely come to terms with herself.

"Helping you? Why?" Sareem furrowed his brow.

Closing her eyes, she instantly felt her magical senses stretch out, building the room in a sight that was beyond sight. She could feel Sareem there, but he was a gray area. Vhalla couldn't help but remember the blazing, brilliant clarity that always surrounded Aldrik, and she suddenly held a whole new appreciation for him as a sorcerer. Vhalla raised her palm, the thimble sitting in the middle of it.

Opening her eyes, she saw it, she felt it, and she understood it. Sareem was about to speak when the thimble shuddered and raised itself above her open hand. She held it there for a long moment, before bringing it slightly higher to eye level. Vhalla was actually rather proud of herself for this. Aldrik would have been too, she was certain. Her attention drifted to Sareem; the shocked and horrified look on his face made her lose all concentration and the thimble fell back into her palm.

Vhalla placed it on the table and slowly turned to him. He was staring at her as if she were some monster preparing to eat him.

"That's why..." Vhalla said weakly, unable to meet his gaze.

"V-Vhalla... Wh-what was that?" he stuttered.

"Exactly what you think it was," she retorted—defensive and annoyed. She didn't know what she had been hoping for from him, but it wasn't this.

He was on his feet in front of her, his arms spread out. "Oh, Vhalla, you're funny, tell me how you did it. It's a great trick. Was it a string connected to your other hand? Some kind of magnetism? A trick of the light?" He couldn't seem to let alternate explanations fall from his mouth fast enough.

"You know what it was." She glared at him.

"No, no, that would make you—"

"A sorcerer," she finished for him, crossing her arms on her chest.

He took a step back from her. "You, you can't be. You're not one of *them*."

"I am," she said sourly. "That's what you want to involve yourself with." She glared at him with all the icy bitterness that she could muster. That's right, she was *one of them*, and *they* were different and scary.

Sareem shook his head and took another step back. He opened his mouth to speak, his jaw quivered, and then he turned and ran.

Vhalla sat back down at the desk and stared at the book. She listened to his hasty footsteps up the stairs and out of the archives.

The soundless scream of hurt and frustration caught on a sob, and Vhalla lost herself to tears. After crying for an indiscernible amount of time, Vhalla peeled herself from the table and sat straighter. Numbly, her hands returned to their work. She should have known better with Sareem. After his reaction to the simple mention of sorcerers, showing him magic had been foolish. There was no way he was ever going to accept her for who she was, and she wasn't about to shed tears over someone with such a narrow mind, over a false friend.

VHALLA STOPPED MID-STEP, the door to the archives closing behind her. She stared at the tapestry that Aldrik had led her through during one of their lessons.

What was she? Was she a library apprentice or sorcerer? She vowed to get serious about figuring out her powers and making a decision soon.

"Vhalla." She had almost made it to the front desk when

Sareem hastily whispered from between bookshelves. She kept her gaze forward. "Vhalla!" She pretended not to hear and walked with purpose.

"Master, I finished the first manuscript. I don't feel well. May I be excused a little early today please?"

The master and Roan both looked up at her with matching puzzled stares.

"Very well, Vhalla. Go ahead." The master nodded.

"Thank you," she said politely, bowed, and left. Vhalla pointedly ignored Sareem standing at the edge of the shelves, watching silently as she strode out of the library.

Her feet battered against the stone floor as she marched back to her room. Curling and uncurling her hands, Vhalla struggled to keep a fresh wave of anger at bay. He was supposed to be her friend; how could he react like she was suddenly less than human?

Vhalla stopped and a nearby candle flickered out, then the next—all at once she was standing in the darkness. She swallowed a cry of surprise, all but running to her room.

Slamming the door behind her, Vhalla dug her nails into the grain of the wood and caught her breath. She was already treading lightly. Any rogue and wild emotions could force her decision, and she felt so close to making it on her own. A scent tickled her nose, and Vhalla opened her eyes, her heart slowing.

Laid upon her pillow was a long-stemmed red rose. Tied around it was a length of black ribbon by which a note was held. Everything melted away, and her hands were soon devouring the token.

Vhalla,

I am sorry I could not steal you away this day. You have my word that tomorrow I shall make every effort.

Sincerely,

A.C.S.

P.S.

When will I see you in black?

Laughing softly, Vhalla curled up in bed holding the flower's head to her face, inhaling its rich scent. Perhaps she could request he steal her back to that rose garden? Vhalla laughed lightly, imagining her ordering a prince. Somehow, it didn't seem so farfetched.

A.C.S. she pondered as her lids grew heavy. Aldrik was the *A*, and Solaris—the Imperial family's name—was the *S*. But, what was the *C*? Vhalla shook her head, closing her eyes and giving herself to the relaxing scent, a mystery for a later time perhaps. It was barely dark but all she wanted to do was lie there, and stretch her mind as far as she could, to find that place that smelled of roses.

CHAPTER 14

Moonlight streamed through the glass overhead, and Vhalla tilted her chin to the sky, watching the moon float by. The rose garden was no different at night than it had been during the day. The darkness didn't bother her; she saw everything brilliantly clear around her. There was a mysterious fuzziness to it if she moved her head too quickly, which was easily explained away as the moonlight playing tricks on her.

She stood and walked to the gazebo door, attempting to open it. It wouldn't budge. She tried the handle again but found it unwilling to move. Vhalla wanted to be outside.

With only that thought, she was standing on the steps and looked behind her. She didn't recall opening or closing the door. Vhalla walked lightly down and over to the iron gate. He was there, but she didn't know her way through that hallway; she only knew enough to return to the servants' quarters. It surely was locked.

Vhalla leaned against the gate and slid down until she was sitting on the ground, looking up at the stars again. On a night so cool and clear it seemed a shame to be shut up in the palace. She wondered if he knew that. It was better outside. Her eyelids felt heavy. She would *simply have to wait for him, she reminded herself again. He would come out eventually. For now though, she would sleep while she waited.*

Vhalla opened her eyes as though someone had pinched her awake. A headache pounded in her skull. She rolled over into a ball, not even noticing that she had crushed the beautiful flower she had slept with all night. Clutching her temples, she took a deep breath and let it out slowly, as if she could will her mind to stop hurting. Vhalla squeezed her eyes back closed; the daylight was making her sick.

Slowly, her body began to relax and the sharp stabbing subsided to a dull throb. The light no longer caused a rebellion of her senses, and she attempted to sit. She dressed slowly. Everything had a delay and a sickening blur to it.

She hid the note in her closet—with the rest. Vhalla put the half-smashed rose with them. It was pointless to try to save it. Flowers began dying the moment they were cut, and she had only helped the process along. Petals hung at odd angles, and its leaves were broken. Her fingers lingered on the soft velvety red. She couldn't bring herself to throw it away yet.

She paused. Didn't she dream about roses? Vhalla shook her head. It still hurt, and trying to recall her dreams seemed to aggravate the ache further.

Sapphire stole her attention, and another shot of lightning pain shot between her temples. She grabbed Sareem's stupid gloves. With a cry they were on the floor; her feet jumping on them.

The tears and jumping only made her head hurt more. Sareem wasn't worth the pain, she reminded herself. The gloves remained rumpled on the floor as she started for the library.

She stood at the doors of the library, a war waging in her stomach. Sareem was either in there waiting, and she would be stuck alone with him again. Or he hadn't made it to the library yet, and she would be stuck with him when he walked in. Bringing her palm to her forehead, she grimaced. It felt like it was about to split open. The day couldn't get any worse.

Making a decision, she pushed through the doors and was happy to find she was the first. She considered hiding somewhere, but couldn't think of any excuse for when she finally emerged. So, Vhalla simply hoped that he was going to be the last one, and she would already be working in the archives by the time he arrived.

She sat behind the desk and amused herself by rolling a corked bottle of ink across the surface. The doors opened again.

It was Roan. Vhalla sighed and pressed her forehead to the cool wood of the desk. The blonde took a seat next to her.

"Good morning, Roan," Vhalla forced herself to say. Her voice sounded strange to her ears.

"Good morning, Vhalla," she said with a smile.

"Have you seen Sareem yet?" Vhalla mumbled.

"Sareem?" Roan asked delicately. "No, why?"

"Nothing," Vhalla sighed, not wanting to go through the effort of explaining anything.

"Are you all right?" Roan placed a hand on her friend's back. Before Vhalla had a chance to respond, the doors to the library opened again.

It was the master and Sareem, and they were talking. Vhalla was on her feet, pain ignored by her panicked heart. Why was he with the master? Her hands trembled with paranoia, despite her trying to still them.

"Good morning, Vhalla, Roan," the master started. "Today the jobs are much the same as yesterday. Cadance and Lidia are off receiving some final decorations for the Festival of the Sun from the Ministry of Culture. So, Roan, you'll continue transcribing, and Vhalla you're back in the archives."

Vhalla nodded and quickly stepped around the desk. She

could feel Sareem's stare but ignored it like she did Roan's baffled look and the master's quizzical gaze. If the master wasn't kicking her out, then maybe Sareem hadn't told him. All Vhalla knew was she wanted away from them all.

"What is wrong, Vhalla?" the master asked as he opened the Archive's padlocked door.

"I'm fine. My head just hurts today." She rubbed her temples again.

"I'm worried for you," Mohned added thoughtfully, a palm on her back.

"Thank you, but there's nothing to worry about." Vhalla gave the master a tired smile. She looked away before emotion could get the better of her. She wished she could talk to him, but the master wouldn't understand either. *The name in the Tower book likely was a different Mohned Topperen*, Vhalla told herself.

The master led her down to the same location as yesterday, pulling open a few curtains along the way. When she was settled, he instructed her to return to the main library should she feel worse. Vhalla nodded wearily and set to her work, trying to convey—with as much politeness as possible—that she had no interest in speaking. Mohned seemed to take no offense and departed with the quiet shuffle of his feet.

Vhalla tried to focus on the task at hand, but she found it hard to focus on anything. Every time she opened her eyes, the world was blurry—like two things were on top of one another. Eventually, she simply put her head on the table and tried to let the silence cure her brain.

The soft clanks of footsteps down the staircase were like knives to her ailing consciousness. Vhalla opened her eyes, but she didn't even lift her head to see who it was. Aldrik's walk was different, and it would've hurt less, somehow.

"Sareem, go away." Her voice was low.

"Vhalla, we need to talk," he started gingerly.

"Go. Away," she repeated, her patience thin.

"No." His was determined.

She looked up at him, trying to get her eyes to cooperate with her. He stood halfway in the room, clearly unsure if he was making the right decision. Vhalla had the pleasure of letting him know he was not.

"What do you want?" she snapped, putting her forehead back on the table.

"Are you all right?" he asked, taking a few steps closer.

"I'm fine. My head just hurts. What do you want?" Her sentences were clipped with annoyance.

"About yesterday, Vhalla..." he started.

"Did you tell the master?" she interrupted.

"What? No, I promised you I wouldn't." Vhalla looked up at him again through squinted eyes. "I didn't, Vhalla," Sareem insisted and sat with a sigh.

Vhalla put her head back on the table, closing her eyes. "So, what do you want?"

"About yesterday..." He scratched the back of his neck. "You see, you kind of caught me off-guard." He gave an uneasy chuckle, and Vhalla wanted to choke whatever he had to say out of him. "I think—"

A horn rang out from somewhere in the distance. Its call was echoed by one closer. Soon every trumpeter in the palace was heralding the rallying call.

"What?" Vhalla picked up her head off the table. "What is—"

"Horns, Vhalla! Horns playing like that, you know what it means." He was on his feet, already cleaning up her book and supplies without thought. "Come on, we have to go." Sareem was practically picking up her limp body from the chair, and Vhalla felt too groggy to fight.

They made haste through the library. Vhalla squinted, the world was moving by so fast that it unsettled her stomach, and she was forced to rely on Sareem. At least if she was sick she could aim for his feet.

Her eyes didn't know what to focus on. Everything came to a sudden halt as they stood before the circulation desk. The master was talking, and Vhalla struggled to listen. Mohned handed Sareem something, sending the young man running back in the direction from which they had just come.

"—will catch up with us. We should start making our way to the Sunlit Stage."

The master and Roan went for the castle door. Vhalla followed behind them, and Sareem soon joined in tow as they left the library proper. He noticed she was not stable on her feet and linked an arm with her. Vhalla was forced to depend on his support again, as they joined the masses moving quickly through the palace.

The Sunlit Stage was the official entry to the palace. While the stables' entry was more practical, the Sunlit Stage held large-scale ceremonies before the public. It was a semi-circular area where the capital's residents could enter through many golden archways in the outer wall. Giant stands extended up from the wall that were supposed to be reminiscent of the sun's rays. Dignitaries, nobles, and members of the Court sat there, all facing the palace.

White marble steps led up to a large platform with columns set at wide intervals. Behind this stage were golden doors leading into the palace; they were equally large and ceremonial. Four or five horses could ride abreast through them without a problem. Higher on the wall was a balcony, which the Emperor had used once or twice to make short announcements or decrees to his people. Today, soldiers in polished armor and helmets fitted with large golden plumes lined either side of the stage.

Cadance and Lidia joined Vhalla and her escorts along the way, and the whole library personnel positioned themselves upon the outer wall along with most of the other castle staff. With a loud groan, the stage doors opened and two people walked out to the edge of the top step.

The Empress was a short woman with long flowing blonde hair that cascaded to her waist. While she appeared youthful, her stance was modest and motherly. She wore a classically Southern draped gown of white silk that pooled around her feet and extended in a train behind her. It flowed in the air with ease.

Vhalla's eyes shifted to the figure standing next to the Empress. He wore pressed white trousers and a long white coat, which was military in style with two rows of golden buttons running down the front. Its high collar was pinned down by two golden decorative metal plates on the shoulders. A number of military medals decorated the front. A golden rope ran from his shoulder to his chest. Despite all this, his hair was as he always wore it—slicked back and out of his face, flaring out slightly at the sides. The prince regarded the world with poised ambivalence, as he looked down at the people, his nose and high cheekbones accented in the sun.

It wasn't until Roan gave her a quick elbow to the side that she realized she was laughing. Aldrik looked so different in white, but it was still him. Roan shot Vhalla a confused look, and she only shook her head in response. Vhalla wasn't sure why she found it so funny but she pressed her eyes closed, trying to regain control of herself. The sun still hurt her eyes.

The rumble of the crowd quieted and was replaced with a different rumbling: the sound of horses' hooves over stone. It started as a distant noise and slowly escalated to loud thunder. Realization of why they had been summoned swept across the people and soon their cries and cheers matched the horses' clattering hooves.

The first horse blazed through the gates. A pure white stallion held a man wearing golden armor. Every piece of the plate was embellished with careful metalwork and plated with gold. A shrill cry rose through the crowd and the cheers became near deafening.

Vhalla put a hand to her forehead. She didn't have to look to know for whom the commotion was.

The broad-shouldered golden prince stepped down from his horse. He waved his hands to the people, and they reached for him like babes to their mother. Pulling off his helmet, his cropped golden hair clung to his face with sweat and he grinned like a fool as he shook the hands of countless people, making his way to the stage.

For a brief moment Vhalla wondered if she had been one of the masses reaching for him, would he have recognized her from their meeting in the library months ago?

Vhalla looked back to Aldrik. He stood as still as stone, his face offering equal emotion. His hands were folded behind his back as he looked down upon his younger brother, who was slowly making his way forward. Vhalla briefly recalled the unceremonious return of the crown prince. There hadn't been a single cheer for him.

The cry slowly evolved into a unified chant as the main host entered the gates.

"Solaris, Solaris, Solaris."

Everyone around her had given into the cry as the Emperor himself, clad in white and golden armor with a cape draping off the back of his horse, entered the stage area. On the back of his cape the golden sun blazed. He rode all the way up to the first step. Dismounting, their ruler strode toward his family, his walk steady and easy for a man of his age. Prince Baldair had taken his place next to his brother. The Emperor kissed his wife chastely and then greeted his eldest son with a firm handshake.

Vhalla saw nothing in Aldrik's cold gaze and was becoming

frustrated at being so far away—and at her eyes continued refusal to focus.

The Emperor turned to face the crowd; all the people, young and old, fell to their knees before their leader. Vhalla was no exception.

"My most loyal subjects," his voice rang clear through the hushed area, "we have returned from our campaigns in the North with many victories to recount." A cheer rang out again, then quickly stilled.

"The Northern Capital, Soricium, holds out, but they will fall in time. Their country is in shambles before the blazing might of the Sun."

For a brief moment amidst the cheers Vhalla wondered, if the Mother Sun was truly a loving Goddess, then why did she send her people to kill and die?

"We will bring the spoils of war under one unified banner."

People rose to their feet, and Vhalla returned to leaning against the wall. If Aldrik had moved she couldn't tell.

"With this, let a most grand Festival of the Sun begin!" The Emperor raised his hands and a few explosions rang out, fireworks entering sky. Everyone turned their gaze skyward, save for Vhalla and the crown prince. He continued to stare forward, motionless.

Vhalla closed her eyes and focused on her breathing. For a moment, the pain in her head subsided. The world slowly rebuilt itself around her in astounding clarity. She looked forward—but not with her physical eyes—and saw him, a distant point of light. She pushed her vision closer, to see if his face really looked as it had from a distance.

He looked tight-jawed and cold-eyed. Even though he stood among hundreds of people, he might as well have been standing on an island, alone. She didn't understand. They were beginning a festival; this was a time for happiness.

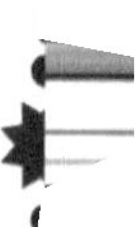

Don't look so sad.

His head quickly snapped in her direction, and Vhalla's eyes opened wide. She cried out, pressing her palms to her face. The sunlight was like fire on her brain. Behind her eyes burned a blazing white light that threatened to rip her apart. She shook her head and stumbled into someone. Vhalla thought she heard a man talking to her, but it was distant and faint, barely registering over the roar in her head.

Lunging forward, she clung to the wall as though it were the only thing grounding her to the physical world. She wanted it to stop; she would do anything to make it stop. There was a hand on her back, and she tried to stand, squinting open her eyes. The cannons fired again, and Vhalla saw the second round of blazing fireworks shoot toward the sky, right before her knees buckled, and her body gave out.

CHAPTER 15

She floated in the air. No, not floated, she was being carried. Her right ear rested against a man's chest, a frantic heartbeat underneath. *Why were they going so fast?* Vhalla wanted to tell him that it was all right, that he could slow down, but nothing seemed to be connected to her mind. It was as though she were trapped in her own body.

But wherever she was, it was warm and the pain had gone. That was good enough for her. Deciding she was tired again, she went to sleep.

She jolted back to awareness when she felt her body being put down. She heard talking again, but she couldn't quite seem to get her ears to work. The man was asking her something. What could he possibly want? Didn't he see she was in no position to give anything? Then he was gone. She could feel that he was gone; something in her just knew.

More darkness and silence. Vhalla sat in the confines of her own mind, wondering how she got here. Her body still refused to obey her.

"I'll be back with help." That's what he had said, her mind put together. More people were coming. He was going to bring more people. She had to wake up, but it was too late. They were already here. More familiar voices, rushed speech, who were they this time?

There were hands, more hands, different from before but not completely new. A woman's hands this time. She was carrying her to another location. Vhalla wanted to feel terrified at the prospect, but she found herself unable to feel much of anything.

The world shifted around her and the air changed. It was once more different, yet strangely familiar. She'd been here before, even if she didn't know where *here* was.

She was placed on another bed. Trapped within her mental prison, Vhalla rallied against the silence. She slowly stretched outward, and the world built itself before her.

The room was unfamiliar, but Vhalla instantly recognized the dragon molding near the ceiling; she was in the Tower. There was a wardrobe. Vhalla had expected it to be black but it was a gray, ashen-colored wood. A small desk, chair; her eyes fell on the bed, and Vhalla panicked.

She was there. Motionless, hardly breathing, Vhalla did not know if she was alive. The foreign room aside, Fritz's and Larel's presences ignored, Vhalla stared at her corpse-like form. Dead, she was dead, and this was the start of the afterlife.

"We need to get the minister." Fritz pulled at his hair, pacing.

"She's breathing. She doesn't look pained. Check her Channels." Larel remained calm, situating Vhalla's legs. The rise and fall of her chest was so minimal it was almost invisible, but Vhalla was relieved to see it was there. Whatever was happening, she wasn't dead, yet.

Larel? Vhalla whispered. *Fritz?* Neither seemed to hear her wispy words.

"No, I can't. I'm not a magical healer, Larel. My lessons have only—" Fritz was breathless in his panic.

"Check her!" Larel demanded sharply.

Fritz finally obliged. His hands rested on Vhalla's throat, fingertips behind her ears, delicate and gentle as though she were made of glass. With closed eyes, he ran his palms over her shoulders, down her arms, flat against her stomach.

"I can't find anything wrong."

The slamming of a door, echoing from the hall beyond, momentarily paused all response from Larel.

"Check her again," the dark-haired woman demanded before dashing out the door.

Fritz returned to his duty. His palms slid down the outside of her thighs and down to her feet. Suddenly Larel's door was thrown open so hard it almost bounced against the wall.

Aldrik stood in the doorframe, both commanding and disheveled. His white coat was unbuttoned and hung loosely around him, a plain shirt underneath. His cheeks were flushed, and his breathing hard. Even his hair looked less than perfect, long strands hanging over his eyes.

He stepped in quickly, and Larel shut the door behind him. Fritz looked as dazed as Vhalla felt. The crown prince did not stand in an apprentice's rooms, but Aldrik did not seem to care. The only thing that bothered him was the sight of her lifeless body.

"My prince," Fritz squeaked.

Vhalla took a step away, a window to her back.

"Out." Aldrik hardly seemed to notice the presence of the Southerner. With one word Fritz had diminished to less than a fly on the wall.

"Larel?" Fritz glanced over at the woman, but Larel only shook her head. "Right, well, I can't find anything wrong with her." He inched toward the door, removing the barrier of his body between Vhalla's form on the bed and the prince. "Should I get the minister?"

"No," Aldrik replied with a glare. His hand shot out faster than a viper, Fritz's collar balled in his fingers. "If I hear you breathing a word of this to anyone, consider your time in the Tower *finished*."

A threat lived in Aldrik's last word. It made Vhalla uncomfortable just to hear. The library boy gaped, frozen to the spot.

"Now, *out*," the older man hissed. Fritz bolted from the room as though his life depended on it. Vhalla didn't want to even entertain the idea that it did.

Neither Larel nor the prince said anything. Fading sunlight filtered through the window behind her, and Vhalla noticed she cast no shadow.

"What's wrong with her?" Larel asked. Her voice had a surprising amount of emotion.

"I don't know," the prince sighed, shaking his head. As though deflated, he leaned against the desk for support.

"How did you know?" Larel folded her arms, her back against the door.

"I will not speak about it," Aldrik said with a pointed stare. His eyes only left Vhalla's corpse-like body for half a moment. Larel followed his gaze with a soft sigh. Clearly, she knew better than to push the prince.

"She's progressing quickly," Larel observed quietly.

"I know." Aldrik took a step forward, his hand outstretched. His fingers hovered in the air above Vhalla's body before falling back to his side.

"You've been teaching her." It wasn't a question.

"Larel," the prince sighed. Vhalla felt a twinge of something she would not dare call jealousy. The prince acted differently around the Western woman, as well.

"It isn't my business," she said with a shrug.

"I will tell you." Aldrik's eyes broke away from Vhalla's body when he added, "Eventually."

"You know that's always been good enough for me." The corner of Larel's mouth curled in an almost Aldrik-like smile. It was strange, and it made Vhalla begin to wonder what their relationship really was.

"Make sure Victor does not find out," Aldrik ordered the woman.

Her hand hovered on the door handle. "He will, eventually," she murmured.

"I want him away from her." Aldrik nodded toward Vhalla's comatose form on the last word.

"You know I'll protect her." Larel smiled.

"I know I can trust you." Aldrik nodded.

Without needing to be asked, the woman slipped out of the room, leaving Vhalla alone with the crown prince.

He stood, looking nowhere but on her physical body. As though each movement were exhausting, he dragged the chair from the desk and sat heavily in it. Putting his elbows in his knees, Aldrik buried his face in his hands. It was a strange motion that she had never seen from him before. His hair was a mess, his clothing unbuttoned, and his figure slumped.

Aldrik, she whispered softly.

His head snapped up and looked over directly at her. The prince squinted briefly against the light of the sun streaming through the window at her back. Raising a hand slowly, he guarded his eyes against the brightness. She saw the moment realization dawned across his features.

"Impossible," he breathed.

You can see me? She tilted her head. He nodded, attempting to smooth back the stray pieces of his hair. *You can hear me?* He nodded again. *So I'm not a ghost?*

"No, you are not. But you have gotten yourself into quite the mess." He sounded tired, annoyed, but somewhere she could have sworn that she heard relief.

How did you know to come? she asked.

"I knew something was wrong. After you pulled the stunt you did at the festival's ceremony." He frowned and stood, walking over to her.

Vhalla recognized that when she asked, he answered— unlike Larel.

I don't know what I did, Vhalla whispered. Her fear was almost a palpable quiver between them.

"I will explain when you are back where you belong," he said reassuringly. "I asked you to trust me, Vhalla. Do you?"

She stared up at his obsidian eyes. These were the eyes of the man who pushed her from the roof, who spoke of mysterious purposes for her powers with the Minister of Sorcery, and who was now keeping her from that same Minister for unknown reasons.

I do. It was an impossible truth.

"I believe this will work, but it will seem terrifying. I promise you that you will not be hurt," he reassured her.

What are you going to do? she asked hesitantly, not sure if she wanted the answer.

"I will explain it to you when you are properly awake." He reached a hand straight into her. Vhalla looked down, the sight was terrifying enough. His hand was directly in her abdomen, her body faded and hollow. In that moment she thought she really must be a ghost.

"Do not be afraid," he whispered soothingly right before he closed his fingers into a fist. A roaring fire soared out from his hand, and she felt it consume her body before her very eyes. Everything was aflame.

Vhalla sat up in bed with a scream. She began to attempt to

pat out the imaginary fire all over her limbs. Aldrik was at her bedside with a fluid movement, sitting directly on the mattress. He grabbed for her shoulders and held her tightly in his hands. His face was white and tense. She struck at his arms, still in a frantic daze.

"Vhalla!" he nearly shouted over her panic. "Vhalla, breathe!" He shook her forcefully.

She grabbed onto his arms and felt the uncomfortable sensation slowly fade away. Her eyes locked with his, and she stared shamelessly into those ebony depths, seeking his stability. She dug her fingertips tightly into the sleeves of his coat, feeling lean muscle beneath.

"Breathe with me," he whispered, and she obeyed.

They sat for over fifty breaths, simply staring at each other. His hands clutched her shoulders, her hands clutching his arms. Both of their features relaxed, and she wanted to collapse into him, but common sense and who she was meant that such contact would be extraordinarily unwelcomed on his part. She slowly relaxed her grip and let her hands fall.

"Vhalla," he breathed, gently taking his hands off her shoulders. "How do you feel?"

She took a breath and assessed herself. Now that the terror and the frantic beating of her heart had subsided, she felt the best she'd felt all day. "Better." Her voice came out as normal; even her eyes were obeying her and not seeing double.

He smiled weakly. "I am glad." Aldrik wiped sweat from his brow with the back of his hand. He placed his forehead in his palm and rested his elbow on his bent knee. "I did not know. I did not realize you had already progressed that far. I would have..." he trailed off into his thoughts.

"Progressed how far?" She put her hands politely behind her, leaning back to give him some space.

"Do you remember how we met?" Aldrik glanced at her.

"The library?" she asked.

He nodded. "You were doing it then too, but you thought they were dreams."

"Doing what?" she asked, a small trepidation growing in her.

"I have only read about it and, even then, the literature is sparse," he started, running a hand across his hair, trying to tame escaped tendrils back into place. "It said that Windwalkers were invisible sentries for their causes. Of course, there are a number of ways that could be read. I only briefly entertained that it would be literal." He sighed.

"Where to begin?" He paused a moment. "Every Affinity has a literal, elemental Affinity. But some scholars have theorized that this is only the tip of what sorcerers can really do. That underlying every elemental, worldly Affinity is an Affinity of the self."

"I remember you explaining it some, about Groundbreakers." Vhalla tried to keep up.

"Indeed, you have a good memory." He gave her a tired smile. Vhalla's stomach did a little flip at his praise. "Windwalkers were said to have an Affinity for the mind. That the real power of the Windwalker was based within their mental abilities."

"I am not that smart," she said lightly.

He rolled his eyes. "You are, but it is not in that way. Intellect and this skill are different. Either way, I would say what you have done is more in line with the mental side of your powers, complemented by the physical," he finished.

Vhalla made a note to find a book on this topic from somewhere.

"And what have I done?"

She was missing the point.

"You are separating your consciousness from your physical body; it is called Projection." He looked at her. "You were doing it in your dreams. But that is only a quarter as impressive as doing it when you are awake."

She stared back at him, accepting it all with a nod.

"Today you did it at the ceremony. But you startled me." He shifted and looked away uncomfortably. "I lashed out at you. I tried to draw back quickly. I just felt someone there. I think it was that which knocked the link with your body out of line and ended up locking you out of your physical body."

"I think it was a little messed up before that." She sat up straighter, looking at his profile thoughtfully. He turned back to examine her curiously.

"All day I was having trouble focusing my eyes; it was as if I were seeing two things," Vhalla mused. Realization dawned on his features. "I also had a throbbing headache."

He looked away again and stood. She heard him mutter something under his breath. Vhalla shifted her feet onto the floor and sat at the edge of the bed. She took in his tall lean shape against the light of the late sun in the window.

"Vhalla." Her name sounded strained against his lips. "It would likely be best if we do not see each other for some time, at least not until you decide if you wish to be in the Tower or not."

His words hit her directly in the gut and knocked the wind from her. Suddenly she was on her feet. "No," Vhalla said firmly, unwavering as he turned.

"The Bond... Being near me is not good for you now." He pinched the bridge of his nose. "Your magic is progressing faster than I can teach you and—"

"Do you want me to go away?" she asked directly.

Aldrik looked at her with parted lips. "No, I do not," he confessed with a small shake of his head.

"Good. You are my teacher," she said firmly. "You can't leave me now."

He turned and crossed the room, standing inches from her,

bearing down upon her with his commanding form. But she stood defiantly against him, trying to meet him inch for inch.

"And," Vhalla started slowly, turning her head away. She hardly had the courage to say what she wanted; looking at him while doing so was far too much. "You are my friend, whatever this commoner's friendship is worth."

His hand reached up, and he placed his fingertips under her chin. Moving nothing but his hand, he guided her face back toward him and up to meet his eyes. He stared at her for a long time. Vhalla felt her heart beat in her throat, and she tried to swallow it back into her chest. He removed his hand, letting it hover in the air uncertainly for just a moment before it fell, featherlight, upon her cheek.

When he spoke it was slow and deliberate, little more than a whisper. His voice had a richness to it that she had never heard before. "It is worth very much." His eyes consumed hers.

Whatever spell they were under broke the moment Larel slipped back into the room. Aldrik's hand dropped away from her face with such precision and poise that even Vhalla questioned if it had been there at all. If Larel had seen anything she was completely unfazed by the prince standing in close proximity to the common girl.

"The halls are fairly clear. Fritz is making a scene in the dining hall." She gave a small nod to Aldrik, which he returned.

"Thank you, Larel." He vanished through the door, pulling Vhalla with him with barely enough time for Vhalla to offer her own quick thanks. Larel gave her a small smile that promised secrecy.

They were down the winding hallway of the Tower and into another side door before Vhalla could assess what level of the palace she was on. The prince's strides were long, and Vhalla struggled to keep up with them. She almost fell into him as he stopped suddenly before another door.

"Vhalla, listen." Aldrik's hand paused on the wood. His profile was lit by a single flame bulb and the lighting outlined his angular features. "Victor will catch wind of this; when he does, I am certain he will try to force you into joining the Tower."

"What will he do? What exactly does he want from me?" She didn't know why she was whispering, but it felt right.

"I..." Aldrik froze, debating his next words. "Do you know the history of the Windwalkers, yet?"

"I know about the West." Suddenly, Vhalla was trying to recall everything she read with Fritz.

"Then you know that there are people in this world who are *greatly interested* in your powers." Aldrik's eyes darted down the hall toward the Tower.

"That was over a hundred years ago." Vhalla didn't want to believe what he was implying. "It's not—"

"Not so long ago," he warned.

"Why are you telling me all this?" Vhalla asked. It finally dawned on her the cause of all their secrecy. Was the crown prince protecting her? If so, from what? Or, from whom?

"Because I was led to believe that Victor gave you a month to choose magic," Aldrik answered.

"Only because I threatened to Eradicate myself." Vhalla leaned against the far wall.

"Still, you have a choice," he reinforced. "I would like to see you choose this life."

"And if I don't?" Vhalla was unable to say the words with any strength. She couldn't even meet his eyes. The silence felt like it was crushing her skull.

His voice was gentle, but there was a quivering restraint, as though his words were forced. "Then," Aldrik began, "I think that would be the saddest thing to happen to the magical community in a long time."

Vhalla sighed softly. Of course, it was the magical

community. She was the Windwalker, first of her kind in almost a century and a half. The one with powers people wanted for reasons still unknown to her. She turned to the door without a word.

"I would miss teaching you." Everything stopped as the sentence crossed his lips. Vhalla turned back to look at him, suddenly aware of how small the connecting passage really was. As if realizing the same thing, the prince quickly broke eye contact to smooth his coat before slowly buttoning it. "So, when will I see you again?"

"What?" Vhalla blinked at the sudden and strange question. He had been doing well at seeing her by stealing her away. "You're the crown prince. You can see me whenever you want. Isn't that what you've been doing?"

"Yes, well," he muttered, running a hand over his hair. "Lunch, then, tomorrow? No, wait; I have business with Egmun." He cursed at the foreign name. "The day after tomorrow, I will have time. But this is not an order from your prince."

Something crept on the edge of Vhalla's mind. He wasn't stealing her away or leaving her with little choice—not that she had minded. He wasn't ordering her as her prince. He hadn't mentioned training or discussing sorcery or her future. If it wasn't business or obligation, then what exactly was the reason behind this meeting?

"I'd love to." She smiled, and the mask that the prince normally wore slipped long enough for her to see a flash of joy in his eyes. "I'll meet you in the garden?"

He nodded, a little smile playing on his lips, causing a warm honey feeling in her stomach. Vhalla pushed on the door before the feeling spread into her blood and overpowered her senses. She emerged into the cool night air, the mysterious portal closing behind her to disappear as if nothing more than a stone wall.

She couldn't stop a giggle from escaping as she all but skipped back to her room. *There's no reason to be so happy*, she reminded herself, and yet she was. She was going to have lunch with the prince.

Vhalla noticed nothing amiss as she pushed open her door. All her lightness vanished with one shift of her gaze.

Sareem sat on her bed holding the wrinkled gloves in his hands. He looked up at her with a mix of emotions flashing across his features. Dropping the gloves to the floor, he pulled her into a tight embrace and rested a hand on the back of her head.

Vhalla stood there pressed against him, his one arm tight around her arms, the other hand holding her face to his chest. After the initial shock wore off, a strange sensation spread through her, and Vhalla didn't know if she wanted to hold him or push him off. Her arms stayed limp at her sides as a middle ground.

"I was so worried," he whispered hoarsely. "You just, you screamed, and then you were on the ground." He stroked her head as if to offer her comfort, but he was clearly more distraught than she was. "I didn't know what to do. I told them I'd get a cleric, but after—after what you showed me, I knew it wasn't a cleric you needed." He rested his cheek on the top of her forehead a moment with a soft sigh. Vhalla remained still, allowing him to piece together his story.

"I went to the Tower entrance—a Tower entrance? I don't even know the names of the people who answered. I simply said your name and they knew; they came without question, and I gave you to them. I didn't even know their names." His voice cracked. "And then they were frantic, and they took you. Vhalla, you didn't move. You were hardly breathing. They took you and I-I didn't know if you were alive, so I waited." He sounded so hopeless and pathetic that Vhalla couldn't help but put her arms lightly around her friend's waist and pat his back in a friendly manner.

They stood together as he slowly regained his composure. Eventually he released her and wiped his face with his palms.

"Sorry about that." Sareem tried to laugh.

"I appreciate it, Sareem. Obviously, they did help. You did the right thing," she tried to reassure him, and it looked like it worked. "Did any of the others ask?"

"Yeah, but I told them I found a cleric, and that it was the heat getting to your head. I also stayed to kick anyone out, saying you were here but needed rest," Sareem added with a small nod.

Vhalla felt guilty for putting her friend through all this, no matter how unkind he had been to her about her magic.

"I'm sorry that you have to keep lying for someone like me." She took a step away from him.

"Someone like you?" He looked honestly confused, which annoyed her slightly.

"A sorcerer," she said directly, watching him hold back a wince at the word.

"I tried to tell you earlier. Even if you are a-a, someone with magic, you are still Vhalla." He took a step closer to her. "You're still the girl I met when I first came here. The girl who is always so lost in her books that she can never spare a boy like me a glance." Vhalla took another small step to avoid his encroaching presence. Her back found the door. "The girl who I never had the courage to ask anywhere because I always thought I was too daft, too boring, too plain for her."

"I'm nothing better than you, Sareem," she whispered as he took another step forward.

"To me you always will be. I was frightened," he whispered as he placed his hand beside her face, palm against the door. "I was frightened that your *development* would take you away from me." He looked away for only a brief moment before staring her down with his gray-blue eyes. "And then, today, I thought I really had lost you. As I sat here waiting, I realized I can't keep waiting, or else I really will lose you."

Frantically trying to think of a way to divert the conversation, Vhalla didn't even have time to close her eyes before his lips were pressed against hers.

CHAPTER 16

Sareem was kissing her.

It seemed the most improbable, impossible, farfetched thought, but as Vhalla stood pressed against her door—his right hand beside her face, his left having found her hip—it was an undeniable truth. His lips were soft, and his breath hot against her cheek. As time stretched, something seemed odd.

Vhalla tried to close her eyes; she tried to enjoy the kiss. But her mouth refused to move, and in the end, as he pulled away, she leaned against the door feeling rather stupid. It had been some time since she had last been kissed. Perhaps that was it; her awkwardness came from being out of practice. It wasn't as though she ever considered herself an adept kisser in the first place.

She stared at him. He had a nice build; while not overly muscular, he was not portly either. He was tall and handsome with long hair. Logic forced Vhalla to admit that he really was one of the best matches someone like her could hope for.

It was frustrating that logic couldn't force her to feel any chemistry with him. Perhaps it would grow in time. His devotion had been heart-warming and charming, in spite of his blatant issues with her magic. Vhalla knew plenty of people in long-term, happy relationships without fiery passion.

"Sareem…" she finally managed, breaking the silence.

"Vhalla, I-I hope I wasn't too forward." He straightened and looked away.

She felt like she could breathe again. "I-your-I am moved by your compassion." Vhalla hoped she was off to a good start. He looked at her hopefully. She tried to swallow the odd guilt that sprung up at his hopeful stare. She wanted to refuse him, but she had no logical reason to. It wasn't as though she were spoken for, and time was ticking for her if she were to assume the natural roles of womanhood.

"If you can accept me, even as a sorcerer, then I'm sure we could find some time to do something, just the two of us." She forced her tongue to form words.

"I would very much like that." Sareem beamed. "How about tomorrow?"

"Tomorrow?" she repeated. He was certainly eager.

"It's the start of the festival. Everyone will be in the streets for the events. I would love to be there with you." Be it from nerves or excitement, he spoke faster than she had ever heard.

Vhalla's head spun. "Tomorrow." She tried to shake away the dizzying feeling. "Sure, tomorrow."

"If you're up to it," he said suddenly. "I know of your complications right now."

"It's fine." Vhalla was eager to show him the door.

"Excellent. I'll stop by in the morning." He paused in the doorframe. "Are you sure you're well? I could stay tonight."

"I will be fine," Vhalla said firmly, allowing the comment to pass as genuine concern.

"All right." He placed a hand at the top of her neck and kissed her forehead. Vhalla tried to smile nicely. "Take care, dear Vhalla," he said gently. "I will dream of you." With that he departed.

Vhalla stood in a daze for a long time, trying to take in everything that happened. Sareem had kissed her. It had to go up on her not-so-short list of the most impossible things to have happened to her lately. She had also agreed to a date of some variety. Vhalla rubbed her eyes. *This will all work out*, she told herself.

As she lay in bed, Vhalla gave herself to the darkness. *I will dream of you*, Sareem had said. Vhalla wasn't sure what she would dream about. But were it to be anyone in the whole world, something told her that person would not be Sareem.

Vhalla woke the next day and again felt exhausted. She had a suspicion that it was not entirely from the previous day's magical exertion. Rolling into a ball, Vhalla did not even try to bite back a groan. She had actually agreed to a date of sorts with Sareem. Sareem! But what else was she to do when he kissed her?

Staring at the ceiling was no more interesting than staring at the wall. Stone and more stone, she existed in her small, insignificant little box. Vhalla took a slow breath—it was suffocating. Her world was nothing, and she was nothing in it.

A strange feeling surged in the tips of her fingers, like a beat of her heart. There was one place she wasn't insignificant, one place where the rooms were not tiny even for someone of her rank.

The Tower.

The thought was a breath of fresh air. Suddenly, the shutter over her window flew open and let in the crisp autumn breeze.

Startled by the sound, she was up and gripping the window sill in a heartbeat, staring out into the vast expanse that was the Empire's capital. Timidly, she extended a hand into the sunlight.

With a pulse of magic from core to fingertip she felt the wind respond to her command, slipping around her open palm.

Vhalla stared in awe. The wind bent to her will. She spun in place, starting for the door. She had to find Aldrik and tell him. This was not little pockets of air she created to push or levitate things. This was the very wind. There had to be something new they could try, something he would teach her. Vhalla grinned like a fool, the expression on his face when she told him would be worth an artist's rendering.

Her fingers slipped from the door handle with a deflating sigh. No, there would be no prince today. Vhalla turned back into the room and began stripping off her sleeping gown and readying herself for what did await her—Sareem.

Vhalla decided to see how much she could do with magic—by herself. Raising her hand, she flicked her wrist a few times and a pair of tan leather leggings and her best dress flew across the room onto the bed.

She uncertainly studied the unassuming garments in her hands. Her father had sent them to her when she had her coming of age birthday. It was a date, after all. Vhalla discovered using magic to dress herself would take practice, and succeeded only in working up a small sweat and pulling on her leggings by hand.

A challenge for another day.

Next was washing. Vhalla attempted to raise the water out of its bowl, but it resisted her. She even tried closing her eyes and reaching out to it like she had to do when she was first being taught. But it kept slipping through her fingers and sloshed around in the bowl. Vhalla frowned. Water was another challenge for later. Maybe Fritz would have some advice, she mused. He was a Waterrunner, after all.

Vhalla looked at her hair in the tarnished scrap of metal that served as her mirror. As usual, her hair was a frizzy, knotted mess. If she could use magic on her hair, her life would be complete. Vhalla took a breath and prepared herself for a fight. She stared at the mirror and thought of a simple style she'd seen some of the Southerners wear before. It was a bun with a braid around its base.

Letting the breath out slowly, she focused on her hair and thought of what she wanted it to do. She squinted at it, tilted her head, closed her eyes, blinked seven times, and waved her hands like a fool.

Nothing.

Vhalla took a breath and sat back. Sareem would likely be here soon, and she needed to have something. Resolved, she insisted her hair would move. Vhalla was rewarded with a small piece lifting near her face before falling back limply. Apparently, her hair was so stubborn it even refused magic. Resigned, Vhalla held out her hand and watched a leather hair-tie float into it from her desk. She did her hair by hand with some mild success —and a handful or two of pins—before deciding it was good enough.

She passed the rest of the time levitating random objects in her room. Aldrik had been an adept teacher, and Vhalla found herself inventing things that she could accomplish with ease. She was working on levitating two things in the air at the same time, her quill and journal, when there was a knock.

"Come in, Sareem." Wrapped up in the bobbing items, she didn't even look to ensure it was he.

He slammed the door shut behind him. "Vhalla," he hissed, "What are you doing?"

She looked at him dumbly. "Trying something out. Look, look! I just got it—two at once!" She grinned, oblivious to his displeasure, pointing at the quill and journal.

"Stop that." He plucked them from the air as though they were anti-Empire propaganda.

Vhalla's expression quickly fell to a frown. "No one taught

me how to do that. I was making it up all on—" She didn't even try to hide her annoyance.

"And what if it hadn't been me at the door?" he snapped. "What if someone who doesn't know saw?" Her features relaxed a little thinking of that.

"Vhalla," he cooed, walking over to her, "you look absolutely stunning. Let's go have a perfectly *normal* day; just you and I?"

She almost refused, her stomach suddenly felt unsettled. But his hand was at the small of her back, leading her out into the hall beyond. Taking advantage of Aldrik being nowhere nearby, Vhalla wrung her hands with purpose.

They walked out of the staff gate nearest Vhalla's room. It was called a gate but it was little more than a back door with a guard stationed outside. It led into the middle class area of the city. The houses were clean and well kept, but the roofs were simply thatched, rather than possessing clay or wooden tiles that could be found higher up the mountain. Some had peeling paint, if painted at all, and only about half possessed any glass in their windows. It was the home of the common folk.

Everyone seemed to be in a spirited mood for the Festival of the Sun. Women walked around in frocks and simple dresses. Children begged to attend this or that event. Men laughed and played music in the streets. Every fountain was flowing with water from the city's aqueducts, no matter the time of day. Judging from the swagger of some, not only water was flowing.

Vhalla smiled at the white and gold pennons proudly displayed; the golden sun, symbol of the Mother and the Empire.

She saw one group of men hunched around some form of dice game. Shirts hung loosely about their shoulders with open ties in the front. No one wore coats or jackets, and none seemed to be bothered that a portion of their chest was easily visible. Vhalla's cheeks felt hot, and she could hardly stifle a nervous laugh as she tried to imagine Aldrik dressed so plainly; his chest on display.

"What is it?" Sareem had taken her hand while she was lost in thoughts.

"Oh nothing," she murmured, still smiling at the image in her mind. "It's just a lovely day."

"It is. But you, my dear, are far lovelier than even the Mother Sun."

Vhalla smiled nicely at Sareem; he was trying. "So, what will we be doing?" she inquired, trying to avoid the silence from stretching on for too long.

"Well, there is a wonderful bakery not far from here; I've frequented it often since I was a boy," Sareem began. "Then I was thinking we could go watch the jugglers in the square."

"There are jugglers?" Vhalla hadn't been keeping track of the events very closely.

Sareem nodded. "A troupe of refugees from the North, I hear. They came South under the declarations of peace to find a better life and escape the war. I've heard the entertainment is their thanks for their liberation."

Vhalla pondered this a moment, wondering if she too would willingly perform for people who took her home from her.

Sareem continued, "Then I was thinking that we could watch the procession of the senators. It's a bit out of the way, but they're dressed up like roosters and it is always good fun to laugh at them."

"Haven't we done that before?" Vhalla wondered aloud. She was struggling to remember if they had terrorized the senators, or if it had been the Court escaping from its grand meeting hall in the palace.

"We have," Sareem affirmed. "If I recall correctly, I was able to make you laugh so hard you snorted like a pig." Vhalla blushed, and pursed her lips in embarrassment. Sareem chuckled. "You have a lovely laugh, Vhalla, and I enjoy hearing it."

She watched as he moved her hand up to his mouth, kissing it. His fingers were intertwined with hers. Vhalla wanted to find a way that she thought they looked good together, but every time she did, she kept remembering his prior reaction to her magic. But, if he was to be believed, his actions were purely shock.

"Well, if I enjoyed it so much last time," she agreed weakly.

"I will make sure you enjoy yourself again, my dear," he promised.

Vhalla forced a smile. She wasn't about to let the unsettling feeling at the very pit of her core ruin everything. It was a nice day, and Sareem was a good friend. Knowing she had several hours with him, Vhalla was inclined to give Sareem the benefit of the doubt.

They settled at a bakery called The Golden Bun. It was not far from the main square, and Sareem sat her down at an outside table, at her request. He pulled out her chair, placed a small kiss on her temple, and then went to fetch the food. She wished he wouldn't be so forward in public.

Sareem returned with a plate of hot lemon cakes. Vhalla blinked. Even though lemons were in season in the West, they were still expensive to transport South.

"If I recall, your favorites are lemon things." He settled across from her.

"They are." The corners of her mouth tugged in a determined smile. He had been paying attention to her for longer than she realized. Pinching one of the dense cakes with her fingers, Vhalla popped it into her mouth.

"These are good," she said with a hint of surprise.

"Are they?" He rested his chin in his palm, reaching for her free hand. "I'm very glad; I had them made especially for you."

Vhalla blinked and blushed faintly. "Thank you, Sareem." To make a point she quickly grabbed for another and took a more girlish bite.

"You know, I've wanted to do this since we were fourteen." She made a small questioning sound and he continued, allowing her to chew. "You're that girl, Vhalla. The one that you just know is special. So much so that it's almost something you feel like you can't touch or you'll break it." He let out an embarrassed laugh. "It must sound silly."

"No, no it doesn't. I know that feeling exactly," she said softly.

He beamed. "I always hoped you felt the same." He squeezed her hand, and she realized he had misunderstood her. She had not been referring to him. "All of this is like a dream, and I want to give you everything you could ever want." He picked up a lemon cake and took a bite himself.

Vhalla attempted to say something in return but she fumbled over her words. They all sounded cheap or false. In the end, she changed the subject. "Why do you live in the palace?" He made a noise of confusion and tilted his head. "Your father came here from Norin in the late Empress's gift party to the Empire. Why don't you live in your family's home?"

"Ah, well, my family lives down in Oparium," he answered. Vhalla only knew about the town at the base of the Southern Mountains because it was home to the old port of the Empire, before they conquered the West and took Norin's port. "My father lived in the palace, initially, but he met a girl down in the shipyard and, well, his business trips became more frequent until he moved to be with her. Funny how that happens, you wed those you work with."

"Funny, right..." Vhalla mumbled and desperately wanted to change the topic from marriage. "Do you enjoy living in the capital?"

"I do," Sareem answered with a nod. "Oparium gets some exotic things through the port, but nothing is quite like living in the capital. I hope to someday raise my children here."

"Your parents—are they still alive?" Vhalla was growing tired of changing the subject and busied her mouth with the last of the lemon cakes.

"They are," he replied. "And yours?" Vhalla shook her head. Sareem's eyebrows rose in surprise.

"My father is, but my mother died when I was ten, while my father was doing his duty to the Empire during the War of the Crystal Caverns." She paused. "I was sick with Autumn Fever. My mother fell ill after me; she never recovered."

Sareem frowned. "I remember you telling me you had the illness before, but I never realized... I am so sorry." His voice was low and his expression serious.

"I've had a long time to come to terms with it." If Vhalla said it was easy now, it would be a lie. There were times when she wanted her mother more than anything in the world. But she had reached a place where it no longer hurt to the point of tears to think on it.

"Let's find a good spot for the jugglers. I don't want any sad thoughts today."

He stood. She followed, and Sareem took her hand again.

The central square of the capital was a large area that could hold hundreds of people. It had a mosaic of the sun and moon in their eternal dance sprawled beneath the feet of those gathering around a central stage. The crowd was beginning to thicken, and it was soon shoulder-to-shoulder.

Six people, men and women, took the stage. Vhalla was entranced. She had never seen Northerners before, she realized. Vhalla was certain she would have remembered a green person. Their skin was a deep forest viridian, with swirling dots and embellishments in silver. Combined with their masks, carved from tree bark, they were like mystical creatures and completely mesmerized her.

A woman walked across the edge of the stage, then faced the crowd who had gathered on all sides. "Good people of the South." Her accent was thick and muffled through the faceless mask she wore. "We have come under flags of peace to break bread with you. For your fine hospitality, we would like to provide some light entertainment in honor of your Mother Sun."

They started juggling simple objects: sacks of beans and leather balls. The crowd began to *ooh* and *aah* as they added daggers and swords into the mix. The Northerners began moving and tossing the variety of objects to each other until all six were involved in a circular pattern of thrown objects. Vhalla was stunned by their control and deft hands. They made it look easy with their fearlessness.

When the show came to a close, a roar of applause rang out and the six took a bow. The same woman walked to the edge of the stage again.

"Good people, I hope you enjoyed today's show. We hope you can make it for all of our shows leading up to our grand finale on the night of the gala." The woman held out her arms. "Tell all your friends!" She gave a wave with both hands and led her companions off the stage.

"I wonder what they'll do for the finale," Vhalla pondered aloud.

"We can find out, together. Come with me." Sareem smiled and took her hand.

"You know I'm not one for the crowds on the last night of the festival," she murmured a half-hearted excuse.

"Two isn't a crowd." Sareem began leading her away from the square in the slowly dissipating mass of people. "It would only be you and I."

"That's not what I meant." Vhalla bit her lower lip,

conflicted. Sareem hadn't been doing a poor job, and the advice of the older ladies from the palace resonated back to her. Marry young and fulfill the natural role of a woman. Sareem clearly cared for her. She glanced up at him and was rewarded with a warm smile.

"All right," Vhalla agreed softly. "I'll meet you."

"Meet me at The Golden Bun." He pointed to the bakery as they passed down the road. "When the moon is one third in the sky. The finales normally happen at the moon's apex so that'll give us plenty of time. I know how girls like to get ready."

Sareem laughed, and Vhalla tried to laugh along. She had no interest in *getting ready* for a second date with Sareem. Doubt was already tinting the edges of her decision, but he seemed so happy about it all that she had not the faintest inkling for how to back out of it now.

"Speaking of getting ready and fancy clothes and all..." Sareem looked up at the sky. "It's almost time for the noon procession of senators."

As they climbed up the sloping, winding roads into the nicer area of town, the houses began to shift from white plaster to stone and solid wood construction. He led her in a direction she had never been before and the houses became even more opulent. Iron fences and tall hedges enclosed homes that actually had a rare small yard or garden. Almost every house had a noble seal upon it bearing a region of the Empire or a family crest. Most, Vhalla did not recognize nor have any interest in. Some houses had two flags; one that was the signet of the Empire, and another that was the signet of a country or region.

"The ones with two flags are senators' homes. Those without are simply members of the Court," Sareem pointed out. "It's not a bad job; get a house and all with the position." Vhalla stared in awe. Some houses even had colored glass window designs like the library. "Of course, you have to be elected to the Senate, so I'm told it's not an easy job to get."

"Well worth it, I'd say." Vhalla was still taking in the wonder about her.

"It's annoying how well some live, isn't it?" Sareem chuckled.

She nodded mutely, instantly thinking of Aldrik and the glimpses she had gained into his world. Vhalla did not know for certain, but she would guess that nothing in the houses they passed compared to the gilded, stained wood, and rich carpeted parlors of the prince's home. In the back of her mind she wondered if he was there now, reading at a window. She wondered if there was anywhere else in the world she'd rather be.

Eventually, the houses gave way to a wide open expanse. The side road merged with a large marble street that matched the building at one end. It was a large circular structure with columns around the outside. Vhalla had never cared much for politics, and she didn't recognize any of the names written on the plaques bolted to the pillars.

A good few others had lined up alongside the road. Vhalla looked at them curiously.

"When did politics become a spectator sport?" she inquired.

"Since always." Sareem grinned. "I imagine some are here to lobby for a cause, others will likely scream dissent at the senators as they leave, while a few probably came for the same reason we did." He shrugged. "The Senate is meant to keep the common folk happy by dealing with small things on behalf of the Empire, but that doesn't mean they always do a good job."

"Doesn't it seem rather pointless?" Vhalla mused. The Emperor always had the final say.

"The Empire's always been at war. Maybe, when the Emperor has time to focus on matters of state, it will be," Sareem joined in her musing. "But I think it's nice to have some way that the common folk get a voice. Otherwise it'd only be the Court, and it's not as though the highborn really care for our plights."

A bell rang out from over the top of the Senate Hall.

"Here they come," Sareem whispered on the thirteenth ring.

It was indeed a spectacle. Men and women of all ages and shapes trickled out of the marble building by ones and twos. He told her there were thirteen in total, so the show wouldn't be over too quickly. Some made speedy departures through the crowd and off down side streets, presumably making a quick retreat home. Others took a more leisurely stroll. Just as Sareem had predicted, some people shouted while others shook hands with their elected officials.

But it wasn't this that kept the smile on Vhalla's cheeks. It was their clothing. Clearly, drapery was the order of the day, a traditional Southern style that was quickly going out of fashion for the tailored looks of the West and practical sensibilities of the East. Every senator bore a golden medallion on a heavy chain, but the similarities ended there. The first was a man swathed in Eastern purple silk with a gold hem. He wore his whitening hair up in curls with peacock feathers sticking out at odd angles.

The next woman had a pinched face and a pointed nose, one that Sareem couldn't help but comment on.

"She looks like she's been forced to smell her own waste," he whispered eagerly into her ear. Vhalla bit her knuckles to keep from laughing.

The next man had a pig nose, and the one after Sareem jested about rolling down the steps, as his shape was far better suited for such than walking.

Vhalla was having such a fun time that she didn't even mind it when Sareem draped his arm around her shoulders, pulling her close for more whispering. She simply kept giggling like a fool and let Sareem continue his roll of taunts in her ear.

"Look there. Look, look, all the ruffles make her look like a chicken."

Vhalla turned her head away from the building to examine one of the ladies in yellow. She had made some very unfortunate choices with all the ruffles of her dress piled upon her ample rump. Vhalla was having more fun than she expected. She beamed at Sareem, and he grinned back at her. It felt like they were kids again and could simply laugh and be silly without the pressure of anything more.

Then the wind shifted, and the smile fell from her face.

She knew he was there before she even turned her head. She *felt* him. It was a subtle temperature shift carried on the breeze, or the sound of his boots on the marble road. Vhalla turned her head slowly to see Aldrik walking alongside a Southern man with darkening blond hair and piercing blue eyes. They were still a few steps away and were deep in conversation.

"Sareem, this was fun, but I'm really hungry, so let's get going," she pleaded, trying to shrug off his arm.

With a laugh, he pulled her closer; his lips pressed against her ear uncomfortably. "But the best part is now walking toward us; the Head of Senate and the dark snob prince." He snickered.

Her lips parted and shut again quickly, barely catching a vehement defense on Aldrik's behalf.

"The Emperor has ordered certain crystal relics be brought back from the North." The senator's voice gave Vhalla the same feeling as ripping paper, a chill uneasiness at its quiet yet harsh sound.

"I have not heard of this," Aldrik responded. Even though they were whispering, Vhalla could hear their conversation along the wind. Their words grew louder with every nearing step.

"Sareem, please," she begged. Vhalla reached up and grabbed

his hand to pull Sareem's arm off her shoulders and drag him away herself. But it was too late.

Aldrik's eyes fell on hers. He considered her a long moment, clearly no longer interested in whatever the senator was saying. His brow furrowed and a shadow darkened his face briefly, before his expressionless mask slipped back into place, and he looked forward once more.

Vhalla opened her mouth to speak but couldn't come up with words to say. Sareem was still muttering like a fool in her ear, but she couldn't hear him over the words of the senator and prince.

"Was that someone you know, Prince Aldrik?" the Head of Senate asked suddenly with no subtle interest.

"Hardly," Aldrik's voice was cold and fading. "Why would I associate with common-folk?"

Then he was gone. Aldrik kept walking until he was out of sight. He never looked back.

Sareem remained oblivious to the turmoil raging within her chest. Vhalla tortured herself with the notion of running after him, but anything she did would only make a scene. What had that look meant? Even the senator had noticed the subtle shift in the crown prince. She chewed it over as Sareem continued prattling away, leading her wherever he wished. Did it matter to Aldrik how she spent her time? Vhalla barely contained a scream of frustration.

She was poor company all the way back to the palace. But Sareem didn't mind, as he filled the silence enough for both of them. Vhalla refused his offer for dinner, heading straight for bed. Food would taste like ash in her mouth anyway.

CHAPTER 17

Vhalla stared at her doorknob. She agreed to meet Aldrik today. He had invited her to lunch in the rose garden. Vhalla replayed the memory in her head with doubt. That was what happened. His confused gaze flashed through her mind as he had stared upon her and Sareem.

She twisted her fingers around each other. *He will still want to see me*, she assured herself. Vhalla grabbed her improvised mirror and fussed with her hair. It was the frizzy mess it always had been, and she stared at it hopelessly. He was the crown prince; she had no doubt he had been with women older, more beautiful, more experienced, and more refined than she. For all she knew, he was with one now.

Poking her finger through a new hole in her maroon tunic, Vhalla sighed. She was fussing over nothing, the apprentice in her scolded. The prince knew who she was. He had said it himself. Why would he associate with commoners like her?

The halls of the palace were mostly empty due to the festival. Those who were working flitted about carrying large trays of lavish food and pitchers of frothing drink. She kept her head down, wandering the passages washed in the afternoon sun.

Eventually, the people in the hallways faded one by one until Vhalla was alone. The garden appeared before her, and Vhalla entered through the same window as last time. It was a nice fall day, perfect for the festival. Some of the smaller plants had already begun to go dormant for the winter, and she wondered how long until the roses also began to fall.

The gardens and gazebo were deserted. Vhalla assured herself that she had only beaten him there, that he hadn't forgotten. She wandered uncertainly throughout the gazebo, inspecting the roses. Thankfully, Aldrik did not keep her waiting long.

Vhalla turned away from the center post of roses as she heard the click of his boots up the steps. Her heart pounded, and her mouth was dry. The prince fumbled with the door a moment before pushing it open. In one arm he balanced a decently sized wicker basket that emitted a tempting aroma.

They stared at each other, as though in disbelief. Vhalla swallowed. He straightened, adjusting the box.

"Hello." She smiled. They had spent countless hours together. *Nothing is different about this meeting*, she reassured herself. Even if this meeting seemed to have no other purpose than for him to see her.

"Good afternoon," he responded. Something in the resonance of his voice gave Vhalla pause. "You are fast this morning."

"I had nothing else to do," Vhalla replied, denying any kind of excitement—even to herself—over the meeting. He crossed the room, sitting on the far bench. Vhalla followed and took her prior seat at his side.

"I am beginning to think you never work. I will have to have a talk with our Master of Tome," he declared in his princely tone.

Vhalla playfully stuck her tongue out like a child. "If I am not working, I think it may be because a certain Imperial Prince keeps taking me from work," she retorted.

"Ah, you have me." Aldrik grinned.

"It's the festival, anyway." Vhalla shrugged to hide her defensiveness at the notion that Aldrik may think her lazy.

"It is," he agreed. Opening the basket, Aldrik revealed multiple trays of food, stacked upon each other. Vhalla had only heard the kitchen staff speak of preparing such luxuries, and the house servants whisper about sneaking bites in-between dinner for nobility. "I thought, perhaps, you had not eaten."

Vhalla stared at the rows of carefully cut tea sandwiches. There was white bread, tan bread, bread with oats, and small rolls with brown crusts. She saw slices of cured ham and peppered turkey sneaking out from the sides, resting in beds of fresh produce. It seemed to practically glisten.

"Are you sure it's okay?" she had to ask. "That food isn't really meant for me." He gave her a peculiar stare. "Staff, servants, we don't eat food like this."

"Well, now you do," Aldrik said easily, lifting up the top tier to her. Vhalla's stomach growled loudly enough to remind her that she had skipped dinner last night. Her face flushed bright red. "You cannot argue with that." He chuckled.

Vhalla decided on an egg sandwich. The egg did not have the rubbery flavor or consistency as when they had been sitting for too long. There was not a mass of cream or butter sauce upon it either to hide the stale ingredients. Every flavor shone, and she stared at the small morsel in awe.

"What do the servants and staff eat?" the prince asked.

She regarded him curiously. "Sometimes stews, sometimes a rice hash, sometimes bread and meat." Vhalla shrugged. "Normally whatever the kitchen has on hand. *Two day old nights* is how we refer to the worst nights. It's things that the kitchen really should've discarded a day or two ago but covered in some kind of gravy or salt, and passes it off as food." He'd stopped eating to stare at her, and she laughed at his still, almost horrified, look. "It really isn't so bad. What do you normally eat?"

"Whatever I ask for," he said, obviously.

Vhalla laughed louder. "It must be nice to be the prince." She grinned, grabbing a few grapes from the tray and popping them into her mouth before starting on another sandwich.

He paused, his eyes fixed somewhere in the distance. "I suppose, in some ways," Aldrik spoke slowly, and Vhalla swallowed her food to listen. "In others, I think I would rather be more common."

"Other ways like what?"

"You are free to make your own choices. I have *obligations*," he said cryptically.

"Obligations? Such as?" she asked, taking a small bite and listening intently.

"Well, my parrot," he retorted and grinned at her scowl. "Lately, I have done a lot in my father's absence. I have approved this or that, checked on the state of the Empire and capital, met with most of the ministers and senators," he explained.

Vhalla was reminded of the prior day. She busied her mouth with another bite of food. Aldrik uncorked a bottle and passed it to her. What she had expected to be water was actually tea with a fruity flavor. It was refreshing and delicious; it almost made her forget the embarrassing moment from the procession of senators.

"I was at the Senate meetings yesterday." He was apparently not going to let the possibility for an uncomfortable confrontation slide. It was his turn to avoid her stare. She watched him shift uneasily on the bench, completely ignoring the food. Could the prince even feel genuinely awkward?

"I know." Vhalla instantly wished she had thought of something better to say.

"That boy you were with..." Aldrik began slowly, his spoken grace suddenly failing him.

"He's my friend," Vhalla responded quickly, her lips on overdrive. "His name is Sareem. We've been friends for years. He's like a brother, really. He asked to take me out, and I agreed because I thought it was the right thing to do but, well, of course I had fun, he can be a laugh. But he's just a friend."

The prince stared at her intently through her uncomfortable and hasty proclamation. Obsidian eyes pinned her to the spot, and Vhalla met them with all the honesty she could muster. Sareem was only a friend, she realized as she looked at the prince. He was nothing more to her. Vhalla swallowed hard, keenly aware of a dangerous feeling that had taken root in her chest over the past months without her consent. What was she doing?

"He is only a friend." She didn't know why she was whispering, or which one of them she was reassuring.

Aldrik's eyes relaxed, the intensity in them fading into a warm heat that pulsed down to her toes with each beat of her heart. The corners of his mouth came next; instead of relaxing into their normal thin line, they eased upward into a small smile. Vhalla bit her lip, trying to hide her reaction to his joy—and failed.

"Friends are good to have," the prince said suddenly, turning away and resituating the trays. He reached for a sliced strawberry. Vhalla did the same and they chewed away the moment.

"Are you and Larel only friends?" She wanted to hit herself the moment the question slipped from her lips. It wasn't any of her business, and the prince's answer wouldn't matter. It didn't matter how comfortable he had seemed in the other woman's room. *He could be with whomever he pleased*, Vhalla reminded herself.

"Larel," Aldrik said after a thoughtful second. Vhalla shifted uneasily at his pause. Heat began to rise to her cheeks, *she had been so foolish*. "I suppose she is like Sareem is to you. I have known her since I was a child. She was different from the others and seemed to be willing to speak with me, work with me, without fawning over the prince."

Vhalla inspected the hem of her shirt. *They are both Western*, she mused, and Vhalla had no idea if Larel had a noble background or not. Most apprentices had some connection to nobility, which was how they became apprentices rather than servants.

"Do not fidget," Aldrik said gently, resting his fingertips on the back of her hand. Vhalla jumped at the contact. "Yes, she is *just* a friend."

The heat of his fingertips burned like the weight of his eyes, and Vhalla was entranced by both. They danced around something that neither seemed ready to admit. Vhalla did not think on it. The only thing she thought of was how close the prince's face was to hers, as he reached to touch her hand.

"Do you ever practice your sorcery?" Vhalla asked suddenly, diffusing the moment.

"I used to practice more frequently." He straightened away and placed a hand on his hip. Vhalla instantly remembered his wound. She busied her mouth with another bite of food to avoid asking another stupid question. "Will you join the Tower?"

Vhalla stopped mid-chew. Untutored in decorum, she placed the half-eaten sandwich back in the box and wiped her palms on her knees. Aldrik's eyes grazed over the action, but he said nothing as she worked through her response.

"Aldrik," she whispered softly, staring at the crimson roses that were their only company.

"Vhalla?" Confusion about her demeanor was evident in his voice.

"If I am Eradicated, what will happen to you?" When had the word Eradicated begun to make her uncomfortable?

"What do you mean?" He arched a dark eyebrow.

"The Bond." Vhalla looked at him, placing a palm on the bench between them. Her fingers almost touched his thigh. "You said it's a magical connection, that it saved your life. If I am Eradicated, what will happen to you?"

"Do not concern yourself with that." He shook his head. The motion caused a stray piece of hair to fall forward to arch around the side of his face.

"Do you know?" she asked with pursed lips. There wasn't any point to her asking. Vhalla acknowledged to herself that Eradication was no longer an option.

"I do not," he relented with a small sigh. "But I wish for you to make your decision for yourself, not because—"

"I don't want to hurt you," Vhalla interrupted the prince. He blinked at her. "Aldrik, I couldn't make a decision if I knew it would hurt you."

"Why?" he whispered.

"Because—" The sharp cry of an iron gate followed by the loud clang of its closing interrupted her. Vhalla looked to the door.

Heavy footsteps ground upon the gravel path. Vhalla barely recognized the gait of the step, but Aldrik did instantly. He straightened, and Vhalla did the same. The man that she had just spoken with so casually suddenly wore a face as hard as stone.

"Brother!" another male voice called energetically. "Brother, are you here?"

Two shadows appeared outside the fogged glass of the greenhouse, their outlines blurry and indistinguishable. The door to the gazebo opened, and a stocky prince walked in boldly.

The man Aldrik had been with the day prior entered with him—the Head of Senate. Prince Baldair looked across the room to Aldrik and then to Vhalla.

"I did not realize you had company, brother." A slow smile crept across his features.

"Baldair, I believe we have discussed—at length—that I am not to be disturbed within my garden." Aldrik's voice was tight and tense.

Vhalla missed the awkward exchange of the princes as the senator's stare sent a shiver down her spine. The older man squinted his eyes, and a satisfied smirk grew from the corners of his mouth. The senator recognized her.

"I suppose I can now see why." Baldair laughed. "Please forgive me, miss..." The Head of Senate was not the only person to recognize the library apprentice in their midst. "You're the girl from the library, the clumsy one! Vhalla, isn't it?"

"Y-yes." She couldn't stop a stutter as the prince crossed the room and took her hand, kissing it.

He had remembered her, though she wished for something more than her clumsiness. He had a brilliant smile, and Vhalla relaxed under his icy blue eyes. Her memories of the Heartbreaker Prince's radiance didn't do him justice.

"I didn't expect a prince to remember my name," she murmured in reply.

"No!" he gasped. "One as lovely as you should never be forgotten. And if you're in the garden, I am sure my brother has not once forgotten your name." He nudged Aldrik playfully.

Aldrik simply stared up at his brother, unmoving from his seat. She looked to the elder prince, confused by his dark glare.

"Baldair, what do you want?" Vhalla could almost see the tension in Aldrik's jaw as he forced the words between his lips.

"Forgive your brother, my prince." The senator gave a small bow. "There was a bird this morning. The eastern front of the southern host has crumbled in its attack. The Clan of Houl is now pressing on the East. I thought it an urgent matter for the war council."

"A messenger would have sufficed." Aldrik stood, glaring at his brother.

Vhalla rose stiffly, everyone else was on their feet, and she did not want to stand out any more than she already did.

"My sincere apologies for interrupting your lunch." Nothing in the senator's words sounded like an apology as his eyes assessed the half-eaten box of food. Aldrik looked back, following his stare.

Vhalla brought her hands together before her, grabbing her fingers with white knuckles to keep from fidgeting. Turning away from the senator and his brother, Aldrik's eyes were significantly softer, but the trace of worry between his brows did not reassure Vhalla.

"It was nothing," Aldrik responded, his voice void of emotion.

Vhalla knew he could not admit to associating with her. He was the crown prince—as if he would want anyone to know he had spent time with someone so lowly. She stared at her feet. She could never be anyone to him.

"My apologies to you as well, Vhalla." The senator held the end of her name, waiting for her to fill in the empty space.

"Yarl," she responded, purely out of obligation.

"Vhalla Yarl," the senator repeated thoughtfully.

If Vhalla could rip her name from his tongue and his mind she would have.

"I will be in attendance at your war council in a moment, Senator Egmun." It must have been her imagination that Aldrik took a half step between her and the senator.

"I'll see her out." Prince Baldair smiled, offering Vhalla his elbow. She stared at the appendage before looking back to

Aldrik. His face was stony again. "You have more pressing matters, brother."

"Indeed." The crown prince turned, and Vhalla was left with no option but to take the golden prince's arm.

The head of Senate, Egmun; Vhalla committed the name to memory. Aldrik walked out first and the dark prince did not even look back at her. The two men began talking halfway to the gate, but Vhalla only heard the wind as her prince left her behind with his brother.

CHAPTER 18

If Vhalla counted the reasons for her to be escorted by Prince Baldair, she would use zero fingers. Yet she strolled with him through the garden and past the gate. Her hand rested in the crook of his elbow and Vhalla realized that, despite his size, he was not as warm as his brother.

She stole a glance down the hall where Aldrik and the senator had turned. They were nowhere to be seen. Not even a faint echo of their voices could be heard. To add to her discomfort, Prince Baldair led her in the opposite direction. The opulence was the same as the last time she walked with Aldrik, but the servants must have been ignoring their cleaning duties due to the festival, for it did not shine as brightly today.

"So," the prince finally started. His voice was higher than Aldrik's, less gravely. But it was a rich and full sound—almost song-like. "How does someone like you end up in my brother's garden?"

"Someone like me?" Vhalla asked carefully. She knew exactly what he meant, but perhaps answering his question could be avoided if she turned it back on him.

"A library apprentice." Baldair grinned. He ran a hand through his ear-length wavy blond hair. His easy response told her he had seen through her efforts to dodge his inquiry.

"I..." Vhalla looked at the thin cracks between the tiled marble beneath her feet. She wished she was small enough to slip through one and fall to the center of the earth. *You're a bad liar*, Sareem's words echoed in her treacherous mind.

"He's not blackmailing you or anything, is he?" There was genuine concern in his voice.

"What?" Vhalla blinked up at the prince. "No, of course not."

"Well, I know you weren't enjoying his company." Prince Baldair gave a full laugh as though he had made a great joke.

Vhalla frowned. Aldrik would not want her to disclose that they enjoyed each other's company, or, at least, she did his. But she felt strange standing there without defending him in the face of a blatant insult.

"I think he has an astoundingly sharp mind," she answered delicately.

Prince Baldair looked at her sideways. "That may be one of the nicest things I have ever heard a staff or servant say about my brother. Let's see, I've heard egotistical, a royal pain, his head stuck in a variety of places that I don't think are anatomically possible..." The prince laughed again.

Vhalla felt her whole body tense. "I doubt those people took the time to understand him," she mumbled.

Prince Baldair stopped laughing and looked at her strangely. "You're so polite, Vhalla." Prince Baldair chuckled. "Fine, fine, I won't push you to be anything but the good girl... for now," he added with a wink.

Vhalla's cheeks were stubbornly hot. The younger prince seemed to love jesting. "How is the front?" she asked, struggling for a change of topic that wouldn't reveal too much to the Heartbreaker Prince.

"Much like my father said, the Northern capital refuses to fall. A few clans continue to resist, but we will have them in time." He spoke as easily about it as if it were the weather.

"Is what's happened serious?" Vhalla asked, glancing over her shoulder. They had long since passed the entrance to the servants' and staffs' quarters, and Vhalla's tension slowly ebbed due to her curiosity over the towering walls of glittering gold and carved stone around her.

"What's happened?" he repeated. Prince Baldair held out his arm as she was momentarily distracted while inspecting a fresco. He remained close enough to maintain contact; Vhalla did not realize how close.

"The war council—" She turned and almost bumped face-first into his wide, muscular chest.

"Oh that." The younger prince chuckled. "I'm certain it'll be fine. I have no doubt Father wants to ensure Aldrik understands everything that has occurred for when he returns to the front."

Vhalla stopped. Everything stopped. Only her breathing and heartbeat moved in the whole world. As Vhalla stared at a distant point, she missed the blond's quizzical gaze. It was as though she could see the moment Aldrik would leave. He would go back to war.

"Vhalla?" The golden prince turned. Much more forward than his brother, calloused palms wrapped around her shoulders, completely covering them.

Her head snapped up at the handsome man who now filled her vision, her trance broken. She struggled to form words, and he seemed content to wait.

"Sorry." Vhalla shook her head, pressing her eyes closed. How had she not realized it before feeling the crippling horror at the idea of the prince leaving? How had these emotions crept up on her? "I just, felt dizzy."

"Dizzy?" The prince made a low humming noise in the back of his throat. "Now, we can't have any of that."

With a laugh and a surprisingly graceful motion for such a mountain of a man, he lifted her small form into the air with ease. There was no hope for Vhalla as she blushed. She fumbled clumsily with her hands, not knowing where to place them as her entire side was flush against the royal's chest.

"I'm fine!"

"Nonsense. I interrupted your lunch; I'm certain any lightheadedness is from that. Allow me to remedy such." The prince grinned, and Vhalla sat helplessly in his arms.

Vhalla was distracted from her awkward position as they entered a central atrium with a beautiful stained glass dome, the sun at its apex casting a kaleidoscope of colors on the floor. A gold staircase spiraled around the atrium with several halls leading off at various levels. On the floor was a mosaic of the palace done in painstakingly small tiles.

Vhalla gazed upward in awe as the prince carried her through its center. She stared up at a picture of the world cast in sparkling yellows. A crescent shaped continent was off to the side of the Empire's mainland, barrier islands in emerald dotting the space between the two land masses. Oceans were cast in sapphire blues, and she saw hints of land upon the edges of the dome; lands she had never heard of and wondered if they even existed.

"It's astounding, isn't it?" the prince asked.

Vhalla hadn't even realized they had stopped walking.

"It is," she agreed easily, beginning to find herself comfortable in his arms.

"My father wakes every day and sees his Empire shining down upon him," the prince mused, surprisingly eloquent.

"I can't imagine what it would be like," she whispered.

"Just ask my brother." Baldair laughed and continued on down a hall covered in a plush white carpet.

Her mind began to spiral down a staircase of thoughts surrounding his suggestion. Aldrik would be the Emperor. After spending so much time getting to know the man, it suddenly seemed impossible. Her teacher, her friend, the man she had come to...

Baldair placed her lightly on the ground before a door large enough for two people to fit through side-by-side.

"Where are we?" There was nothing to mar the white walls and golden vaulted ceilings of this particular hall, except for the door she stood before and one mirror opposite.

"My chambers," the prince replied.

"What?" Vhalla practically jumped out of her skin. "My prince, I do not think that this is appro—"

The door swung open under his large hands and light flooded the hall. Vhalla blinked, her eyes adjusting to the brilliance. She was pulled in with hypnotic curiosity.

The largest windows she had ever laid eyes upon dominated the entire wall opposite the door. He had said they were his chambers, but Vhalla did not see a bed in sight. She did however see two separate sitting areas, a fully-set table for six, a well-stocked full bar to her right, instruments, carcivi boards, darts, a harp, a lute, and every other form of entertainment.

"What do you think?" He leaned against the doorframe.

"It's..." There weren't words to describe it. "This is where you live?" Vhalla felt it must be taboo for her to be in this space, that were she to touch anything it would burst into flames under her fingertips.

"Where else would it be?" The prince chuckled, pulling a rope that hung behind the bar.

"Where is your bed?" Vhalla tried to count the number of her

personal chambers that could fit in the prince's main entertainment room. She lost count at fifteen.

"Through that door." The prince pointed.

"There's more?" She tried to consider the length of the hall they'd just traversed and how much could be hidden away behind the other doors.

"A fair bit." He nodded. Crossing over, he assessed her with his hands on his hips and a wicked little grin between his stubble clad cheeks. "Would you like to see my bed?"

Heat was back on her face, and Vhalla opened and shut her mouth like a fish trying to find air above water. She was in over her head with this man, and there was no hope for escape.

The moment a servant appeared in the doorframe, and Prince Baldair's eyes were off her, she said a prayer to the Mother.

"My prince?" The man gave a low bow. Vhalla glanced at the rope the prince had pulled.

"I would like lunch for two, please," Prince Baldair commanded.

"What would you care for?" The servant dared not even raise his eyes. Vhalla realized how bold she had become before royalty.

"Anything is fine." The prince waved him away, and the man stepped backward with another bow before disappearing down the hall.

Before Vhalla could voice an objection, the prince had her seated in a plush chair at one end of a long dining table, which seemed perfectly proportioned in its corner of the massive room. He opted for the seat next to her rather than the chair at the other end. Vhalla had never been served before, and she did not know what to say or do as servants began to fill the table around her. Guilt tickled the back of her throat and she bit her lip, avoiding their eyes.

"I know why you were with my brother today," Prince Baldair said finally when the help had left.

Vhalla stared at him open-mouthed. Food hung off a fork before her.

A rumbling chuckle resonated through his chest at her expression. "There was a letter."

"What did the letter say?" Vhalla asked cautiously, easing her food back onto its plate. Aldrik had been so adamant that his father shouldn't know of her. Wasn't he keeping her magic a secret out of concern?

Noticing how he held the fork and knife, she let herself be distracted. He held a utensil in one hand, index fingers outstretched over their backs. Comparing it to how she was cutting her meat with a fork stabbed vertical, fist grip, she felt like a barbarian from the Crescent Continent.

"The clerics reported that the library staff had been integral to saving his life. I could tell you were a smart one from the moment I met you. It was you, wasn't it, Vhalla?" It was phrased as a question, but Prince Baldair wore a knowing smile.

Vhalla stopped chewing. She had no idea what to say either.

The prince laughed and saved her from herself. "I knew it. Well, that explains it then; even my ass of a brother would need to give some appreciation to someone who helped save his life. Can't say I'm surprised it took him so long to humble himself."

Vhalla folded her hands in her lap over the napkin, the one she had only placed there after the prince had placed one in his lap. The inside of the meat was pinkish, and she wondered if it was safe to eat. Wondering about the food was better than talking to the prince about his brother. She poked one of the many forks, pushing it up the table. *Why did anyone need more than one fork?*

A low humming noise came from her left, pulling her back from her continual withdrawal. Baldair had placed his elbow on the table, his chin in his palm. He assessed her thoughtfully. She wanted to say something, but Vhalla was fighting a losing battle against the cerulean eyes before her.

"You're not like most of them, are you?" Prince Baldair's voice was softer than she had heard it before, the jest and levity absent.

"Most of them?" she repeated, bracing herself for a parrot comment.

"You're not the first lowborn I have invited to lunch." He leaned back in his chair, food forgotten. "They come in, swoon over my chambers, prattle about the food endlessly, try everything they can to make eyes at me. By the end of it all, they're belly up and bare on the bed."

Vhalla gaped at him. This prince was nothing like the other. She stood, her napkin falling to the floor without a thought.

A firm hand closed around her wrist.

"Don't worry," the prince cooed softly. "I know you're not like that, and I would *never* force a woman into anything she didn't want and ask for."

Her arm relaxed as he held her in place. His command over her was different than his brother's. Where Aldrik could transfix her with a single look, Prince Baldair captured her with gentle words and soft touches.

"What do you want from me then?" Vhalla asked. If he knew she wasn't about to fall between his sheets, then there was little point in her being there any longer.

"I have an idea." He finally relinquished her wrist, but Vhalla did not move.

"What is it?" Judging by the look on his face, she may not want to know.

"Even if my father wants my brother's injury to go unsaid, and Aldrik would never admit to actually needing help, saving the life of the crown prince should not go unrewarded. And a lunch is not nearly a sufficient reward." The prince smiled. "So tell me, what does your heart desire, my little library apprentice? I am a prince; mostly anything is within my power to give."

She brought her hands before her and gripped the pads of her fingers. What did her heart desire? After Sareem, after Aldrik, things didn't add up in her heart anymore.

"Nothing," she replied with a shake of her head, starting for the door again as though she knew the way out.

"You must want something." The golden-haired man was quickly in step beside her.

She looked up at his expression. Something in his eyes told her that he was only playing dumb.

"Nothing you can give," Vhalla whispered, thinking of the news that Aldrik was leaving. If she could have one wish, it would be for the crown prince to stay in the South. *He would be safe here*, the rapid beats of her heart whispered. He would be near her. Vhalla pressed her eyes closed.

"The gala," the prince said suddenly.

"What?" She waited for an explanation.

"At the end of the Festival of the Sun there is a gala in the Mirror Ballroom," the prince began.

Vhalla knew of it. She had friends who had worked the gala over the years. It was a celebration reserved only for nobility.

"Come to the gala tomorrow."

"What?" That seemed to be the only word her tongue could form.

"Think about it—the best food, music, entertainment." He grabbed both of her hands in his. Vhalla followed him as he took a step back into the room. "I'll see you fitted in a fashionable gown. And the dancing!"

He spun her in a circle beneath his arm. Vhalla tripped and stumbled. With a laugh, the prince caught her in both hands and she found herself pressed close to him for the second time in one day.

"We can work on the dancing." Prince Baldair grinned down at her.

"I can't go to the gala." She shook her head, trying to find bones in her legs once more.

"Why not?" The prince seemed undeterred.

Vhalla pried herself away from him in frustration. "Because I don't belong there." She grabbed her elbows, hugging her torso. "Apprentices don't belong with nobility."

"You don't belong in my brother's garden either," the prince retorted with a shrug.

Vhalla wished she could have kept the frown off her lips.

"He's dangerous and silver-tongued. Don't give him an opportunity to weave you into some scheme, Vhalla."

"I would like to return to the servants' halls now," she said with a quiet firmness that she didn't know her voice was capable of.

The prince stared at her for a long moment. He implied that Aldrik would weave her into a scheme, but Vhalla only felt skeptical about the man standing before her. She resisted fidgeting—barely—but didn't like the knowing glint in his eyes.

"I'll give you a fake name," he said finally. She couldn't believe he was still persisting with this insane plot. "No one will know who you are under the powder, gown, and hairdo."

Vhalla shifted her feet and braced herself to object a second time.

"It will likely be the last night before my brother and I return to the front," Prince Baldair revealed, shattering her resolve.

The last night before Aldrik would leave was the gala, tomorrow. She looked toward a far corner of the room, churning this over in her head. That was it, all the time they would have together. No matter how much she wanted to refuse the prince before her, a question remained: What if she had no other chance to see Aldrik?

"You're sure it won't be a problem?" she finally asked the waiting prince.

"No one will be wise to who you are." Baldair nodded. "Unless you think my brother will tell."

Vhalla looked askance at the prince and swore she heard a soft chuckle.

"And if people found out?" She shifted her weight uneasily from foot to foot.

"No one will." It wasn't the answer she wanted, but it was the best she was going to get.

"All right. If you wish to bestow this upon me as a secret thanks, my prince, then I shall accept it." Vhalla gave him a resolute nod.

The prince smiled, and she noticed that where Aldrik's smiles were small and normally just a turn of the corners, the Heartbreaker Prince's moved in a beautiful symmetry.

"First then." The prince extended a hand to her. "We dance."

CHAPTER 19

She did not have time to object before the prince had half-pulled, half-picked her up and led Vhalla into the center of the room. It was immediately obvious by the first turn that she had no clue what she was doing—her foot landed on top of his toes. The prince laughed, assuring her that her *dainty feet* could not harm him.

Vhalla did not enjoy dancing at first. It was awkward and it made her feel ignorant, an emotion that she generally resented and avoided at all costs. But the prince was a surprisingly gentle and encouraging instructor.

"You need to relax," he soothed.

Vhalla was very aware of his palm on her hip. "Why are we doing this again?" she mumbled.

"What do you think people do at a gala?" With a toss of his head, he cast aside a chin-length blond lock.

"I wouldn't know." Vhalla was stubbornly focused on her footwork; conversation was secondary.

"We dance." The prince laughed. He took a step back and twirled her again. This time, Vhalla understood that an extension of the arm meant she was to turn and, while she was not graceful, she did not trip. "You're getting it."

"Barely," she muttered, her eyes still on her feet.

Once she had grasped one infuriating step where they were supposed to glide across the floor in each other's arms, they moved onto a group-style dance with which Vhalla's feet had a significantly easier time. She had grown up going to harvest festivals in a neighboring town, and all the common folk knew the simple four-step that was a variation of this dance.

The prince praised her quick learning, and Vhalla kept the source of her abilities behind a small smile. After that, the Heartbreaker Prince began to have an easier time earning smiles from her.

If she did well, he would squeeze her hand. When her eyes finally lifted away from her haphazard movements, she was rewarded with a wink. Slowly, under the prince's hand and earnest encouragement, Vhalla began to enjoy herself.

It was a different kind of enjoyment than what she felt when she was around Aldrik. This feeling lacked the tension or twitching to break through the skin that she felt with Aldrik. This was simpler. It was as though the golden prince wore everything on his sleeves, and his cerulean eyes promised nothing but the truth. Vhalla stumbled when his lips barely brushed against her cheek.

"You're beautiful, you know," the prince whispered thoughtfully.

"I am not." Vhalla looked away, but their proximity did nothing to hide her hot flush.

"You are, and I wish to ensure everyone will see it at the gala." Sliding his palms down her forearms, the prince stepped away from her with a squeeze of his fingers.

Vhalla's heart was beating a bit harder than normal from the dancing.

The prince pulled a bell cord by the door, and a servant arrived a moment later. The prince engaged in a series of low-voiced orders that meant nothing to Vhalla. Sensing she was not intended to hear the conversation, she wandered to the massive windows that consumed the opposite wall.

The panorama was magnificent. The afternoon sun had the world ablaze, and she could almost feel the palpable joy of every fluttering festival pennon dancing on the breeze in the city far below. Streamers that hung from windows and were posted upon rooftops made the capital glitter.

Vhalla gave a wistful sigh.

"What's wrong?"

She hadn't heard the prince return to her side. "Nothing." Vhalla took a quarter step away, overwhelmed by his abrupt appearance at the end of her thoughts.

"Ah, Vhalla," he hummed thoughtfully. "I know when a woman says *nothing* it is always *something*."

"I don't want the festival to end," she confessed softly.

"And why is that?" There was a knowing glint to his eye.

"No reason." Vhalla shook her head, and the brief image of Aldrik vanished.

"The festival is a magical time," Prince Baldair agreed, following her gaze over the city. "Do you know anything of magic, Vhalla?"

She looked up in surprise, his eyes catching hers again. The prince's mouth swept up into a smile that made Vhalla uneasy. He knew something; he'd put things together too easily for her liking. Vhalla's words began to fail her and she was saved only by the door opening.

Prince Baldair asked nothing more about magic for the rest of the afternoon. Vhalla quickly forgot he'd asked in the first place as bolts of silk, velvet, cashmere, chiffon, fur, and fabrics she couldn't name were carried into the room by a small entourage of servants. Once more, Vhalla attempted to keep her face down, but it did little good as her curiosity got the better of her.

At the end of the entourage a portly, balding man strolled in as though he owned the entire palace. The prince introduced him as Chater. Vhalla shook his hand in a daze, the hand of the man who was the founder of the most prestigious clothing shop in all of the South. He looked her up and down.

Before she could ask a question, the fabrics she had lusted over moments prior were being held up against her skin to assess her complexion. Vhalla stood dumbly, a living model for the men surrounding her, prattling on about the gala. It was the lilac silk on her cheek that finally pulled her out of her daze.

"Black," Vhalla said suddenly, unaware she just interrupted the famous couture designer standing before her.

"Pardon?" The rotund man was startled into silence at her sudden interjection.

"I want something black." Vhalla followed the thought that had possessed her to its logical conclusion.

"My lady, black is not a customary color for a gala." Chater frowned.

Vhalla brought her fingers together, picking at her nails. She wasn't a lady. Even though she had discarded her apprentice robes for the festival, she was certain Chater knew it also.

"Well, I suppose that, if it's improper..." she mumbled. Vhalla glanced away wondering if Aldrik would be wearing black. She couldn't imagine him dressed up like a peacock, even if it was a gala.

"Now, about the purples. They're very Eastern; your complexion... you are from the East, right?" Chater was back to rummaging through bolts of cloth.

"Let her wear what she pleases," Prince Baldair said suddenly.

"My prince—"

"It'll be a special night, and the lady here has someone she wants to impress, I'm sure." Cerulean eyes caught hers, and Vhalla could do nothing more than swallow.

"Well, I will need to get additional fabric," Chater said uneasily, keen on the fact that his companions had some unspoken communication.

Vhalla's eyes followed the round man out of the room, until the muscled form of the prince broke her vision.

"Vhalla," Prince Baldair spoke softly.

"My prince?" she whispered. Just like the last time, his palm was on her cheek before she was even aware of the movement of his arm.

"Chater is right. It *is* unconventional for a gala," he noted thoughtfully.

"How unconventional is black?" Vhalla didn't shy from the prince's touch.

"Very." She was vaguely aware of his thumb moving over her cheek as he spoke. "Vhalla, you're a pretty girl, you know. You don't need to go down the unconventional road to be noticed. Good men will notice you without all that; the men you want to notice you. I'm sure good men have already noticed you."

"I-it's not that," her voice wavered. Vhalla struggled to find an explanation.

"I will show you." The golden-haired prince smiled encouragingly. "You can have your black, but I will be the one who shows you how dazzling you are."

The designer returned, and Vhalla's face flushed red hot as the prince made no haste in removing his hands from her person. She took a chaste step away. Chater was unbothered by what he had seen and continued to talk on about silhouettes and skirts. Vhalla found herself focusing more on the prince's easy smiles and his input, during the process, than the designing. What men did he think would be noticing her?

When Chater left, the sky was ablaze and she was uncertain what dress had been designed for her.

"Now remember, Vhalla," Prince Baldair offered her his elbow. She took it and they started for the door. "Come back to the servants' entrance around noon tomorrow. I'll have someone there ready to help you prepare."

"My prince, that isn't necessary," she denied with a shake of her head.

"It most certainly is!" Prince Baldair chuckled. "You don't think I'd put you in a Chater dress and have your hair and makeup be left undone, do you?"

"No, of course not..." Vhalla's free hand went up to her head, feeling the frizzy mass that was her hair.

"Don't fret, you'll be beautiful." The prince smiled, his hand on the door latch. "Just remember to save a dance for me when every man of the Court is begging to be your partner."

"I doubt that will happen." Vhalla laughed, looking up at her companion with a light smile.

"Then I have a dance?" Prince Baldair asked again, as they stepped into the hallway.

"You've already had one." Vhalla's lips pressed together in a little grin.

"Another?" He leaned closer to her.

"How could I refuse?" She laughed lightly, beginning to grow more accustomed to his proximity and casual nature.

The prince's footsteps paused, and Vhalla's gaze swung forward. Standing little more than five steps across the hall was a tall silhouette that made her jaw slacken. She felt Prince Baldair's bicep tighten under her palm, trapping it. Aldrik's eyes flicked from her to the golden-haired man at her side.

"Hello, brother," Prince Baldair hummed sweetly.

Ebony eyes bore deep holes into Vhalla. If Aldrik had heard his brother, there was no response other than a twitch under his eye. Vhalla suddenly felt very small, small enough to fall off the earth. It was uncomfortable. It hurt.

"How did the war council go?" The golden prince seemed to be pleasantly unaware of the tension that resonated between his company and his brother.

"Fine." Aldrik's voice brought her cowardly eyes back to him. The word was as cold as it was curt.

Vhalla opened her mouth to speak but there was nothing she could say, not in front of Prince Baldair.

"I look forward to marching on the North again as soon as this nonsense of a festival has ended." The elder prince's words were punctuated with the slamming of his door and the laughter of the younger.

Vhalla must have missed the joke because she didn't feel like laughing. If she tried, she may end up being sick.

With a kiss on a numb cheek, Prince Baldair left her at an entrance to the servants' quarters.

Agony, her blood had been poured out and replaced with something cold and painful. Vhalla raced through the halls and when she reached her door, she shut it as loudly as possible, which made her feel no better. She threw herself onto her bed, fumbling for her pillow to muffle a cry.

She didn't want any more princes. She was finished with nobility, and the last thing she was inclined to do was go to that pointless gala. Vhalla rolled onto her back, her eyes stinging with something resembling anger. Everyone was right. Prince Baldair was the better of the two princes. He was kind, thoughtful, lighthearted, and simple to understand.

But he didn't have the same wit as his brother. He didn't possess the same flair with his words nor grace in his step. He couldn't command a room in the same way. He certainly didn't have shoulder-length raven hair nor wonderfully pronounced cheekbones.

Vhalla groaned. She was a foolish girl. Mixing with princes only led to pain. She was done.

A knock on her door pulled her to her feet.

"Just a minute," Vhalla called, running her palms over her face. She was pleased that no tears had escaped, whatever the tears would have meant. But she was certain her eyes were red. The person knocked again and each rap sent a small tickle of pain between Vhalla's temples. She yanked open the door. "What?"

"We need to talk." Roan pushed her way through the doorframe.

"Roan, now is not—" Vhalla began to sigh as the blonde rounded on her.

"Not a good time? Too busy fraternizing with the golden prince?" Roan's finger was in her face.

"What?" Dread seeped into each beat of Vhalla's heart.

"The servants were all abuzz. Library girl with the Heartbreaker Prince, in his room, eating his food." Roan crossed her arms. "Did you think you wouldn't be noticed?"

"I didn't. I can explain."

"You don't have to explain to me." Roan shook her head, sending her curls bouncing in every direction. "It's Sareem you'll need to explain to." Vhalla shut her gaping mouth for a moment. Did Roan's eyes look red? "Vhalla, did you even think about how this will make him feel? You running off with a prince? He's a man, and he's head over heels for you. He went out of his way. He planned a whole day just for you. He arranged food and entertainment, and now you're breaking bread with another man? With a prince known for his bedroom conquests? How will that make Sareem feel?"

Vhalla's arms were limp at her sides as her shoulders sagged. Went out of his way? Planned a whole day? She brought a palm to her forehead, remembering a dark pair of accusatory eyes.

Was that what Aldrik thought? She groaned for even wondering. If that had been what Aldrik thought, did that mean the crown prince was jealous about his brother and her?

"I see you have enough sense to feel bad now." Roan threw her hands up in the air. Vhalla had never seen her friend so annoyed. "Really, he's a good man. I wasn't going to say anything, but now, after today..."

"What? What is it?" Vhalla wasn't sure if she was prepared for more.

"I don't know what you're into right now or why, but I caught Sareem in the section of mysteries today, on a festival day, of his own accord," Roan hissed. "Do you know what he was doing there?"

"What?" Vhalla asked cautiously.

"He was reading books on magic!" Roan snapped. "Something about Eradication. I don't know, he seemed really eager—too eager. Sareem has always stayed on the right side of things. I've always known you to be curious. The first to go out of her way for knowledge. I tolerated it just like I tolerated you and him. But this, I can't tolerate this. I won't let you wrap him up in magic for your curiosities."

Vhalla stared at her friend blankly, wondering if she had ever really seen the woman opposite her. Roan, her friend, the girl she had grown into a woman alongside, the person who she had shared her secrets with. When had they become so different?

"What's wrong with magic?" The defensive words escaped as fast as Vhalla thought them.

"What's wrong with magic?" Roan took a step back as though threatened.

"Really, what's wrong with it?" Vhalla persisted, taking a step forward. "Have you ever read about it? Have you ever taken the time to learn about it? Have you ever spoken to a sorcerer without closed-minded fear?"

"Why would I?" Roan squared her shoulders and planted her feet. "It's not something good people should bother with; I thought you knew that. Your father served in the War of the Crystal Caverns."

"That wasn't the fault of magic, if you'd actually read—" Vhalla began.

"I can't believe it," Roan interrupted sharply. "What happened to you? I thought we were the same. I let you have Sareem because that's what friends do. I thought you would treat him well. I let it slide that you lied to me about you and him, but I was fine because I wanted him to be happy."

"What?" Vhalla breathed. "You *let me* have Sareem?" Roan's sudden anger, her looks over the past weeks, the sense of betrayal, it all came into focus. "You like him."

"What?" It was Roan's turn to be taken aback.

"You, you're in love with Sareem." It wasn't a question. Roan shot her a seething glare. How hadn't she seen it sooner? Vhalla laughed at herself.

"What's so funny?" Roan asked defensively, no denial of the accusation in sight.

"It's funny, because you should have taken him. I don't *want* him, not as a lover."

"What? How could you not? Then why?" Roan was flabbergasted. "What do you want then?" The blonde's prior anger and frustration melted into confusion. "Your books? The Heartbreaker Prince?"

"No," Vhalla said softly. "I want a place you hardly dare to even whisper. I want the bravery to not only read, but to do. I want a man, not a library boy. A man who is tall and witty and knows more about the world than you would ever dare dream.

"So listen, I am going to go into this world, and I don't care if you and your narrow mind cannot be a part of it. Go to the Golden Bun tomorrow when the moon is a third in the sky. Meet

Sareem there in my place. Tell him you love him, tell him I don't, and go live your lives." Something in Vhalla's gut ached. She wasn't sure what from. Be it her harsh words or the harsher truth they stemmed from. She had loved these people, and they attacked her without asking her what the changes in her life meant, what the truth was. Vhalla had never known the pain of rejection like this and all it made her want to do was reject them just as coldly in return.

"What are you wrapped up in?" Roan whispered. Her anger and frustration had shifted to a sympathy that grated Vhalla.

"I'm simply learning where I'm meant to be." It was the only response, because it was the truth.

"Vhalla, listen, I—"

"I think you should go, Roan." Vhalla motioned out the door she held open before the other girl could finish her sentence.

"If you're in trouble, we can help." Roan stopped in the doorframe.

"I don't need your help," Vhalla responded coolly.

Roan met her gaze, and they stood a long moment. In all their past tiffs, this would be the time when one of them would smile, crack a joke, and they would laugh. This would be the second that they hugged and flopped onto the bed to talk about how stupid they were and then share gossip before running off to dinner.

The sun sunk lower into the sky. Vhalla wasn't about to be that girl. Apparently, neither was Roan.

The second the door closed, Vhalla rushed to the small portal that was her window, gulping in the evening breeze. Tomorrow, she would speak to the master before heading to the gala. Vhalla stared off at the horizon and wondered if she could have a window as big as Larel's in the Tower.

CHAPTER 20

It was easy to wake up and get ready the next morning. Vhalla hadn't actually slept. Her mind had spent the whole night processing everything that had happened. Things were moving faster than an avalanche, and it felt like her only option was to run *with* the moving ground under her feet—or be swept away by it.

The master would be heading to the library about now. Even during the Festival of the Sun, someone had to tend to the books, and if the majority of the apprentices were off enjoying the celebrations, then it fell to the master.

Vhalla tugged on the hem of her shirt as she made her way through the mostly-deserted halls to some of the better levels of the palace. She would have to make her conversation short and direct.

Soon she found the courage to knock on Mohned's chamber door. She waited, shifting her weight from foot to foot and fidgeting until she heard a soft shuffling sound right before the door opened. The timeworn and hunched frame of the master was swathed in a crimson robe.

"Vhalla?" Mohned adjusted his spectacles.

"Master, I need to speak with you," she said before her resolve was lost and all hope along with it.

"Very well." The master stepped to the side, permitting her entry.

Vhalla had been working with the master for seven years, but every time she entered his room she would still feel a sense of awe. Her time with princes had diminished some of that awe, but here she still felt some wonder as she looked at the bookshelves that ran the length of one wall. Each leather-bound spine seemed to look at her, as if betrayed by what she was about to do.

"What do you need, Vhalla?" The master occupied one of three chairs around a small table, motioning at one opposite.

"I, well." She sat as though pins and needles awaited her. "Master, I am so thankful for everything you have done for me all these years."

"You are welcome." The master's beard folded around his weathered smile.

"But, you see, I..." Vhalla stared at the milky eyes of the man who had taken care of her since she had first set foot in the palace. She was going to betray all he had ever done for her. He had given her everything she had, and now she was to tell him that she would leave. "I can't."

"What can you not do?" the master asked thoughtfully when words failed her.

"I can't be in the library anymore," Vhalla whispered. She saw nothing as the confession slipped past her lips and across the point of no return. The master's silence worked her into an instant frenzy of fear and guilt. "Master, I want to be. I mean, part of me wants to be. But, you see, there's this other part. There's this part of me I never knew I had—and it may be something, something special. Master Mohned, I wish I could have both but I don't think I can and I don't think I can stay as a library apprentice."

"I know, Vhalla," he said softly, cutting off her rambling.

"You know?" she blurted in surprise.

"I do." The master nodded.

"No, master, this isn't—"

"You're a Windwalker," the master said simply.

Vhalla's chest tightened. She suddenly felt raw and exposed, as though everything she knew had been stripped from her.

"M-master, that's..." She couldn't deny it, and the master did not make her.

"The prince came to me." Master Mohned leaned back in his chair. "A few months ago he came to me and asked about you by name."

"Prince Aldrik?" she whispered.

"The same." Mohned nodded. "He came to me because he thought I could help him."

"How?" Why hadn't the prince told her that he had shared her secret with someone outside the Tower?

"Well, when I was a young man, about your age, I engaged in a certain kind of research," Mohned began. "I wrote books, though many have since been confiscated, if they still exist at all."

"Books about what?" Something was on the verge of clicking into place.

"About Windwalkers," Mohned said easily.

"*The Windwalkers of the East*," Vhalla breathed. "It really was you who wrote it, then?"

"Indeed." The master nodded.

Vhalla's head spun. Her world had suddenly entered into a backward-land that made less and less sense by the minute. It was a world where not everyone in the library was fearful of who, of what she was. The master knew enough about her magic that he had written books about it, enough that a prince had spoken to him personally. She was so off-balance that Vhalla did not even have time to feel anger or betrayal at the master for not telling her sooner.

"Vhalla, do you know where I am from?" the master questioned. She shook her head. "I am from Norin."

"The West?" she pointed out dumbly.

He chuckled. "I know you have not forgotten your geography due to a day or two off work. Yes, I am Western." Vhalla had never seen Master Mohned's hair any color but white. His eyes were milky with age, and his skin had turned pale and ashy from years indoors. He could have been from anywhere.

"I was born in Norin to a poor family who lived on the edge of town, and not the good edge, mind you. I imagine my childhood wouldn't have been unlike your own had I been in the country. But I was in the city, and the city is a harsh place for anyone to grow up."

When she nodded her understanding, he continued, "My father was a guard, and my mother a kitchen maid in the castle of Norin. My parents did not have many prospects, but they always put food on the table and a lit fire in the hearth. They also knew the value of literacy for the prospect of advancement. So, one spring my father told me that he was going to take me with him to work. There was a man who was willing to teach me my letters." The master shifted in his seat, adjusting his robes before continuing.

"What started out as an occasional lesson quickly evolved into daily practice. But I soon realized that these lessons were not free." Mohned looked through her as he recounted his tale.

Vhalla thought back to her own parents. If her mother had not been able to teach her to read, Vhalla had honest doubts her parents would have been able to pay for a tutor.

"I did not want to be a burden to my family, so I began to

help my father and the guard to earn small amounts of change here or there. I was only a boy, younger than you were when you joined us, but the other guards were kind enough to keep things off the books." Mohned stroked his beard a moment. "Eventually, my father began telling me strange stories on the way home. They were stories of a land far to the east and people who could control the wind, like our own sorcerers controlled the flames. For a while, I thought my father was making up tales to entertain me."

"But one day, when I was delivering lunch, I found him sitting outside a prison cell deep in the dungeon." Mohned sighed softly. "In the cell was an old man, he was hunched and frail. He had a long beard, and his hair was uncut. He had never seen the sun. His parents were taken when they were young, and he had been born in captivity."

"A Windwalker," Vhalla whispered faintly.

Mohned nodded. "The *last* Windwalker," Mohned corrected.

"From then on I began sneaking to the dungeons in my free time," Mohned continued his story. "I'd steal lead and scraps of paper from my writing classes and take notes on what he said. Some days were better than others. Men were not made to live in cages, Vhalla; it does things to the mind that are unlike any other hardship. But I recorded his words faithfully—including his insanities. For my final project with my teacher, I compiled the stories and knowledge the Windwalker had given me into a book titled, *The Windwalkers of the East*."

Vhalla stared at her lap, unsure of how to process everything. There were forces at work that she barely understood. Men and women enslaved in the depths of the West. Aldrik's Western black eyes flashed before her mind.

"I tried to warn you." The master's shoulders hunched and his eyes seemed dull. "I saw your growing distractions. I knew the prince had confirmed what you are."

"Master," Vhalla whispered her borderline treasonous words. "Is he as dangerous as they say?"

He looked at her for a long time, just stroking his beard in thought. Vhalla swallowed and wondered if she really wanted the answer to her question. She balled her fingers into fists to keep them from shaking or fidgeting.

"I suppose it depends on who asks that question," he finally said.

"*I* am asking," Vhalla pressed. "I know what they say about him. I know they call him silver-tongued and a Fire Lord, that his eyes glow red with rage. I know he can be thoughtless when it comes to something he wants. But he's not, he's also... different."

"I think—" the master gave her a tired smile "—you already know the answer to your question."

"I want to join the Tower." Vhalla finally found enough courage to say it aloud.

"I figured as much." The master nodded, and then shook his head. Vhalla tried to make sense of the conflicting movements. "I should have told you all of this sooner. Forgive me for being a selfish old man, Vhalla, but I suppose I didn't want to see you go." She smiled softly, as if that would ever upset her. "I envisioned your opportunities in the library; I wanted you to replace me someday."

Vhalla inhaled sharply. There was a time where that would have been her dream. But her dreams had changed.

"Thank you, master," Vhalla said thoughtfully. "I wish I could have been that for you."

"No. You are destined for far greater things." The master began to struggle to his feet, and Vhalla stood as well, realizing their conversation had reached its natural end.

She wanted to think of something else to say, overcome with an overwhelming desire to continue their discourse in any way possible. There had to be more to talk about, things she needed to tell the master and he needed to tell her. Perhaps they could order a light breakfast and reminisce. Vhalla thought frantically for something to elongate their discussion—at the fringe of her thoughts was the frightening realization that she had just set change in motion.

"It is the last day of the festival," the master pointed out thoughtfully, ignorant of Vhalla's internal turmoil. "I will contact the Minister of Sorcery tomorrow. No one intends to do any work today."

"That's fair," Vhalla agreed with a nod.

A gnarled hand closed around her shoulder. "I wouldn't look so scared if I were you." The master was not as ignorant as she thought. "I think your shadow is looking out for you."

"My shadow?" Vhalla whispered.

The master only smiled. "And Vhalla," he continued without further explanation, "You have been like a daughter to me all these years. Don't think you can walk out with any expectations of visiting me often."

"Of course not, master." Vhalla's eyes suddenly burned.

"I will tell you one more thing." The master paused at the door. "The prisoner told me that it was a shame the East and West could not have worked together. He said, 'Fire needs air to live. Air fuels fire, stokes it, and makes it burn brighter and hotter than it ever could alone. But too much air will snuff it completely, just as too many flames will consume all the air. They are far greater than the sum of their parts together, but are equally as dangerous to each other's existence.'"

CHAPTER 21

Vhalla ate breakfast alone. Sareem was nowhere to be seen, which was easier than the looks and silent treatment from Roan. The blonde sat with Cadance and let the young girl jabber on as though she were interested in the inner workings of a twelve year old's mind. Vhalla glanced over from time to time but Roan never made eye contact.

It was for the better. Roan may not understand now, but Vhalla was out of her life. After learning that Sareem had been looking up books on Eradication, she had no doubt that the two would go on to live their happy little normal lives as far from magic and her as possible. Vhalla left her tray and mostly untouched food at the receiving window. She stole one last look at Roan.

Yet, despite it all, Vhalla wished she could have told her friend goodbye. Roan looked over suddenly and Vhalla quickly stepped out of the hall before any exchange could happen.

Apologize to Roan after things were settled with the Tower, Vhalla decided. After the initial shock had faded and people had a chance to absorb her transition, she would find Roan alone, and explain everything. She would apologize to her friends for the secrets and harsh words.

Maybe, Vhalla paused to look through a window at the rising sun, she would even tell her friend about the prince. Aldrik would be in the North by then and who knew when, if ever, he would be coming back. Her gut felt like it had been stabbed by an ice-cold dagger. The last time he had gone to war he almost died. Vhalla gripped her shirt above her stomach.

It made her walk all the faster to the servants' entry to the royal halls. She had to see him tonight. She had to tell him that she had decided to join the Tower. She had to thank him for helping her all the weeks they had been together. Vhalla leaned against a wall for support. She had to tell him how she felt— whatever that was.

Vhalla tilted her head back, taking a slow breath. Too many things needed to be said. She could only pray she would find the time to say them.

Less than an hour later, Vhalla was ushered through the small door that blended seamlessly with the wall beyond.

The servant waiting for her spoke little and locked the passage behind them before leading her down the vaguely familiar hall. Vhalla said nothing, skeptically wondering if this was one of the people who had spread rumors of her and the Heartbreaker Prince.

The man turned away from the prince's chambers and walked up some narrow side-steps. Vhalla wondered if Aldrik was just beyond reach, preparing for the gala himself. These thoughts, and anything else, were lost as she was brought to a guest chamber.

While not as lavish as the prince's quarters, Vhalla was mesmerized by the large sitting area with an attached bedroom. Connected to that was a private bath. Vhalla's hands touched every inch of white marble, porcelain, and gold within reach. It was physical verification that the splendor before her was not a magnificent dream. Her fingers rested on two gold handles attached to matching hot and cold spigots.

Turning the knobs, Vhalla sat in wonder of the magic that was hot water on demand. The servant and staff baths had running water, but it was whatever temperature happened to come out of the tap that day. Sometimes there were only large barrels to fill smaller bowls to take a sponge bath with.

"Ouch!" Vhalla snatched her hand back from the steaming water.

"Be careful, my lady," a servant girl said from the doorway. Vhalla stood, looking at the two silent shadows who had taken over her care. Her flesh was pink, but it wasn't a bad burn.

"I'm not a lady," Vhalla said softly, opening and closing her tingling fingers.

"We know," a darker skinned girl replied, clearly from the northern regions of the West. "Would you like help washing?"

"No, I can do it." Vhalla shook her head, looking away in shame.

Vhalla drew her own bath and stripped—after the servants had left the room. She wondered if it was customary for royalty and nobility to have assistance while bathing. In the servants' baths everyone bathed together, so it was not the idea of eyes on her that left her wondering. Just the notion of what nobility was unable to do on their own.

She wondered if Aldrik needed help while he bathed. Vhalla laughed aloud, blowing bubbles into the water with her giggles of amusement. *No*, she decided, *Aldrik most certainly did not need help bathing.*

The servants provided her with towels once she finished. The cloths were perfumed, and she smelled of flowers and sweet soaps. Vhalla wore a silk robe and sat in a chair in the center of the room, toweling herself dry.

The darker skinned of the two servants began tugging and pulling at Vhalla's hair, vigorously shaking the water out. The Eastern woman began filing Vhalla's nails. Vhalla looked disappointedly at her fingers. She really should stop picking at them when nervous.

"Why are you doing this?" Vhalla finally asked, unable to handle the silence any longer.

"Because you are a noble lady from a mysterious and foreign land." The Eastern servant grinned up at her. The servant behind her snorted, and Vhalla rolled her eyes.

"You know who I am," Vhalla said, unsure of what made her so determined to find out the answer.

"Well, that's why we're helping you," the woman with her fingers in Vhalla's hair said thoughtfully. Vhalla attempted to turn and look at the person speaking, but she was only left immobile as her hair snagged on something. "Don't move, idiot." The servant sighed. "Listen, even if we weren't ordered to help you, we still wouldn't mind."

"Mmhm." The Eastern servant had shifted to Vhalla's feet. Vhalla wondered why she needed her toenails done as well. Wouldn't they be in shoes? "We asked around after Chater was called in. The Heartbreaker Prince has entertained lots of ladies for lunches and, well, you know what else."

Vhalla shifted in her seat at a look from the servant. They all thought she had slept with the prince. Every one of them assumed she had crawled into his bed. Vhalla frowned, even Roan must have.

"I didn't sleep with him," Vhalla said defensively.

"You don't have to be so modest around us, we've been here since we were ten." The woman was rolling Vhalla's hair around strange circular spools.

"I didn't," Vhalla insisted.

"Well, if you didn't, it makes it all the more peculiar," the

Eastern servant continued. "Prince Baldair has never ordered one of his common women to be prepared for a formal function. It's all on the wrong side of the sheet, hush between the pillows. You're the first he's ever brought out in public."

"But, I, this is not..." Vhalla wished she had something to quench her dry throat. She and Prince Baldair? Was there more than she had previously thought?

"So, we want to show all those stuck up nobles that we're just as good as they are." The woman who had previously been working on Vhalla's hair went over to a large wardrobe. The doors thrown open, Vhalla saw a single garment: a long black gown with a bustier top, capped sleeves, and a skirt of endless draping.

"Is that mine?" Vhalla barely heard her own words. The wonder of it sounded like a chorus in her ears.

"A Chater original," the girl affirmed with a nod.

Vhalla said nothing during the process of getting into the dress. Her ribcage was squished into the most frustrating garment that she had never even seen before. It was laced in the back and tightened to accentuate her figure. The servants called it a corset, but Vhalla could think of a handful of other colorful words to use.

They painted her face and applied lotion to her whole body. Vhalla was like a living doll and equally clueless. So she sat, mostly silent, and allowed the servants to accomplish their tasks.

The dress fit her perfectly. The bustier top was silk with velvet sleeves and skirt. Vhalla shamelessly ran her palms over the fabric. It felt soft, like what she imagined clouds felt like.

By the time the girls pulled the last curler from her hair, the sun hung low in the sky. They touched up her curls with a rod stoked over coals, after much assuring to Vhalla that it would not burn her hair. Skeptical by the steam and scent that her hair gave as they wrapped locks around the poker, Vhalla obliged them.

Eventually, the servants took a step back and assessed their work. They would touch up this or that before reassessing. With a final nod, they pulled her to her feet.

"Are you ready?" The Easterner helped her slip her feet into heels. Vhalla's ankles wobbled unsteadily.

"Am I?" Vhalla asked, thankful the young woman had not yet let go.

"There's a mirror behind you," she said with a small smile. There was a wistful longing on her cheeks, and Vhalla felt a twinge of guilt for having this opportunity. She turned in the direction of the mirror. Awkward in the tall shoes, she tripped on her skirt—almost toppling forward were it not for the Eastern servant's support. The young woman laughed loudly. "You need to work on that, Miss Lady."

Vhalla didn't even hear the jest. Staring back at her in the mirror was a woman who Vhalla could not recognize. Frizzy and untamable hair had been curled, falling over her shoulders in almost ringlets. In the black gown, her amber-hued skin almost seemed to glow golden. The hazel of her eyes lit with the touch of smoky shadow upon her lids, enhanced by a dark liner. Vhalla took another step closer.

It wasn't like her palm mirror in her room. She didn't have to bob her head around to attempt to see her whole face. Vhalla could see her whole body, and she stared in awe. Her arms were scrawny and her chest wasn't much to speak of, even with the help of the corset. But her waist was small and her neck looked long and regal. She looked—

Vhalla couldn't bring herself to even think it.

"You're beautiful." The woman who had done her hair filled in the word for her.

"Thank you," Vhalla whispered. There wasn't anything else

she could say, but it wasn't nearly enough for what these people had given her. She looked like a lady, a real lady.

"Let's practice walking in those shoes before we turn you over to the hounds of polite society." The Easterner took her hand and began to lead her around the room.

Vhalla walked around the guest rooms, hand in hand with each of the young women. Like children learning their first steps, it was a slow process but Vhalla eventually took to it. By the time they called for a servant to escort her to the gala, Vhalla hadn't tripped in over fifty steps.

"Will Prince Baldair be escorting me?" she asked the servant who led her down a small side hall.

"He is already greeting the gala's attendees." The servant kept his eyes forward.

"Am I late?" Vhalla wondered if her walking practice had gotten her into trouble.

"No, my lady, you are on time," the servant responded.

Vhalla wondered how she could be on time if the prince had already arrived to greet others, but she kept her ignorant questions to herself.

Eventually the hallway merged with a major hall of the palace. On one end, two doors stood open wide. Vhalla saw the fabled glittering chandeliers of the Mirror Ballroom hanging from the ceiling before its second story entrance. The servant who escorted her gave a nod to a different man positioned at the door before turning away without a word.

"Wait, where are you going?" Vhalla asked, suddenly aware of how alone she was.

"You didn't think I'd walk in with you, did you?" The man turned with a chuckle. "Good luck, Lady of the Common Folk."

Vhalla stood dumbly, watching the man walk away. She listened to the sounds drifting up through the doors. It sounded like half the city was in that bright and mysterious ballroom.

Vhalla looked down the opposite end of the hall. A few people were making their way up, but nothing would stop her from turning and running back to her room.

Taking a step away from the doors, she looked at where the servant had disappeared. *This wasn't her.* She wasn't some lady from a foreign land. She was Vhalla Yarl, the farmer's daughter whom no one expected to be able to read or write. Her feet stopped.

That wasn't all she was. Vhalla turned and started for the doors before her resolve failed her. She already had secrets. She was the first Windwalker. She was something the crown prince had claimed he would protect. Vhalla's toes stopped at the edge of the light in the doorframe. She didn't yet know what she was about to blossom into, but it was far greater than a library girl.

"Are you ready?" the servant asked softly.

"Yes. No." Vhalla swallowed and nodded. "Yes."

"Listen to the name I say." He took a step out into the light, drawing a deep breath. "Presenting, Lady Rose."

Vhalla stepped out into the light and was almost blinded. If one full-length mirror had been overwhelming, the walls of the Mirror Ballroom were enough to make her feel dizzy. A long stairway challenged her footing, and Vhalla descended, trying to keep a smile on her face.

The room was reduced to hushed whispers, even though the ambient music continued. People were multiplied by the reflective walls and Vhalla began to feel her resolve diminish under all the prying eyes. Why had Baldair chosen the name Rose? It clearly was a fake name. Who was actually named after a flower?

She walked slowly, determined not to fall, her eyes darting throughout the room as she tried to hear the hushed words from the crowd.

They were not whispering about the name, Vhalla quickly

realized. It looked as though all the colors of the library's stained glass ceiling had come to life. Vibrant hues dotted the large dance floor waiting beneath her. Southern blue seemed to be the preferred shade, with a few reds of the West; there were even purples of the East sprinkled in. There were no other dark colors.

Vhalla scanned the crowd almost frantically until her eyes fell on a white marble dais far opposite the stairs. There, standing with the royal family was a prince, her prince. Although the rest of the royal family wore gold and white silks, he stood all in black, as if a waiting counterpart for her ensemble.

Aldrik's face was dumbstruck. He hadn't even noticed, or didn't care, that his jaw had fallen loose. Vhalla smiled brightly at his wide eyes as she strode over to the royal family. The crown prince gaped at her openly the whole way.

CHAPTER 22

The whole room faded away. The high society could keep their judgments and jeers; they would not touch Vhalla tonight. For several long steps the only person she saw was him, the only judgment that mattered was his—and it felt amazing. The smoldering pair of dark eyes hungrily fed on her every movement.

Alone, she approached the dais and stopped at ground level. Vhalla attempted to dip gracefully into a curtsy, just as Baldair taught her. She had no doubt that one day of training would not make her a graceful swan of high society, but she didn't fall upon her nose. That was good enough. Vhalla began a mantra in her head to get her though the night, *smile, grace, pose, float, smile.*

"Welcome to our gala, Lady Rose," the Emperor boomed warmly, *not unlike Prince Baldair,* she thought amusingly. Vhalla tried to find Aldrik in the muscular and weathered man. She tried to imagine Emperor Solaris without the closely cropped beard along his jaw, seeing if she could see any of the eldest prince's striking features. "We hope you enjoy the celebrations."

"Thank you, my lord." Vhalla kept her eyes averted. She had

just become accustomed to speaking with princes. The idea of exchanging words with the Emperor himself was still overwhelming.

"Baldair," the Empress's voice interrupted. "I thought you told me you invited this one yourself."

"I did," Baldair announced loud enough to earn some not so subtle stares from a group of ladies at Vhalla's right.

"Did you not also inform her what was proper to wear to a gala?" the Empress sniffed in her airy tones. Nothing about her speech sounded like Aldrik. "Lady Rose, my son is well versed in fashions, you should have taken his input to heart."

Vhalla opened her mouth, unsure of what to say. The whispers around her resumed, and her tongue had gone fat and limp. Cerulean eyes stared her down.

"I think she looks stunning." Aldrik finally spoke and his voice was soothing to Vhalla's sizzling nerves. Their eyes met and the corner of his mouth curled up slightly as he looked at her. Vhalla looked down again to hide a blush.

"Oh my, dear." The Empress turned to the Emperor in a hush. "See, he is a bad influence. People will begin to think such dress is acceptable."

"Come, let us relax and enjoy our evening." The Emperor dismissed his wife, as well as Vhalla, with a wave of his hand.

Pleased to no longer be the center of attention, Vhalla fled quickly to the outer edge of the room. People parted to make way for her, though no one addressed her directly. She dared a look back at Aldrik, who was greeting the guest announced after her.

He looked closed off again and sounded curt, but she savored the image of his face in her mind, replaying that stunned look again and again. If she went back to her room right now, the evening would be a success. As the sky grew darker outside, more of the finer players in society began to filter in. Vhalla pretended to be interested in their greetings to the royal family, but really it was an excuse to look at Aldrik.

He wore a long black, double-breasted coat. It fell to right above his knees and had a slit in the back for movement. It was unbuttoned at the top and a perfect triangle was pinned open to show a white-collared shirt with a wide, black necktie that was tucked into a vest beneath his jacket.

It wasn't quite like the neck ruffles some of the men were sporting, but it did have a bit of volume to it. The jacket was stitched with patterns of the sun, all in black that caught the light perfectly as he moved. Golden rope decorated his cuffs and arms. Beneath, he wore a pair of black trousers—Vhalla was beginning to grow suspicious if he actually owned any other color—with more golden piping down the sides. His normal boots were replaced with well-polished, black dancing shoes. Aldrik's hair was the same as he'd always worn it, save for a golden circlet that was simple in design, a flat rectangular band across his brow.

She found she much preferred his fashion to the colors and pomp of everyone else. Even Prince Baldair had ruffles coming out of his sleeves and peeking out around his coat, ruffles that bounced when he moved; the Southern styles made Vhalla want to laugh.

From time to time, Aldrik would glance in her direction. She'd give him a small smile in reply and enjoy the heated darkness of his eyes. After the formalities had been exchanged and most of the guest list was in attendance, the Emperor called for the gala to begin.

The minstrels paused, adjusted their instruments, and picked up a new tune. Vhalla attempted to count the beat as the golden prince had told her to do, but she was hopeless at the technical aspects of music. Instead, she simply hummed along to the instrumental of a classic Southern ballad and tapped her foot as the dance floor filled. She didn't even notice the royal family had stepped off their pedestal until Prince Baldair was upon her.

"My lady, fairer than the flower of her namesake, will you grant me the honor of this dance?" All his charm was mustered as he dipped into a half bow. Vhalla blinked at the idea of a prince bowing to her. He looked up expectantly at her silence.

"The first dance?" she hissed nervously. Suddenly aware of how many eyes were on her, Vhalla quickly nodded. It was only the expected thing to do when a prince asked you to dance. "Of course, my prince."

Vhalla curtsied and a calloused hand pulled her onto the dance floor. It was the dance he had taught her, three steps and repeat. Vhalla struggled to remember his steps, but her feet did little more than clumsily shuffle along.

Luckily, Prince Baldair had years of training and was a stunning dancer. He guided her effortlessly, navigating her across and between other dancers as they turned. His showmanship made up for her clumsy feet, so much so that she actually felt like she could dance. His hands were gentle and soft as they guided her and his arms supportive to prevent her from falling.

"What are you doing?" she whispered.

"You promised me a dance." He flashed her a dazzling smile.

"Yes, but everyone is watching." Vhalla glanced over his shoulders at the people lining the dance floor.

"What else would they do?" Baldair chuckled, extending his arm. Vhalla turned as expected before he drew her close once more. He smelled of something warm, like vanilla, and Vhalla wondered if he could smell the sweet perfumes that the servant girls had applied behind her ears. There was no question as he leaned in, his breath ruffling her hair over her ear. "If you walk into this gala in black, you will leave the-strange-lady-that-knew-nothing. Dancing with the Heartbreaker Prince for his first dance? That makes you a dark and mysterious woman everyone wants to meet."

He pulled away, and Vhalla looked up at him, allowing the rest of the room to dissolve for one moment. Her feet moved without thought, and she simply looked at the man who led her across the floor.

If she had more time to get to know the man known as Heartbreaker, what she would learn?

"Smile, Vhalla. You're stunning when you do," the prince encouraged with a smile of his own, and Vhalla relaxed under his hands.

They danced the rest of the song and halfway into the next before there was a tap on his shoulder.

"My prince, may I cut in?" A gentleman gave a small bow.

Prince Baldair pulled her close to his side by her waist; he leaned in dramatically as if he were sharing some dark secret. "I told you so," he whispered in her ear. Then he continued more loudly, "You may, good sir, but only so long as I do not see you acting a fool, or I shall have to claim the lady back from you!" Both men chuckled and Vhalla was passed along.

She danced with three more men she had never met, all of whom seemed nice enough and complimented her attire. They seemed fascinated with who she was and where she was from, apparently looking to pin the color choice on some foreign and peculiar cultural difference. She answered as vaguely as possible, keeping the illusion. For one night she could be this mysterious lady.

Four songs later, the band struck up a large group dance in which people were paired at random before turning, circling, doing a small dance, and exchanging partners. After her first two partners, Vhalla found herself eye to eye with the Head Elect of the Senate.

"Lady Rose." Egmun smiled as their palms and forearms

touched. They circled around each other. "Or should I call you Vhalla Yarl?"

He gripped her hand and pulled her to him roughly. Vhalla made a small squeak of surprise, but everything else was lost as the man leaned in close to her. She was trapped between decorum and a sincere wish to push the man away with force.

"Look at you, playing the part of a proper lady. But we both know who you really are." He held her too closely; she needed air. "Just a library girl, a commoner of low birth and no title to speak of. Then again," he sneered at her as they linked arms, "you're not just a library girl, you're a library girl who takes secret lunches with the emotionally stinted crown prince."

"I don't know what you're talking about." Vhalla looked at the other couples dancing around them, praying they weren't overheard.

"Oh, don't play ignorant. Tell me, is *Lady Rose* Prince Baldair's pet and Vhalla Yarl Prince Aldrik's?" Vhalla's mouth fell open. "I've hardly even seen the crown prince with a woman, and I have known him for quite a few years more than you. Are you someone special? Tell me, has Prince Aldrik finally taken another lover?"

Vhalla's cheeks flushed against every scrap of will she had, and the senator watched each growing shade of red with a dangerous glint to his eye. Taking a deep breath, she shook her head and dug deep for her diminishing supply of courage.

"Please excuse me, senator, I fear I have overheated from all the dancing," Vhalla announced boldly.

"Certainly." The senator released her, save for her hand; she fought a grimace as his lips brushed upon its back. "Perhaps you may retreat into the gardens for some air. I hear those dressed in black prefer the darkness."

The music shifted and partners changed. Vhalla stepped out of the dancing reel. She couldn't stop herself from looking back.

Egmun was smiling and carrying on as though nothing had happened. Vhalla started for the balcony that overlooked the water gardens. She felt a pair of eyes on her back, lifting the hairs at the nape of her neck. She turned, but couldn't find anyone's gaze to pin it upon. Vhalla brought her hands together and fidgeted as she plunged through the crowd and into the mostly unpopulated night.

The terraced water gardens had a grandeur that she had never seen before, with wide semi-circular structures overlapping at different intervals of height. The wall of each was thin white marble and the water contained within was flawless and still, reflecting the night sky like a mirror. Marble stairs led down from the balcony and cut a winding path through the inky blackness of the water. Small, circular plant gardens had been placed at varying intervals along its lazy way, before it wrapped back around again on the balcony's other side.

She clutched the railing and took a deep breath of the clean night air. How dare someone speak of her and Aldrik in such a manner! It wasn't as though they were... Vhalla looked out across the garden with a small sigh, *what were they anyway?* Briefly, something in the darkness shifted before leaning back against a tree. Vhalla was down the steps without glancing over her shoulder.

The stars stretched out above and around her as she walked to that small oasis of marble and greenery. She stepped up onto the platform, holding her dress, careful not to trip, and smiled faintly. This was what she had come for.

Aldrik stepped away from the tree's trunk.

"What are you doing here?" The question was slightly accusatory, but there was no aggression in the prince's voice.

"Your brother invited me." Vhalla walked under the shadow of the foliage.

Aldrik snorted in disgust. "A woman comes at my brother's

call." He took a half step away from her. "I have heard every variation of that before."

"I didn't come for him," Vhalla whispered softly. The gardens were surrounded by a tall palace wall that blocked most of the mountain winds. The prince heard her with little problem, his retreat stalled. "I came to see *you*."

"Me?" He looked back in disbelief.

"Yes, you." Vhalla laughed softly. Her chest hurt, and she couldn't decide if it was from happiness or heartbreak. "And you're out here trying to skip the party."

"I could not stand watching all of them, my brother, dance with you," he said defensively.

"Well, why didn't you ask me then?" She tilted her head to the side, a touch coy.

"Fine. Vhalla Yarl, may I have this dance?"

He held out his hands, and she crossed the remaining distance. His right hand timidly landed on her waist and her right hand settled in his left. She placed her free hand on his shoulder and, ever so faintly, they heard the echo of music across the water. He stepped first.

It was a slow dance with deliberate steps. He didn't possess the flair that his brother did, but he didn't need to. Vhalla felt his movements through his palms, the shifts in his waist, the closeness of this way or that. They danced together to a faint melody drifting across the water, among the star-filled pools, with the heavens shining down upon them. She closed her eyes and felt him with every sense she possessed.

He turned and pulled her a half step closer. She obliged with a full step. It was impossible to move without touching somewhere. Each brush of fabric or turn of the head sent chills through her. When his hand shifted from her waist to the small of her back, gooseflesh dotted her arms. She looked up at him and he met her eyes. The silence wasn't awkward or stressful; it spoke more eloquently between them than they had ever been able to speak with words.

The song finished, but he held her there. Looking away, she clutched the seams of his jacket and rested her left cheek on his chest. Aldrik stiffened briefly, and Vhalla held her breath, expecting to be pushed away. He let her hand go and trailed his fingers down her arm to her shoulder, before it rested with his right on her lower back. His skin was warm, almost hot, and she could feel the outline of his hand even through the corset and dress. Vhalla moved her free hand to his other shoulder, and they stood there together for a long time in silence. He rested his cheek on her forehead and took a breath. Vhalla willed with everything she had for the world to stop, so she could linger in the moment eternally.

In those fleeting moments, the complexities of titles and who they were faded into base emotion. She wanted, she *needed* him. This man, who was regarded as little more than a curt and dark monster, had somehow claimed her without ever truly touching her before this night.

"Vhalla." Her eyes fluttered closed at the mention of her name. "First the library boy, then Baldair. I am envious of them."

"Why?" She needed to hear the answer.

"Because they seem to have no trouble finding reasons to be around you. And I..." A deep chuckle resonated through the crown prince's chest into the ear she had pressed against it. "I struggle to find a reason, and when I am with you, I struggle still."

There was something strange about his voice. It held a barely audible huskiness that sent heat to the pit of her stomach. Vhalla tightened her grip on his clothes.

"You shouldn't struggle for anything. You're the crown prince," she breathed into the crisp autumn air.

"I may be a prince," he said as his lips brushed her ear lightly.

"But I would trade it all to be a common man, even if only for tonight."

His lips made her knees feel weak. Vhalla shifted her head to look up at him; Aldrik wore an unfamiliar and heavy expression. She wished she had years with him to hear his stories, to talk about his pains and his joys, to continue to enjoy slow afternoons together, to work out the strange struggle between them that was both irresistible and undeniable. But a clock ticked in the back of her mind. Dawn would come far too soon.

"Are you really leaving?" she whispered faintly. He sighed and glanced away. Vhalla lifted her hand and cupped his cheek, turning his face back toward her. He didn't resist her touch, and she searched his pained expression.

"I do not know the exact hour. But yes, soon," Aldrik confessed in a deep rumble.

She bit her lower lip and shifted her hand up his face. Her fingertips grazed his pronounced cheek, his brow, and forehead. Vhalla paused, stopping on the golden crown that was nothing more than a barrier between them.

"Then, for one night, if I can pretend I am a lady of noble birth—" She grabbed the circlet gently with her fingertips and lifted it off his brow. He stiffened as she dropped it to the ground "—can you pretend you are a common man?"

Vhalla wasn't sure what she fully implied as his eyes grew wide. Aldrik's lips parted in surprise. All she knew was that if he was to leave, she didn't want to leave without experiencing his closeness and warmth.

"I'm afraid, if you leave..." she choked out, thinking of a rainy night that seemed so long ago.

Aldrik lifted his hand to her cheek and lightly ran his fingertips down her face, as if he was worried she may break at any moment. Very briefly, his thumb touched her lips, and his arm tightened around her waist, eliminating any remaining distance between them. Vhalla felt him along her whole body; his warmth, his presence enveloped her.

"Vhalla," he whispered with a voice as dark as midnight. His nose was almost touching hers.

"Aldrik," she breathed faintly, as though it were a prayer. No word had ever tasted sweeter on her tongue.

As she felt his warm breath on her face, he paused and turned his head toward the city, his expression drastically changed. Vhalla looked over, frustrated and confused.

The first fiery explosion rang out through the clear night, sending shockwaves across the capital of the Empire.

CHAPTER 23

A second before the blast, Aldrik turned his body so that his back was toward the explosion. His hand was buried in Vhalla's hair as he pressed her protectively to his chest. She clung to him, trembling. Her ears had not yet stopped buzzing when the second explosion rolled across the mountainside, and Aldrik's arms pulled her tighter. She cried her fear into his chest at the mind-numbing sound. For a moment there was silence, and she tried to catch her breath. However, the stillness was short-lived as slow-growing noise began to float up from the city below.

Screams, cries, and wails carried up the mountainside, and Vhalla pressed her hands over her ears. Aldrik continued to hold her tightly while she regained a shaky control.

"Wh-what?" she asked frantically, all words and thoughts falling to the rising panic. His grip loosened as he looked over his shoulder. Vhalla shifted her body so her eyes could follow his.

A fire was already beginning to sweep through the city, jumping from house to house. Smoke began to blot out the stars and cover the city in a foul, orange haze.

Vhalla took a step away from him, toward the scene.

"Where—" she stammered "—where is that?" Her brain felt scrambled from noise and shock.

"Vhalla, you need to return to the palace. *Now*." Aldrik's tone was sharp and he grabbed her forearms, refusing to let her wander from him.

She resisted his tugs, glued to the scene. Something fitted into place in her mind.

"Vhalla." Aldrik moved in front of her, a hand on her cheek. "The guards will be mobilized. I'll go help, myself," he said, trying to be assuring, but his voice sounded strained and panicked. "But I *need you* to go back in the palace where it's safe."

Vhalla stepped to the side of him and looked back at the scene. Her eyes widened as her brain returned to life. She inhaled sharply, her breathing rough.

"R-Roan, Sareem."

"What?" She barely heard Aldrik ask, he sounded far away.

Vhalla pointed. "That's where the square of the sun and moon is, isn't it?" her voice raised in fear.

"I don't know, Vhalla." Aldrik tried to take her hand again.

"It is." She looked back, and there was no doubt. "Roan, Sareem! Aldrik, my friends are there!"

"So were half the commoners in the city. Now, *back in the palace*," he snapped and grabbed her wrist with force.

"No!" she cried, wrenching her hand back. "No! They need my help." Vhalla turned and felt a hot wind rise up to the sky, carrying the smell of fire. She remembered her confrontation with Roan, telling her of Sareem's plans to meet her at the bakery near the plaza. Vhalla had never told Sareem anything different, and Roan most certainly would have gone to claim the man she loved. Vhalla's chest tightened. She hadn't apologized to either of them. She hadn't even had a chance to explain what was happening to her.

Without any thought, Vhalla was running, ignoring the prince's cries at her back. Her fancy heeled shoes were soon left behind on the marble, and Vhalla moved quickly in her bare feet. One of the terraces stretched outward to the top of the wall and Vhalla sprinted across the shallow water, her skirts quickly growing waterlogged and heavy. She heard a splash and looked behind her. Aldrik had given chase.

"Vhalla! Stop this! You're not going to be able to help them!" he cried.

But she wasn't ready to hear reason. All that filled her ears were the sounds of screams. All that filled her nose was smoke and death. All that filled her eyes was a burning inferno closing upon two people she had known for half her life—friends she had foolishly shut out.

Vhalla reached the wall and hoisted herself up. It was much taller on the other side, taller than even the bookcases of the Imperial Library. She looked down a moment, uncertain.

"Vhalla, they may not even be there." Aldrik had caught up with her. His breathing was fairly easy where hers was labored.

Vhalla began to rip at the gathering on her skirt, starting a tear between her calves and knees. "They were there," she insisted.

"You don't know. Come down."

"Sareem would have waited all night for me!" She choked on a sob of guilt as she looked at the sky. It was past their arranged time to meet. If she had just told him the truth, he and Roan may have spent the evening in the palace as the three of them had so many years prior. Burdened with guilt and grief, Vhalla jumped off the other side of the wall.

The air rushed past her ears and around her, blowing the remaining skirt this way and that. Vhalla braced herself but she landed lightly in a crouch.

"Vhalla!" Aldrik called from atop the wall.

She stared up at him, offering an apologetic expression before plunging herself into the chaos of the streets.

While she had lived in the capital all of her adult life, Vhalla had spent most of it in the palace. The alleyways could be tricky and maze-like even on the best of days, but now they seemed like passageways through the horrors of the afterlife for evildoers. People pushed against her from every which way, fleeing from the place she was struggling to reach. Some had burns covering their bodies, their clothing hanging in tattered rags. Others had open wounds with blood flowing from them.

Vhalla stepped in something warm and soft that squished between her toes. She looked down in horror to see the remnants of a man who had been trampled to death by the stampede of people. His skull had been crushed and his bones shattered on the street. Unable to handle the sight a second longer, Vhalla darted down a dead-end alley and vomited, screamed as she stared at her bloody feet, and her stomach heaved again.

A third explosion thundered through the air. Vhalla cried out and dropped to the ground covering her ears. She was much closer this time, and she could hear the houses groan around her as the earth shuddered with the force of the blast.

"Vhalla! Come here!" a man's voice cried loudly, and she looked up. Aldrik stood atop the palace wall. He had run parallel to her as she descended into the city, but the wall was going to make a turn.

She clutched her knees to her chest and trembled, her mind going numb momentarily. A woman's cry pierced the air, jolting Vhalla back to her senses. Roan and Sareem were still out there. She stood and looked back again at Aldrik with apologetic eyes.

"You stupid girl!" he roared and then jumped from the wall.

First, he landed onto a thatched roof not too far below, ran along it to a single story home that lined Vhalla's alley and rolled down until he caught the edge of the roof. Releasing himself, he landed fairly easily and stomped over to her. Vhalla could almost feel his palpable anger as he grabbed her arm.

"You—are—completely—mad," he ground out through gritted teeth, shaking her.

"You didn't have to come!" She shrugged him off with a step back.

"You must think me soulless if you really thought I'd sit back and watch you gallivant to your death!" he shouted, though in the mayhem she could still barely hear him.

"Are you forcing me back into the castle?" Vhalla asked, ready to turn and run once more.

"I should," he snapped. "But I can see you desire nothing more than to be the martyr, and since no one else is here to prevent that, the task falls to me. So lead on." She looked at him in shock. "Go!" he snarled.

She ran with him at her back.

Back in the pandemonium, no one seemed to notice—or care—that the crown prince was among them. Vhalla saw women clutching babes to their breasts, struggling to escape from the horrors below. She saw an old man simply sitting on a step, waiting for his fate to come.

Slowly the crowd began to thin and the temperature rose.

"Vhalla." She turned. Aldrik pulled off his coat and handed it to her. She looked at him strangely. "For the heat, and for some protection from the flames." Vhalla considered the orange glow on the path before them and took his coat with a nod. He rolled his eyes and pulled off his shoes and socks.

"Don't you need them?" she asked as she quickly donned the garments. The shoes were too large, even with the laces as tight as possible, but they were better than nothing.

"Remember who I am before you ask stupid questions." He rolled up his sleeves and stood barefoot in his trousers, white shirt, black vest, and tie. She might have laughed at the sight, if the world wasn't ending around her.

Vhalla turned back to the road ahead. Soon they began to pass more dead bodies than living ones. The smell of burning flesh assaulted her senses. After they were six flaming houses deep, the scent forced her to stop and retch again. Aldrik placed his hand on her back and she looked at him weakly.

"I don't smell it anymore," he explained. His face had taken on a freakish stillness, whereas Vhalla felt she was slowly losing herself to madness. There was no choice now but to press on.

The fire popped and cracked around her, and she heard a building collapse not far away. The square wasn't far now. Aldrik used his magic to gain control over smaller flames, to extinguish fires with waves of his arms as they went, clearing their path.

Vhalla came to a sharp halt.

Bodies littered the square. Men, women, children scattered about with their remains twisted in unnatural positions, their faces locked in horror even in death. Some of the corpses were aflame, others soaked in pools of their own blood. They had been blown apart, limbs scattered this way and that, disconnected from their previous owners.

"By the Mother..." Vhalla raised her hand to her mouth, a renewed panic pulsing through her veins. The street with The Golden Bun was off to the left. At first, she tried to step carefully over the bodies, but in the end she ran over them, a horror rising in her gut with each sickening soft spot her feet landed on. She was crying, despite the heat and the flames, tears streamed down her face.

Then she was falling.

Tripping on an arm, a leg, or over her oversized footwear, Vhalla landed across a woman's body, face-to-face with a girl who had a piece of wood lodged in her skull, one eye staring at her blankly.

Vhalla screamed and tried to move away, but all around her was death and carnage. Two strong hands helped lift her up and back onto her feet.

"It is not far now, is it?" Aldrik asked, almost mechanically. She shook her head. "Go on." He pushed her gently, and Vhalla found her feet again.

She rounded the corner and broke into an all-out sprint. Half of The Golden Bun had collapsed, the rest was aflame. The building next to it had been reduced to rubble, and a small crater in the street suggested one of the explosions' epicenters.

"*Sareem!*" Vhalla put her hands to her mouth and called frantically. "*Roan!*"

Her voice was raw after shrieking three more times. She looked at the bodies on the ground, turning them over or trying to imagine what their faces may have been. By the outside patio, she shifted a fat man and saw a tuff of familiar, cropped, blonde hair beneath.

"Aldrik!" Vhalla screamed frantically. "Aldrik, help me!" He was at her side in an instant, pulling the fat man off Roan. Vhalla looked at her friend, she was bruised and broken but in one piece. Vhalla put her ear to the other woman's breast.

"She's breathing!" Vhalla cried. "We have to find Sareem."

Vhalla looked around; if Roan was here, Sareem had to be close. She began to shift more bodies, treading closer to the former bakery. Vhalla tore at the rubble, leaving bloody handprints behind, no longer sure if the blood was hers or others. Aldrik took control of the nearby inferno and kept the fire at bay while she searched. Larel had said that Firebearers could not feel heat, so the beads of sweat that rolled down his temples could only be explained by exertion.

"Vhalla," he said faintly, looking around.

"He's here somewhere," she pleaded, more with the universe than her companion, hoping that she was not wrong.

"Vhalla." Aldrik's voice was sterner.

"I know he's here. He wouldn't leave Roan, and he was waiting for me." Her voice was frantic as she lifted a rock and heaved it aside. "I-I never told him I wasn't coming. He thought I was still going to come for him."

"Vhalla!" Aldrik shouted.

She let out a scream.

Underneath the rock was a face—half of a face—that she had known since she was a girl. A face who had made her laugh, who had taken care of her, who had been a friend—like family. Vhalla fell to her knees over Sareem's burnt and debris-battered body, her shoulders heaving with sobs.

"Sareem, Sareem, I'm sorry. *I'm so sorry.*" She placed a hand on the cheek that wasn't crushed and oozing. "I..." She hiccupped, snot dripping from her nose. "I didn't want this. Oh, Mother, I-I-I'll never keep anything from you again, Sareem. See, see I came, so wake up now, Sareem. Please, *please.*" Her stomach hurt from her sobbing and her shoulders ached, as though all the nightmares that she had endured threatened to tear apart her body. Vhalla leaned back on her feet, not caring who or what else she sat on, and stared hopelessly back at Aldrik.

"Aldrik, how do I save him?" she asked, tears staining her soot-covered cheeks.

"Vhalla," he said faintly, taking a step closer.

"How do I save him?" She rubbed her nose with the back of her hand.

"You can't do that." There was a sorrowful kindness under each word.

"I saved you." She took a shaky breath. "How do I save him?"

"It doesn't work that way." He knelt down next to her, putting a hand on her back. "You can't fix this."

"Then why have magic?" she screamed at the prince as her

tears forced their way out again. Aldrik spread his fingers across her back.

"Because," he said very softly, his voice strained and tense. Aldrik glanced over his shoulder, careful to move only his eyes and not his whole head. "You need to get down."

Vhalla hiccupped. As the words registered in her brain as not making any sense, his hand was pushing her down forcefully into the bloody carnage of her friend. Aldrik ducked, too, as a quiet swoosh cut through the air above their heads.

He pushed off her back and spun upward, his hands alive with fire, and Vhalla heard a woman's laugh.

CHAPTER 24

Vhalla turned to look at their attacker. The silver embellishments on the woman's arms glittered in the firelight. She wore base leather armor overlaid with a strange piece of clothing over her shoulders and chest, like a rectangular pennon with a hole cut in the center for the head. Embroidered upon it was a foreign script that Vhalla had never seen before. At the woman's waist was a large belt, an empty sword sheath hanging off of it.

"Well, well, this makes things easy," the woman spoke, her voice barely audible from behind the faceless mask. If the green skin wasn't enough, the attacker's accent was proof that she was one of the jugglers. "I never expected the mighty Crown Prince Aldrik to come running all by his lonesome. It's too noble for the man who torches babes in their beds."

The woman rounded them slightly. To the couple's backs were piles of rubble, to their side was an inferno, and before them was a sword-wielding Northerner. Vhalla knew nothing of combat, yet she was able to see that they were not in a good position.

Aldrik was silent. He stood straight and tense, his hands clenched in fists, fire crackling and hissing around them. It trailed up his arms and singed the bottoms of his rolled sleeves.

"Vhalla," the prince said roughly. The other woman raised her eyebrow and glanced over to her. "Go! Get out of here."

"What about Roan?" she asked weakly.

"*Go*, that is an order." Even though flames raged around her, Vhalla suddenly felt cold.

"It's rude to leave a party early," the woman chimed in.

"Here I was, merely trying to spare you the embarrassment of dying a pathetic death with an audience," Aldrik lashed out.

The woman growled and lunged.

Aldrik stepped to the side, the Northerner ducked below his flaming punch and twisted, shifting her weight to bring her sword up. Aldrik jumped back, the tip of the blade missing him by a hair's breadth. She pursued with a backhanded slash, targeting his opposite shoulder. Aldrik spun around her side, grabbing the arm holding the weapon. Flames burned brightly, licking up the woman's skin.

At first, Vhalla thought her immune to the flame. But as she watched the flesh changed color before her eyes, it dawned on her that the green color was actually a fire-resistant paint. She stared in shock as the woman's mask was thrown off during a vigorous spin to land a sword strike into Aldrik's side. He cried out, losing his balance and stumbling. Vhalla struggled to find her feet and escape the rubble.

"Vhalla, *go*!" he grunted.

As the woman raised her sword arm again, Aldrik reached up and grabbed the dark bare skin with his hands. Fire seared across her flesh and she cried out as it began to ripple and bubble under the heat. Her agony rose to a torturous scream unimpeded by any mask, and she dropped the sword. She twisted and fought with her free hand, but Aldrik held fast.

He stood slowly and released his right hand from her arm, which had almost burned away to the bone. Taking advantage of her shocked state, Aldrik pressed his palm to the woman's face and her body seized. It jerked and contorted as flames licked around her eyes, boiling them in their sockets. Her throat swelled with the internal blaze, and she finally went limp. Aldrik tossed the charred corpse aside and looked to Vhalla.

Vhalla stared on in horror. Her hands were over her ears, trying to block out the echo of the Northerner's last desperate noises before death. She stared at the charred corpse. That was what they were fighting in the North? Certainly her skin had been slightly darker than a Westerner's, and her hair curlier than a Southerner's. But she had been human. She had been no more or less than Vhalla, and Aldrik had killed her.

Her eyes swung up to the man who had both saved her life and burnt a person alive. He had killed this woman and countless others. Aldrik took a step forward, and Vhalla took a step back. She swallowed. Why were they fighting these people at all?

Aldrik laughed darkly. "What did you think I was?" he snarled. "Did you think I went to war and read books?" Vhalla took another step back. "You ran head-first into my daily hell. Would it not be more convenient if weapons of death and torture could not talk back?" Vhalla forced herself not to tremble as she looked at him. He glared at her; the orange of the fire reflecting in the black mirrors of his eyes.

With all the bravery she possessed, Vhalla crossed the distance between them. He straightened and looked down at her, imposingly. Vhalla swallowed hard and tried to muster her last scrap of confidence. There would be time later to ask him about the real reasons behind the war. For now, they needed to go home.

She grabbed his hand, praying it didn't burst into flames at her touch. It didn't.

"Quit being stupid, Aldrik. Let's go." His features barely softened, but it was more than enough to know she had made herself clear. Whatever this man was, he wasn't a monster. Vhalla took a step back, turning to grab Roan and start the gory trek home.

With stunning clarity, she heard the distinct twang of a bowstring piercing the air. Vhalla moved instinctively in front of her prince.

She screamed a noise worse than any she had ever made before as the arrow pierced her shoulder.

"*Vhalla!*" he roared as she fell to her knees.

She gasped for air. She gasped to make a sound. The pain seared through every nerve in her body, across every synapse in her mind. It seized her muscles and forced her to blink dizzying blackness from the edges of her sight. His hands were supporting her but his attention was elsewhere. Vhalla turned her head to try to see what he saw. But when she caught sight of the arrow sticking out of her body, she instantly struggled with consciousness.

"My, isn't this charming?" Vhalla tilted her head over her other shoulder to see the source of the voice. Her vision was becoming tunneled and she willed her eyes to focus.

There were three of them.

"It's the jugglers," she murmured.

"Don't talk," Aldrik whispered harshly, his thumb caressing her shoulder as he supported her.

"Careful, they're, they're missing..." She struggled to count. "They're missing two, still."

He glanced at her and then back at the people.

"Don't you think it's charming?" a man asked.

"It really is," came a nasally woman's voice.

"The noble prince, defending the damsel. Who knew the Fire Lord had it in him?" the man snarked.

Vhalla heard the ring of metal on metal as a sword was drawn. These people truly wanted to kill them, Vhalla realized, as she felt blood soaking down to her waist. She wasn't in a position to run anymore; if he carried her, she would only burden him.

"Aldrik," she whispered. He didn't move but she knew he'd heard. "Go, go and leave me." It was her fault he was there in the first place. The last thing she could do in her life was to ensure the heir to the throne did not die on account of her stubbornness. Vhalla closed her eyes and dipped her head.

"No," he replied in a soft and low voice.

"Your life is worth more than mine. It's the life I partly gave you, isn't it?" She smiled faintly as she heard footsteps and the crunch of bodies across the street. Aldrik said nothing. "I should have some say over whether you throw it away or not. So, go." His fingers gripped into her arms. She was fairly sure he was bruising her.

"You know, we thought it was a lie you were alive at all." It was the man's voice again. Aldrik still hadn't moved. "Our leader brewed the poison that was on the dagger. One prick should've killed a large Noru Cat, and I hear you had the whole damn thing in your side."

Aldrik's breathing had become heavy. Vhalla was confused about the mention of a dagger.

"Then again, we also hoped that if the poison failed to kill you, the shame of one of your dear sweet brother's men stabbing you in the back would be enough."

Aldrik stood, and she swayed without his support. *Yes*, Vhalla thought weakly, *go*. She propped herself up with her uninjured arm and turned to sit on rubble so she could face her attackers.

Unfortunately, Aldrik hadn't run. He stood, fire surrounding his fists again.

One of the women laughed. "He's still injured. Look, that pathetic little spark is likely all he can muster." This woman was holding a bow, and Vhalla hoped she could keep her eyes open long enough to watch the woman's face be burnt off. "Come, let us end this now." She notched an arrow on her bowstring.

The man held his sword with both hands and the other woman followed suit. Aldrik took a few steps toward them, and Vhalla's stomach twisted in agony. He wasn't going to run. The three advanced slowly.

"Careful, he may be a beast with clipped claws, but he's still a beast," the man warned.

"If he's still a beast, can we shave him when we're done and wear his skin as a pelt?" Nasal voice asked.

"I'd rather hang it off my bow and wave it like a flag," the archer chimed, glancing at her comrades.

That was all it took, and Aldrik seized his opportunity. He charged and grabbed at her bow, immediately setting flame to both the hand and the weapon. The man was upon him quickly, however, and Aldrik was forced to relinquish his hold in order to dodge. He moved his fingers through the air, creating a curtain of flame. The man's momentum caused him to step into it. The swordswoman dashed around and lunged from the side. Aldrik twisted his body and brought his elbow down hard on the back of her neck, sending her reeling. In a horrible way, he was like a song of death and flame.

"You bastard," the man groaned as he found his footing again, swinging his sword in a wide arc. Aldrik stepped back, but into the archer's blow as she snapped the remains of her weapon across the back of his head. Aldrik gave a cry, falling to his knees. Vhalla felt her heart stop.

The man advanced on him with a satisfied grin—prepared to

deal his fatal blow. Aldrik stuck out his hand and grabbed the man's ankle; flames burned up the side of the man's body and not even the paint could protect his skin. Aldrik rolled out of the way of the crash of the swordswoman's attack and gained his footing again. Vhalla could see he was already winded, his posture hunched slightly.

The archer charged. Aldrik dodged easily and responded with a punch to her gut, but there was no more flame. The swordswoman spun, Aldrik dropped to a knee and held out his hand before crying out in anguish, his hand on his hip where she had seen a dark spot on his magic months ago.

The man chuckled darkly. Vhalla looked upon the Northerner in horror. Half of his clothes had been burnt off, large chunks of flesh with it. He looked like a corpse returned to life.

"See," he heaved roughly. "His magic fails him."

Aldrik glared up at the Northerners. His hair had fallen out of place wildly and it clung to his sweat-drenched face. His features were twisted in pain, but he was still proud and defiant. The crown prince's hands clutched his hip as he looked up, the sword at his throat.

"This is how a prince dies." The man snickered and drew back his sword.

Vhalla opened her mouth to cry out.

"Wait!" the bow woman said, throwing off her mask. "I have a better idea." She wore a wicked grin.

"Let's just kill him and be done with it," the nasal woman breathed, still catching her breath.

"Death is no fun without pain," the archer said darkly.

"I will not scream." Aldrik chuckled. "Whatever you do, I will not scream or beg, so it will be very boring."

Vhalla studied the prince. His posture was relaxed and his voice calm. There was something almost inviting in its deep tones. As much as she wanted to believe he was bluffing, the tiny smirk told her otherwise. She hurt, and not from the arrow protruding from her. He had come to terms with his own death, and Aldrik was prepared to meet it at this moment. Her breath hitched in her throat.

"I didn't say I was going to make *you* scream." The bow woman turned and looked at Vhalla.

Vhalla straightened as best she could, instinctively scooting away from her assailant, ignoring the stabbing pains in her wounded shoulder.

"I don't doubt you, prince. I'm sure your pain threshold is very high. But there are many different kinds of pain, aren't there?" The sadistic woman almost cooed, her emerald eyes gleaming. "I wonder if hers is as high." With a cold smile, the woman walked over to Vhalla.

Vhalla looked at Aldrik helplessly before staring up at the Northerner who was about to decide her fate.

Grabbing the shaft of the arrow sticking out of Vhalla's shoulder, the woman pulled upward, dragging Vhalla to her feet. She shook with the pain and the effort of keeping in her screams. Vhalla didn't want to die like this, and she didn't want to give these people the satisfaction of her anguish. Still gripping the arrow, the woman pulled Vhalla along over to where Aldrik knelt. His eyes wore a tormented mix of fury and sorrow.

Vhalla's foot caught on a piece of rubble and she tripped. The fall ripped the arrow, fletching and all, clean through her shoulder. Vhalla cried out as she rolled in pain among the debris and human flesh littering the ground. Aldrik attempted to jump to his feet, but the man pressed the sword against his throat.

"Down," he grunted, like Aldrik was a dog.

"Come, girl, we're not done yet." The woman grabbed her by the hair and pulled Vhalla over the rest of the way. She was dumped an arm's length from Aldrik, but it seemed like half the world as Vhalla stared at him blankly, shattering at the sorrow of his beautifully dark eyes.

Pulling Vhalla up into a seated position, the woman plucked an arrow from her quiver.

"Tell me, prince, what is it you like about her?" The archer's voice was rough.

"I like nothing, really; she is little more than a cheap whore I found," Aldrik forced out with a flat voice.

"Is that so? Very fine clothes for a cheap whore. Do you like her face?" The woman ran the point of the arrow down Vhalla's cheek, leaving a dripping red line in its wake.

Vhalla winced softly, her lower lip trembling.

"Why soil your weapon with her blood?" Aldrik tried, attempting to glance away casually.

"She has a nice figure. What about her breasts?" Two more cuts were upon her body and Vhalla felt tears on her cheeks.

"Enough," Aldrik said softly, his eyes were back on her.

"Enough? She's not just a whore?" the woman sneered. "What about her legs? Want to see them?" The woman lifted the hem of his jacket and Vhalla's tattered skirts with the arrow, making a deep incision along the way.

"Enough!" Aldrik cried.

Vhalla looked at him and saw the panic in his eyes. The woman had won. The Northerner knew it too as she let out a laugh and released Vhalla, the broken library girl falling to the ground.

Vhalla stared at the world lifelessly. It would be torture for Aldrik to watch her die. They would kill him next. His, Sareem's, and Roan's deaths would all be on her hands.

"Don't kill him," she whispered.

The woman's laugh quieted and she leaned over Vhalla. "What was that, you little shit? I didn't hear it," she snarled.

"Don't kill him," Vhalla repeated. She never took her eyes off

Aldrik. "Do what you will to me, but don't kill him, please." Vhalla struggled to sit.

The woman laughed again. "You are nothing," she snarled. "You are less than nothing. You were only something because it was amusing to hurt you."

"And now it is no longer amusing," the man said, raising his sword.

"No," Vhalla whispered.

Aldrik stared at her, unmoving. He didn't try to run or flee—he simply stared.

"This ends now!" The man brought his sword down over Aldrik's head.

"*No!*" Vhalla screamed. In less than a second, the only sound that filled her ears was the wind of the man's sword cutting the air.

CHAPTER 25

Vhalla shifted on the cracked and uneven stone floor and cried out in pain. Her shoulder felt swollen and hot; simple movements were agonizing. She tried to prop herself up but she fell back to the floor with a dull thud. Dried blood and smoke were crusted around her eyes; trying to rub it off was pointless as her hands were coated as well.

The room was a simple square, and the air was heavy with the stench of excrement and bodies. One wall had a large portal with a great iron door made of interlocking bars fastened with a padlock larger than her fists. She saw the shoulder armor of two palace guards on either side.

"Hello?" Little more than a dry rasp escaped her throat.

The guards turned and looked through the bars. One had a large mole on his left cheek. The other had two front teeth that caused him to look like a rat.

"Oh, she's awake," mole man said. "Better go ring the bells." Rat man scampered off.

"Where? Where am I?" Vhalla asked, trying to make sense of her surroundings.

"What does it look like? A prison cell." The man picked his nose and flicked it at her.

"Why?" Vhalla's head hurt and the warm pulsing of her shoulder didn't help either.

"Oh, clever. I see you're trying to play the innocent right away." Mole man shook his head. "The Senate'll see right through that."

She sighed and placed her head back on the floor, closing her eyes. This man was frustrating, and not in the charming way that Aldrik managed. *Aldrik.* Vhalla opened her eyes as the night began to replay in her mind: Roan, Sareem, the woman, the arrow, Aldrik on his knees with a sword to his throat, the man raising his blade for the final blow. Then—nothing. She had no further memories.

"Sir, sir!" Mole man looked back at her with mild annoyance. "The crown prince." She struggled to sit. Vhalla wanted to stand, but she ended up mostly crawling to the bars, gripping them for support. Her whole body felt so exhausted it could barely move. "Prince Aldrik, he, where is he?"

"Why do you want to know? Going to make another attempt on his life?" The man looked at her queerly.

"What?" she exclaimed in shock. "No! I want to know if he is all right!"

"To my knowledge the prince is alive and well."

Vhalla let out a large sigh and rested her forehead against a bar. It was cool on her flushed skin. Aldrik was alive and safe. She must have passed out, and he overpowered them somehow.

"Thank the Mother," Vhalla breathed before a choked strangle escaped at the memory of her friends who had not made it. Her moment was interrupted by the clip of two pairs of boots down the hallway.

"Yes, she just woke." It was rat man from earlier. She tried to listen carefully to hear the other set of footsteps. They fell heavily. It wasn't her prince. Aldrik would come soon. He'd sort this out and she'd be on her way. Vhalla looked up as the men stopped before her cell. Anyone, she would take anyone over the man who stood before her.

Egmun grinned gleefully down at her, and her blood curdled. He wore his golden senatorial chain over a blue robe.

"Well, I can't say I am entirely surprised to meet you here." He picked lint off his sleeve nonchalantly. Vhalla stared at him blankly. "It was only a matter of time." Losing interest in his clothing, he approached the door of her cage, his words as slow and deliberate as his movements.

"You common folk are attracted to the glamor of noble life like—like a moth to a *flame,*" he said with a wicked smile. "So sad you often fly too close and simply burn away."

Vhalla couldn't keep her face from dropping into a frown as he spoke. She was growing to detest everything about this man, and every time he opened his mouth, he succeeded in reminding her why. He was smart, and she quickly realized that it made him dangerous.

"What do you want with me?" she asked, attempting to force her voice to stay as level as possible, to not portray any fear or panic.

"Oh, it's nothing *I* want with you. I honestly just want you to crawl back under the rock you came from and never come out again. But, well, you made that difficult for yourself when you attacked the crown prince." He put his hands in the air before dropping them. "Now, we will need to see you properly punished for your transgressions."

"What?" Vhalla's voice rose sharply. "I didn't—"

"Denials?" the senator hissed. "You must sing a different song before the trial."

"But I didn't *do anything,*" Vhalla repeated.

"Guards," Egmun sighed. "I think our prisoner may need her memory jarred."

Rat and Mole exchanged a look that Vhalla had a difficult time reading, before they started for the cell door. The moment the door opened and the two armored men entered Vhalla knew it hadn't been a good look. Vhalla put as much distance between her and the men as the cell would allow, ignoring the screaming pain in her shoulder.

These men were there to protect her. But they stared down at her with the same look of contempt the Northerners had.

"Don't," Vhalla whimpered out of instinct.

"Denials still?" the senator hummed, leaning against the wall beyond.

Mole heard a command that Vhalla hadn't in Egmun's voice and his fist was in her hair. She cried out in agony, grabbing at his tense wrists as he practically lifted her off the floor. The man threw her against the wall and the back of her head cracked loudly.

She slumped, blinking away stars in a blurry daze. Mole was on her again before she had time to decide which of the four of him was real. His boot connected with her stomach, again and again. She tried to lift her hand to blow them away with magic, but no sorcery crackled beneath her fingertips. There wasn't even time to panic as Mole stomped upon the appendage, the bones crunching. Vhalla didn't feel the next strike to her ribs; she could only feel the dirt and gravel covering the floor pressed against her cheek.

"Do you remember now?" Egmun called.

"Why?" she wheezed. *Why were they doing this?*

Rat picked her up by the front of her dress. The sound of the seams exploding as he pummeled a fist into her face were louder than her screams or cries for help. The garment could only endure two strikes before tearing and Vhalla fell onto the floor in an undignified heap wearing nothing but her underclothes.

Her consciousness was smaller than a pin by the time their beating ended. She existed in such a tiny portion of her mind that the outside world was only tangible through echoes. Yet, somehow, their cruel words still made it to her fracturing psyche.

"That's sufficient, I should think. Unfortunately we cannot take the Empire's justice." Egmun walked to the entrance of the cell. "Remember this. For I will. This is how I will always see you —worthless trash."

She blinked up at him, unmoving, unflinching. Hatred had always been described in her books like fire—a hot and uncontrollable inferno. This hatred felt like ice. It numbed her empathy and sharpened her resolve to survive at any and all costs, if for no other reason than to spite him.

Egmun took a slow breath, as though he could feel the daggers she was mentally flaying him with. "Now get dressed." He tossed a burlap sack atop her and left the cell.

Vhalla's limbs barely heeded her demands for movement and sitting was agony. Phantom pains from her fall seeped from fractured bones and torn tissues. The sack she had been bestowed had some slits cut into it for her arms and head and Vhalla crawled into it with as much dignity as she could muster.

She had endured worse. The once library apprentice struggled to her feet. She had survived a fall from the palace spires and warriors from the North. Her limbs trembled with pain and fear as Vhalla reminded herself of those facts and faced the three men.

Mole grabbed her and yanked her forward. Vhalla stumbled and cried, instantly hating herself for it. She hated them and she hated her treacherous body for feeling the pain caused by them. His hand dug into her shoulder, and she felt a drip trail down her back. Rat retrieved shackles and bound her hands and feet together. The last fastenings to her sanity were snapping, and they sounded like a raspy laugh.

"As if I can run." She smiled madly at Egmun.

This sudden emotional contrast almost seemed to shake his perfect poise. He adjusted his robes and said nothing before starting down the hall. Rat and Mole practically carried her as they held her up with each arm.

It was after a short flight of stairs upward when Egmun left them. They walked the rest of the way in silence. A numbing chill crept from her extremities inward. *Sareem was dead.* The blood dripping from her skull reminded Vhalla of his shattered face. Roan likely was too. The prince had somehow lived, but Vhalla expected him to blame her—rightfully—for everything he shouldn't have had to endure. The pendulum of her emotions swung far into guilt. It was her fault. All of this was her fault. She was suddenly laughing again.

Why was losing her whole life so *funny*?

"Shut up," Rat hissed, slapping her across the face.

Her craze left her, and she hung limply. Blood dripped down her chin, adding to the trail she left on the stairs they were ascending. They opened a door, and threw her into a brightly lit room. She hit the floor with an ungraceful clank of chains, waiting for her eyes to adjust to the light.

She had been thrown into a square cage welded into the wall behind her on all sides. Rat and Mole assumed guard duty to the left and right of the door. There was no other visible entrance into this section of the room—her temporary prison.

To her far left was a different door and empty seating. To the right stared thirteen people, Egmun at their center. The senators had been lined up neatly in two rows. Before them, on the floor in the center of the room, was a dais made of a golden sun. Across was a raised area with three seats—no, not seats: thrones.

In the smallest throne to the Emperor's left sat Prince Baldair; it was the first time she'd ever seen him without a smile. In the middle sat the Emperor, his expression unreadable. On his right, was a face she knew well. Vhalla choked back a sob of relief at seeing Aldrik alive. She shut her eyes before she could see whatever was written on his features. She didn't want him here; she didn't want him to see her like this. She who had killed her friends and endangered his life didn't deserve his gaze, even if it held justified anger.

The Emperor raised a large staff and brought it down onto the floor three times. The sound of metal on stone echoed through the silent hall.

"I, Emperor Solaris, on behalf of the Mother, call this special trial to order. Senate Head Elect?"

Egmun stood, and Vhalla kept herself from screaming the worst obscenities she could imagine.

"Vhalla Yarl, we the Senate have charged you with recklessness, endangerment of your fellow citizens, public destruction, impersonating nobility, heresy, murder, and treason in an attempt on the life of the Crown Prince Aldrik."

Vhalla opened her eyes weakly and dared to find the man whom she was said to have attempted to kill. Aldrik sat unmoving; he may as well have been carved from stone.

"How do you cry?"

Vhalla's world slowed as she waited for the prince to make a movement. She wanted him to stand, to smile, to tell Egmun he was wrong. But Aldrik did nothing.

Vhalla thought about the idea of pleading guilty. They would kill her and this would all end. All the pain that her body and mind were steeped in would be gone. There would be no more choices, no more princes, and no more senators. If she was lucky, they would make this temporary prison her tomb, striking her down before she returned to the cell with Rat and Mole. Vhalla closed her eyes with a sigh, taking a ragged breath.

"Vhalla Yarl, how do you cry?" Egmun repeated.

No, Vhalla sat straighter, pulling her shoulders back despite the pain of the irons around her wrists. If she was to be judged, then let her be judged by the ones whom she had wronged. Aldrik's eyes glittered with a barely contained inferno. She would endure his judgment, and Roan's, and someday Sareem's. Vhalla may have been a sheltered library girl and she may be a yet-realized sorcerer, but she would not allow Egmun—or anyone— to turn her into a coward.

"Not guilty." Her voice was raw. Vhalla turned to Egmun and his mouth twisted in annoyance. "Senators, I cry not guilty."

CHAPTER 26

The rest of the first trial day was spent detailing her crimes and explaining how the verdict would be reached. The next day would be the start of evidence, people speaking on her behalf, witnesses, and testimony on the Senate's side. Vhalla wondered if Aldrik would be speaking for her; he was the only true witness she could think of. The third day Vhalla would answer their questions and speak for herself. Then, the last day, she would not be present until they had reached their verdict.

"Vhalla Yarl, it has been determined that you Awoke as a sorcerer months ago," Egmun started. Vhalla felt her mouth drop open. "In this time, you have not reported to the Tower of Sorcerers for training and restriction. Nor have you been Eradicated, allowing your powers to run wild and dangerous.

"In doing so, these powers have progressed so far that they have destroyed public property and likely contributed to the death of multiple citizens."

A chill ran down her spine. The death of multiple citizens? She'd killed someone? Blood dripped down her neck from her head and oozed from the wound in her shoulder as she struggled to find some memory that would make the senator's words truth.

"Some also consider your powers to be a form of heresy against the Mother," Egmun continued.

"There's a reason why we killed them all!" a Western senator shouted. "They're twisted, evil. Give it to the Knights of Jadar, they will know what to do!" He was on his feet raging at Vhalla.

She looked at him numbly.

"Silence!" The Emperor's voice echoed across the room. "Head Elect, please continue."

"This almost pales in comparison to an attempt on the life of the future Emperor Solaris—an attempted murder on our Crown Prince Aldrik." Egmun gave a small bow in the direction of the prince.

Aldrik's expression remained unchanged. Pain and fury were burning in the aura around him, but his eyes had a restrained coolness in the brief moments he allowed himself to glance at her. Whatever the truth was, he did not really think she had attempted to harm him.

But what had happened? She was on trial for a whole list of things. These men and women looked at her as though she was a rabid animal. The hatred she was drawing strength from was still strong, but her spine was weak and began to curl as tears fell from her cheeks.

They were talking again, arguing over this or that but it all sounded like buzzing to Vhalla's ringing ears. She was tired. These people clearly did not care what happened to her. No, they cared, but what they cared about was seeing her dead.

Vhalla opened her eyes and looked at Aldrik, his head had turned slightly to listen to whatever discussion was now occurring, but he took no part.

Vhalla wanted to blame him. Had it not been for him, none of this would have happened. If it weren't for him, her magical powers would've never Manifested, she would've never been involved with the Tower, and she would still be blissfully unaware of one senator's name.

But Vhalla couldn't blame him, because she had been happy. For a moment she thought back to the night before, his arms around her waist. The memory was so perfect it almost broke her. Vhalla tried to mentally rejoin the conversation but it seemed to be wrapping up.

"The trial will commence at sunrise tomorrow then." The Emperor looked to her. "We have already assembled a list of witnesses and people to speak. Is there anyone the prisoner would like to name on her behalf?" He didn't even use her name.

"My-my friend, she was alive when I found her. Her name is Roan." There was a murmur through the senator's benches at this. "Does-does she live? She's known me a long time." In truth, Vhalla wanted to know the answer to her question more than she wanted to demand that Roan speak for her. Her friend likely, rightfully, wouldn't have the warmest words about her presently.

The Emperor looked at his youngest son.

"I'm afraid I don't know her status," Baldair confessed.

Maybe she had only imagined hearing Roan's shallow heartbeat.

"If this Roan is unable to give testimony, is there anyone else?" the Emperor asked.

Vhalla thought, swallowing more tears when she thought of Sareem and the glowing testimony he would've given her. Her mind filled with images of his crushed body.

"Master Mohned," she choked out, struggling to keep the sobs that shook her shoulders at bay. The master would come for her.

"It shall be done." The Emperor knocked his staff again three times and stood. The princes and senators followed suit.

Vhalla didn't try to stand again. She looked at the ground. Rat and Mole seemed to be content to assist her, wrenching her roughly to her feet in a way that wrung a small cry of agony. Vhalla's head dipped forward, and her hair covered her face.

"This session is adjourned."

Royalty left first and the senators began to stream out one by one as Vhalla was dragged back to the cells below.

After removing her shackles, Mole threw her back into her cell with a rough laugh. Vhalla fell to the floor like a rag doll and didn't move—her energy expended. She heard the door slam behind her. Her body may not survive long enough to see the end of the trial. The darkness that crept behind her eyes had a heaviness to it that she'd never felt before. It wasn't sleep her body craved, *it was death.*

Just as she was closing her eyes, Vhalla heard the echoes of boots down the stairs. For one heart-pounding moment she thought Egmun had come again to punish her for crying not guilty. But the walk was even heavier than his. Too heavy to be Aldrik and yet something about it sounded familiar. Vhalla heard the clink of the guards' armor as they brought their right fist to their breastplate in salute.

"My prince!" Mole said, Rat echoed. Vhalla struggled to turn her head. Prince Baldair stood just beyond her cell door carrying a large box. He still wore a frown, and his brow was scrunched and lined.

"What was that sorry display, men?" he asked, his voice having all its normal melodic tones but none of its mirth. "You're supposed to be taking care of our prisoner; she was ten times worse in that courtroom than when I brought her."

"Sh-she tried to kill your brother, th-the prince," Rat tried.

"She's been found guilty of nothing yet, and until that time, she is to be kept alive and *well*." Prince Baldair turned with a glare in his direction.

"She's alive," Mole offered.

The prince sighed. "I will assume you have simply never been taught how to tend field wounds. I'll show you myself. Open the door," he demanded, full of regal poise.

"Senator Egmun gave us clear instructions that—" Mole began.

"Egmun is your senator, and I am your prince. Do we need to go over the chain of command?" Baldair snapped.

"No, no, my lord, of course not." Mole fumbled with the keys. The door unlocked and he pushed it open. "Be careful, my prince. She already tried to kill one member of the royal family."

Prince Baldair ignored him as he entered the dim cell. The only source of light came from a torch on the wall outside, so his face was cast in shadow. He set the box down with a small clanking sound not far from her.

"Can you sit?" Prince Baldair's voice was even softer than his tired smile. Vhalla said nothing and struggled into a seated position with only a few whimpers. "Good," he encouraged and reached out for her shoulder.

Vhalla flinched as his fingertips grazed her skin.

"Vhalla, I have to dress your wounds properly or they'll fester."

She tried to sit still as he reached for her shoulder again, but her whole body wouldn't stop trembling. All Vhalla saw was a man's hand coming for her in the same, dark, cramped space as before. The energy pulsating through her muscles snapped and she swatted his hand away.

"Don't touch me!" she hissed, her body overcome with shivers. His hand paused in the air. "Please..." Vhalla wanted to break down then and beg him for safety, but she was reduced to sobs and coughing blood through split lips.

"Vhalla," Prince Baldair murmured faintly. "What happened to you?" He looked and absorbed her battered form for the first time.

Vhalla's breathing was short and fast, giving her a lightheaded sensation. Her eyes struggled to focus through the rage that was blinding them, but they found their targets. Rat and Mole took a step backward as the force of her glare pressed upon them.

Prince Baldair followed her stare, his body gathering tension like an archer's bowstring. He took a long inhale of air before exploding upward. The prince crossed the short distance to the door in two quick steps. Mole and Rat had been wary under Vhalla's glare, but now horror consumed their faces as the prince barreled toward them. Prince Baldair put a hand on each of their breastplates and pushed them into the far wall of the hallway.

"Did you touch her?" he roared, pinning them both in place.

Each guard seemed too shocked to move as the prince's largely muscled frame held them easily.

"M-my prince, w-we..." Rat stammered.

"You see, the senator..." Mole tried.

Prince Baldair shook his head and gave a small chuckle. "I'm very proud to be a man. Men have duties, honors, which we can stand behind and take pride in." He raised his eyes to look at them. "Abusing a woman—abusing anyone—violates all of those. You know what I do with men under my command who ignore their duties and honor?" The two men looked on in terror. "I make them no longer men, so they can't give the rest of us a bad name."

"But-but she's not a person. She's a freak."

Vhalla finally looked away; Rat shouldn't still be able to hurt her.

"Go! Out of my sight!" Prince Baldair roared, the rage in his voice echoed down the corridor after the two fleeing guards.

Letting out a sigh, he watched them flee. Prince Baldair turned and looked down at her with large, sad, apologetic eyes. His whole face gave into the expression. Vhalla looked at the floor; she didn't want his pity.

"I'm sorry. They're Egmun's men; he recommended them. We should've known better." He cursed under his breath. Vhalla looked up at him warily. "Vhalla, I know this will be difficult, but I must clean and bandage your wounds. I'm sorry but I can't do that if I can't touch you."

She looked down again.

"You understand, you will die if we let them fester," he added.

"I know." Vhalla drew a slow breath and reformed her resolve. Egmun had wanted her to give up and give in. "Go ahead."

Prince Baldair absorbed the woman before him, paying subconscious respect to the creature clawing her way from the dark hole she kept being forced into. With a nod he returned to his box, popping open a latch and fishing through clerical supplies. When his hands made contact with her skin Vhalla didn't even flinch. *This is Prince Baldair*, she told herself, *he won't hurt her.*

"I was the one who found you." The prince didn't look at her as he spoke. "When the first whirlwind landed, I went running. It doesn't just happen like that. If something weird, horrible, and magical is happening, I normally find my brother close by."

"A whirlwind?" Vhalla asked softly.

The prince nodded. "The wind was insane. It ripped those Northerners into tiny bits."

Vhalla stared at him blankly. "Wait, that's why..." She was putting the pieces together.

"You really don't remember?" he asked, stunned.

"I don't remember anything," she told him honestly.

"Vhalla, you summoned a windstorm. It was almost as big as the entire square nearby," the prince explained.

"Did I really hurt Aldrik?" She stared in horror.

Prince Baldair raised his eyebrows. Vhalla's hands went to her mouth and she realized her mistake.

"He lets you call him by name?" The prince chuckled softly. Before she could attempt to answer he continued, "Aldrik was a little battered by this or that in the wind, I think more than he confessed to me afterward. But he doesn't blame you. The wind did not hurt him like it did the Northerners." Vhalla let out a breath. "I could only make it to you when the gale stopped." The prince ran a hand through his hair.

"My brother was clinging to you with all his might. As though you were... I don't know what..." Prince Baldair shifted, as if the memory made him uncomfortable. Vhalla stared at him in shock, and he chuckled uneasily. "Jaw open, eyes wide," Baldair summarized the expression she was giving him. "That must've been my face when I saw him holding you like that."

Vhalla looked down at her bruised hands and wondered if Aldrik would ever want to touch her again. "Why are you here?" The prince hadn't come only to tell her all this. Another cleric could just as easily have tended to her.

"Because I owed my brother, and he called in a favor," Baldair answered honestly. A frown crossed her face; she was a burden to them. The prince shook his head, as if reading her mind. "Because I was worried about the beautiful, charming woman I had danced with."

"Why didn't he come?" She tried to keep the pain from sneaking into her voice.

"There's a war council occurring right now to discuss the safety of the city. He had to be there." Vhalla nodded mutely. The prince wrapped some clean gauze around the fresh wound at the back of her head. "Why didn't you fight them off with your magic?"

"I tried." She choked on nothing in her throat, suddenly overwhelmed. She felt more deserted by her sorcery than by anyone else failing her. "But my magic... it isn't... I don't know why it didn't work."

"That's okay, Vhalla. You'll be safe now," he mumbled, knowing that words were not about to fix it. Prince Baldair shifted her burlap to inspect her shoulder. "This one is bad. It's going to hurt," the prince said apologetically.

Vhalla laughed and he looked at her queerly. "What doesn't hurt?" she asked bitterly.

His brow furrowed again. "Lie down," he instructed.

Vhalla obliged. She stared at the ceiling as the prince found a tall bottle of clear liquid.

"Do you want something to bite on?"

Vhalla shook her head.

He uncorked the bottle and poured its contents through the wound. She hissed and arched her back. Vhalla gripped at her clothes, forcing herself to stay still with slow deep breaths.

"You're a lot tougher than you look." The prince put the bottle aside.

"Am I?" she asked, looking back at the ceiling as he changed to a jar of creamy salve. "I don't feel tough."

The prince shrugged and dipped his fingers into the salve, applying it liberally to the wound. She winced at the pressure.

"Sorry," he murmured.

"It's fine," she murmured. "You and Aldrik." She noted her use of Aldrik's name made him glance at her weirdly. "Do you get along?" Talking kept her mind away from the pain.

"We—" the prince sighed "—we have a strange relationship."

Vhalla glanced at him; she could gather that much on her own.

Before she could follow up, he turned the conversation on her. "And you? You and Aldrik clearly get along. What's your relationship exactly?"

Vhalla stiffened, and not from his fingers probing her wound. She stared at nothing. The funny part was Vhalla didn't know how to classify her relationship with the crown prince.

"I don't know," she said truthfully.

He glanced at her as he threaded a needle before leaning over her. Golden hair fell in front of the prince's face, and his eyes had none of the laughter she'd seen in them before. Vhalla wasn't sure if she'd ever met this Prince Baldair. He looked exhausted.

"That's it? You don't know?" he mumbled, stitching up her wound.

"That's it." She kept from shrugging. "How often do you know what your brother is thinking?" The corner of Vhalla's mouth tugged upward by a fraction, and the prince actually chuckled.

"I just knew you were going to be amusing." He motioned for her to sit so he could stitch up the back.

"How did you learn to do this?" she asked, finding conversation easier than expected, given the circumstances. It was something about Prince Baldair, the same easiness she felt in his room.

"My brother played with spellbooks, I played with swords. One gives you paper cuts, the other removes your fingers. I saw so many clerics that I learned the basics." Baldair held out her arm and wrapped the wound closed. "Careful. Don't rip your stitches."

"Tell that to my guards," she bit out.

The prince didn't even try to hide a grimace. He pulled out a rag and another large leather bladder from the bottom of the box. Wetting the cloth, he handed it to her.

"Here, it's only water." He took a small sip, as if to encourage her. Vhalla didn't think he'd spend so much time patching her up if he was about to poison her. She took the rag and wiped her face, pausing a moment to look at the mix of black and red that smeared it.

"I must look like death itself," she mused at the soiled fabric.

"Worse than death." He did not even try to flatter her. "After seeing you in the courtroom, my brother broke a mirror and a vase, and set a chair on fire on his way to the council rooms. I couldn't get a cleric's box fast enough."

Vhalla laughed faintly and smiled for the first time in what felt like weeks. He pulled out a different cream and ran a thumb down her cheek. She stiffened slightly but she didn't find his touch unsettling anymore, at least in this limited capacity.

"There we go. You're prettier when you smile." The prince reflected her expression on his face but the moment was short-lived. She had no reason to be happy.

"They're going to kill me, aren't they?" Vhalla asked calmly.

His smile faded. "They're going to try," he replied with a nod.

She respected him more for not lying to her. "Why?"

"I don't know. Egmun was calling for it before Aldrik had even carried you back to the palace."

Vhalla was distracted a moment, imagining Aldrik's arms around her. Prince Baldair cleaned up his box, leaving her the bladder of water, a group of clean rags, the jar of cream he'd used on her face, and a small vial of green-looking syrup. She returned her attention to him as he stood.

"I figure, you have more you'd like to scrub off without me here. The salve you can use on any other cuts." The prince motioned toward the items.

Vhalla glanced at the gash running up her thigh that

disappeared under the sack dress and nodded. "Thank you," she said honestly.

"The green stuff, Deepsleep, it'll ease the pain and help you sleep."

Vhalla looked at it uncertainly; she wasn't sure if she wanted to be in a drug-induced slumber around Rat and Mole. "Please, don't go," she begged faintly.

"I'm not really supposed to be here." He sighed and picked up the box.

"Then lock me in and take the key with you. Give it back to Mole tomorrow," she pleaded with him. "Lock them away from me. If I have to be here all night with them, I'll..." A shiver ran through her.

"Mole?" The prince asked. Vhalla put a finger on her cheek where Mole had his unfortunate facial feature. "Ah." Prince Baldair considered her request for a moment and then locked the door with the key Mole had left in the lock earlier. He showed it to her before slipping it into his coat pocket. She nodded.

"My prince," she said quickly. He looked at her. "Tell Aldrik..."

He glanced down the hall. Tell Aldrik, what? She hadn't thought that far ahead. That she'd never forget their dance, for however long the rest of her short life was? That she enjoyed his company more than she ever expected? That she had yet to still sort through all the complex feelings surrounding him? In the end, she simply had to hope he knew.

"Please tell him, thank you, and I'm sorry." The prince gave her a strange look and nodded. "And thank you too, Prince Baldair, for whatever reason you did this."

"Be careful," the golden prince cautioned. "You seem sweet, Vhalla. Clearly you have something magical about you, and while I don't really understand it all, I do understand that Aldrik has fire in his veins."

"He is a Firebearer," she explained dumbly.

Prince Baldair chuckled softly. "I know what he's called." The prince shook his head, glancing away. "I don't want to see you getting wrapped up in my brother's dark world and hurt again. That's all."

He wasn't interested in giving her a chance to formulate a response. The prince left with the key, and Vhalla heard his footsteps disappear down the hall. A cold shiver ran through her.

Alone, she was left with her thoughts and the demons that lived there. The memory of Sareem came back to her, and Vhalla made a futile attempt to catch her sobs with a palm over her mouth. It was pointless, and she was soon doubled over, her sobs echoing through the halls. Every time she blinked, she saw his face, his twisted and broken face staring at her with its one good eye.

Knowing the prince walked away with the key, she grabbed for the bottle of green liquid and took a large gulp. Before Mole and Rat returned, she used a little more water and the rags to finish a near pointless cleaning of herself, choking down tears. Vhalla applied the cream to all the surface wounds she could find and then laid down.

She was exhausted and the potion set in quickly. Her whimpers soon faded into silence, and Vhalla passed out on the stone floor with little problem.

CHAPTER 27

Surprisingly, Vhalla slept fairly well. Extreme exhaustion did wonders for sleeping through the night, no matter the conditions. Sitting up, Vhalla's head throbbed as she rubbed the stiffness from her joints.

She used one of the damp cloths the prince had left to freshen her face, even if it made it no cleaner. Vhalla glanced at her doorway and saw the shoulder of a man standing there. Likely Mole. She lay back down and closed her eyes, not wanting to alert them that she had woken. Another set of footsteps strolled down the hall.

"You got assigned here too?" It wasn't Mole's voice.

"Like he'd separate us." It wasn't Rat. "Crazy story, isn't it?"

Vhalla sat up, confused.

"Who's there?" she asked, and two new faces stared at her.

"I'm Craig," said a Southerner who appeared about Aldrik's age.

"Daniel." An Easterner. Something about his relaxed and youthful eyes made Vhalla feel marginally easier.

"What happened to Mo—the other guards?" she asked.

The two exchanged a look. "Last night, the crown prince found them stealing from the bond coffers. He put them to death on the spot." Craig made a shivering motion. Vhalla's eyes widened as her jaw dropped. "It's a little crazy. I knew he had a temper, but it takes a special rage to kill two of your own men standing in their boots."

"Keep your voice down," Daniel hissed. "Last thing you want is his wrath on us."

Vhalla stared in a stunned silence. Rat and Mole—Aldrik had killed them. She remembered the face of the Northerner melting off, but found her stomach strangely calm.

When her stomach finally churned it was not over the idea of their deaths, but the likely reasoning behind it. Regardless of what people believed about him, Aldrik would not kill without cause; Vhalla wouldn't believe anything else about him. There was only one reason she could think of.

"Did you really make that windstorm?" Daniel asked, drawing her from her reeling thoughts.

"I-I'm not sure," she replied, uncertain of the look on his face.

"It was huge!" Daniel's eyes grew large. She felt uneasy; was he friend or foe?

"You are not supposed to sound excited." Craig thumped his partner's head with a fist.

"If she did, that'd make her a Windwalker. You don't understand what that means." Daniel rubbed the crown of his head with a grin.

Vhalla moved a little closer to the bars.

"You read too many books." Craig rolled his eyes.

"And you don't read any books at all!" Daniel laughed.

"You know about Windwalkers?" Vhalla asked timidly.

"Not until recently," Daniel confessed, turning back to her.

"Not until last night you mean." Craig rolled his eyes. "He

gets assigned here and tries to become an expert on magic overnight.”

“At least I have an interest.” Daniel shrugged.

Vhalla stared at them uncertainly. The door at the end of the hallway opened, and her mind was instantly racing with panic at the footsteps. Both guards snapped to attention.

“Senator.” Daniel saluted. Craig stayed silent but mirrored Daniel’s motions. Vhalla glared at Egmun. She could feel every last bruise as his eyes took a leisurely assessment of her body.

“Where are her assigned guards?” Egmun asked.

“We are her assigned guards, sir.” Both Craig and Daniel held their salutes.

Egmun rubbed his temples with a sigh. “I realize that their standards for guards are astoundingly low, but I would have hoped you could read your assignments.”

The two men exchanged a look. “This is our assignment, sir,” Daniel said with confidence.

Vhalla’s mouth curled into a smirk at the confused and enraged expression crossing Egmun’s face.

“Where are Salvis and Wer?” the senator demanded. Vhalla tried to guess who Mole was.

“They’re dead, sir,” Daniel answered.

Egmun lost his composure to his surprise for a brief second, and Vhalla wanted to cackle.

“*Dead?*” he repeated.

“Parrot,” Vhalla mumbled under her breath.

“How?” Egmun’s teeth were grinding.

“They were found stealing from the bond payment chest,” Craig jumped in. “Imperial Justice.”

Egmun paused and laughed.

“It would be, wouldn’t it?” His eyes fell on Vhalla and she was happy to have the bars keeping him out. “It would be...” He chuckled and turned. “Her trial starts soon. Make sure she’s on time." Egmun clicked away down the hall, his emerald robes swishing about him.

Vhalla let out her breath.

"He seems about as pleasant as a rabid weasel in a bag of vipers," Craig noted dully.

"Craig!" Daniel hissed, but didn't argue.

With that remark these guards became acceptable. She remembered Prince Baldair mentioning something about the previous guards being Egmun's men. If that was true, whose men were these? What luck was looking out for her? Vhalla struggled to her feet.

Daniel fumbled with the keys, opening the door. She looked at them expectantly.

"I think you're supposed to cuff me." Vhalla held out her wrists, hoping they wrote off the abuse that painted her arms as having been caused by the Northerners.

"Are we?" Daniel asked uncertainly.

"I-I think so?" Craig ran off to grab some shackles hanging on the wall. They were only over her wrists this time.

"It seems rather pointless," Daniel mused as they started down the hallway. "You're a sorcerer, right? What's cuffing you supposed to do?"

"Daniel!" Craig groaned, "Let's not give the person standing on trial for treason any ideas?"

Vhalla shifted her hands; he had a point. She dared an attempt at her magic. Tears of relief escaped when she felt a weak little flicker around her fingertips. Knowing it was returning reduced her resentment for its absence to help against Rat and Mole.

Daniel went to grab her arm.

"No!" She frantically jerked away, taking an instantly defensive stance. He jumped back, startled. "I mean, I won't run. Please, let me go on my own."

The walk to the courtroom was slow, due to her mad determination to do it without their help. In her mind, she shifted it from an issue of paranoia over their potentially harming her to an issue of pride. She wanted to show Egmun that she could walk in there on her own two feet.

They opened the door, and she appeared to be early. The thrones stood empty and only about half the senators had arrived. They looked at her with a whole spectrum of emotions, from horror and anger, to fascination and skepticism. Vhalla walked up to the edge of her cage, standing as tall as she could manage.

As the room began to fill with people, it also began to fill with light. A large, circular, overhead window let in the morning sun. On occasion, the senators walked in with other people whom they sat with at the benches by the door before taking their own seats. Vhalla tried to see if she recognized anyone. It wasn't until Minister Victor took a seat that she felt a glimmer of hope. He caught her eyes and nodded his head by a fraction.

When the last senator had settled into their seats, the doors to the courtroom were opened and the three male royals strode in. They each wore a white jacket; the Emperor and youngest prince donned in light blue trousers, whereas Aldrik wore black. Clearly, compromises had been made.

Upon the Emperor's brow sat the flaming crown of the sun, each of its points a spear of golden light rising toward the heavens. Vhalla wondered how it would look on Aldrik. It led to the reminder that if she made it through the trial, she would someday find out. Something deep within her, under the broken and jagged pieces of who she now was, ached at the thought.

"Let this high court be called to order. On trial is Vhalla Yarl for the crimes of recklessness, endangerment, heresy, public destruction, murder, and treason. The prisoner has made a cry of not guilty. We will now hear those who will speak on behalf of the Senate and the prisoner. Let their testimonies be true or may the Mother strike them down with her divine justice." The Emperor settled back into his chair. The princes sat as well, sparking the rest of the room to sit with them.

Vhalla's shoulders ached from holding up her shackles, and she decided to sit also. She looked across the room at Aldrik. He wore an emotionless expression today, much like the day before. He didn't look like a man who had created wanton destruction between official duties. He didn't look like a man who had killed two guards the night before. He looked almost bored.

He briefly flicked his eyes over to her, but he looked away equally as fast, his mouth pressing into a thin line. Vhalla swallowed. Was he angry with her?

Egmun called the first witness to the stand. It was a Southern woman who had a very average build and plain looks about her. Vhalla tried to determine if she had ever seen this woman before, but she didn't recall.

"Thank you for coming today," Egmun started, "I realize this will likely be a great trauma for you to recall, but I will need to ask you questions about what happened two nights ago." The woman looked uncertainly at the powerful people surrounding her. "Do not be frightened, you are not on trial. Tell the truth before your Emperor and the Mother above; that is all we ask." The woman nodded. "Tell us, what did you see that night?"

"Uh, well, my, Emperor, princes, lords and ladies." The woman gave a small curtsey. "As ye know, first there was the explosion and I be tryin to run. Seemed like everyun in the city was tryin to get away." Vhalla's heart began to beat faster, remembering her frantic sprint through the masses. "I noticing the prince was runnin."

"You noticed the prince in the crowd?" Egmun asked.

"I was in such a hurry I dun bow or nothing." She gave a small curtsey to Aldrik. "No offense, milord."

"I'm sure the prince took none."

Vhalla felt offended on Aldrik's behalf that Egmun would presume to speak for him. If Aldrik was bothered by Egmun's words, his face betrayed nothing.

"You're sure it was the prince?" Egmun asked.

The woman nodded quickly. "I noticing because he was running *toward* the fire, not away. And he was all in black, as he oft is, in fine things, so I knew it was the prince."

Aldrik shifted in his seat, and Vhalla instantly noticed the movement after he'd been so still. He rested his cheek on his fist and reclined back in his chair, his knees spreading open slightly.

"Senator," Aldrik drawled, "I already said I was there. As amusing as it is to hear my story repeated through a commoner, it hardly seems a relevant way to spend our time."

Some of the other senators chuckled uneasily. Egmun only had a cool smile on his face.

"My prince, I was merely attempting to establish that the woman was indeed there and thus her testimony is trustworthy," Egmun explained. Continuing his line of questioning, he turned to the witness. "Good lady, when you saw the prince, was he alone?" The woman shook her head. "Who was he with?"

"He was followin' her." The woman slowly raised a finger in Vhalla's direction.

"See, my fellow senators. I called this witness to account for the malicious intent and the heresy of the prisoner." Egmun turned to her and Vhalla frowned. "Why else would a prince be following a plain girl of common birth *into* the center of danger? Why else would she lead him there if not to kill him?" He looked at the Emperor and senators, raising his hands dramatically.

"Because she had bewitched him with her magic; she placed our prince into a trance that even he did not realize and she brought him into her den to strike him down. For all we know, she plotted with the Northerners." Vhalla clenched the bars tightly; ignoring the pain the tension in her muscles caused her shoulder. "A magic that bewitches men and steals freewill alone should be a crime punishable by death. There is no other—"

"I did no such thing!" Vhalla cried.

"The prisoner will keep quiet!" the Emperor bellowed, slamming his staff down with a large clang.

Vhalla shrunk back and dropped her head.

Egmun could take anything people said and turn it into whatever he wanted. He had the Senate eating from his palms by the time the witness was done. Vhalla was fairly certain he could claim that she had a second head springing from her navel that sucked out people's souls through their noses, and they would gladly believe him. She raised her head half an inch to look at Aldrik through the curtain of her hair.

He'd yawn from time to time and made a show of looking bored with all the proceedings. She wondered if it was hard for him to sit through. It was insulting to say someone like her could command him in any way, just as it was insulting to imply that she could affect him as a master sorcerer. Then there were the rest of the lies. Vhalla rested her forehead on the bars as Egmun called the second witness.

The second witness was a man, a builder, who was saying that the demolished houses showed signs of wind and not explosion damage. That they may have been standing today, otherwise. The third was a woman whose daughter had died in the square, and Egmun made the point that perhaps her daughter had survived the explosion but, instead, the wind killed her.

"The Minister of Sorcery, Victor Anzbel," Egmun called.

The minister took the dais. He had a fist on his hip and stood easily. "It's been a while, Egmun." Victor grinned.

The senator sneered. "This is hardly a social call, minister. We have serious matters to discuss." Egmun was stiff.

"I can see that. I very *seriously* wonder why you locked away one of the most promising apprentices the Tower has ever received like some common criminal."

Egmun raised his eyebrows.

Vhalla tried to keep the surprise off her face. She was officially an apprentice of the Tower? She glanced to Aldrik. A spark in his eyes directed at Egmun had been lit. He was amused.

"An apprentice of the Tower?" Egmun seemed to have the same questions she did. "There are no rec—" He was shuffling through papers on a small desk nearby when the minister cut him off.

"Of course there aren't. Nothing had been made public yet. We were waiting until after the festival to announce it. She had friends in the library, and we wanted them to enjoy the celebrations. It seemed rather ill-timed to do it during the festivities," Victor explained easily.

Vhalla blinked.

"If this all occurred, then where are the documents?" Egmun asked in haste.

"Oh, my apologies, senator." Victor fussed in his bag and produced an official-looking paper. He walked over and Egmun met him at the bottom of the steps leading to the senatorial seats. "You should find it all in order."

Egmun glanced over the parchment with a frown.

"This bears the seal of the prince," Egmun growled.

"It certainly does," Victor said matter-of-factly. "He is very active in the Tower, as you know."

Vhalla looked across at Aldrik. He had a small smirk curling up the corners of his mouth. His confidence fit on him like well-tailored clothing.

"And of the Master of Tome..." The paper trembled like an autumn leaf in Egmun's hands.

Vhalla blinked. It had Mohned's mark?

"Senators, I think you will find all the necessary signatures, mine and Vhalla's included."

Her signature was on there? It had been forged, and she had a suspicion she knew by whom. The master wouldn't, even if he knew it was her wishes, and Victor didn't know her writing.

Aldrik allowed his eyes to meet hers levelly for a moment, and she knew. He was asking for her silence with that dark gaze. She closed her eyes for half a breath and looked back at him, hoping he understood. While she had never told the prince her final decision, she had to assume that somehow he knew. Vhalla wondered if Mohned's signature was a fake too, or if the master was also stretching the truth on her behalf.

"We had actually started working with her; it would have been irresponsible of us not to. She's been in the Tower quite a bit since her Awakening. She even has a mentor." He produced another piece of paper, and Vhalla realized Larel was also fighting for her. It was a relief to see that Egmun wasn't the only one who could paint pictures with words.

"If she was in such control by the Tower, then what happened the Night of Fire and Wind?" Egmun said roughly, his annoyance showing.

"Everyone Manifests differently. There hasn't been a Windwalker in almost one hundred and fifty years. We can only operate on the best knowledge we have," Victor said casually.

"That lax attitude may have gotten innocent people killed," Egmun sneered.

"I believe the prince was doing his best to keep an eye on our promising apprentice and those around her. We can only make adjustments going forward. But as a point of reference, were there any confirmed deaths from the cyclone?" Victor asked.

Egmun paused.

"Quite the contrary," an old and sagely voice called from the back of the room. All eyes turned and Vhalla smiled; Mohned had come. "Forgive my tardiness, good ladies and sirs of the Senate, your graces of the Empire." He walked slowly to the edge of public seating on the left. The master stood at the short fence that blocked off the area from the central testimony dais.

"Only one witness is to speak at a time," Egmun scolded, glaring at Mohned.

"I would like to hear what he has to say, Head Elect," an Eastern female senator called.

Mohned turned to the Emperor. "If it would please your highness?"

The Emperor looked to the Senate and received motions of approval, so he gave Mohned a nod. Master Mohned crossed through the gate to stand on the dais with Victor. Vhalla looked at him; he was hunched over and looked every year of his age.

"Please explain what you meant," the female senator asked, taking some control from Egmun.

"I just came from the clerics. Unfortunately, one of my apprentices died in the explosion."

"*Sareem,*" Vhalla breathed his name faintly, his face clouding her vision in an instant. Would she ever have a chance to mourn him? Or would she soon meet him in the Father's realms beyond?

"But another was with him. The girl's name is Roan."

"Is Roan alive, master?" she called frantically.

The Emperor seemed to let the outburst slide, much to Egmun's annoyance.

The master gave her a nod. "She will heal in time, the clerics say."

Vhalla didn't try to hide her tears of joy. "I'm so glad," she rasped.

"Well, this is just touching, but I fail to see how it is relevant." Egmun was trying to regain control.

"Roan, my apprentice, was discovered right next to the epicenter of the windstorm," the master pointed out. "I have been told the storm had such force it ripped apart the attacking Northerners and tore down buildings. If she was right next to it, would she not have been tossed to shreds also?"

A murmuring coursed through the senators. Egmun looked around, his face twisting in rage.

"Now that you mention it," Baldair joined the conversation with a thoughtful rub of his chin. "None of the bodies were moved, alive or dead. They hardly seemed touched by the wind at all. They still littered the road. I would've imagined them blown about."

The murmuring became louder, and, for the first time, Vhalla breathed a little easier. Not only because it seemed like Egmun's control was wavering, but because she realized she hadn't hurt anyone, save for the Northerners who tried to kill her and Aldrik.

Egmun stomped down the stairs and up onto the dais, clutching the paper Victor had handed him earlier.

"Is this your signature, master?" He shoved the paper in Master Mohned's face, forcing him to take a step back to try to read it. "Tell me, had it been decided that Vhalla Yarl would join the Tower?" The senator took another aggressive step forward, thrusting his fist and the paper at Mohned.

"Let me read it." Mohned took another step back, and the hem of his robes caught on the small lip that surrounded the inner circle of the sun dais. The master's old, frail frame began to tilt, and Egmun made no motion to stabilize the older man. Victor was too far away, and Vhalla saw it happen, as if ten seconds slower than everyone else. The master couldn't correct his balance and, with pin-wheeling arms, he began to tumble backward.

"Master!" Vhalla cried and thrust her hand out from between the bars, the chain of her shackles clanking loudly. She felt a tingle in her fingertips. Her magic still felt exhausted and barely strung together, but enough had replenished to heed her command.

The master's fall slowed with a ruffle of his robes, and he was eased onto the floor gently. Mohned turned his head and smiled at her as the rest of the room sat in a stunned silence.

She took a shaky breath as Victor helped Master Mohned carefully back onto his feet.

"Thank you, Vhalla," he said gently, readjusting his stance.

She had just enough time to breathe a small sigh of relief before chaos descended upon the room.

CHAPTER 28

"Guards!" Egmun cried.

Vhalla glanced back at Craig and Daniel. They were frozen in place, and the odd sense of wonder on Daniel's face as he looked at her told Vhalla their stillness wasn't entirely from fear.

"*Guards!*" Egmun bellowed and they sprang to life, roughly pushing her to the ground, their swords drawn. The tips pressed into the back of Vhalla's neck.

"Calm down!" Victor cried, his hands in the air.

"She's a monster!" shrieked one senator.

"We're not safe here!" wailed another.

"Vhalla wouldn't hurt anyone," the master attempted.

"It isn't natural," a man shouted.

"You old fool, it's amazing," came a lone voice, though one or two others muttered agreement.

The shouts and arguments became more heated, and Vhalla felt the boots of the guards on her back. She'd made a mistake. Without thinking or planning, she'd used her magic in front of everyone. Vhalla struggled to twist her head to see, very aware that sudden movements could be permanently detrimental to her health.

"We should kill her now," one man bellowed.

"How can we kill such a power?" a woman snapped back. "It has utility!"

"The most important thing about power is how someone uses it!" Victor attempted, though Vhalla wasn't sure if he was heard. "She can do great things!"

The Emperor began banging his staff.

"We will rue the day if we let her out of here alive," one senator said.

"Kill her now!" screamed another.

Vhalla looked out at the scene; most of the senators were on their feet. Some were fighting with each other, more were arguing with Victor on the dais below. Egmun stood silently, a mad smile creeping up on his features. He'd won. He showed she didn't have control over a different and frightening power.

"*Silence!*" the Emperor roared, and the whole room fell into a startled hush. Everyone realized, all at once, that they had forgotten themselves. He rose to his feet and descended from the royal platform. Mohned, Victor, and Egmun parted with a bow of their head as he stalked through, but his attention was glued on her.

Vhalla twisted her head slightly; one eye was squinted shut against the floor, and the other was partly covered by her hair. He knelt down before her on the other side of the bars, and placed a hand on his raised knee. The Emperor regarded her curiously.

"Let her sit," he ordered.

Vhalla felt Craig and Daniel remove their feet from her back. She eased up slowly, their sword points still at her neck. Vhalla risked a movement to pull her hair from her eyes.

"My lord, I don't think—" Egmun started.

"Silence, Egmun." The Emperor held up a hand. The most powerful man in the realm considered Vhalla for a long moment, his blue eyes searching her for something. Eventually she looked down at her hands folded in her lap, unsure what he wanted to see. "Could you strike me down where I am now?"

"My lord?" Vhalla couldn't believe her ears. Was it a trick? Or a test?

"You are shackled, with swords at your neck, behind bars. Could you still strike me down?" Though his eyes looked nothing like Aldrik's, she felt a familiar intensity in them and it gave her pause.

"I've never thought about doing something like that, and my magic seems strange right now, but I suppose I may be able to," she answered honestly.

The Emperor nodded. "Did you try to kill my son?"

She met his eyes. "No," Vhalla's voice was small, but strong, like a finely forged rapier. "I would only ever want to save your son."

She thought back to Aldrik on his knees, not unlike how she was now, with swords at his throat. It rattled her from the inside out; it fueled her resolve. Even under the Emperor's searching gaze she did not look away. In this one moment, Vhalla had nothing to hide.

The Emperor nodded. "Take off her shackles." The Emperor stood and Daniel quickly sheathed his sword to fumble with the locks on her wrists.

"My lord, we should consider—" Egmun began to protest.

"Egmun, if this girl wanted to kill any of us, she could have and would have by now." This realization seemed to rattle some senators as much as it calmed others.

Her chains removed, Vhalla stood on doe-like legs and rubbed her wrists gently. Even if she was still in a prison, she felt marginally better without being cuffed and chained.

The Emperor continued to study at her. "Vhalla Yarl."

She looked up; it was the first time he'd used her name.

"Have you ever conspired to harm my Empire?"

"No, of course not," she answered directly.

"Did you conspire with the Northerners on the Night of Fire and Wind?" he asked, his eyes continuing to rest heavy on her.

Vhalla's mouth dropped open. "No!" she snapped, not caring to whom she spoke. "They killed my friend, they threatened my home, and they—" She stopped herself and his eyebrows rose. Vhalla's eyes flicked over to Aldrik. "They..." she repeated again. How much would he want her to say? "They did something unforgivable."

"What happened that night?" the Emperor asked.

"I was at the gala," Vhalla began. "I was... there when the explosion happened. I saw where it happened. My friends were near its center; I had to go help them. So I ran through the city. I found them, then the Northerners were upon me a-and..." She was struggling with leaving Aldrik out of her story. "I thought they would keep hurting people. They were going to kill me and I only wanted them to die."

"And the crown prince?"

She cursed inwardly. Of course that wouldn't be forgotten easily. Vhalla took a deep breath, finally looking away. "He..." He, what? He had been a supporting and guiding figure since the summer? He inspired her? He was someone who made her smile as much as he had made her want to kick something? Vhalla shifted her gaze to the senators, who seemed to be hanging on her every word.

"He's a much better person than I've heard people give him credit for. He's worth a lot more than many of the people in this room, and it's not just because of the crown on his head." She looked back at the Emperor. "He wanted to help. If I am guilty for anything, it was putting him in a position where he felt compelled to do so."

A stunned silence filled the room. Even Egmun couldn't seem to find anything to comment on. She wasn't sure if she had damned herself, or if Aldrik would be enraged at her for it, but she didn't regret her words. Eventually, she looked down and grabbed the sides of her sack.

Without a word, the Emperor relinquished his stare, turned and returned to his throne. Vhalla felt the eyes of everyone in the room on her but her attention sought out the gaze of only one.

Aldrik made no motion. He concealed his emotions even from her. Vhalla sighed softly and looked down again; it was hopeless. Everything she thought she knew about her and the prince was wrong. Why else wouldn't he speak for her?

"I think we have enough to reach our decision. Do you have any more to say on your behalf, Vhalla Yarl?"

She shook her head, not raising her eyes again.

"I propose a motion that we reach our verdict tomorrow. Our Empire is at war and has more pressing matters than this. If there are no objections?" Naturally, no one stepped forward to speak against the Emperor. "Guards, take the prisoner away."

Vhalla turned and Craig pulled open the door. She followed Daniel out, not looking back for a moment. The walk back to her prison was in silence. But they made no motion to return her shackles.

Within her cell, the walls closed around her. Vhalla sat by the door, her back against the bars to avoid giving the impression she wanted to speak. She rested her head against a bar gently; the pressure on the back of her skull was a welcome pain.

She sighed and closed her eyes. It would be another day of waiting—and then, her fate. At least she would be out of here soon. The end of the trial seemed to have gone in her favor, but it had started so poorly. Their cries, calling for her death, echoed through her ears.

The next morning, Vhalla woke to the same dim light of her cell and wondered what time it was. She rubbed her eyes, blinking away sleep. They fed her last night, but it was only scraps of bread. Her stomach wasn't in too much pain though, her sparse eating habits paying off.

The sack was beginning to itch, and she desperately desired to bathe and change. Even if they put her back into a burlap thing, she wanted to get out of this one. A heavy sigh relieved a small amount of stress and tried to keep the sanity-threatening memories at bay. She had to compartmentalize and lock the thoughts away to survive.

"Oh, you're up." Daniel had heard her. "Want breakfast?"

Vhalla nodded.

"I'll see what I can find," Craig said before running off.

"What time is it?" she asked, moving closer to the bars.

"I think an hour or two past dawn." Daniel turned and knelt.

"Have they begun?" She didn't need to clarify *they*.

He nodded. "Yeah, not too long ago. I've no idea how it's going," he said apologetically.

"It's all right." She picked at the stray threads of her sack, suddenly feeling less hungry thinking about the men and women in the courtroom.

Craig returned with a small roll and a handful of grapes. "It's all I could get; they weren't really planning on feeding you, apparently." He passed it through the bars and she began nibbling and picking at the food.

"I wouldn't be surprised if Egmun told them part of my powers was not needing to eat," she said bitterly, certain he was spinning lies about her right now. Both men chuckled and she forced down the last of the bread.

"We're going to take you to the Chapel of Dawn today,"

Daniel said. She looked up curiously. "Baldair told us that normally a prisoner likes to pray before their verdict, asking for fairness and wisdom from the Mother. Or absolution from their crimes."

Vhalla had never been a particularly spiritual person, but she would take any excuse to leave her cage. The Chapel of Dawn was the official place of worship for the Imperial family and capital. It was one of the highest public places in the palace. To get to the chapel, the common folk used an outdoor stairway not far from the Sunlit Stage. It was where the Crones of the Mother were ordained and where coming of age, weddings, and other religious ceremonies were held for the Imperial family.

The day passed. Vhalla inspected her wounds and found them red and puffy, but no worse. It was the not knowing that began to drive her mad. If she could walk outside of her body like Aldrik had once implied she could, then perhaps Vhalla could listen in on the courtroom. But the idea of being stuck out of her body again kept her rooted firmly in place, doing little more than rolling pebbles across the floor and back.

"Let's go," Craig said finally. Vhalla pulled herself to her feet and ran a hand through her hair, snagging on tangles almost immediately. "I'm not going to shackle you, so please don't run."

"I promise," she agreed, not sure if these guards were exceptionally smart, or extraordinarily stupid for trusting her. Whatever the case, she was glad they did and that they allowed her to walk silently between them.

She'd done little all day, but Vhalla found the walk exhausting. The path was entirely underground, up dimly lit stairwells, and cobweb cluttered halls. They passed no one else, which led her to assume she was in some kind of temporary holding and not the labyrinth of dungeons that were rumored to exist beneath the palace.

Eventually they came to a rather plain door. There was a

blazing sun upon it, crafted from bronze but tarnished with age. It protested Daniel's attempts to open it, starting to budge only when he put his shoulder into it.

"Are you sure this is the right way?" He coughed up dust.

"It's what the prince told me." Craig shrugged. "Maybe it's been a while since the last person?"

"It's been a long while," Daniel muttered.

She was thankful that Craig had thought to grab a torch a while back. For a brief moment, Vhalla's heart raced as she realized that she was very far from anyone else, alone with two guards. But as the muted lights of the chapel began to stream in through the door, she breathed easy.

They walked into a small sub-room of the chapel that Vhalla had never seen before. There was a large altar. Over it was a sculpture of the Goddess holding out her arms. She was swathed in life-giving flame and had a firm, but kind, expression on her face. On the altar were a series of ritual artifacts, a golden mirror supported by white marble, a steel dagger, and black and white candles. There were only four kneeling pillows set out and they looked old and worn. Vhalla assumed the pillows were once white, but now they were threadbare and gray with dust.

There was another door that Vhalla surmised led into the main area of the chapel. It seemed to be in better care and was reinforced with iron and a golden lock. Daniel kicked off his boots before entering the sacred space to try the other door. This door did not budge either, but gave a telltale clank of a lock engaging.

"I guess we'll wait outside here then." He shrugged, yanking his shoes back on. "It's the only access, so we know you can't run."

"Give you privacy in your prayers," Craig offered.

Vhalla gave them both a small smile. They couldn't give her

much, but what they could they did. With a nod both departed, leaving her alone.

They hadn't given her shoes, so she had nothing to strip before entering the hallowed ground—but she wished she had something to wash her feet and hands with. Walking over to one of the pillows, Vhalla sat listlessly, watching the dancing flames envelop the sculpture of the Mother. It was hypnotic and, while it did not resemble prayer, there was something peaceful to it. The Crones said the Mother looked after all her children; Vhalla wondered if she had been lost or forgotten. One mother had already left her, maybe that was simply her fate.

The sculptures turned into reliefs around the outer walls. Each held a story of Mother Sun and her eternal dance with Father Moon. The Mother crafting the earth; their false child, the dragon of chaos; their splitting of the world to keep the disorder from their true children, humanity; she knew all the stories. Every tale was a memory of a book she had read on that beloved window seat. Her eyes began to burn.

Quickly wiping her cheeks, Vhalla turned in place as the chapel door opened slowly and silently. A figure swathed in maroon glided across the threshold. The Crones of the Mother wore a deep red color to signify the departing light of the sun, a symbol that their vigil would last until the end of their days. The door closed silently and the Crone locked it again.

"Crone," she said uncertainly. "I've come for my prayers before my fate," Vhalla tried to explain, concerned she would be presumed to be somewhere she wasn't supposed to be.

Two hands reached up and pulled the hood backward.

"I know," it was a deep masculine voice.

"Aldrik?" Vhalla gasped in shock.

The brim of his collar on his white jacket extended beyond the top of the large hood, and he wore his golden crown.

"Do not speak too loudly." He glanced around before walking

over quickly. Aldrik knelt down on a pillow across from her. "Are you well?"

"Aside from the obvious?" She grinned weakly.

He frowned. "This is not a game, Vhalla," he scolded her lightly.

"Oh? I'm sorry, I thought it was. I don't know about you, but I've been having so much fun." She wasn't in the mood to be spoken to in that tone.

He looked at her with a frown, chewing over his words. "Your new guards, are they treating you well?" Aldrik finally asked.

It confirmed her fears. She was a broken little thing to him. Vhalla inhaled sharply as anger rose within her. Nothing compared to the hatred the thought of Rat and Mole put in her stomach. Remembering Egmun's eyes on her made her want to die. Every negative emotion compounded as she thought of Roan and Sareem, the guilt she had struggled with for days since parting with them before their deaths—or near death in Roan's case. Even anger at the master and prince for consorting behind her back sent a pang of frustration through her. Every last thing Vhalla could have been angry about came to her then in the wake of her fear and shame.

"What do you care?" she spat at him. Aldrik blinked as though she'd slapped him across the face. "You, you've gone behind my back; you've become a puppeteer in my life; you lied to me; you threw me off a roof; you taught me recklessly; you forged my signature." It was hopeless, the tears came freely. "You wouldn't even speak for me!"

He grabbed her upper arms fiercely, and Vhalla twisted frantically.

"Don't touch me!" she shrieked in horror. Aldrik released her, shock and pain across his face. She held herself, feeling every emotion come tumbling through her eyes. "I-I'm just a pitiable thing to you, *worthless trash*, why would you touch me?"

Vhalla pressed her eyelids closed and curled into a seated ball of sobs.

By the time he finally moved, her stomach hurt from crying. Vhalla expected him to leave. She wanted him to hate her so that she could validate the hate she felt in herself. However, he didn't go. Hatred would have been easier than the frustration and pain that was rife upon his face.

The prince's mouth opened and closed, but his silver tongue failed him. Frustrated, he grabbed the pillow next to him and stood in a half turn, throwing it toward the wall. It incinerated in a burst of flame before hitting anything. He stood with his back to her, panting softly.

"I," his voice was deep and ragged, "I am not a good man. Maybe I have never been a good man. Out of that sham of a trial the hardest part was to hear you waste words to defend me when all I wanted you to do was defend yourself."

"I would've let the city burn had it not been for you." He chuckled, and it was a crazed and crackling sound, void of its normal velvety hues. Vhalla struggled to believe his words. "I was in no position to leave the palace, wounded as I am, so I would have sat in the safest place I could find and waited it out." He turned, searching her face.

"Does it shock you? Aren't you disgusted with your prince? I would've been happier watching the flames consume half the damn city to purge the filth, even if it meant sacrificing the good with it. Those are my subjects! People I am sworn to protect!" He threw out his hands. "You're right, about it all. I wanted you. The moment I found out what you were, I wanted you like a prize to be captured and put on my shelf. And you, Vhalla, you made it so easy to manipulate you to walk right where I wanted you. You, with your transparent innocence."

"Stop," she whispered. His words stung deeply.

"Like an ignorant fool, you trusted me and never once

questioned my guiding hand—even knowing my reputation!" Vhalla looked away; she didn't want to hear any more. "You're right, I had it all lined up. The master knew as soon as I suspected, but he would not go against the will of the crown prince, not even to warn you. The Minister of Sorcery didn't know what he had in you, he may have let you go! It fell to me to ensure that you fell and Awoke to your powers. You may have gone to the master in your own time, but all those *choices* you thought you had? That paper was signed while you were still recovering from your fall! The master knew you were already gone, even if you did not know it yourself. All I had to do was keep pushing you along, being your guiding and caring teacher, and I could've had your magic doing whatever my will desired!"

"Aldrik, please..." she begged him, tears choking her.

"And then..." His voice audibly softened. Aldrik's shoulders slumped and his arms hung limply. "Then I realized I just wanted you around. My days were better when they involved you. I enjoyed your thoughts. It was thrilling to see you discover magic. You had a mad hopefulness about sorcery that I have not felt in almost a decade. I started finding excuses to take you away, not because you *needed* my teaching but because, because I wanted to see you. I looked forward to our meetings and—like that, Vhalla—your opinion mattered to the crown prince of the Empire. You mattered for who you were, not for your magic and what some dusty texts say Windwalkers may or may not be able to do."

She blinked up at him, speechless.

"I wanted your forgiveness, as though that innocent acceptance would absolve me of all the blood on my hands. I wanted to see you well and happy. I wanted to see you flourish, and I wanted only a small piece. To know that, in you, I had made something good. And I truly wanted to keep you from pain." He balled his hands into fists.

"I knew the best way would have been to remove myself from your life and, by the Mother, I tried. But I was still too self-centered to tolerate that library boy. I should have encouraged you to go off and be with him. Then, despite my efforts, my brother had to meddle—only to torture me—and you wore that damn dress." He fell down to his knees before her, his fists on the ground and head bowed. Aldrik took a deep breath, it wavered just slightly.

Vhalla's head swirled as she tried to absorb everything.

"I spoke for you today," he confessed. Vhalla's heart skipped a beat. "I did not speak before *not* because I did not care, but because—because, I am not a good man, Vhalla. My voice is more likely to damn you than save you. There are people in this world—in that room—who will hurt you for the sake of hurting me." He dropped his head again with a few bangs escaping from the perfect comb set his hair always had.

"People who already have." He punched the ground with such force that Vhalla jumped and knew, without a doubt, his knuckles were bloody. If they were, then the pain was nothing to the prince as he continued to kneel rigidly.

Vhalla's tears had stopped, and she wiped her cheeks with her palms. He made no motion; he barely seemed to be breathing. She took a deep breath and rubbed her nose.

She mattered to Aldrik, Vhalla didn't have the energy to process the how or why.

"Did those guards really steal from the Empire?" Vhalla asked, finding her voice surprisingly stable.

He sat down again. His knuckles were indeed bloody. "No," Aldrik answered directly.

Vhalla closed her eyes, and took a breath. "Aldrik," she said weakly. "What do you want from me, *really*? What am I to you? Am I a conquest? A trophy? A project? An amusement? A tool?"

He needed to tell her now. Guessing would tear her apart,

and his slew of confessions was too muddled for her exhausted brain to sort through. They were nothing until she knew.

"You," he paused.

She searched his face, trying to understand all the complex emotions that hung upon his lips. Aldrik glanced away with a small sigh, but he returned his eyes to her with a softness they had not possessed in some time. "You are a dear friend. For whatever my royal ass of a friendship is worth."

Vhalla smiled weakly. She reached out and his body went rigid. "It is worth very much," she whispered.

He barely seemed to breathe as she leaned over the distance between them to tuck the stray bangs back with the rest of his hair. He reached up and caught her hand gently in his.

"Don't," she protested weakly.

He stopped her from withdrawing this time, his grip warm but not painful. "Why?"

"Because I-I." Vhalla's lower lip trembled and her cheeks burned.

"You foolish girl," he murmured. "As if anything could make me not want to touch you."

She tensed but allowed his gentle caress to wipe away the remnants of Rat and Mole's abuse and Egmun's words. There was something about his skin alone that was therapeutic. No matter what the world did to her, his warmth remained.

"My magic," Vhalla said after a long moment, feeling electric tingles under the pads of his fingers. "Is it—broken?"

"Broken?" he asked, the talk of magic relaxing him.

"It hasn't felt right since I woke up," she explained.

"Ah." Aldrik shook his head. "No, not broken. You're likely exhausted from the exertion. It is a wonder you did not use it up completely, then you would really be in trouble."

"It's all trouble, isn't it?" She laughed weakly and was rewarded with a small smirk from him as well. Vhalla took a deep breath and gathered her strength. "Aldrik, I need your honesty. I don't care about your reputation. I want you to be open with me." She paused, swallowing hard. "For however long I may continue to be alive."

"You shall have it." The crown prince nodded. "Do not be afraid, Vhalla. I will not let them kill you." He made two dangerous promises in two breaths. Yet something in his voice told her he was ready to go to great lengths to keep both. Aldrik squeezed her hand gently. "I should return. The break for lunch will be over soon, and, after my testimony, I am sure they will want me accounted for."

She gripped his hand as though her life depended on it, feeling tears protest his departure. He stopped all movement. Even after his confessions, after the anger, after all she'd been through, he remained. Aldrik, her prince—good or evil—remained with her. They both stared, waiting for the other to make the first move. Vhalla would have given anything for time to stop.

"Please don't go," she whispered faintly. "I don't want to face their verdict alone." Her shoulders trembled, and she struggled to keep the tears contained. As the time ticked down, Vhalla realized, with earth-shaking horror, the notion of dying terrified her.

"Vhalla," he breathed faintly. "You are never alone. I will be there." He took her palm and placed it on his hip, his body was even warmer than his hands. "Never forget, we are Bound."

Vhalla remembered that dark and ugly spot from the day in the garden. She looked at where her hand now rested on the prince's side.

"We will face it together." His tone was sincere and serious. She looked for reassurance, and he lavished it upon her with only his eyes. One more time, Vhalla let herself shamelessly fall into those dark depths, before he rose to leave.

CHAPTER 29

If Craig and Daniel had heard anything, they made no indication when she met them shortly after. They also had the decency not to comment on her eyes being red and puffy. Vhalla replayed the surreal conversation in her head as she followed the guards.

The prince was ever an enigma.

He had said he was her friend. Vhalla wondered exactly how he had been taught the meaning of friendship. The lines of truth and lies were blurred with him and her life hadn't exactly improved since he had entered it.

She resumed her seat by the door after Craig and Daniel locked her back in. *Aldrik*, she thought, not daring to say his name aloud. No matter what had happened, she couldn't find it in her to regret meeting the dark prince.

"Friends, huh..." she breathed, remembering how he held her beneath the stars. Vhalla opened her eyes before her mind betrayed her.

The door at the end of the hall banged open. Vhalla heard the scampering of small feet and turned. A servant boy dressed in a dull gray tunic came running.

"The prisoner is requested."

Craig and Daniel exchanged a look before turning to her. Vhalla nodded and stood; it was time. They unlocked the door and she walked unshackled to the courtroom. No matter what happened, she found relief knowing this was the last time she would make this walk. The door opened before her, and Vhalla plunged herself into the light, squinting as her eyes adjusted to the late afternoon sun.

The Senate was there and seated. Some stared at her in anger, others regarded her with calm. Vhalla tried to determine if the senators who had called for her death looked angry or happy. She couldn't decide. Egmun sat in the center, and he stared at her queerly. His eyes made her uncomfortable. Vhalla's skin crawled, and she looked away.

The royal family sat on their thrones. Prince Baldair wore a conflicted frown. The Emperor was banging his staff

again, but Vhalla barely heard it as her eyes met Aldrik's. He wore a tortured expression on his features and looked away quickly when he saw her stare. Vhalla's stomach turned upside-down.

"Vhalla Yarl." The Emperor stood. "After much deliberation and review of the evidence—" Vhalla noticed he glanced at his eldest son for a brief moment "—this high court has come to a verdict. Head Elect?"

Egmun stood. He held out a large piece of parchment before him that he read from. "Vhalla Yarl, on this day two hundred and thirty-four years after the birth of the first Solaris, you have been judged for your crimes against the people of the Great Solaris Empire."

She shifted her weight from foot to foot, forcing her hands to stay at her sides.

"For the crime of recklessness, we have found you guilty."

Vhalla breathed sharply through her nose.

"For the crime of endangerment, we have found you guilty."

She clutched the sides of her burlap sack.

"For the crime of impersonation of nobility, we have found you guilty."

Vhalla looked sideways at Baldair. Clearly he had not offered much defense for his role in that particular offense.

"For the crime of public destruction, we have found you guilty."

She began to feel dizzy.

Egmun continued to read as they looked down upon her. "For the crime of heresy, we have found you *not* guilty."

It was a start.

"For the crime of murder, we have found you not guilty."

She gripped the bars, taking a slow breath.

"For the crime of treason." Egmun's eyes flicked over to her for a brief moment. "We have found you not guilty."

Vhalla rested her forehead on the cool iron of her cage. She wanted to feel relieved, but something about the pain in Aldrik's eyes cautioned her otherwise.

"To atone for your crimes, it is the will of the Senate, the people, that you will be conscripted into the military to apply your abilities to the war in the North."

Vhalla blinked. They were making her a soldier. She didn't know anything about fighting; sending her there was a death sentence. Her eyes widened; that was the point. Either way they would win. If she succeeded they would claim the glory, or the Northerners would kill her for them.

"You are to be considered property of the Empire for the remaining duration of the war and will be deployed to the front in one week's time," Egmun continued.

"I don't know anything about combat," she said meekly.

The Head Elect looked at her slowly. "We have been assured your powers are special, beyond compare. If that is the case, I am sure you will learn quickly," Egmun sneered at her.

Vhalla looked about frantically; Aldrik clutched his seat so hard his hands shook.

"Should you be found to disobey an Imperial Order, partake in any treasonous activities, or flee your duty, you will be put to death by the righteous flames of the leader of the Black Legion —" Egmun paused with a dark grin in her direction "—the Crown Prince Aldrik."

Her mouth dropped open.

Aldrik's expression hadn't changed. Vhalla looked to Prince Baldair next, who glared at his brother. She turned to the other senators, but, unsurprisingly, there was little love there.

"This is the will of the Senate, on behalf of the people." Egmun rolled the parchment and began to descend the risers of the Senate. His footsteps echoed like a hammer against her brain.

Vhalla felt numb; she wasn't sentenced to death, but she might as well have been.

When Egmun was halfway to the Emperor, starting up for the Imperial Platform, she allowed herself to look at Aldrik. He shifted in his chair and for a brief moment he placed his hand on his hip. His message was clear.

No matter what, he couldn't kill her because of the Bond.

This was an order just as dangerous to him as it was to her. She wasn't sure if she was glad, or tortured by knowing where this placed him. If he was told to kill her and he refused, Vhalla had no doubt these very senators would turn it against him. Vhalla gripped the bars and barely kept in a scream. They did not know the true gravity of what they had done.

Egmun handed the parchment to the Emperor and slowly returned to his seat.

"Vhalla Yarl, before the Light of the Mother I have heard your crimes, your evidence, and the people's will in your fate. I find this to be a fair and just punishment for the offenses you have committed against the Empire." A servant brought a small bowl of hot wax and a large metal seal on a platter. The Emperor dripped the molten liquid onto the parchment and pressed his seal onto the paper that held her future.

"So it has been written, so it shall be."

"Guards, return her to the palace via the care of the Tower," Egmun said with a gleeful grin.

Vhalla was ushered away by Craig and Daniel. She didn't even have a chance to see Aldrik once more. Instead of turning back to her cell, they began heading upward.

They ascended through an inner passage, the stones of the wall and floor slowly became more polished and carefully laid. The torches lining the walls became more frequent and the hallway began to be bathed in more light than darkness. After a series of doors, they reached an archway that emptied into a larger hall. A girl waited; her hands folded before her.

"Larel?" Vhalla blinked.

The Western woman smiled faintly, turning to Craig and Daniel. "I will take her from here. I am her escort to the Tower," Larel informed Vhalla's companions.

They nodded. "We will leave her to you, then," Craig said.

Vhalla turned. "Thank you for your kindness," she said in earnest.

"Take care, Miss Windwalker," Daniel added, with a sad but genuine smile. "Maybe we'll see you on the march?"

"You'll be there?" Vhalla asked as Larel took her hand gently.

"We will," Craig affirmed with a nod.

Vhalla opened her mouth but there wasn't time to say anything else. She gave her guards one more nod of appreciation before allowing Larel to lead her away. Vhalla had never been more ready to leave anywhere in her life. Her head was still reeling from the verdict.

Larel lead her quietly and efficiently through the hallways of the castle. They wove between main halls and down small side passages, avoiding all people. Eventually, they arrived at a large painting of the Father. He was leaning against a pile of rubble, lusting after a distant point of light in the sky. Larel pushed it to the side, motioning for Vhalla to step through.

Vhalla immediately knew she was in the Tower, as the candles and torches had been replaced with flame bulbs. A wave of emotion washed over her, and she leaned against the stone, trying to catch her breath. It hadn't sunk in yet. Larel rested a hand gently on her shoulder.

"Your room isn't far," Larel spoke softly, focused on one task at a time.

"My room?" she repeated.

"And your black robe," she said very matter of fact.

Vhalla followed her numbly to the main stairwell. They turned left and proceeded upward. They passed the door that Vhalla knew led to the room where she had healed; then they continued up. A few doors after, they reached one that looked much like any other, save for a unique steel plaque in its center. She rested her hand upon it, feeling the letters engraved on its surface—*Vhalla Yarl*. Larel produced an iron skeleton key and unlocked it.

The room was an upgrade from her previous quarters. It had similar standard-issue furniture. There was a decent-sized wardrobe, mirror, desk, and chair. None of this attracted her attention.

Vhalla walked over to a large floor-to-ceiling window, unhooking the latch. She stepped out onto a small balcony, barely more than a window ledge with a railing. It was the first time she had been outside in days, and the cold crisp air greeted her like an old friend.

"Is this really my room?" she asked in awe.

Larel nodded. "The minister thought, given your Affinity, that a room like this would be good for you."

Vhalla wondered how many other apprentices in the Tower —in the whole palace—had a room with outdoor access, however small and limited.

She walked back inside. Opening the wardrobe, she found all her clothes neatly hung inside.

"I brought your things," Larel explained.

Vhalla noticed a familiar trunk beneath her bed. The rest of her meager possessions had been neatly organized at the base of her wardrobe. Vhalla bit her lip when she noticed a thick pile of notes, organized and bound tightly with a piece of twine. She looked back at Larel.

"I didn't read them," Larel said softly. "Your correspondence with the prince isn't my business."

"How did you know they were from him?" Vhalla asked dumbly.

"I've known the prince a long time. He is a talented and powerful Firebearer. It's hard for him to make anything without leaving a little trace magic on it. It's faint enough that even most magical people wouldn't know much by it, but..." She shrugged, not really finishing.

Vhalla ran her fingertips over the top of the stack wistfully. If only she could return to those days.

"Did you hear the verdict?" Vhalla asked, shutting her wardrobe.

"No, the minister just told me you were part of the Tower now."

"I was found not guilty for half—the better half—of my crimes. But for what I was found guilty for... I've been drafted into the army. I'm property of the Empire now. I will leave with the soldiers as they head back to fight." Her tone was level and dull, the numbness hadn't worn off yet.

"*Property?*" Larel gasped. Vhalla simply nodded at her. "Do you know anything about combat?" Vhalla shook her head. "Have you ever fought someone before in your life?" Vhalla shook her head again. "They're trying to get you killed." Larel was brave enough to say it aloud.

"Yes, I think that's the plan," Vhalla agreed weakly.

"They march soon, I hear." Larel sat heavily in the room's single chair and took a moment to let it sink in.

"Well, you can have my room when I'm dead," Vhalla remarked darkly. It wasn't as though she deserved as nice a room as this.

"You will not die," Larel announced, determined. "We will heal you and then, when you march, you will be trained in the legions. I'll speak with Prince Aldrik and Major Reale."

"Major Reale?" Vhalla swallowed. She wanted to share the woman's determination, but that would mean everything happening to her was real.

"Major Reale is one of the leaders of the Black Legion under Prince Aldrik and Head Major Jax, though I think Jax is still at the front. Major Reale is here, and she will be marching back as well. The march will take two or three months headed north," Larel explained. "It only took a month to get here, but the men were lighter loaded with enough horses to go around. This time there will be new recruits, so they will be marching on foot. There will also be heavily burdened pack horses and carts bringing food and supplies. And the army will stop to pick up additional soldiers from the West at the Crossroads, I hear. You'll gain some time there also. All that time you will be training."

As Larel elaborated, her confidence became infectious. It seemed less impossible and marginally probable that Vhalla might learn enough to keep herself alive. That is, until the memories of the Northerners in all their ruthless resolve came back to her. Vhalla bit her lip; it was hopeless to think she would be able to do anything.

"Come, we'll speak on this later." Larel stood as if sensing her shifting determination. "Let me show you the baths. I'm sure you'd like a wash."

Vhalla nodded; there was little that appealed more in the world than bathing. Perhaps she could scrub her skin away and find a new person beneath it.

Just like everything else in the Tower, the baths were a significant upgrade from the servants' baths. It was communal, unlike the lavish private room she had used to bathe in before the gala. But here too, there were spigots with hot and cold water; two in each of the ten stalls that sat ready for people to wash with before soaking in a steaming pool that covered the back third of the floor.

Vhalla hadn't even wanted to touch her clean clothes, she felt so filthy. Larel had been kind enough to carry them for her, and the other woman placed them in a small changing area before a large mirror. Vhalla stopped and looked at herself for the first time in almost four days.

Her hair was a bird's nest, sticking this way and that. It was a good three inches shorter with all the knots. Her face was streaked with blood, soot, and caked makeup. Her eyes looked tired and worn, and her cheeks more hollow than she remembered. Vhalla ran a finger down the gash that ran between a black eye and a split lip, beginning to laugh.

"Vhalla?" Larel asked gently, her concern evident.

"I'm a mess. No wonder the senators had little difficulty

seeing me as a crazed killer." Vhalla continued to laugh. It echoed through the empty hopelessness she found within her.

"I need to see your wounds, Vhalla." Larel pressed her fingertips together. "I'll go get whatever salves are necessary once I know their status."

Vhalla paused a moment as the other woman waited expectantly. Larel was telling her to undress, she realized.

With a breath, Vhalla pulled the sack over her head. Her hands trembled as the air hit her skin, and Vhalla forced herself to be brave. With an angry grunt she threw the burlap ball and underclothes into a corner.

"Burn it, Larel," she barked, a dark tone in her voice that tasted heady and almost sweet in its rough tang.

Larel nodded, and, with a glance, it was consumed in an orange flame until nothing was left but a small black spot on the tile.

The Western woman rounded her and seemed to be making a mental list. She looked closely at Vhalla's shoulder, pulling away the remaining bandage that Vhalla hadn't fussed with. She moved to her head next, taking off the soiled gauze. Vhalla saw the remnants of Rat and Mole's assault, the purpling of her abdomen, arms, and legs. Larel spared her any unhelpful coddling or pointless anger, saying nothing of the abuse.

"All right, they don't look too bad, physically at least," she said thoughtfully after another turn. "I'll go get a few things and be back. Go ahead and start washing up. I asked the other girls to stay away for a bit, so you should have privacy."

Vhalla sat in a stall and turned on the hot water. She doused herself the second the bucket was full. The water was scalding, and Vhalla took a breath, repeating the process. It couldn't be hot enough, and after the fourth bucket her skin was bright pink and slightly steaming.

Working a bar of soap to a lather, Vhalla found a small

pumice stone and used it liberally. She applied all the pressure she could. At first, it was for the thick layer of grime, but each time she stopped, the thought of Rat's and Mole's assault raining down on her consumed her. Eventually her skin was splotchy with raw—almost bleeding—spots where bruises once were. Vhalla threw the stone away before she could harm herself further.

She poured water over herself again and turned to her hair. She lathered in soap with delicate fingers, working on the tangles and scabbing at her scalp. The water ran red with dried blood, so Vhalla washed it again. After the third washing, she found a small brush and attempted to comb through the hopeless mess.

It was slow going. Each time she put the brush in her hair, it hit a snag. Vhalla started with the crown of her head and began working downward. Around halfway, all the knots began to stack on each other and she couldn't work the comb through. Vhalla attempted to brush from the bottom, to no avail. She tried the left side, then the right side, but found no luck.

Vhalla threw the brush against the wall and buried her face in her hands. She didn't want to cry anymore; she was tired of feeling weak and sad. She was tired of feeling hopeless, tired of fighting, and tired of feeling like the world was against her. Standing, she walked back over to the mirror, looking at the mass of knots halfway through her hair.

A glint of silver caught her eye, and Vhalla picked up a razor. Grabbing a hunk of hair, she took a breath. The wet clump that fell to the floor was one of the most psychologically beneficial things she'd done in some time. Vhalla grabbed the next fist of hair and the razor glided through it effortlessly, then the next, and the next.

She would cut it away. She would cut away the anger, the pain, and the frustration. She'd cut and cut until she was sculpted into something better, something stronger. They wanted to kill her, so this Vhalla would die, she resolved, and a new Vhalla would be born from her ashes.

"Vhalla?" Larel's faint voice broke the silence. Vhalla wondered why her shoulders wouldn't stop shaking.

"It was a hopeless mess; I didn't really like it anyway." Vhalla shrugged at the pile of hair on the floor, as though she were indifferent to the length she had always carried on her head. Her fingers went easily though the remaining hair now, short enough that the nape of her neck showed.

"Sit," Larel instructed, motioning to the stool in the stall while retrieving the straight razor. Larel proceeded to apply a more masterful hand to her hack job. "Do you want bangs?" Larel motioned across her own forehead at the hair that landed right before her eyes.

Vhalla shrugged. "Anything is fine." She didn't care much now; the healing part of her haircut was over.

Larel hummed a moment and then worked with the hair around her face. Vhalla thought she should feel nervous with someone holding a knife so close to her eyes, but she felt completely calm near Larel. The dark-skinned woman cut a low swoop that left the hair almost falling over her right eye, and began to touch up her work.

"There." Larel stepped back. "Come here and look."

Larel held her hand, gently leading her to the mirror. Vhalla did not recognize the person staring back at her. Dull skin and listless eyes had a dangerously piercing quality about them. She brought her fingers up to her hair. Vhalla had never worn it this short before, and she wasn't sure who she was with it cut so severely.

"Thank you." Vhalla didn't know what else to say.

"You're welcome." Larel smiled kindly and placed a large towel around her shoulders. It felt like silk after the burlap.

Larel instructed her to sit again on the small bath stool and began to apply salves to her wounds. Larel handed her a bottle of liquid to drink that created a momentary fire in her veins. Her shoulder required closer inspection.

"Who stitched this?" Larel asked, reaching for a small tub of white paste.

"Prince Baldair," Vhalla answered.

"Prince Baldair?" Larel repeated, raising her eyebrows. "That sounds like a story."

"He said his brother called in a favor," Vhalla repeated his words, but left out the remark of his wanting to do it for his own reasons, as well.

"Those two... One of them is always claiming a debt of the other." Larel clicked her tongue and shook her head.

Vhalla decided to let her questions slide.

She pondered her own relationship with the crown prince. Was she indebted to him? Could he be indebted to her? Either notion made her feel uncomfortable. She didn't enjoy feeling like there was a score being kept. She would do almost anything for Aldrik, *it didn't matter if she owed him or not.*

Larel finished putting clean bandages and salve on her wounds. After inspecting Vhalla's head, she left the wound bare. Vhalla dressed slowly, savoring her clean clothing.

The dark-haired woman held out a piece of black fabric to her. Vhalla looked at the dangling garment for a long moment. This was who she was now. Taking it, she studied the short black jacket. It had slightly longer sleeves than Larel's, reaching to right before her elbows, but it had the same short upward collar and stopped at her waist.

Vhalla swung it on one arm and then the next, adjusting it with both hands. She looked in the mirror at the new person staring back at her.

A sorcerer with battle scars, lost friends, and blood on her hands occupied the mirror. The frightened faces of the senators came back to Vhalla with vivid clarity. They were sending her to war, so she would go and become something they had every right to fear.

~

Vhalla's story continues in *Fire Falling*

**Grab your copy and keep reading:
https://www.elisekova.com/fire-falling/**

DISCOVER MORE FROM
ELISE KOVA

THE COMPLETE AIR AWAKENS SERIES:

Vhalla's epic saga of love, loss, triumph, and growth continues across five books. All out now!

Book 1 - Air Awakens:
    https://elisekova.com/air-awakens/

Book 2 - Fire Falling:
    https://www.elisekova.com/fire-falling/

Book 3 - Earth's End:
    https://www.elisekova.com/earths-end/

Book 4 - Water's Wrath:
    https://www.elisekova.com/waters-wrath/

Book 5 - Crystal Crowned:
    https://www.elisekova.com/crystal-crowned/

Are you a binge reader? Get the complete Air Awakens series in one bundle:

https://www.elisekova.com/air-awakens-box-set/

~

VORTEX VISIONS

How did the Crown Princess Vi Solaris open up Meru? How did she fall in love and win the hand of the Voice of Yargen? Find out by reading her story today.

Get your copy: https://elisekova.com/vortex-visions

Vi Solaris is expected to rule an Empire she's barely seen... but her biggest problem is the dangerous magic that's awakening within her.

Now, alongside her **royal studies**, she's training in secret with a sorcerer from another land. From his pointed ears to foreign tongue, he's *nothing* like anyone she's ever met before. But he just may be the only one who knows what's happening to her.

As Vi fights to get her magic under control, the Empire falters from **political infighting and a deadly plague**. The Empire needs a ruler, and all eyes are on her as Vi must make the *hardest choice* of her life: Play by the rules and claim her throne. Or, break them and save the world.

~

DRAGON CURSED

"Pulse-pounding romance, vivid world-building, and badass dragon hunters make for a bloodthirsty and brutally fun read. The stakes couldn't be higher—I devoured every page. This is the YA fantasy I've been waiting for!"
~ Brigid Kemmerer, New York Times bestselling author of *Forging Silver Into Stars*

Learn More:
https://www.elisekova.com/dragon-cursed

❧

ARCANA ACADEMY

A woman who has devoted herself to learning forbidden tarot magic to thwart the crown. A prince who claims her as his bride to use her skills to seize a legendary power. Enter the mysterious halls of ARCANA ACADEMY, where strength is survival and your future is your tuition.

An adult, epic fantasy by bestselling author Elise Kova. Ideal for readers looking for dark academia, intricate magics, slow burn romance, enemies to lovers, found family, and twists you never saw coming.

Learn More:
https://www.elisekova.com/arcana-academy/

❧

A DEAL WITH THE ELF KING

Looking for a fantasy romance with a happy ever after? Read the story of Luella and how she falls in love with the magical king of the elves.

Get your copy: https://elisekova.com/a-deal-with-the-elf-king/

Perfect for fans of A Court of Thorns and Roses and Uprooted, this stand-alone, fantasy romance about a human girl and her marriage to the Elf King is impossible to put down!

The elves come for two things: war and wives. In both cases, they come for death.

Three-thousand years ago, humans were hunted by powerful races with wild magic until the treaty was formed. Now, for centuries, the elves have taken a young woman from Luella's village to be their Human Queen.

To be chosen is seen as a mark of death by the townsfolk. A mark nineteen-year-old Luella is grateful to have escaped as a girl. Instead, she's dedicated her life to studying herbology and becoming the town's only healer.

That is, until the Elf King unexpectedly arrives... for *her*.

Everything Luella had thought she'd known about her life, and herself, was a lie. Taken to a land filled with wild magic, Luella is forced to be the new queen to a cold yet blisteringly handsome

Elf King. Once there, she learns about a dying world that only she can save.

The magical land of Midscape pulls on one corner of her heart, her home and people tug on another... but what will truly break her is a passion she never wanted.

A Deal with the Elf King is a complete, stand-alone novel, inspired by the tales of Hades and Persephone, as well as Beauty and the Beast, with a "happily ever after" ending. It's perfect for fantasy romance fans looking for just the right amount of steam and their next slow-burn and swoon-worthy couple.

~

See all of Elise Kova's published and forthcoming works at: https://elisekova.com/books

About the Author: Elise Kova

ELISE KOVA is a *New York Times*, *USA Today*, and *#1 Sunday Times* bestselling author. She enjoys telling stories of fantasy worlds filled with magic and deep emotions. When not writing, she can be found playing video games, drawing, chatting with readers on social media, or daydreaming about her next story.

She invites readers to get first looks, giveaways, and more by subscribing to her newsletter at: http://elisekova.com/subscribe

Visit her on the web at:
http://elisekova.com/
https://www.instagram.com/elise.kova/
https://tiktok.com/@elisekova
https://www.facebook.com/AuthorEliseKova/

ACKNOWLEDGMENTS

Foremost, I'll say it again—Thank you to all the people who were mentioned in my dedication and everyone else who supported me from the very beginning. I had no idea what Air Awakens was going to turn into and I'm so glad you all didn't let me give up on it.

Michelle—thank you for your endless support. You have been irreplaceable in my journey into the publishing world and I'm really not sure where I would be without you. All your criticisms and insights pushed me harder and made me better, things that you had no reason to do other than because you are an amazing friend. Your edits and story revisions were mind-blowing to me and this book would not be what it is without you.

My editor, Monica Wanat—I knew from the moment I met you that it would be the start of a beautiful relationship. You cut words that I did not even see needed to be cut and made the story better for it. Thank you for helping fix my flaws and polish my tale.

My original cover artist, Merilliza Chan—you shattered my every expectation for artwork and gave me something that I could not have conceptualized in my wildest dreams. People say, "Don't judge a book by its cover." But with the cover you've created I hope they do! You made Vhalla come to life in a way that I could not. For that, I am eternally grateful and I can barely contain my excitement for the next cover in the series.

Jessica—without you there really may not have been an Air Awakens at all. It was you and all of our discussions and endless car rides filled with talk of books and really epic music that put the passion back in writing for me. I hope you know the important role you've filled in my life and what an amazing friend you truly are. Thank you for reminding me to be patient and torture my characters.

Katie—where would I be if I didn't have you to geek out with? In a very sad place, that's where. Your enthusiasm kept me going long after the initial glamor of penning these words faded. Were it not for you I may have never found the courage to press on. You inspired more than you know in Air Awakens.

Meredith—the other half of me, my "octurnal twin," thank you for your confidence, your love, and your pragmatism. You're always there when I need it most and you've always been a nurturing force for everything that's positive in my life. You're the person who taught me the true depth of familial love and inspired relationships in this story.

My parents—I don't have enough words to say thank you. Not just for your support in Air Awakens and your thoughts about my drafts, but for everything you both have ever done for me as a person. I am not perfect, and I will always have more to learn and grow from, but I would not be half the woman I am today without you both. I hope you enjoy all the revisions to this and future installments of Air Awakens.